SHORT FUSE

Also by Kit Craig

Strait
Gone
Twice Burned
Closer
Some Safe Place

SHORT FUSE

Kit Craig

HEADLINE
FEATURE

First published in Great Britain in 1999
by HEADLINE BOOK PUBLISHING

10 9 8 7 6 5 4 3 2 1

British Library Cataloguing in Publication Data

Craig, Kit
  Short fuse
  1.Detective and mystery stories
  I.Title
  813.5'4 [F]

ISBN 0 7472 2086 7

Typeset by
Letterpart Limited, Reigate, Surrey

Printed and bound in Great Britain by
Mackays of Chatham plc, Chatham, Kent

HEADLINE BOOK PUBLISHING
A division of the Hodder Headline Group
338 Euston Road
London NW1 3BH

www.headline.co.uk
www.hodderheadline.com

0747 220 867 2340

For Mack, who gave me the first line
with love

Prologue

If you want to bring a building down, first you have to break its knees. You do this with hundreds of little explosions. They come seconds apart. The strengths and weaknesses of the building determine what kinds of explosives a company uses, and every company has its secrets. Certain supports are weakened ahead of time. The charges have to be placed exactly. A vertical implosion is a masterpiece of precision. In the seconds after detonation it looks as if nothing is happening. Then an end wall begins to go. The building falls in on itself in an amazingly timed progression. In seconds, some architect's dream is reduced to a neat stack of rubble.

In the abstract, it is beautiful. Film crews are here to watch the famous Revenaugh family bring down a department store today. Their implosions draw crowds. Including Tom Devlin's worst enemy.

This isn't a Devlin Dismantling job but he is here anyway. He haunts these demolitions like an angel of destruction. He came in as the building was being prepared, supports sawed and stairs torn out – before the crew brought in the explosives and laid wire. Stalking the site like a tiger, he found the best vantage point. Now he crouches on a rooftop, waiting. It is seconds to detonation.

Thousands watch from behind police barriers. Somewhere, a band is playing. At a signal it stops. Then with a sharp, regular crack-crack-crack, explosions march through the building.

The doomed department store stands still for a long minute. Then it shudders and begins to fall. It is like watching a mammoth die. Orgasmic. The crowd cheers.

But this particular watcher is different. He twists in an ecstasy of pain. Reliving the other blast, he roars 'Didn't you see him hiding in there?' And twists as if he's been gored. *Then* gets all mixed up with *now* and, howling, he wonders: *Is he still in there? When it blew, did I hear him scream?*

1

'You should have seen it Tommy,' Lexie says with that blazing smile he loves. Her eyes widen and her hands fly. 'Blam! I'm telling you, it was gorgeous.'

You know a person well enough to want to marry her and it turns out you don't know her. You love her more than anything and it isn't enough to keep her safe. The woman Tom Devlin flew two thousand miles to see is curled up in a chair by the window, enclosed in something strange. All he wants to do is hold her. He wants to hear her tell him it's OK, they're OK, and she is talking about something else. She's talking about everything else. He says, 'What is? What's gorgeous?'

'Implosion, right here in Chicago! Didn't you see it? It was all over the TV.' Grinning, Lexie looks at him over scraped knees. It is both sexy and disconcerting.

'I was on the plane.'

'Oh well, you know what I mean. You've blown up enough buildings.'

'You never told me why you quit.'

He says, 'You get sick of seeing buildings die,' but it's not what he means.

'I'd never get sick of it.'

'Could we talk about something else? Is there something going on I don't know about?'

Her voice curls around him and clings. 'Oh Tommy, I missed you so much!'

'Me too.'

'But you're back now.'

'I am.' He wants to get past this and lose himself in a long hug but his lover sits in the brocaded hotel chair with her feet drawn up and her fingertips raw from the cement ledge, smiling at him. The Chicago hotel she chose for this meeting is an old one with twelve-foot ceilings and tall windows, inch-thick panes in heavy sashes that rumble up and down on old-fashioned chains. When he came into the room tonight he found her poised on the windowsill. Alexandra McQuarrie, surprised in transition. He doesn't have the foggiest idea whether she was climbing out or coming in. When she saw him she smiled and slipped back into the room as gracefully as a dancer, closing the window on the soft May night. *Oh. I'm so glad you're here.* 'Three months is too long.'

'I should have come with you.' Her smile is warm but she's still sitting over there and he's still standing here.

'I wish you had.' He thinks the window behind her opens on an airshaft,

2

blank wall. When he came in all he saw was Lexie framed in a black rectangle. She jumped down and pulled the curtains so fast that he has no idea what's out there. Balcony? Fire escape? There is the outside possibility that it's a sheer drop and it makes his teeth squeak. 'Lexie, are you OK?'

She smiles. 'Don't worry, sweetie. I'm cool. It's cool.'

'Then why won't you come to me?' After three months, this is not what he expected. Flying in from San Francisco to meet Lexie he was excited to see her, he was scared to see her after being away for so long. They're getting married – big wedding in September – but when too much time comes between you, things start to change. Some stuff has come down since he left. Things he doesn't want her to know. And there's something going on here that he needs to know. Her outlines are shimmering: the butterfly in the middle of the change. He's trying to be cool about it but he loses it and feints for the curtain pull. 'Is there somebody outside, Lex? Somebody on the fire escape?'

Smoothly, she slips out of the chair and intercepts him. 'Oh Tommy, don't scowl like that.'

He touches her face. Static electricity strikes sparks. It is like walking into a force field. 'Lexie, what's going on?'

'Just you, Tommy, I'm so glad to see you.' She drops in the setup line to an old routine, her signal that they should kiss and lighten up. 'Smile, you look like a dead president.'

'And you're coming on like Godzilla on skates.' In ordinary time they would start laughing. In ordinary time they would drop their force fields and move closer, but this is not ordinary time. 'Oh, Lex. When we get married I won't let you out of my sight.'

'Try and lose me,' she says, thank God she is laughing. 'Just try.'

So Devlin puts his arms out and this time Lexie moves into them; they slip into the familiar magic like a pair of children agreeing to run away from the world. Then she sighs and puts her hands on his chest. 'I'm so sorry, we have to wait. Somebody . . .'

'What?'

'Something's come up.' She trails her fingers down his arms and drops into the chair, tucking her legs under her as if she's a package that's just been shrink wrapped, neat and untouchable.

He gulps. Did she find out about his one night stand with Zee? He says carefully, 'Are you going to tell me what's the matter?'

At least she doesn't torture him with that *Nothing* that women use to signal that things are bad with worse to come. 'Don't worry, Tommy,' she says at last. 'It's just some family stuff.'

'Your weird Uncle Kieran.'

She says too quickly, 'No.'

Troubled, he looks around the room for signs. Her things on the dresser are the same: lipstick, comb. Gold necklace, a gift from her father. The binder with her script sitting on the table by the untouched bed; she would have come to San Francisco if it hadn't been for the play. *When you see it, you'll understand.* Well, he doesn't. What else does she have here in the hotel? Notebook. Magazines, the usual: *Scenarios, Daily*

Variety, *The Voice*. Book: *One Hundred Years of Solitude*. If there's a subtext he is damn well going to have to guess. He repeats her 'Family. Is it about the play?'

'What makes you think it's about anything?'

Wild, she looks wild. He blurts, 'If only you'd come with me.'

'San Francisco? I wish.'

'No, I wish.'

'You can't walk out on a workshop situation, Tommy. My play . . .'

'If you'd only come.' He means: *if you hadn't left me alone.* 'Three months!'

'Shh.' Her voice is soft and sad. 'I know. I had to stay with it, Tommy. Have to. I can't quit until I know how it comes out.'

He groans. 'Family secrets.'

'I think so. Half memories, bad dreams, I have to figure out which.' She looks up at him, bemused. 'I can't walk away until I know'

'If you don't know, how can you write the play?'

'It's my way of smoking them out.'

Three months. Then Zee. 'I wish you'd never started the play.'

'When you see it you'll understand. I love you, bear with me.' Then she surprises him. 'This isn't about the play, Tommy. OK?'

'What is it about, then? That stupid job?' Pat McQuarrie owns this money pit of a hotel that he wants imploded. He's pretty sure the Revenaughs won't touch it. Otherwise why come to him? McQuarrie pressured Tom to bring in Devlin Dismantling. Leaned on him, played the father-in-law card. *Now that you're part of the family.* 'He offered twice the going rate. I refused.'

'Daddy told me.'

Don't be mad. 'You know I quit the business.'

'It would help if we knew why,' she says absently. It's clear her mind is on something else. Whoever's coming. Whatever is outside. Someone on the fire escape? What if it's a sheer, unbroken drop?

If he tells her why he quit Devlin Dismantling, will that get her attention? If he tells her about the kid who died on his watch, will it be enough? 'Nobody needs that kind of responsibility. My God, Lexie, do you know how hard it is to sweep a building? You can sweep a dozen times and still overlook something, street person, stray cat. I never wanted it. I want to build things, not tear them down.'

'What happened?'

'Family pressure.'

'You don't have to tell me about family pressure,' Lexie says with a *been there* smile.

'I know.' Devlin has seen them: the McQuarries with those tight Irish glares, massed against the universe. Prosperous Pat McQuarrie keeps his family in line. His children, his brothers, his wife. The man walks point like a Marine going into combat. Nothing like the ragtag Devlins. 'My story is a little different.'

'Every story is a little different.'

'Three generations in demolitions,' he says. Again. Things are so weird tonight that it seems safer to talk about something they both already know.

'Pop had his two boys, then he had the vasectomy. They then had me. Nobody likes a surprise. Mom takes one look at me and she bails.'

'I know what that's like. Maggie was a surprise. Shock, more like,' she says and does not go on.

'But you're a good sister to her.'

She gives him a conflicted look. 'I hope so.'

'Tony and Bro and I are almost twenty years apart. When our mother left, they blamed me.' There's no explaining what it was like, growing up with those two stern brothers in that empty house. He had to be an A student, win trophies, shine at Harvard, all to make up for it. Pop made the brothers front for him. Tuition, clothes, everything he needed, no wonder they hate him. 'I was supposed to go out and get famous to make up for it.'

'The next rung up the ladder,' she says with that beautiful smile. 'Been there. Know that.'

'Maybe they just wanted one Devlin with clean fingernails.' When he first met Lexie at a party they bonded over family histories. Two controlling fathers, two families on the march. *Not us*, they promised each other. *We're going to be different*. Now he's given her everything he has and they're still half a room apart. He holds out his hands. 'I love you, Lex.'

'Soon, OK?'

'Should I be worried about you?'

'Why?'

'I don't know, it's just!' Listen, he's brought the ring. A classic solitaire, Tiffany setting; he spent too much. He wants to give it to her but she wants to go on having this conversation.

Instead of closing the distance between them, she feeds him his next line, 'Your brothers don't like you much.'

Something's changed and Devlin has no idea what. He'll do anything to keep this from getting any worse. Tell his story one more time and hope she'll tell him what's going on. 'It cost them. Harvard. Architecture at Yale. You bet they don't like me. "Look who's here, Joe College. He thinks he's too good for us." I had an internship at IM Pei! Then Pop got sick and Bro and Tony called in all their markers. They hauled me back to work for them. They said if I didn't, it would kill Pop. The minute I walked in he got better. They said, if I left he'd get sick again. They said it would kill him. They said it wasn't for long. Five years! Then.'

She stirs but does not speak.

He gives her everything he has. 'Something came down and I quit anyway.' One smile and he'll give away the works. The bad old secret that he's kept to himself. The dead boy and the nightmares that don't stop. God, if she asks, the fling with Zee. He'll tell her anything because he can't sit here wondering if she knows. 'If it isn't me and it isn't the play, what is it? What's going on? If you won't tell me what this is about . . .'

'You don't want to know what this is about.'

Her tone is so dark that it surprises this out of him. 'Look, if somebody told you . . .'

'Told me what?'

'. . . anything about Zee . . .'

5

But Lexie says, 'Who's Zee?' so carelessly that she can't possibly know. And glances at her watch. She's been using him to pass the time!

'You're shivering!'

'Tommy, you have to go. Oh, don't look at me like that. It's only for an hour.' She gets up like a hostess saying goodbye to a houseguest who's overstayed. Smiling, she frames his face with her hands. 'Go have dinner, sit in the bar, whatever, and when I'm done . . .'

'Done with what?'

'Nothing major. It's just something I have to do.'

'Lex!'

Now that she has him at the door she trails soft fingers across his lips. 'I promise, it won't take long.'

'Lex!'

'Really, it's OK! As soon as I'm done, I'll come get you and then we can make up for everything.'

He wants to hug her but the force field goes up. This is worse than he thought. 'Who's coming, Lex. What are you expecting?'

The phone bleats and Lexie jumps. She turns away. 'That's it. You have to go. And don't lurk outside, it'll only string this out. If they come out of the elevator and see you, they'll go right back down and they won't come back until you're gone.'

2

The guy at the far end of the hotel bar isn't necessarily watching Devlin but there's no proof that he isn't. He came in shortly after Devlin and he hasn't left his post. They are stranded here in the dismal blue light. The stranger with the alfalfa hair could be your ordinary businessman passing the time, but the cut is all wrong. The brown suit is wrong. The beard is wrong. The pants are highwaters and the coat sleeves stop short, exposing wide, knobbly wrists. It's as if Dr Frankenstein went out and bought a suit for his monster without caring how it fit. Scowling, he curves his hand around his drink like a heavy smoker lighting up in a high wind. He is not at home in bars.

Neither is Tom Devlin, tonight. Two hours trapped on a zebra skin stool have left his teeth clenched and his belly sour. He is sick of running his sweating drink around on the black glass counter, working on a smile to flash Lexie when she come in. If she comes in. He has no idea what's going on upstairs. He can't shut off the worry, any more than he can filter out the cocktail Muzak drifting in from the lounge. He can't keep his mind on the ballgame on the overhead TV. He can't unclench his teeth far enough to talk to the bartender, who shoves the beer nuts at him with that bored, say-something look. So what if Lexie kissed him as she pushed him out the door. They only have tonight, and he's cooling off his heels in a bar. Angry, he slides the beer nuts aside and slips off the stool. Movement may not be action, but he can't keep sitting here.

At the far end of the bar, the guy in the bad suit gets up.

Fine. If he heads for the door and that hick tries to stop him, he'll know. Testing, Devlin sits down.

At the far end of the bar, the guy sits down.

Devlin orders another drink.

The guy orders another drink.

So. What? If he starts upstairs, will the hick in the cheap suit try to stop him? Follow? Use a flip phone to call reinforcements or walk away? He doesn't know.

OK, asshole. Are you working for Pat McQuarrie? My brothers? Who?

He ought to go down to the end of the bar and ask the damn question. Yank the stranger up by that shiny green tie and choke until the truth falls out. Threats of violence aren't Devlin's style, but growing up in the demolitions business has taught him how. He's big enough to back up any threats he makes. He gets to his feet, rumbling.

The bar phone rings. The bartender hands it over the counter. 'It's for you.'

He shouts into the receiver. 'What!'

It's Lexie, sounding as easy and natural as rain. 'Tommy, don't bark. Should it be the month before the wedding or closer to the time?'

He shakes the phone. 'Should what be what?'

'My opening. You know. The play.'

'Two hours, and you're asking about dates?'

'It's important, Tommy. I want everything out before we get married.'

'Why?'

He can hear her scrambling for words. 'It's hard to explain. When you see it, you'll understand.'

'You kept me waiting for two hours because of the play?' *Three months and now this.* He's been patient. He has.

'Not exactly. I. It's family business.' There's somebody in the room with her. He can hear it in her tone. Slightly elevated, as if she's working a room full of strangers with no way of knowing if her act is going over or not. 'Look. The timing is up to you.'

'I don't care when it opens, Lex.' He is straining to hear. Is that a man muttering in the background. 'Lexie, I'm going to ask you a couple of questions now. Just answer yes or no. Is there somebody in the room with you? Somebody you don't want to see?'

'Are you crazy?'

'Just tell me, Lex. OK? Are. You. All. Right?'

'All right? Why wouldn't I be all right?'

He can hear her voice skittering. 'That's it. I'm coming up.'

'No! We're almost done, Tommy. Really. I'm practically on my way down.'

Devlin waits another fifteen minutes. He's wasted half the night watching the door and the minute he gives up on her and turns away, the guy at the end of the bar goes rigid. He can almost see the back hairs rise – somebody in the doorway, somebody the hick in the cheap suit doesn't want to see; he wheels and dodges into the hall just off the bar. Devlin's first instinct is to follow. Throttle the truth out of him. But soft fingers sweep the back of his neck. His love has sneaked up on him. 'Lexie!'

'OK, that's over,' Lexie says. Love in her eyes.

He hugs her and then stands back, looking for signs. If she's in trouble, it will show. He'll see it in that chiseled wedge of a face. 'You took forever.'

'I know.' The only think he sees in her face is desire. It's been three months! Her voice is wonderful. The pressure of her hands is wonderful. 'These things take time.'

'You were going to explain.'

'It's nothing, just family stuff.' Smiling, she turns him, drawing him upstairs. 'I'm so glad you're here.'

'You're not going to tell me, are you?'

'Not really. It's OK now. These things are always hard.'

'Well this one is making you really weird.' He sets three fingers on her jaw, lifting her chin so she has to look at him. 'Who was it, Lex? Who came to see you tonight? Is there trouble with your rotten sister?'

8

'Lally?' She grimaces. Lally the drunk is a continuing story. 'Not this time.'

'Your underground uncle?'

'Kieran? How could it be Kieran? I haven't seen him since Maggie's christening, and even then he had to sneak back.'

Lexie's uncle is a renegade pacifist, dropped out in the early Seventies – Pat McQuarrie's personal thorn. Weatherman, he thinks. Some war protest group. 'You never said what he did. Did he blow up a building?'

'He was there.'

'If it wasn't Kieran, who was it?' He takes both her hands holding her in place so he can study those opaque violet eyes. 'Knowing is always better than not knowing, Lex.'

'Don't, Tommy.' They've been together for too long for her to lie to him. After some thought, she says, 'OK, I was just trying to spare us some embarrassment. If you've got to know, it was a cousin, trying to put the bite on Dad's company. I came out here to blow him off.'

'I thought you came to see me.'

'I had to tell Dad *something*,' she says. 'Right now he's kind of pissed at you.'

Tight-jawed Pat McQuarrie with that flinty, spiteful smirk he calls a smile. Devlin growls, 'He'd better get over it. We're getting married soon.'

'He will. This wedding is a very big deal for him.'

'Too big.' Four hundred and counting. That's another thing.

'Shh, we're together! Look, he was going to send Uncle Kevin to handle this until I convinced him Kevin's too soft.' She grins. 'How do you think I finagled the trip?'

Devlin has seen Pat McQuarrie's brother Kevin, Fordham Irish with a buzz cut and a big square jaw, in the old days he would have been earmarked for the priesthood or the FBI. Instead he leeches off the McQuarrie Development Corp., all the McQuarrie brothers do except for Kieran, and Kieran's long gone. 'I thought this trip was about us.'

'It is.' She is still grinning. 'What Dad doesn't know won't hurt him.'

'Is everything you do about your father?'

'My father? No! I hope not. I don't think so. No.'

'He thinks he owns you, Lex.'

'Don't start with this, Tommy. Not now.'

'You're with me. I don't own you, but you're with me.'

'Shh, Tom. We own each other.' She slips her hand into his.

'Yes!'

For the first time Lexie takes in their surroundings: black glass and black mirrors, the banquettes upholstered in fake zebra skin. 'God, I'm sorry I stuck you down here. This place looks like the inside of a bad movie. Come on, I've ordered Room Service. Steak and champagne.'

'Lexie, did you see that guy when you came in? The one at the end of the bar?'

'Filet. Chandon.' Her fingers curl and drag across his palm, wriggling in the cleft his lifeline makes. 'Us.'

'Is he one of your father's clowns?'

'It's been forever, I love you. Let's go.'

'I love you, but we've got to talk.' They should, but the strongest magic is old magic. The more he is with Lexie, the less talking matters. They're together again. It's all he needs.

'Shh. Come on.'

Devlin scopes the lobby as they pass through like a honeymoon couple running for the barn. Whatever the hick in the bad suit came to do must be finished. There is no sign of him.

3

Upstairs, there are more important things to do than talk. When they're done in the shower and have slid into every embrace they've ever known and some they are still discovering, they roll the table over to the bed and giggle and eat and talk. When they're together they never run out of words. Crazy, the two of them, so close and so stupid that they thought they could survive for a while in separate beds on opposite coasts. But things happened while Devlin and Lexie were apart. Now they're together and he wants to pretend that together is the only thing. Keep his eyes closed and maybe the rest will go away. But it doesn't. Lexie's secret, whatever it is. Zee. He can't let it go by. Sitting up, he touches her face. 'One more thing.'

She smiles drowsily. 'Anything.'

'You were . . . Lexie, when I came in tonight. What were you doing up there on the windowsill?'

'Oh,' she says, still smiling. 'Oh, that. It's no big deal. If that's what's bothering you, I'll confess. I bought you a present.' She's trying not to laugh. 'It was too big to hide in the room.'

Devlin traces her outlines. He moves with great care, like a test subject learning a maze so he'll never get lost again. He is happy for the first time in months. He should be pressing her but at this point in their night together she could tell him anything and he'd just nod and smile sleepily, oh yes. Dreamily, he repeats, 'A present? On the fire escape?'

She laughs. 'OK, I got you a dog.'

'A dog?'

'A border collie, OK?'

'But Lexie, the windowsill!'

'It's a wedding present, silly. It was supposed to be a secret and the carrier was too big to hide in the room.'

'Can I see it?'

'After the wedding, OK? It's only a baby dog and the breeder has to take it back to the mom.'

'You had the breeder out on the fire escape?'

She doesn't answer. Laughing, she pushes him down and knuckles his ribs until he starts laughing too. 'Tommy, Tommy, is anything ever enough for you?'

In one of their favorite old movies, Danny Kaye has to be knighted in a hurry and the palace knights go through the ritual double-time. They get everything in but they have to do it so fast that their legs blur. Tonight is like that. Devlin has to leave at dawn to make a seven a.m. plane. He and Lexie want to do everything they always do together – laugh, talk, eat, but there's

11

not enough time. They talk and share a meal with a sense of urgency that makes it particularly sweet. Nuzzling in front of late-night TV like any close couple, they talk in the glow of the electronic fire. Making gags about the shows, they slide lazily from point to point in their never-ending conversation, touching each other's lives – families, their work. Exchanging confidences. If they can't tell each other their troubles, who can they tell? Lexie's worried about leaving her baby sister Maggie alone with Lally because the woman was born mean. If they keep talking long enough, Devlin will offer to let Maggie come live with them. They don't need any more family; he wants Lexie to himself but he likes the kid and he wants to help. As for the Devlin brothers – he pretends that he's free now that he's out of the family business, but he's still caught up in a tug of war with Tony and Bro. Devlin, who goes by his last name because Devlin sounds tough and his big brothers used to call him Tommyboy to put him in his place.

'The guilt police,' he says.

'They know where we are and they know what we did.'

'It's like you have to fight for your freedom every day.'

'It is.' Lexie says without explaining, 'You do things for your family that you wouldn't ordinarily do. You of all people ought to know.'

'My Life in the Business.' He is waiting for more from her.

She sighs. 'Stuff you do for your family.'

Devlin trails the bait. 'If it's bad stuff, I want to help.'

'I know you do.' But Lexie doesn't pick up on it. She smiles and curls her finger in his ear. 'It's not heavy lifting, Tommy. Just. Stuff. Like this wedding.'

'Like this wedding,' he repeats, surprised. 'I thought you wanted a big wedding.'

'Not me. Daddy. It's transactional. I do what he wants, buy my freedom and we're out of there, but not before I have my say. See why the play's so important?'

'I wish I did. You won't even tell me what it's about.'

She touches his face. 'When you see it, you'll understand.'

For a year now the wedding has been shaping up and it's going to be a monster. Four hundred guests. Pat McQuarrie spent a million moving his family into a showplace big enough for this event and another half-million renovating the house. The man had a three tier terrace bulldozed out of the hill behind it and carpeted with sod. Trees got plopped into place. Full-grown topiaries, already clipped into animal shapes, came in on a flatbed truck. By Labor Day weekend there will be a colonnade of flowers flanking the marble walk down to the tents. At the bottom, the marble dance floor is already in place. When Pat McQuarrie dances with the bride he doesn't intend to do it on a rented wooden floor of splintered pine. What else: tent on the top tier for the receiving line, tents on the second tier for the caterers, kitchen tent to the rear and bordering the walk, long tables with hot *hors d'oeuvres* for Pat McQuarrie's guests as they wander down to the big tent where tables will ring the dance floor and guests will use bathrooms with marble fittings. But the four hundred are Pat McQuarrie's guests, not theirs.

And time is running up their heels. 'It's almost five. I have to go.'

'I wish you'd never leave.'

12

'Me too.' Devlin presses her hands to his face. 'Oh Lexie, come with me. Let's get married now.'

'We can't. The wedding. Daddy's got a lot riding on it.'

'But we're in love!'

'If I walked out on the wedding it would kill him.'

You can't leave the business, it would kill Pop. He winces. 'Fathers don't die from that. Look at mine.'

'Please, Tom. This is the last thing I have to do for him.' There is a long pause that he doesn't like. 'That and my play.'

He snaps to attention. It would help if he could see into her but Lexie is staring straight ahead, her profile sweet and smooth as an image on a coin. If she's reading the writing on the wall, there's no telling what it says. 'Stop beating yourself up, Lex. Come with me.'

'I can't. My job.' She means the play. She always does.

He tries, 'Put it on hold. We can stop in LA. I know a great phone number. 1-800-IMARRYU. After we're married it won't matter what comes down! Look,' he says, trying to cover all the bases, 'Your father can have his damn party, he can even have us. For the day.'

For a minute Lexie catches fire. Excited, she shuffles through the possibilities like a pack of cards and then sighs and settles back. 'No, Tommy. It'll never work. Whatever happens, we'll handle it. Just let me pay my dues so we can walk away.'

He should be asking what she means but now that he has her, he's desperate to keep her. 'I love you. Let's do this.' He can see her wavering. 'We can run away.'

'Don't. We'll be together as soon as you're done on the coast. Unless.' Lexie is skimming his face, smiling at what she sees. The bed is warm, she is warm and this is wonderful and he holds his breath, waiting to hear what comes next. 'Unless. Oh Tommy, what if you just quit and came back to New York with me?'

'I have to finish this job.'

'See?' Lexie gives him a clever grin. *Fair's fair.* 'We both have priorities.'

'My first priority is you!'

She touches him. And touches him. Her lips slide down his cheek and she murmurs, 'It's only two weeks.'

'Two million years.'

'Then we'll be together. Forever, I promise. It's only two weeks.'

'I don't know if I can live that long.' Why does he feel like he is bargaining with God?

'Don't.' She takes his hands. 'Be cool, engagements are always hard.'

'Engagements! Lexie, I forgot!' Before she can ask, he dives off the bed and rummages in his coat until he comes up with it. 'I'm so messed up I forgot the ring!'

'Tommy!' It's talismanic. Brilliant. It took a long time to pick out. The minute he slips it on her finger he feels better. Once he puts it on her hand they are bonded. Safe.

'Now go,' she says. 'We've got the rest of our lives together, and that's how we're going to spend them.' She fixes on him with her smile bright and her eyes filled with promises. 'Together. We will.'

4

When they come out of the movie Maggie McQuarrie's fat old sister is all clingy and weird. 'That was scary. All that blood.'

Maggie says, 'Like, you don't think that's chocolate syrup?'

There is too much distance in their family, with Maggie in junior high and her favorite sister Lexie grown up and living in New York. Lally's back living at home, but Lally is forty – whatever, mention her age and you die. In spite of which, she is shoving thirteen-year-old Maggie into the mall parking lot like she's the mom and Lally is the kid. 'You go first, Maggie. I'm too scared.'

'Movies aren't scary,' Maggie says under her breath, 'I'll tell you what's scary. Families are.'

A movie, when it's over you can walk away. Your family is forever. It's like being yoked to a huge idiot twin that pushes you along even while it's hanging on your arm, dragging you down. The whole family is like that except for Lexie, and Lexie's gone.

Lally is the worst. E.g. for instance. Maggie is stuck here in the parking lot when all she wants to be is home. They're going along with Lally squirming in her leather mini skirt and giggling like she's thirteen. 'That was so scary that I need a drink.'

'Like you need a reason to get a drink.'

Sarcasm doesn't even slow her down. Lally just gets in the car with that happy face. Her tone is all: don't bother me, la la la. 'When Daddy asks where we were you just tell him I took you to Brigham's for ice cream.'

Maggie says, 'I'd rather go to Brigham's than some stupid bar.'

'One drink. We'll go as soon as I'm done.'

'Like we ever do like you say. What about my ice cream?'

'I'll give you the money.' Lally thrusts a five at her. 'Here!'

What is Maggie supposed to do with a five, locked in the car outside her old sister's favorite bar? Lally can't drag her inside because of her age, but it's scary out here. Depressed, Maggie scrunches down so guys won't see her and come tapping on the glass.

It takes too long. It always takes too long. When Lally comes out she is three-quarters drunk. Maggie says, 'Maybe I should drive.'

'You're too young to drive.'

Some guy comes lurching out of the bar and across the parking lot. He is yelling. Maggie doesn't know what Lally gets up to in those places, but guys follow her and they are not guys anyone would like. This one is shaking his fist. Maggie sticks her head out of the window and then turns to her sister. 'Who's that?'

'Oh shit.' Lally goes a little nuts starting the motor but finally she gets the car in *Drive* and we roar.

'Lally, my God!' She doesn't know if Lally meant to do it but when they scratched off she almost hit the guy with the car.

Daddy is in the front hall. Leather slippers. Smoking jacket. Matching pants and an angry scowl that doesn't fit into the picture he is trying to make. *You,* he said to her once, *why did you have to come along and spoil everything?* 'Where've you been?'

'At Brigham's.' In spite of everything Lally is still, la la la.

'It's after twelve.' He gives her a look and turns to the girl. 'Margaret, where have you two been?'

'Brigham's,' she says. Daddy will kill her if she lies. Lally will kill her if she doesn't. Maggie calls the shot and growls, 'Why do you have to know where we are every minute of the day?'

And her father comes back so fast that it scares the crap out of her. 'Because bad things happen when I don't! Now go upstairs.'

Maggie has no idea what Lally and her father say to each other when she's not around, but given the way their voices are rising down there, she's just as glad. Still, when they fight like this, everybody feels bad.

When Lally comes upstairs Maggie tiptoes out into the hall and whispers, 'Are you all right?'

Lally doesn't exactly say. She just goes into her room like a cat walking on glass.

Maggie follows her in. 'Are you? OK?'

'Go away.'

'All right for you,' Maggie says.

And then, wow! Out of nowhere, Lally turns on her and lashes out. 'Shut up!'

'I was just trying to . . .' Every time, Maggie thinks, it happens every time.

'I told you to shut up!' Lally tangles her fingers in the girl's hair, twisting hard enough to pull it out of her skull. Then she grinds her knuckles into her scalp. 'You're in the way.'

'Ow!' Maggie hates it when Lally makes her cry.

Then her big sister who's *supposed to take care of her* pushes her against the wall so hard that her head bangs. 'Get out of here, bitch. You're in the way. You're always in the way.'

15

5

Devlin calls Lexie as soon as he gets off the redeye from San Francisco. 'I'm home. I'm at JFK.'

Her voice is happy and bright. 'Oh Tommy, I just missed you!'

'Me too.' It's only been two weeks. Chicago made it worse.

'No, I really mean I really just missed you,' she says in that sweet, bright voice. 'I'm on my way out.'

'You can't be! I tried to call from the plane, but the rotten phones were on the fritz.' He banged on the receiver and badgered the flight attendants and still couldn't find a working phone. The more he tried to get through, the more he needed to make this call. Memorial Day weekend, and the airport is a zoo. The background noise makes it hard to catch her tone. 'If it's the office, phone in sick. I'll be there in an hour.'

'I can't, Tommy. I have to . . .'

'I can't wait to see you.' Devlin is gritty from cramped seating and bad air on the redeye, vapors coming off all those people failing to sleep enroute from the coast. It's light out here in the east but in his heart it's five a.m.

'I can't either. I wish . . .'

'Then stay home and play with me.' Playing pretzel in the half light of that flying coffin has left him in a weakened condition. He has a wild, hyped vision of Lexie shimmering on the windowsill. Testing, testing. 'How's the puppy?'

'Oh sweetie, I talked to the breeder and he's fine!' Lexie is so easy and immediate that he buys everything, even her apology. 'I wish I could stay, but this about me calling in sick.'

'Come on, Lex. I'll die if I don't see you.'

She laughs. 'No you won't, you'll be fine.'

'When we're together, not before.' Then even though he knows how this conversation is going to come out he says, 'Stay. We can get married!' He'll hold her close and never let go. City Hall. Rush the license, do it today. Then he can keep her with him and — he's not clear where the next thought comes from. Keep her safe.

'We are getting married.'

'Today.'

'You know we can't. The invitations are out. Daddy would . . .'

She doesn't have to finish. This wedding is like a blind dragon, roaring to completion with them in its teeth. His fingers are clenched on the phone; his mouth is dry. Why, when he's here in New York, talking to the person he loves the most . . . Why is he crazy with worry now? 'Wait, I'm on my way.'

16

Lexie laughs. 'Ack, I'm not being clear. I meant, I really just missed you, or maybe it's the other way around. It's timing. I'm already late. The minute I hang up I'm out the door.'

'Lex!'

'Shh. It's a kind of emergency.'

'Emergency!'

'Don't freak, I mean fashion emergency. Oh Tommy, we're saying all the wrong things to each other today.'

'Sorry. It's early out. It's been too long.'

Her voice is soft. 'It has.'

'And this is hard.' It's hard talking to her without being able to see her but he's afraid to hang up. Right now it's the only connection they have. 'Don't hang up!'

'I have to. Gotta go. Don't hate me, I don't have any choice. The mother is halfway up the wall and I have to get her down. She has two dozen things we have to get done to the wedding dress.'

'In Boston.'

'In Boston.' She sighs. 'They have to be done on me.'

He looks at the board. The ticket desk. 'Fine. Are you taking the shuttle? I'll wait for you.'

'No. This is hard enough. Having you there when I can't touch you will only make it worse.' The Catholic thing: until they're married, they are expected not to sleep together in Pat McQuarrie's house. She says, 'Besides . . .'

He rushes in. 'Then we'll get a room at Logan. Airport hotel, your folks will never know, they'll think you came in on a later plane.' He is surrounded by three months' luggage – duffle bag, two-suiter, bootbag, laptop – everything but a flip phone. Juggling the receiver and his phone card, he set the computer between his feet; it means a quick fifty bucks to some junkie. His files are eighty per cent backed up but the rest . . . Weird, having a detachable brain. He has appointments in the city today. Never mind. He'd walk away from it all to be with her. Anything to keep her. Anything. 'What plane are you on?'

'I'm not flying, I'm taking the car.'

'Then I'll ride post. Hang on, I can be there by . . .' His watch is still on California time. 'Eight-thirty. Nine, tops.'

'My appointment's at noon.'

'Three months. Plus!'

'Shh. We had time in Chicago.'

'That. That wasn't time.' It was negative time. Suspicion is like a snail; it leaves tracks on you. He's listening hard.

But Lexie sounds like Lexie – no subtext, no overtones. 'Twenty-four hours, that's all. Then I come home and we have the rest of our lives.'

'The thing is, I'm getting bad vibes.'

She laughs. 'Sleep deprivation, that's all. You have your own key. Just let yourself in and get a nap. Everything will look better and you'll be fine.'

'And you'll be gone.'

'Not for long. I'm coming back in the morning, first thing.'

'Why not this afternoon? It's only a dress, Lex. How long can it take?'

'You don't know these women. Hours!'

'Even dressmakers have to quit sometime. If you love me, do the dress and come straight back.'

'It's the dress plus dinner. It's the last family get-together while I'm technically a virgin,' Lexie says. 'With Mom and Dad and Lally and Maggie, your nuclear family plus uncles.'

'But not me?'

'Dad wants just family.'

Wounded, Devlin sticks in the knife. 'They don't want me and they asked Kieran?'

He can almost hear her flinch. 'As if. We don't know where Kieran is.'

'So this party of your father's might, like, draw him out?'

She moves on quickly so she won't have to answer. 'Family dinner, just us. Afterwards we have to go see Aunt Costanza.'

'Oh, I get it.' The secluded convent just outside Boston. The ninety-year-old aunt. 'The nun doesn't approve of me.'

'Nothing like that. She's old, too many people get her confused.'

'You wish!' Exhaustion makes him wheedle like a kid. 'Admit it. She doesn't approve of me.' None of them approve of him. Pat McQuarrie didn't want Lexie marrying into the Devlin family. Until he needed their services. Before that, he shoved her into Boston society. Driven, successful, he expected his daughter to marry up.

'Don't knock Aunt Costanza. It's not her fault she thinks only married people have sex. Tell you what. I'll take my car and after we finish at the convent I can split. I'll head back as soon as we're done.'

When you get what you want sometimes you have to refuse it. He loves her too much. 'No.'

'Why?'

'Holiday weekend. Too many drunks bombing around. I miss you like hell, but I don't want you driving alone at night.'

'I've done it before.'

'Bad vibes. 'It's a hard enough drive when you're not night blind.'

'That isn't true!'

'You drive like a mole under kleig lights. Squint and blink.'

She laughs. 'OK, tomorrow. See you around noonish. Sleep late and when you wake up, I'll be there.'

6

Families are all alike, Tony Devlin thinks sourly. A forced march over hard ground in bad company. You may like some of them but there's one you never asked for and don't want, and you're yoked for life. It's like the goddam vineyard in the Bible. Tom is the last one in but he gets everything that was supposed to be yours.

Your mother shackles the baby to you with a kiss. *Take care of him.*

And you promise, because it's her.

Keep your head up, Tone, you are being watched. Step lively, smile as if you're not dragging him along. And you thought you were free.

He will always both love and hate Tommy.

Fuck Tommy. He glares into the computer. The demolition problem Pop has given him, like this is third grade and he's back in study hall. Specs on some old hotel that went down years ago, like Tony is not smart enough to plan a real implosion and bring it off without taking out everything surrounding. Training, at his age! Hours past dinner and he still hasn't figured out how to start. You bet he's bitter. *I could have been doing this stuff all along.*

Tommy is his millstone on this forced march. Even with Tommy miles away, Tony can feel the weight.

Before they had Tom, the family marched along smooth and fine, lovely Mom and Pop and Tony and Bro. Nice, although Bro's always had a dangerous edge to him. And then, just when the brothers are starting their lives, wham. Before Tommy, Tony and Bro were Pop's glory and his pride.

And this is one proud family. Born to bring down great buildings, brought up with it. Eat it, drink it, love it. Devlin Dismantling. They're nowhere as big as the biggest, no branches here or abroad, but the Devlins have been in demolitions almost as long as the Revenaugh family. Pop keeps it small to keep his procedures secret. Stone Devlin started the company but when they got into implosions Mike Devlin developed his own techniques. Pop's not about to let anybody rip him off. He strung Tony along with promises. *Bro's solid but you're the smart one, Tone. When it's time I'll turn this part over to you*, he said. *Let Bro run the business end, you can plan the jobs.*

Look at him now, staring into a computer, at a problem he can't solve.

While they were still in high school, Pop bought them suits. Took them to ISEE meetings. Introduced them to the big fish and the small ones with that great big Devlin grin. 'My boys, my future.' Two sons born and bred to carry on. He bought them jackets with The International Society of Explosives Engineers seal on them. Clip boards. Pens He bought them

19

hard hats and took them to all the sites. Introduced them to every one of the on-site contractors, 'It's my boys you're going to be working with one of these days.'

Controlled demolition is an art and the joy is in vertical implosion. Pop's implosions are beautiful. Buildings collapse in on themselves with amazing grace. Devlin Dismantling is a little company, but it's among the best.

And Pop had sons to take over DD. Still in their teens and Tony and Bro were walking through buildings with him. Taking core samples. Checking the supports. Which do we have to saw through? If we're tearing out all but one staircase, Pop would say, which one should we keep? The planning, he kept secret. Every company does. He'd hole up with photographs and blueprints and elevations and decide just exactly how to bring each building down safely and neatly, top to bottom, everything pegged to that one fantastic moment when the walls shudder and everything starts to go. When Pop went back to the site he took Bro and Tony with him, they were part of his crew. They would lay the charges and set the timers, badda bing, badda boom.

Just before detonation he would make a little speech to the crew and the local contractors and whoever else was allowed this close to the barriers. 'My sons, my pride.' Tony and Bro both heard: *Some day all this will be yours*. Before Tom.

BT. It's bigger on Tony's personal calendar than BC.

Proud family, marching into the future. Then Tommy comes smashing into the ranks. The key person in the parade gets on the last train for the coast.

Mother came to him in the night. *I want you to look out for your baby brother, Tone. Mama's going to be gone for a little while*. The baby was tiny. Tony was eighteen. The next morning she was gone.

'Mom!'

It almost killed Pop. He isn't the only one. Fifty years old and Tony misses her so much! As if she left yesterday. After Tommy, one by one Tony lost most of the best things in his life. Girl he was seeing at junior college – night classes, sure; he was at DD all day – ISEE scholarship pending, everything lost because he had to quit to babysit. Never mind that the kind of woman you want always turns out to want a college man, something about the gloss. Like that beautiful, actressy thing Tommy is engaged to, but of course Tommy went to goddam Harvard. Tony never would have made it into Harvard but he didn't go to college at all. What else did Tony lose? The one girl who might have loved him, when she went to college they went separate ways. All the women he never met. The children he still doesn't have. Everything Pop promised. Pop said he'd turn the planning over to Tony as soon as God told him it was time to quit. Well, Pop lied.

It came down this way. Tony babysat most nights. Days he was pulling a man's full weight on the job. And Tommy, he got everything because he was the baby and the pet. Baby Tom is six feet something now, he tops out at 180 pounds and Pop doesn't like him but he made him the star. So this is the other big thing that Tony and Bro have lost. They lost their place in the food chain in that lump of coal that Pop calls a heart. Bro and Tony stayed home and got their hands dirty while Tom got drunk with those pink-faced snots at Harvard. Harvard! Architecture school!

'This boy,' Pop said. 'He's going to do us proud.'

'I thought we were doing you proud.'

Pop got that look in his eyes. 'Tony, Tony, he's going to be an architect. When I'm old and dead, there will be Devlin buildings around so the world will know I was here.'

Well, look what all that education did for him. Seven years of school and he can't even talk to us. Listen. Anybody can do math and write stupid poems but only we can bring a building down so sweet and slick that thousands of people jump to their feet and howl. He begrudges every cent they wasted on the kid.

But Tony has a naturally sweet nature. It's what got him through. He figured Tom would get his PhD or whatever and go off to make opera houses like he wants. That would be the end of him, after all, wasn't he already too good for them? So whatever the inconvenience, they would get shut of him soon.

That hope went out the window when Pop got sick.

At first they didn't know what it was. His hand started shaking so hard that he couldn't hold the drafting pencil. Half the time he could barely speak. Nothing Tony or Bro could do would help. He'd done all the specs for the next job but there were important details pending. Poor old man could hardly walk but he made them help him to the office. Sitting there at the drafting table, staring at the plans. They called the client and postponed the blast. Tony helped Pop however he could, never mind that Pop took a swing at him and almost fell. It got worse. While the brothers were out at a meeting Pop fell down and couldn't get up. The cleaning lady dialed 911. The ambulance came. The hospital called Tony. They got Bro on the phone. The look Bro shot Tony as he passed on the message tore into him like a buzzsaw through butter. 'He only gets one visitor at a time. He sent for you.'

Tony's heart jumped up. He went tearing into the ICU. 'Pop!'

'Not now.' Pop was strangling on spit but he was warning God. 'Not now, in the middle of a job!'

'Pop, I can do it.'

'What.'

'Draw the plans. Finish the calculations. Time the charges.'

'Tom knows how buildings work. He'll know how they come apart. You don't.'

Tony heard his voice shake. And at the same time his insides made this lunge that he mistook for joy. 'Maybe not, but I will.'

'And rain chunks on everything for miles around? No way.' Sick as he was, Pop raked him to bits. 'Son, son, you're not up to it.' Then Mike Devlin, who didn't cry even when Tony's mother left him, broke down and sobbed.

It was enough to break your heart. 'Pop, I'm here!'

'Not what I want!'

'Tell me what you want and I'll get it.'

Then Pop ripped Tony apart and threw away the pieces. 'I want Tommy. Get me Tom.'

Never mind that Tom gets back and Pop cures up. Like that! 'It happens with Parkinson's,' the doctor said. 'But it takes its time.' Remission, they said. But Pop wouldn't let Tommy go. Tom comes home with this God damned computer and all his fine tricks. And the job that was supposed to be Tony's, that he'd sacrificed a normal life for, went to Tom. Tom, he thinks, smacking the computer. Tom and this fucking unusable *thing*.

Tommy comes home and Pop hands him the world. All his secrets. Tony's job! Then some kid gets killed in a DD blast and Tom leaves us flat. Just like Mom. He leaves the business and he leaves DD and we are stuck with the dead boy's father. We paid him off and the bastard still won't go away. It doesn't look so good, a guy like that hanging around. At the time Tony thought fine, it's a trade-off. What's a little inconvenience. It's my birthright now.

But Pop takes hold as soon as Tom is out the door. Like he'd rather get well than tell his secrets to Tony here. It was bitter, bitter. Pop put the computer back in its box and went back to the old methods, forget it, Tony. Not you. Until now. Now the Parkinson's is creeping back in on him. It's like a monster crouched on his chest. Pop can't hang on to the power forever. The old man knows he's losing it. So what does he do? Drags out the computer and sits Tony down in front of it, Tony, who never had time to play around with this blank-faced poor excuse for a video game. 'OK Tone, let's see if you're up to the job.'

My job. 'What does this thing have to do with the job?'

'Tommy set this thing up for me. He could make it sing and dance,' Pop said. 'It ought to be a cinch. I can still do the calculations but I'm too old for computers and I'm getting too shaky to draw.'

'Pop, I didn't go to Harvard.'

'This isn't a Harvard thing. Sit down. Now, do me these problems. And don't get back until you get it right.'

He gives Tony these practice problems! Practice! And,

a., Tony can't get this computer to do *anything* and

b., when he tries it with the calculator and the drafting pencil, it comes out wrong and Pop shoves all his hard work off the table like a baby pushing spinach off a tray.

Tony doesn't know whether he hates Tommy more for walking out and leaving the computer without even a how-to note, or for squeezing him out of Pop's heart.

The problem Pop set for him is stalled on the screen, what did he do wrong? Reboot the computer, the damn thing is dead as a glass eye. 'Shit!'

Bro pokes his head in. 'You're on top of it, right?' When they were kids Bro used to bash Tony hard every time he got it wrong. He looks ready to smack him now.

'Oh yeah.' A lot hinges on it.

'You gotta be able to jump in when Pop corks.' Bro, with the sharp nose and the sharp chin and the sharp glare.

'He's not gonna . . .' Not until I know how to do this.

'When we take over,' Bro says and slams the door.

Tony's fingers are greasy with sweat. He hates computers and he can't figure out what this one wants.

Damn Pop, setting up paper tigers for him to kill.

Like Tony is too stupid to plan a real job. Well, pretty soon it won't matter. The Parkinson's is wrecking Pop from the inside out. It's moving fast and Tommy is out of the equation. Pop wouldn't let him touch the machine until this week. Like he thought Tommy was going to come back. Tony could probably do this on paper, like Pop, but Pop wants him to do it like Tommy does. Digital imaging, yeah right. Four hours on this fucking thing and he can't make it work! Sure Tommy left them the software. He also left without saying how it works. 'It's easy,' he said last year, 'just access the help menu. If you get in trouble, call me.' Well fuck him, it's hard as hell and Tony is too proud to ask.

For the fifth time the rotten computer screen seizes up and Tony smacks his brother's halfassed machine hard enough to break a normal person's hand. The only thing that cheers him is imagining Tommy is inside it, and he can hear him shriek.

7

'You're Mr Devlin.'

'You ought to know me by now.'

'You just missed her,' the doorman says.

'What do you mean just, she was supposed to be in the car an hour ago.'

The doorman is older than the building by at least forty years. A hair coloring disaster has fried what little he has left to orange frizz. He is holding a mashed package. 'Miss McQuarrie said to say that to whoever came whenever. She said if it was you, give this to you.'

'She's expecting somebody else?'

'How am I supposed to know?'

He doesn't know why he's so twitchy today. 'If she's expecting somebody else, who else is coming?'

'Do you want this package or what?'

'As in, did she give you a name?'

The doorman doesn't like Devlin, never has. It's as if Pat McQuarrie personally put him in place to make sure nobody sleeps over at his youngest daughter's house. It doesn't matter how many Christmas tips Devlin gives the guy or how much time he's spent building character, asking about his family, talking about the Mets, Pat's paid Rottweiler snarls at him all the same. 'She doesn't tell me everything.'

'Are you going to let me in?'

'You're already in.'

The package is wrapped in brown paper bags taped together the way Lexie tapes things, every which-way. Crazily, he thinks she may have bundled up some of her clothes like a shucked skin – something for him to put his face in while she's gone. He stuffs the thing under the strap of his duffel and starts for the elevator. When he left for San Francisco he closed out his apartment and put everything in storage. He thought he'd be comfortable staying with Lexie while they looked for an apartment together, but he was wrong. He should have eaten the deposit and three months' rent on a new apartment big enough for both of them. He needs to get her out of this place! Never mind that she can't move until after the wedding, they could camp out on what little furniture he has. This isn't her place. It's Pat McQuarrie's choice. The building is relatively new for this part of the city, a dull, yellow brick box filled with dull, boxy apartments just this side of genteel. Anything Lexie could afford, Pat said, would not be safe. Devlin knows gifts of money aren't really gifts. They are transactional. One more reason to move into their own space, and soon.

The old lady across the hall from Lexie sticks her head out the door as soon as he puts his key in the lock. 'Oh, it's you.'

'Hi Mrs Steegmuller.' Does Pat pay her too?

'I was hoping it was Mr McQuarrie. I love it when he comes.'

'Always nice to see you too.'

Interesting how much time people spend outrunning their families. Devlin is rescuing Lexie from hers. Well into his thirties and he's still trying to outrun his. He'd like to find an island where no relatives come. Where people are themselves and not their histories. He'd take Lexie there and never come back. As it is they both drag families like dead vines snarled around their ankles. He and Pop and his brothers have a long history. The McQuarries, he's only begun to unpack.

Most days he wakes up thinking he's a free agent but he's not. Wherever he goes he's hounded by Bro with his angry eyes and the pinched look that comes with lowered expectations. Then there's Tony's soft, reproachful smile. Plus Pop. He'll never understand what it is with Pop. At least it's a small family, he thinks, putting his stuff down in Lexie's front hall. There are so many McQuarries that he's only met half of them. He's doing his best to help her separate but he may need to move her to Mars. *And I won't get shut of mine when I'm old and they're all dead.*

Empty apartment, yesterday bleeding into today with no sleep to mark the division, Lexie's bed waiting with no Lexie in it. If he showers and crashes now he can sleep until his afternoon meeting. He'd like to sleep straight through and wake up tomorrow, with today behind him and Lexie home. Forget it. Just sleep.

The phone bleats. Fine. Let it go. The machine kicks in. He hears his oldest brother's voice. 'Tommy, is that you?'

He tells the machine, Go away, don't bother me.'

'I know you're there.'

'Fuck off, I'm not doing this.'

'Pick up, it's an emergency.'

He grabs the phone. 'What, is it Pop?'

'It isn't Pop, asshole, it's me.'

'Bro.'

'Who did you think it was?'

'Who told you I was here?'

'You're not in San Francisco, where else would you be?'

'Look, I just got off the redeye. Can I call you back?'

'No need, this will be short. It's about the wedding.'

'The wedding is months away.'

'Never mind when it is, we need to settle this.'

'Could we do this later? I'm dead beat.'

Two hundred miles away and Bro is passive-aggressively shoving him around. 'Your brother and I have been thinking. Let's do this while it's on our minds.'

He puts down the laptop but the package Lexie left is clamped under one elbow, not sure why. 'Whatever, Bro.'

'We're thinking to leave Pop home from the wedding, so's we don't embarrass you. He's losing it and he drools.'

25

This carries two messages, both meant to make the baby brother feel bad. Tom says through clenched teeth, 'I'm not getting married without Pop,' so it comes out grudging and all wrong.

'We don't any of us have to come, you know, if you'd be easier without us.'

Lexie's wound the package with so much tape that he'll need a knife to get into it. 'Why would I be easier without you?'

'You and your smartass college friends. The McQuarries, too good for us until they need a job done. Do you know what your father-in-law calls us?'

Devlin does know. *The dirty Devlins.* 'He's not my father-in-law.'

'So, we don't want to embarrass you in front of your new . . .'

'Be cool, Bro. I'm cool with you.'

Then Tony slips into the conversation with that smooth phone manner he picked up in voiceover class, another of those Tony get-rich schemes that never came to anything, they took his money and botched his audition tape. 'Wish you all the best, Tommy.'

'Tony!'

'Just wanted you to know no matter how far you go from us, we're on your side.'

'What are you doing, are you both on the phone?'

'Life's too short to pay for two long distance calls.'

Tony says, 'What Bro means is, life's too expensive.'

'For a ten-minute phone call? Hang up, I'll call you right back.'

Bro, on the extension: 'We're cutting costs, what with Pop getting too sick to plan the jobs.'

'He should train somebody up.'

'Get real,' Bro says. 'He only trusts his own blood and he only trusts us half the time.'

'Well he shouldn't have trusted me.'

Tony says, 'What, because you bungled one job?'

'I don't bungle. This was worse.'

Bro's voice is pinched tight, like his expression. 'If you're talking about that kid that got killed in the blast, you were looking for an easy out. It was like you took the first excuse. Now I'm not saying you *arranged* it, I . . .'

'I'm not going there with you, Bro.'

'We need you back. Somebody's got to plan the jobs.'

'Tony can do it.'

'Yeah shit.'

'Tommy . . .'

Don't whine. 'It's all in the machine, Tony. I left everything behind.'

'If you mean that computer, it's a piece of junk.'

'I wrote some help into the program. Once you get your head around it you'll do fine.'

'That and two bucks won't even buy me a beer. College boy.'

'This isn't a college situation,' Devlin says. Fifty years old and his big brother is wheedling. 'Tony, it's all right there in the machine.'

'Like I can find anything on the damn thing without you.'

Bro cuts him off. 'Come back in with us, we'll make it worth your while.'

26

'Is that what you called me for?' Devlin is distracted by the package. He has made a triangular tear in the paper. Tweed, he is looking at a scrap of tweed. *Present for me*?

'More than worth your while.'

'You know where I am with that.'

They are hunting him in pairs, Bro first. 'All that tuition. We sacrifice and now that you're educated, you're too good for us.'

'No. He's too good to do the job.'

'Not good enough,' Devlin flashes on the kid's body in the rubble. The job went down fine, perfect implosion, no fallout. The removal crew went in to pull out the steel for recycling. The crane lifted a vertical support and there he was. Poor Freddy Slade.

'Too good to waste his time on us.'

Anger surges. He opens his mouth to shout.

But quick as you are, big brothers are always quicker. Devlin can't be sure which of them delivers the punchline as they break the connection. 'Too good for the ones that made you who you are.'

Leaving him dead empty, standing there in Lexie's empty apartment with the brown paper package she left for him still clamped under his arm. It takes him a while to remember to put down the phone. All his life Tony and Bro have been like a pair of hunting dogs working in tandem, wearing him down. They're his brothers and he loves them but he'll never get shut of them, not even when they're dead. He needs to deal with this package and he's too tired. All he wants to do is get in the shower and forget. Crash in Lexie's bed and wake up thinking about something else.

He trips on his duffle bag and the package flies. 'Shit.' The thing skates under a table and lands against a wall. If he gets down on his hands and knees to grab it, he'll fall asleep right here on the floor. Better deal with it after he's gotten some sleep.

8

It isn't Gerald Slade's fault that he lives in his office now. With no fixed address, he sleeps, eats and washes at the junior college where he teaches accounting. At least the office is easy to take care of. On alternative Thursdays, the janitor comes. Gerald showers at the school gym. He has his main meal of the day in the cafeteria at noon. Most nights he eats graham crackers and Lipton's Cup O' Soup out of their neat shelf-to-table Styrofoam containers. His clothes, he hangs in the book closet. Every morning he rolls up the single-sized futon and wedges it into the knee hole under his desk. At this stage in his grief, it is important to keep the particles to a minimum.

There used to be more objects in his life. He used to be able to handle them. The house. The yard. The furniture. The phone books and newspapers and junk mail and political fliers and food containers that drop into an ordinary life. Then Freddy got killed and he lost interest. His only son. Barely fifteen. Alive one day. Missing the next. And weeks later, found dead. All right, Freddy was in a place where he didn't belong but kids of fifteen are always in places they don't belong. Doesn't everybody make allowances for that?

Grieving takes the blood out of you. Gerald gave up shaving. It was hard enough staying on his feet. Getting to work. Pursuing his case. He did what you do when Freddy got taken away from him. He went to the law.

Without Freddy to care what he did, the house went to hell. No time for that now. He was too busy grieving. Collecting evidence. That kind of thing can eat up your life. Things got out of hand. At first Gerald didn't notice. The he noticed, but he was too preoccupied to do anything about it. He lost control of small objects. They came into the house at the same rate they had when Freddy was alive. Compounded by law books and paper work – his case, his case. Objects accreted. It was relentless. Thousands of things passed through Gerald's fingers and lay where they fell, waiting for some cosmic recycle truck. When he lost the house the removal people had to shovel out the halls to get at the furniture. Nothing sinister, really, nothing that rotted or corroded and nothing that smelled, it was only four years' worth of magazines and newspapers and unopened mail, empty bottles and grocery sacks and cartons he had tossed wherever because he didn't care enough to cope. What's the use with Freddy gone?

The mail was the worst. With no encouragement from him it just kept coming, the death certificate and funeral bills and sympathy notes at first, then junk mail, four years' worth of Publishers' Clearing House notices and unsolicited credit cards and sweepstakes announcements got mixed in with the property tax bills, fire and water tax bills, overdue notices from the city. The tax bills got lost in the flood along with catalogs for International Male and Victoria's Secret and The Sharper Image, fat brochures for a thousand other products he would never order. As it turned out the mail included warnings from the city about his unpaid bills but grief filled Gerald's mind. There was no room left for details. It was all he could do to keep his job and deal with lawyers. Lawsuits eat you to death.

The city foreclosed on the house.

At least the office is easy to keep neat.

As if neat mattered. As if anything mattered. When you lose your only son you have lost your life. Poor Freddy, so what if he was a little wild. Dead under a hundred thousand tons of crumpled steel and broken cement. Nobody deserves that. The only person Gerald Slade ever cared about dead, deep in the belly of a ruined building, like an Egyptian prince.

He didn't have a son any more, he had a case. Against the advice of his lawyer, he sued Devlin Dismantling. They wanted to settle out of court. He wanted to sue their brains out. No. He wanted to sue the Devlin family to death. It never got to court. The company wanted to settle. To Devlin Dismantling, Freddy was worth a hundred thousand dollars, it was the best they could do. Gerald took it as an admission of guilt. His lawyer told him to settle, after all, company security had chased Freddy out the night before the blast. It wasn't their fault Freddy snaked under the fence and went back into the abandoned hotel because demolition or no, it was where he always went to shoot up. Right before Gerald fired him the lawyer said, 'Listen, for all you know the kid OD'd.'

If he OD'd they should have found him. Rushed him to the hospital. Look. They should have stopped him going in. They could have saved his life! In an odd way, the Devlins killed his Freddy twice.

His lawyer said his case would get thrown out, so settle. He wanted to kill the Devlins all the way to the Supreme Court but he couldn't do it alone. The Devlins cut a check and forgot. Well, Gerald Slade can't forget what happened to Gerald Frederick Slade Junior and he won't let the Devlins forget it either. When you've lost your only son you've lost your life. Settlement is never enough. It isn't the money, money is nothing. He wants them to pay. What can he take from them to make them even? Another life?

With Freddy dead, Gerald has exactly one reason to go on living. Revenge. It fuels his nights and gets him through the days.

He is still mulling the ways. Of course the Devlins and all their employees are to blame, but in things this big there is always an accountable party. Over time, Gerald has found out who, He has learned a little something about vertical implosion. Gerald, who haunts DD blasts. The point man is the job designer. He walks the sites and takes core samples and decides what kinds of explosives. More: he blueprints the job: when and where and how the charges will be planted. There are other people tearing out staircases and weakening supports but the planner is responsible for the sequence of timed detonations. He triggers the blast and he is the man who killed Freddy and Gerald wants to rip out his heart and watch it bleed.

Last year he drove from Waltham, where the junior college is, to New Haven. Company headquarters. He pretended to be a reporter doing a story. Said he'd seen the implosion of the old Armbruster Hotel on a TV documentary and knew the public would be interested in how it was done. The receptionist said company techniques were trade secrets. Controlled demolitions is a tight business; companies keep their methods to themselves.

Well, Gerald has a secret. He is working on a plan. When he insisted, she asked him to leave. He waited until she went to lunch and tried again. He told the lunch-hour substitute that he was the former manager of the defunct hotel and he was looking for old photographs of the implosion. She called security.

He went back to the building after hours. Did he plan to break in? He isn't clear. Devlin Dismantling was locked but there was an old man in a wheelchair parked out front, waiting for his car to come around. Gerald said he represented a Canadian demolitions company and he had come to study the Armbruster job, the design was brilliant, who was responsible? All right, he came on too strong.

The old man glared. 'Who wants to know?'

'I do,' Gerald shouted. 'I do!'

The old man sat there with his mouth working, fragile and defiant. As Gerald raged, a car shot out of the underground garage. The skinny Devlin brother jumped out, shouting. When he refused to go, the slick-looking heavyset brother came at him with a jack handle. He ran.

Never mind. When you need to know something, you go where you have to go to find out. It cost him a portion of the DD settlement check to find out, but Gerald found out. A Thomas Devlin ('Mr Devlin isn't with us any more') killed Freddy, this is clear. After all, didn't he plan the job? That made it his responsibility to make the final sweep of the building. An hour before detonation? Not minutes or seconds before? God damn you. Didn't you see him? If you didn't see him, why didn't you keep looking until you found my boy? So, fine, you swept the building, you God damned murderer. Why didn't you sweep it again? Again. You should have found my Freddy no matter what he was doing or where he was hiding. You should have found him and carried him out. He was only a kid!

Gerald Slade sees a hell with this Thomas Devlin in it, searching the building into eternity and finding Freddy over and over again. Again. He will make a hell for Tom Devlin, but not yet. He is only beginning to figure out how. He is already working on ways. He found out there is a fiancée, he has taken steps to get close to the family. Not in any of the usual ways because Gerald Slade is an orderly man, more subtle than you might think. He has been to the neighborhood where the McQuarrie house stands at the end of a lavishly planted drive; he knows who comes and who goes. He has spent some time in the little village – the ice cream place, the bookstore, the news stand where the McQuarrie women sometimes pick up magazines. Not a stalker, not Gerald Slade. Just a man who has developed an interest and will do what he must to protect it. Sweet man. Gentle manner. Nice smile. Taking one light step at a time, he has made a new friend.

Grief makes a man move slowly. He has nothing but time.

The kettle in his office has come to a boil. He pulls the foil seal off his cup O' Soup and pours hot water in. Stirring it with a pencil, he broods.

All right, you bastard. You'll find out how it feels to lose someone.

9

Devlin hates sleeping badly but not as much as he hates strange dreams, and this one is extremely strange. He jolts awake. He can't remember where he was in the dream but the sound of the phone filtered into the mix as a warning beep. Last call to clear the site. Fifteen minutes before detonation. Detonation? It is the old dream but it's not the old dream. Time telescopes and suddenly he is running ahead of the walls in a collapsing building and Lexie is running somewhere farther ahead; he crashes through barriers to get to her but he can run for the rest of his life and never catch up. He shouts at her to wait but sirens drown him out.

Correction. It's the phone. He surfaces with his blood pounding. He is alone in Lexie's room. The only light comes from the blinking digital clock. A temporary power outrage left it winking: 12:00, 12:00, 12:00, no telling what time it is. Totally dark in here, it must be deep night. He shouts into the phone. 'What!' Only bad news comes in the middle of the night.

Her voice explodes the nightmare, but fragments cling. 'Tommy, it's me!'

'Then you're OK!' The nightmares that you can't remember are the ones you have to worry about. Your subconscious, warning you.

Lexie says, 'Of course I'm OK, I just got back from lunch.'

'Lunch?' He can't shake the premonitory dream. The trapped part of him is trying to get off the phone so he can get back into the building, he needs to go back into the dream to see if he can find out what's wrong. 'Lunch? What do you mean, lunch?'

'Well, not real lunch, it was Thai take-out. We didn't have much time.'

'In the middle of the night?'

'Tommy, are you wearing my sleep mask?'

'No.' He blinks. Lexie's room darkeners are too good. Only a thin, brilliant thread around the window shade tells him that outside, it's daytime. 'Sorry. The redeye whacked my clock. What time is it?'

'Two-thirty. Are you OK?'

'Bad dream. Lexie, are you OK?' Somebody trapped in the building and detonation in fifteen . . .

'Of course I'm OK, but I think you'd better go back to bed. You sound like Tom Waits on Pop Rocks.'

She always could make him laugh. Oh, he thinks, relieved. It was never Lexie, it's the old Freddy thing. It's not her fault he can't shake the dream. He chalks it up to guilt and moves on. 'No, it's a good thing you called. I've got a meeting at three.'

'I'm sorry I woke you up.'

'You did me a favor. Reponen and I are meeting the new client today, holiday or no.' He flips on the light. 'I miss the hell out of you, Lex.'

He has no idea how she manages to sound apologetic without apologizing. 'That's what I called about. This is going to take longer than I thought.'

'Come on, I'm dying here!'

'You won't die, you never do. The trouble is, they need me tomorrow too. It's a thing about the dress.'

'I thought today was the thing about the dress.'

'One last thing after they do the thing,' she says, laughing. 'I promise, I'll be through by noon. Oh Tommy, I miss you so much.'

The laughter brings her into the room with him. Times they've had here. It's hard, her voice in his ear and Lexie miles away, but all he can find to say is, 'Me too.'

'Look at it this way, it's the last time I see Boston until the day before the fateful day.'

'You make it sound so – fateful.'

'And we'll be together for that one. Thank God. I really need you for these. Um.' Her pause conjures up a thin, red-haired line of McQuarries. 'Family moments.'

'I can be there for this one in . . .' he checks his watch. 'Four hours.'

'You'll never make it in this traffic. Next time. And every time after that until we die of old age.'

'What if I kidnap you?'

'Dad would have cops scouring all fifty states.'

'And offshore islands?'

'And Bratislava and Ceylon. Look, I'll be in the car by noon tomorrow, promise. I should be home by four, four-thirty, tops.'

Talking, he pulls a clean shirt out of his two-suiter. Gets his shaving stuff. 'I can still make it.'

And Lexie, Lexie knows he's getting ready for his meeting. 'No you can't, you're deciding which shirt for the new client.'

'I am. I can come right after.'

'You know how long those meetings take. Holiday weekend, the roads are jammed. We'll be at Aunt Costanza's and back before you hit Route 128. Incidentally, they're mightily impressed by the ring.'

'Would they be impressed if I came late and sneaked into your bedroom?' Us. Together.

Lexie hesitates just long enough to let him know she's thinking about it. 'Do you believe Daddy's had this heap alarmed? He's redoing the place for quick turnover after the wedding and he drops gazillion bucks on security. First alert kind of thing. One beep brings down the Lincoln cops.'

'If it wasn't that it would be dogs.'

'He's talking about Dobermans.'

'OK, tomorrow.' He feels better, just talking to her. Just hearing her voice is sweet. So whatever the dream was trying to tell me, he thinks, we're getting married and it's OK.

'Tomorrow I promise. Four, four-thirty tops.'

Then his eye lights on the package. If it's a present, she's probably wondering why he didn't thank her. If it isn't, he needs to ask. 'Lexie, wait!'

Too late. He has to empty his wallet to find the McQuarrie phone number in Massachusetts. It's her folks' home number, not one of those things you memorize. He calls back but nobody picks up.

He gets out his knife and cuts through her snarl of tape. Lexie never did know how to wrap packages, this one is a mess. He pulls off the brown paper – four layers of grocery bags, turned inside out so the printing doesn't show.

'OK, what is it? What have you got for me, Lex?'

It's a jacket. It's a man's tweed jacket, more or less his size but worn down to the buckram at the collar and shaggy at the cuffs. *Somebody else's jacket*, he thinks. *For me*? Grimacing, he shakes it out. Nothing in the pockets, but it smells like mildew and pipe tobacco. If she wants him to wear it, fine. After it's cleaned. This is somebody else's jacket. If she wants him to have it, there must be a reason. Like everything else he cares about, this has to wait until she comes home. When Lexie gets back, they'll talk. And talk.

10

Warnings are never specific. When it comes, the evil you were expecting is never what you think. Sometimes it's worse.

Devlin's meeting went well. He and the new client are a good match. As his present for bringing the San Francisco project in on schedule, Reponen has handed him a new client who wants to talk through every detail of the new project before he starts drafting, all billable hours. He went out for dim sum afterward. Comfort food. Then he came back to Lexie's. He called the house in Lincoln, Mass. And even though he thought he heard somebody else breathing on an extension, he and Lexie talked each other to sleep.

The phone drags him out of a long stupor. He breaks the connection. 'Middle of the night!'

It rings again. It may be closer to midnight than morning in San Francisco, but it's closer to morning in New York. The digital clock is still blinking: 12:00, 12:00, 12:00, got to fix that damn thing. One more ring and the machine will take it. Wait a minute. Can't have that. What if it's Zee? Better yank the phone out of the jack. No, he could end up with her at Lexie's door. So at a gut level, he knows what's coming. ''Lo!'

'Thomas Devlin?' That familiar smoky voice.

'Yes.' *Oh, so this is what the nightmare was telling me.* The call is a surprise, but now that it's come he knows it was inevitable. The nightmare wasn't about Freddy Slade this time, it wasn't even about Lexie. It was his early warning system kicking in.

'Thomas Devlin of Reponen Associates. The Evergreen Building?'

'How did you find me?' This is awful. Still, knowing is better than not knowing.

'Do you know who this is?'

'No.' Of course he does. Devlin came back from San Francisco holding a wild card. His secret, that he wants to hold close to his chest so Lexie never has to see. Now, like an adversary in an online card game, a woman he slept with exactly once sits in California, studying the options. Making a remote connection, she clicked on his wild card and took control of the game.

'Aren't you glad to hear from me?'

'How did you get this number?'

'So you do know.'

Of course he knows. 'Why are you calling me, Zee.'

Zee Wellaver, with her caterpillar eyelashes and that seductive telephone voice. If she ever loses her job the woman can set up a 900 number and

35

rake it in. Of the women he knows, only Zee sounds like an overheated Barbie on crack. 'I'm just feeling a little out of touch.'

'We never said we'd stay in touch.'

'Yeah. But we are.'

'I told you I was engaged. I even showed you the ring!' Crazy, but he did. Lexie's solitaire. He showed it to her to get her off his back. Simple setting, beautiful.

'Tiffany, right?'

'Tiffany.'

Zee turned the ring over and over in her hand and did him anyway. *Don't worry*, she said, *it's only sex.*

'The ring.' As if all he has to do is remind her. 'You thought it was beautiful. I told you I was engaged.'

'And I told you I didn't care.' He can hear her stretching like a cat – the rustle of soft flesh under fabric. 'But I do.'

'Why, Zee?'

'We had a good thing going, Tom. Really nice.' She is teasing. 'It was good for you. Was it good for me?'

He says patiently, 'It doesn't matter, Zee.'

'Yes it does.'

'OK, it shouldn't.' This is making him uncomfortable. He wants to tell her it was nothing but it wasn't. It was something. It was something he never should have done. When you're promised to one person and you end up sleeping with another, it is a very big thing. He didn't think so at the time. No, he wanted not to think so. There was a party. They were both drunk.

Zee told Devlin it was recreational. She said she needed it to relieve tension, no strings. The bidding had just closed on interior design for his project. Zee was chewing her nails over whether her company had come in with the lowest bid. She was working Devlin because he was Reponen Associates' on-site person. The dance was supposed to be about business but they got too close and forgot where they had started. He assumed Zee was boffing him to get the contract. The whole thing was hot, swift and transactional.

Lexie never should have sent him off to San Francisco alone.

'I suppose you're going to say it was nothing.'

'Nothing.' Except for the guilt.

Zee says sourly, 'Well, it isn't nothing.'

'Look, you got what you wanted. Your company has the job.'

'And you got what you wanted. Tom, we need to talk.'

'I don't have anything to say.'

'What's that supposed to mean?'

'Stop sounding like a TV soap. Listen. I can't take calls from you here, Zee. Ever.'

'Yeah well, that's OK because I just called to tell you . . .' Zee is waiting for him to beg her to finish. When he doesn't, she says girlishly, 'Guess what? I'm coming to New York!'

'And?'

'I want to see you.'

36

'No. I'm sorry. We can't,'

The next sequence is so calculated that he knows Zee worked it out before she started researching this phone number and well before she made this call. 'You're engaged, right?'

'You saw the ring!'

'To this Alexandra McQuarrie, works at Bledsoe Securities, right? Yeah, at Twenty-ninth Street and Tenth Avenue, I've got the number right here.' She recites it. Lexie's private line.

'No.' Right, he thinks. She's threatening to tell Lexie. I made a mistake when I slept with her. I made a worse one when I tried to hide it.

'Don't lie to me. I can't wait to see you! No, we're seeing each other. You. Me.'

'Wrong.'

'Please?'

'One night, Zee. It was only one night.'

The voice hardens. 'Don't blow me off, Tom. I have ways of making you remember me.'

'Is that a threat?' Zee Wellaver is laying out a chain of rhetoric to haul him in. Fine. Let her get it out of her system. Let it play, let it play. 'Should I be recording this call?'

'No, you should be paying attention to this call.' As if she knows her sexy tone has slipped, Zee goes all soft. 'I just called to tell you how excited I am to be in the city.'

'Wait a minute.' Did she say in the city? Hang up, man. End this.

'I'm really, really looking forward to getting with you, since we're already talking, we might as well set up a time . . .'

'No.' He is doing several things at once here. Cutting this short before it gets started. Neutralizing Zee's secret weapon. It's so simple. Tell Lexie about Zee and do it fast, before this crazy woman can. God only knows what Lexie will do but he had to get straight with her. If they can survive this one, they're linked for life.

'Because if you don't set up a time . . .'

'Stop threatening me, Zee, I'm not going to see you.' Oh, wow, Lexie. *If I lose her I'll die*. At least Zee is keeping him honest.

'Oh, yes you will. Because if you don't I'm going to call You Know Who and tell her everything we did.'

'Don't bother.' He doesn't exactly lie, he just switches tense. Nine-tenths of the act is the intention. 'She already knows.'

Zee snorts. 'As if!'

'Your mistake. We tell each other everything.' God, Devlin thinks, *I was so stupid. What made me think I could keep it from her. Why did I think I could cover it up?*'

'You're lying.'

'Don't count on it. And don't call me back. Nice talking, Zee. Now, goodbye.'

Good. Not good, exactly, but better. Now, do this. Get it over with. He picks up the phone. Then he looks at the clock. Four a.m. A terrible hour to have this conversation. He loves her too much to mess this up. He'll take her hands when she gets here, tell her face to face.

Devlin goes into the lovely, barren living room. The tweed jacket she left for him is hanging over the chair like an extra person. It gives him a start. Then he thinks: *maybe it belongs to an old boyfriend.* It would make confession easier. When she gets back, he'll ask. He turns his chair ready to sit here until she comes in. Penance, he thinks, dredging the word up from his deep past. He sits for a long time, considering.

When Lexie comes in that door he will open up to her. The worst thing he did was not boffing Zee, it was lying. If he and Lexie are going to get married and be well married, they can't have unpacked baggage in the bed with them. They need to tell each other everything. When she comes in that door he'll just tell her. Let her get pissed off at him. If she wants to hit him, fine. He deserves it. If they have to break up for a while before Lexie forgives him, he'll handle it. Whatever it takes, he thinks. He'll hold her and never let go.

As first light comes in the windows he stands. Waiting has gotten too big to handle. If he crashes now, time may come unstuck. Yawning, he takes a Melatonin and stumbles back to bed. With luck he'll sleep until Lexie gets home. She'll come into the bedroom and wake him. He can reach up and pull her into his arms and begin. The sooner he tells her, the sooner he can get through this bad part. Maybe she'll tell him what it was with Chicago. What it is with this coat. She'll tell him what's going on with her and they'll be even. As soon as she comes in.

11

Pat McQuarrie has spent his life making this elegant life for himself and he will spend the rest of his life defending it. Handsome man, silver hair. He is the picture of prosperity. Suave, confident man close to the top and hanging on by his fingernails.

'Alexandra,' he says, looking at the paper he's found. He slips it under his blotter. 'What are you trying to do to us?'

When you have predictions to protect, life is hard enough. Add secrets you never thought you'd have to keep and it's insupportable. Still, his aim in life is to bring off the dance and make it look easy. Witness this house. Fit for a country gentleman. Top of the ladder, which is where he is heading. Everything shelter-magazine gorgeous, for quick turnover after the wedding. A lot hinges on this wedding. Contacts he needs. More.

With photos in *Town and Country*, *Architectural Digest*, with the right vibes, he can turn this place over for five times what he paid for it. Truth is, he is overextended. The game in real estate is good old supply and demand but with the market whacked and the Dow jiggling like an electrocuted lineman, it's a crapshoot. The money's hanging by the thread. *And I thought land was the one thing that wouldn't blow up on you.* But land meant more before property taxes and maintenance went sky high and depreciation and costs on the Florida hotel are eating him alive, he has to get out from under. Meanwhile there are startup expenses on the big mall he is developing, certain short term notes due, where is he going to get the money? The wedding is key to survival, but his wife Moira doesn't know this. He protects her. It's what a man does.

So all she has to think about is which dresses and what color. As if appearances are all they have to worry about. 'Pat? Got a minute?'

'Not really,' he says. He has bigger things on his mind. The wedding. The deal he has to make this weekend. The piece of paper he found in the office copier his decorator stashed in a gutted Beidemeyer cabinet, one more worry. 'I'm working.'

Moira sees that there's nothing on his nineteenth-century English hunting table except the silver ink stand the decorator put there. 'Doesn't look like it to me.'

'I'm thinking.'

'Seconds only, Pat. I have this dress on approval.'

'Please.' When he looks at Moira he sees everything has faded; she looks like the ghost of his favorite daughter. Lexie, who left the paper in the copier, novel or something, about the . . . My God, what was she thinking?

'It's lavender. If you'd just *look* for a minute.'

It's all piling up. 'Lavender's fine.'

'The question is, *this* lavender?'

'Really, Moy. I don't need to see it.'

'It's expensive.'

'Fine fine.' He's in for millions and she's talking nickels and dimes to him? As if she cared about his opinion.

'I just don't want you screaming when you see the bill. I love you.'

'Me too.' It's all she really wanted. Why wait to hear him say his line when it's only one more exercise, like there's a catechism for life. He married the woman because he thought she stood for everything he wanted but she doesn't care about Boston society, she just sits in her room and cries because nothing turned out the way she thought it would when they got married. You love your family because everybody loves their family. Then you learn to hate your family and with reason. They keep sliding out of place!

He carries them on his back. Look, somebody has to take control. Of all the McQuarries, Pat is the strongest. Of all these lallygaggers and weak women, he's the one who knows how to make a buck. He carries them all. Moira. His blood, his daughters, the heaviest load is Lally. Maggie, the dirty secret they all keep.

The others? They are all gimme. This is how they communicate. They ask. He gives and they hate him for it. Then they hate themselves. He carries his brothers Kevin and Aidan and their families. He carries Kieran, but Kieran doesn't know it. Kieran's his favorite and now they aren't speaking. It hurts. Better not dwell on it.

First he pulled strings to get Kieran out of the draft. Out of jail after the demo at the draft board. 'Stay,' he begged after the Weatherman bombing, 'I'll buy your way out of this.' *Then Kieran broke my heart with that stern, proud glare.* 'I don't want your money.' And went underground. Which turned out to be useful, but that's another story. Pat happens to know where Kieran is – God knows he put him there, sends money to keep him in place and Kieran doesn't know. Pat's private eyes found Kieran where the cops couldn't. Then. Things happened. And without wanting to help, Kieran became useful. Too bad about Kieran. *Well*, he thinks, *I showed him.*

He writes monthly checks to the man who owns the place where Kieran works so Kieran won't know where it's coming from. Arbogast adds the extra to Kieran's check. Pat keeps the money flowing so he won't feel bad.

Moira's back. 'We'll need matching dresses for Lally and Margaret and they can't be cheap.'

Pat says in a go-away tone, 'I'm sure you'll find something.'

'About the shoes.'

'Fuck the shoes, just go away so I can think!' He is hanging by a thread here.

Not how the first Pat McQuarrie imagined them, standing in line on Ellis Island, dead broke and new to the country, potato famine Irish hoping for better. He hauled coal, pretty soon he was selling the stuff. He saved every penny he ever earned and left what he had to the first Kieran, who took it and made it grow. A little bit took you a long way in those days. When that Kieran died, his son saw no reason to change the way

McQuarries did business. He put the money into real estate because like the poor, your land you have always with you. When stocks and bonds went down and out the window and people stuffed mattresses with the paper they were printed on, the McQuarries still had their land, and they knew how to sell it. Kieran senior rode out the Depression and when the war started he cashed in bigtime. War plants! He took the profits and on VJ-Day he got in on the ground floor of housing developments. Levittown North, they called it. So it was Father who made them rich and son Pat who made the money grow. He was first into shopping malls. Later it was luxury hotels. He carried on, and his brothers? Two drunks, one school-teacher and a Weatherman. Not everybody's favorite brother was a Sixties radical, wanted by the law. His is.

'Fuck.' Lally slouches past, bumping into things.

'And you.'

'Shit.' Drunk again. Divorced again. She thinks he doesn't hear her, but he does. He says in a low voice, 'Lally, Lally, I'll pay for rehab.'

She sticks her face in. Smirched lipstick, hair a frizzy nest. A dozen twelve step programs, zero results. There is so much history between them that he can hardly bear to look her in the face. She spits, 'Get out of my life.'

She was my first, and God, the trouble. *Your burden, be patient.* 'I'm only trying to keep you out of trouble.'

'You don't care about me, all you care about is this wedding. Fucking Lexie and her fucking six thousand dollar dress.' Lally's had four husbands, but she doesn't have a husband now.

'This wedding is . . .'

'I know, I know, an investment in my future.' Forty-something and giggling like a girl. 'Well, I want my future now.'

'Go somewhere and get sober. Then we'll talk.'

'Lexie, perfect Lexie.' Spiteful bitch. 'I'll purrfect you.'

'Quiet, you'll wake the house.' He glares. She spits and goes.

People say he's a hard man. Well, he has his reasons.

Look at what he has built. The McQuarries have come a long way in four generations, from mud cottages to nice big houses and college degrees – Fordham and Holy Cross and Boston College – and membership in certain clubs where their great-grandfather delivered coal. In this generation, even the deadbeats are distinguished. Welcome anywhere, you'd be privileged to know them. Pat and his brothers traveled up first class. See, their dad went to work straight out of school but he vowed to give them better. Ambition. In a funny way, it's ambition that killed him. The hopes, and what Pat's brothers made of them. Pat has always been the best, but Kieran was the favorite. He got politics like some people get religion, and he got it in the Sixties, at Oberlin. When he made the Ten Most Wanted list it killed Father. Heart attack, and Kieran didn't even come back for the funeral.

Pat pleaded with him. 'Don't go. I'll pay your way out of this!'

'I have to do this. Honor!' He went away.

Well, I'll honor HIM. It's a fulltime job, but Pat McQuarrie keeps his family where he wants them. Lexie is in New York now, but in a place he found. He pays. She couldn't live the way she does on what she makes.

41

And the rest, he keeps out in the open where he can see them. Makes them dance and cut bait and stand on their heads if he says so and they will do it because they'll do anything for money. They'd go down on him if he asked, anything for the money.

But this is troublesome. Lexie, with her thing she is writing, he isn't supposed to know but he's found this page. Never mind, got to keep this show on the road so he'll sweep it under the rug, take it up with her after she and the Devlin boy are good and married and certain deals are made. At first he had a hard time with her marrying Tom Devlin. The Devlins are, to be frank, a couple of links down the food chain from the McQuarries. Pat's great-grandfather didn't haul coal to see his descendants yoked to a family that goes out every day and gets their hands dirty. Pat has met those mugs Tony and this Bro, like the family's so poor that they can't afford a proper Christian name? He doesn't like them any more than they like him but they can be useful, so he accommodates. They think they see money, and they accommodate. Decent, but frankly working class, with those watery eyes and matched *gimme* faces.

That's what money can do for you.

And this Tom has been to Harvard.

Understand where Pat is coming from. *We are all spawning uphill.* There's an old joke that dogs the McQuarries no matter what clubs they get in and what parties they're invited to. Pat heard it standing in line at his first dancing class. Rich Irishman goes in to the Dean of Manhattanville to find out why his daughter isn't doing well at this ritzy Catholic girls' college. The Madam says, that's what they used to call the nuns, Madams of the Sacred Heart. The Madam says, 'Sir, your daughter is intelligent but she's rather uncouth.' 'Sure,' he says, 'and tell me where they sell this couth and I'll buy her some.' Top of the heap now, but it's been a struggle.

When Lexie came home with Tom Devlin he told her the joke again, a reminder. 'We didn't come all this way to slip back into the bog.' She didn't laugh this time either. She got pissed. He said, 'Understand, the snots from Beacon Hill didn't *tell* me this joke, I overhead it!' *What they really think of us.*

'That doesn't have anything to do with me.'

'The dirty Devlins,' he said. 'As I remember, Boston society didn't think much of them. Hauling junk!'

'Not junk,' his daughter said. 'Demolitions. Besides, Tom is an architect.'

'Demolitions?' That got his attention. 'Would he care to do a job for me?'

'Ask him.'

'Bring him in,' he said. Cordial Pat McQuarrie.

See, he's had a bit of a problem with cash flow. This hotel down in Florida, brilliant opportunity, prime location but it's been empty these twenty years and it's bleeding him white. He can't raise the jack to get on with the renovations and without income, how is he going to launch the new mall? If he sells, he'll take a huge loss and he can't afford any more losses. The old ark is eating him alive. Enter Tom Devlin.

He came in with his arm around her waist and a smile Pat *does not like* but he suffered him. After all, Harvard. And certain skills. Pat dropped a hint. 'Is it possible to do a building and make it look like a gas explosion?'

He got busy with his hands and didn't answer.

Damn you, Pat thought. But he advanced to Plan B. 'Buildings come down, they get in the movies. If you brought down a hotel for me, I could get it into the movies.' Packaging!

'Try the Revenaughs.'

'I need this job done.' He stuck it to him. Everything is transactional. 'Before the wedding.'

'Don't expect me to do it.'

But Pat McQuarrie gets what he wants. One way or another. This weekend, he's meeting with the Devlin brothers.

And meanwhile, what? His Lexie, writing on something that she won't show him. The wife and Lally sobbing somewhere in the house. Maggie like an unwanted ghost and Lexie engaged to a black Irish bastard who doesn't have the decency to do a simple job for him.

Speak of the devil. 'Dad?'

'Lexie!' *My daughter my darling.* He is thinking, *this paper should I ask her? Lay back and hope it goes away? Never knew exactly how much the girl knew about what went on the year Maggie was born, judging from this scrap of writing, I don't think she knows either.*

She says, 'In case I don't see you tomorrow . . . I dropped in to say goodbye.'

'But Lexie, the picnic. I thought your boyfriend was coming.' Counting on it. Bring him face to face with the brothers and he'll have to come in on the job.

'No. I have to get back.' Tonight she looks transparent, with that pale Irish skin. Her hair is red, where Moira's has faded. His love, his consolation.

'There are other interests involved.'

'There always are, Dad. I have to go home tomorrow, right after the fitting. I love you, Dad.' She pulls away. His hearts cracks in two pieces.

Don't leave! 'I know you do. Don't go. Get the boyfriend here, Monday's a holiday.'

'I miss him, Dad.'

Sex on the brain, is that all they think about? 'You're engaged.' He offers a big concession. 'It's OK if he sleeps over.'

'No, Daddy, just, no. OK?'

'Then stay and talk to me.'

'Daddy, I'm dead beat. Really. It's all this. Wedding machinery.' She looks exhausted. Frantic. ''Bye Dad.'

'Don't say goodbye, say good night.' But Lexie kisses him and vanishes. 'Lexie?'

He sticks his head out into the hall, goodbye sounds so final. 'Lexie, wait.' If she hears, it doesn't stop her. *I love you, Alexandra, and I'll do whatever I have to, to keep you.*

Upstairs, her door slams. At least he knows where she is. If he had his way he'd keep her locked up until the wedding. Let her write her damn book or whatever it is, he can find it while they're on the honeymoon, read it and burn it.

Then in the night when the house is supposed to be sleeping he catches a vibration. Something going on that he doesn't know about. Something going on beyond his control. Upstairs, somebody is talking. He picks up the phone.

The voice is sleepy and full of desire. It belongs to Lexie. She and that boy are talking deep down and dirty. 'And once we've done that, we'll . . .'

It is obscene. They are going on as if they are alone in bed! 'All that and more. Once I get you where that bastard can't hurt you.'

I hate the way he looks at her. I hate his big, careful hands on her and I hate the heat. I hate the two of them on the phone just now, talking deep down and dirty about things too filthy to put into words. I hate the groom but I need this wedding and I need the rangy bastard's expertise on the Florida job. Still. I would do anything to stop that smile and get his black Irish hands off her. Maybe an accident after the honeymoon, some unexpected disaster after the Cleotha hotel is leveled and this decorator's wet dream that I live in is well and truly sold. It takes more control than Pat has to let it go by. At least he hangs up before he starts screaming. 'Son of a bitch! What's the girl been telling you!'

He wants to kill him, but after the wedding. *Maybe after my books start showing a profit, maybe after McQuarrie Development is stabilized he can arrange something. Mugging gone wrong. Accident. Memo: airtight insurance policy, surprise wedding gift. Unless I get in the car tonight and go down there and rip his heart out of his chest.* But he's a born photo op for the slick magazines with the black Irish hair and the blue eyes, and to get what he wants for this house Pat needs bigtime publicity. He is pitching to the gentry. If he can bring in some sheik or silicon millionaire he'll amortize the wedding and double his investment, and what are they buying? Couth, plain and simple. Look at this place! Eighteenth-century furniture, Ming vases, somebody's ancestors in fancy gold frames, the trashy new rich are willing to pay for their place in society and Pat is going to make them pay a bundle. Plus he has money coming to the wedding, contacts to warm up and utilize for the mall project. Get people into a setting like this and they are yours if you are smart enough to cash in on it. Pat knows it is axiomatic, you have to spend money to get money.

His office phone rings. 'Yes.'

'Daddy, I'm warning you.'

'Lexie, stop crying!'

'I heard you breathing on the line.'

'I'm sorry.'

The last thing his favorite daughter says to him frosts him to the soul. *What is she writing?* She says, 'You haven't *seen* sorry.'

12

Devlin sleeps hard. He tried to submerge and not come up until the waiting part was done. Instead something smashes into him; his head jerks and he thuds into consciousness. The vibes bring him to his feet in the middle of the bright room. No use lunging for the shades and crash diving again. He's dead awake. Marooned in mid-morning, hours from four p.m.

He can always eat. Lexie keeps so much food on hand that this is never a problem, but today the contents of her refrigerator read like a bachelor-pad cliché: six-pack of Perrier, dried out sandwich half, pork fried rice that he's afraid to carbon-date, Greek olives. *Lexie, Lexie, is this how you eat when I'm not around*? He should go out on the avenue to buy food but waiting has built a shell around him. What if he missed her call? There's a one-pound bag of Zabar's coffee beans wedged next to the ice trays along with a freezer-burned half-loaf of bread. Enough for now. Tonight they'll celebrate over the chef's special at Balthazar.

First, there's now.

He lunges for the phone at the first ring. 'Lex?'

'No. This is Veronica. Veronica, from *Death Duties*?'

'*Death Duties*!'

'You know, the play?'

'Oh. The play.'

'You know, I play Eulalia. Who's this?'

'Tom Devlin.'

'Oh, Lexie's man. Why don't you come along tonight and watch us rehearse?'

'I don't think she's rehearsing you tonight.'

'It's right here on the schedule. I called to ask what time.'

'Sorry, it's pretty much canceled.' When she comes in they have better things to do. 'I'll have her get back to you.'

When Devlin gave up his apartment, he moved into his laptop and set up housekeeping. It's the only real home he has. All his records and some of his best thoughts sit on his hard disk, along with three months' worth of e-mails from people he cares about. Images of buildings he cares about. Specs and notes for projects, past and future. Until he and Lexie get their own place he is, essentially, a stateless person. It's good to boot up knowing that on his hard disk, at least, the furniture is right where he left it. Parts of his life sit neatly in document files and image files.

'No run-throughs, Lex,' he says to the empty room. 'No *Death Duties* tonight. Life's too short.'

He pulls up his summary of the San Francisco project and inserts notes

45

from the meeting with the new client. Devlin is one of those architects who learns from what he's already done. Differences between what was in his mind and what's on the page. Variations between the intention and the act: the finished building. The annual report isn't due until December but he starts writing up the Evergreen building. When he finishes a draft he moves on to notes and queries about the new job. He pulls out his portfolio. Might as well start on sketches to show his new client. He works quickly, gets out his computer and starts drawing on-screen. He puts in a long day and when he looks up it's only two p.m.

Against his better judgment he calls Lincoln. Holiday weekend or not, Pat McQuarrie will be at the office – one conversation he doesn't need. He doesn't much need to talk to Lally, either, she either comes on to him or bites his head off, bad news either way. Maggie, he thinks, I hope it's Maggie.

Mrs McQuarrie answers in that sweet, overbred voice. 'Moira McQuarrie here.'

Odd: he won't use her first name even though she's about to be his mother-in-law. Marrying somebody doesn't mean you and her folks are automatically related. 'Mrs McQuarrie, it's Tom. Tom Devlin.'

She goes on in that hostess tone, 'Oh Tom, we know which Tom by this time. We're so sorry you couldn't make it last night.'

This is a puzzle. 'I'm sorry too.'

She says abruptly, 'What held you up?'

'Ma'am?'

'It was supposed to be a family party. We missed you.'

'Lexie said it was just family.'

'But you're part of the family! What kept you, Tom?'

He's trying to make this make sense. He'd have gone; he wanted to; his hands are aching with it. 'I wasn't invited.'

'Of course you were.' Moira is intent on reproach. 'We were all disappointed, Maggie especially. You think she's just a little kid, but – thirteen. You might as well know she's kind of in love with you. And Aunt Costanza was so looking forward to meeting you.'

'She was?'

'After all, the poor old thing is too frail for a big wedding.'

'Lexie said. Um, never mind.' She gave Aunt Costanza as one of her top ten reasons for him to stay away.

'Well, what with you just back, and with that big new building on your mind. We understand. You were just too busy for us.'

'Me?'

'That's what Lexie said.'

'Is she there?'

'Of course not, you know how Lexie is.'

'When?'

'It's hard to keep track of her. When I came out of the boutique she'd already left.'

'For New York?'

'I suppose so.'

'But she'd be here by now.'

'You ought to know by this time, Lexie's unpredictable. I'm sure she'll be along sooner or later.'

'She said four, four-thirty at the latest.'

'I wouldn't count on it. Look, Tom, when she comes in tell her I'm FedExing her wallet but she won't get it until Tuesday.'

'Her wallet!'

'She left it on her dresser. Let's just hope she doesn't get pulled over for speeding.'

'If she was speeding she'd be here by now.'

'Nice to talk to you, Tom. And, Tom.'

'Ma'am?'

'It's Moira. Next time, right?'

'Yes Ma'am.' Devlin isn't sure what he's agreeing to. 'Next time.' Oh, this is not good.

When he tires of ritual pacing he sits down. He can't work so he begins sketching for a magnificent building, the kind that architects love to design knowing that they're too good ever to be built. There's an imaginary city out there filled with architects' unrealized visions. Fantasies like the Tribune Tower. In London Sir John Soane's house is filled with unrealized monuments for an ungrateful city. By the time Devlin is finished the paper city has a new Romanesque bridge leading to a monumental office tower.

That does not exactly use up the day. He makes Lexie's bed with hospital corners, pulls up the quilt, thinks twice and turns the covers back. He is so stupid with love and waiting that he actually considers a few upmarket hotel amenities. Should I find a rose to put on the pillow? After Eight mints? Perfume the room? All he can think of is the Faulkner short story that starts with roses and ends with a desiccated corpse. Lexie hates perfume. She calls it an invasion of her personal space. Furthermore he knows a guy who fell into his hotel bed in the dark and woke the next morning convinced he was bleeding from the ears. Melted chocolate looks like dried blood on the pillow.

Food, he thinks. At least I can get in some groceries. Stuff she needs, favorite things. We'll eat steak and chocolate tonight and stay in and get back to where we were before all this happened. Memory blindsides him. Lexie laughing in the sunshine on Montauk, Lexie baffled by a bookcase that he puts together in five minutes, Lexie sitting on that sofa explaining his life to him. It's like a place that he's homesick for.

After a long night and a day in the apartment, lower Third Avenue is brilliant. It's like being sprung from solitary. Devlin shakes like a wet Scottie puppy. He scores a Beaujolais, steaks and vegetables at the super. He puts them into his leather shoulder bag and moves on to the neighborhood deli for bagels and Nova Scotia salmon – their Sunday morning usual. In his head he's already made things right with her and jumped ahead to tomorrow, when they're as they were before, happy together on a brilliant Sunday morning.

Clay Presnell, the weekend counter guy, is Lexie's director. Clarence Pitkowski before the name transplant. He's also taking the lead in *Death Duties*. Lexie says Clay can solve the worst narrative problems, you wouldn't understand. Devlin hopes so. The thing is eating her up. He's offered to help her talk it through but Lexie says without explaining, *I'm afraid.* When he presses, all she'll say is, *It's very personal. Death Duties.* Until this Veronica's call, he didn't even know the title.

Clay says without looking up, 'Can I help you?'

'Hey, you're still here. I mean, um, a half pound of Nova?' The last time Devlin talked to Clay he was giving notice – big part, hello bigtime. He can't help squinting. If he says the right thing to Clay, will the actor-wannabe tell him what's going on with Lexie's theater piece? 'I thought you'd be on Broadway by now.'

'Wuow,' Clay says, slicing salmon thin enough to see through. 'Long-time longtime.'

'Been on the coast.'

'LA?' Competitive greed flickers. Actors!

'In your dreams. San Francisco.' Let him off the hook.

'Right,' Clay says jealously, 'the San Francisco scene.'

'Not exactly.' Tell him what you were doing.

Clay can't stop himself. 'So, the Lukas operation?'

'Lukasfilms? I think it's a closed shop.'

'There still are a lot of indies there. You were in a picture, right?'

Don't torture him, let him off the hook. 'Presnell, I'm an architect.'

'Oh right, I forgot. Cool.' Clay wraps the salmon in oilproof paper and slaps it on the counter. 'You want house cream cheese?'

'Thanks, I'll just use Philly. When do I get to see you do your thing?'

Clay gives him a funny look. 'Which thing?'

Guys like Clay, you don't ask what else they're into. Actors are full of big, useless hopes. 'You know. *Death Duties.*'

'Oh, that. We're having some trouble with that.'

'Some particular part?'

Clay shrugs. 'You know.'

'Sort of.' Mistake. But fuck if he'll admit he doesn't.

'Then you know it's pretty heavy stuff.'

'I guess so.' He should know, he should have crawled inside Lexie's head and pulled the contents out but the play got between them like an extra boyfriend. He didn't ask because he resented it.

'Plus,' Clay says. 'Letting it all hang out like that. She's afraid of repercussions. *If.*'

'If?'

Clay amends, 'Not if, when. When certain people see it. She's scared shit they'll get wind of it and shut us down. She figures once it's up, what she has to say, it's been said, and there's no way they can shut her down.'

He says angrily, 'If it's that hard on her, what's the point?' *I have to do this. When you see it, you'll understand.*

'She says she's clearing the books before the wedding. Squaring the accounts. By the way, congratulations. Hey, when you get back, ask her what time we're rehearsing tonight?'

'Tonight? I don't think so.'

'She sets the schedule,' Clay says. 'So, will you check?'

'Sure.' *As soon as I see her.*

'We need to know soon. It's almost six.'

48

'It can't be. She was supposed to be here by four.' He stuffs the Nova into his shoulder bag.

'I make it five-thirty.'

The part of his head that's in denial has kept him from noticing how late it is. 'Boy, I'd better get back.'

The next thing that happens is quick and ugly. He is rounding the corner onto Lexie's street when somebody behind him slashes the strap of his shoulder bag and yanks hard. Instead of grappling, Devlin lunges backward. He rams his elbow back and up, into the thief's sternum. Then he wheels, fast, and brings his fist up into the kid's Adam's apple, sending him staggering. Without considering the fact that his kid assailant cut the strap with a knife, which he is still holding, Devlin whacks him in the side of the neck with the blade of his hand, leveling him. Then, shaking, he takes back his bag and steps over the sobbing adolescent. No time for pedestrians moving like figures under water. Not time to wait for the cop. No time to confront his assailant, who is writhing, groggily struggling to his knees so he can stand up and flee. Devlin won't think about what he's doing, only that it feels good to be doing something after so many hours of doing nothing.

He goes in calling her name even though he knows the apartment is empty.

It is after midnight when he acknowledges that Saturday is over and Lexie isn't coming.

13

Sunday is worse.

The person at the door is never the person you want. Not when you are strung out on waiting.

When the bell rouses Devlin he doesn't press the intercom. No need to find out who's down there, waiting to be buzzed in. Lexie, who else? Don't ask why she rang instead of coming right up. Love supplies the logic. The doorman doesn't come in on Sunday mornings until eight. Lexie would do anything to keep from disturbing the super just because she forgot her apartment keys. She left Boston so fast that they're in the same place as her wallet, right? Wedding fever, he thinks wearily. We all have a touch of it. Now that she's here he isn't quite ready to see her. He needs to figure out how pissed he is at her for being so late.

When the apartment chimes go, he still hasn't thought of anything to say. 'Hang on, hang on. I've been waiting since Friday. You can wait three minutes.'

'So, what took you?' But it isn't Lexie. It's not anybody he wants to see. It is his brother Tony.

'Tone!'

In the French blue suit with the gray shirt and the matching tie, dapper Tony looks like the kid brother, even though he's north of fifty. He lounges in the doorway as if he doesn't have a care. Hair that Tony remembered as thick and brown has a reddish cast. Tony has back-combed it to make it look as full as it used to be. Devlin's smiling older brother is using Clairol. The veneered teeth are porcelain perfect. Tie pin. Rolex knockoff. Gucci loafers. Tony, what are you hoping for? Tony makes as if to give him the high five. 'Yo Tommy.'

'Yo Tone.' Devlin slaps his brother's palm. He is not quite glad to see him. 'What are you doing here?'

'I just stopped by on my way to Atlantic City.'

'This isn't on the way to Atlantic City.'

'Yeah well, I just thought I'd drop by.'

'That's great, Tone. Well, it's great seeing you but I can't talk right now.'

'Can I come in?'

'This isn't really a good time.'

'Give me a break, it's time I met the lucky girl.' Tony is looking over Devlin's right shoulder, scoping the spare, elegant room. 'I'm your brother and I can't come in?'

'It's a bad time.'

'After I drove all this way? Oh, I get it.' When he grins like that Tony

50

looks like pictures of the young Frank Sinatra. 'You're, um, otherwise engaged?'

'You might say that.'

'Tell the lady I'm sorry. Tell her I'm here.'

Devlin stands his ground. Worst case scenario on an already bad day: Lexie comes out of the elevator and finds them there. Him and jaunty, unreliable Tony Devlin, in the middle of their messed-up reunion. He won't let Tony in and he can't exactly kick him out. Tony is a non-negotiable part of his life. 'Not this time, Tone. But look, it was really nice of you to drop by . . .'

'So, what. I caught you two in the middle. It's OK, Tom, don't be embarrassed.'

Devlin knows his face is red. 'So. Atlantic City.'

'Big doings.'

'Cool.' He studies Tony. *What is your deal*? 'You gambling?'

'Better. Aren't you going to ask?'

'That's great.' It's time for this conversation to be over. 'So. Why don't we get together on your way back? Lexie and I will buy you a bang-up dinner.'

'Like Manhattan's on anybody's way home from Atlantic City. I drove the hell out of my way especially to see you. I left the car parked God knows where.'

'Why, Tony, What's going on?'

'Aren't you the brother that's getting married?' Tony is craning to the left, to the right, trying to see past Devlin into his life. 'Come on, kid, I know she's in there, all sweet and pink and wrapped in a towel. Why don't you give me some coffee while she puts some things on, OK? I got in the car before five today and my ass is dragging so far that I'm walking on my knuckles.'

'There's a Starbucks a couple of blocks from here but it's really busy so you'd better go ahead and get us a table. Look, give me five to shower and I'll be right along.'

'I'll wait.' Tony looks affable but the tone has an edge to it.

'Don't let me hold you up.'

'I don't mind waiting. Give me a chance to eyeball your lady.'

'I said, not today.'

'What, is there a problem?'

'She isn't.' No. Keep that one to yourself. 'She isn't seeing people right now.'

'Tell her it's me.'

'It won't make any difference.' He's not anxious to let Tony know he doesn't know where his lover is.

'You're not going to introduce us?'

'Not today.'

Tony keeps grinning that Frank Sinatra grin. Did he study old Sinatra movies? 'Bad luck not to meet the bride before the wedding.'

'Bad luck all round.' Devlin steps out into the hall, pulling the door to. 'What are you doing in the city?'

'I told you, it was on the way so I thought, why not?'

'On the way *from*, maybe.' By then Lexie will. Don't go there. 'You can meet her then. Where are you going, Tone?'

'I told you. Atlantic City. Fireworks. All night block party, the whole nine yards. There's an old casino coming down.'

'An implosion.'

'You got it.'

'Cool.' Devlin tried for a best case scenario. 'So. You planned the job and you want me to look over the site plans for you, so great. I knew you could do it.'

Tony shows all his teeth. 'Not us. Revenaugh.'

'Revenaugh.'

'Face it, who's gonna take us on with Pop the way he is? What it is is, Revenaugh and Company, they're gonna walk me through so I can get a handle.'

Devlin tilts his head. The Revenaugh family were early into vertical implosion and they were among the most secretive. They don't give away their methods. Not to anyone. 'You mean they're gonna walk you around the perimeter.'

'Nope. The whole nine yards.'

'You guys are the competition. They'd never let you in.'

'No shit. I get to see everything. What the family's using, where and how they placed the charges.'

'That would be a first.'

'Really.' Phony laugh. 'They might want DD to go in with them.'

So Tony is lying.

'If you don't believe me, come on down.' Tony grins. 'I get to sit in the booth with the family for detonation and you know what? You and the girlfriend are welcome too.'

'In what future?'

'Tomorrow, no shit. And this is a big one. Holiday tie-in, you know. Citywide block party. Marching band, fireworks, the whole deal. And at sunset . . .' His hands fly. 'BLAM!'

'It's been nice talking with you, Tone.'

'So, are you in or not?'

'Not. Tomorrow's a work day.'

'Tommy, Tommy, where you been? Tomorrow's Memorial Day.'

Devlin is standing here talking to his brother – nothing new, but this time it's a long slog uphill over hard territory. *Why am I so tired?* 'You know where I've been. I've been on the coast. So, fine. Thanks for coming. Go get us a table and I'll be right along. The coffee's on me. I'll buy you some biscotti for the trip.'

'If you and the girlfriend would . . .' Tony's smile is as sad as it is sweet. 'I thought if your lady saw what it was like she might want you to . . . Beautiful spectacle. Biggest show in town.'

'Sure, Tone. I knew you didn't come here just for fun.'

'You should be proud of what you come from, and so should she.'

'I quit the business, so back off.' He puts the door between him and Tony. Hooks the chain latch and says through the crack, 'I'm done and double done with demolitions. I was done five years ago.'

52

'Wait.' Tony pokes his face into the two-inch opening that remains. 'Starbucks at which corner?'

'Astor Place, a half block off Broadway. It isn't far. Ask anybody. If I'm not there in time, start without me.'

Old as he is, Tony looks like a mournful child. 'You're coming, right?'

'Coffee with you, yeah. And dinner with me and Lexie on your way back through, sky's the limit, it's definitely on us. If you come back this way. But the rest? No way, forget it. You're not budging me.'

The thing about waiting for someone is that a watched pot, etc., but go out and you'll miss something important. Still, he can't just fob Tony off and leave him simmering at Starbucks. He spends a taut half hour with his brother, double espresso and a muffin, you're a good guy, Tone, but I am not doing Atlantic City. As soon as he disengages from Tony he starts running.

Let your concentration waver and it won't matter how soon you turn back or how hard you run. You can't get there fast enough. When he comes in the red eye in the answering machine is blinking.

In his absence Lexie's left a message. 'Tommy, apologies, I have to schlep the baby sister to pre-frosh weekend at boarding school or she won't go so don't look for me till Monday, it's in this rural hell but if I can get to a phone I promise, I'll call.'

14

So Tony thought Atlantic City would be great. Instead it is bitter. He is waiting for detonation in a glorified parking lot a good quarter-mile away from the hotel the Revenaugh company is bringing down today. He had to come out here at dawn just to get a decent seat. At this distance he should cut his losses and see it on the nightly news. Anthony Devlin, vice president of Devlin Dismantling and official company delegate, is stuck on the asphalt among the common people. He is out here at arm's length, by noon the sun will turn the place into one gigantic waffle iron, while everybody that is anybody, all the city officials and contractors and celebrity guests, take their seats in the stands under the canopy set up by the Revenaugh family for the event. That's what it is when Revenaugh Incorporated brings down a building. An event, like the world is watching and in case you missed it they will show film on CNN. And he thought he and Marcel would get friends.

Blame Tom. One lousy weekend, is that too much to ask? Roll into town with Tom Devlin AIA and the Revenaugh family would be all over him and Tom with their souvenir hard hats and complimentary Martinis. T-shirts. Warmup jackets and souvenir coffee mugs. Front row seats in the shade, yeah right. Face it, the whole weekend is a loss.

Without the touch of baby brother class, Tony Devlin is a null quantity here. No way is he going to get next to Marcel Revenaugh or anybody else in the Revenaugh family with their MIT diplomas, like that expensive piece of paper makes them better than you, Tony thinks bitterly. No, he's sure of it, and if it was him that went to college instead of Tommy, he'd be the power here. People like that, they see Tommy Devlin coming, and they think *Harvard*, which spells *class*, and they're all over you.

When you graduated high school only, they don't see you and they don't think anything at all.

Force it and they squint at you like a bug that got mashed on their sleeve: How did this get here? Polite, though. *Oh, it's you.* 'Hello, Tony.'

Translated, that's 'Goodbye, Tony.'

And he came down here to kill two birds.

Walk into the Revenaugh family party with the junior partner of Reponen Associates and who's gonna squeak if your name isn't on the list? In spite of the accident, Tom is a class act. His credit is good anywhere. Get Tony in and he could knock back a few with the city officials and people from NSEE and the CDC. Plus film crew because the Revenaugh implosions are high-profile; producers love these implosions, half of them end up in bigtime action pictures. Hey, maybe a couple of movie stars laid

54

on to make the special guests feel big. And this morning, front row in the stands for the detonation. Mimosas or Martinis, their choice. If he could get in.

Part two was, let Tom get high on fireworks and champagne and then hit him with it. Look what you left behind. Me and Bro, we gave up everything for you, money, time, whatever it took so you got educated right. Now Pop is sick and the company's on the skids. Is it unreasonable to expect something back?

It was a hard sell, getting Bro to front for the suit and two nights in Atlantic City. Tony stuck it to him. 'You don't want me going in looking like crap, do you? You don't want the Revenaugh family and the McQuarrie girl thinking we look like crap.'

Bro said through gritted teeth, 'I don't care what you look like. All I care is you get Tom back in with us.'

Tough rocks, Bro. Scratch part two of the agenda.

And last night Tony messed up on part one.

Pricey car rental, luxury suite, thousand dollar suit. One little slip last night and this morning Tony can't even get as far as the front ranks behind the barricades. After last night he isn't about to get next to Marcel Revenaugh, either. No way.

But it was close. If he only hadn't put his hand on her breast.

When he checked into Caesar's Palace last night he found out which hotel was headquarters for the Revenaugh operation, Harrah's of course, the Revenaugh family always travels first class, go over there and build some character. Press a little flesh, play your cards right and it's a first class ride for the rep from Devlin Dismantling. He slicked his hair back and put on a clean shirt for the hunt.

It was good luck finding Yvette Revenaugh right there at the bar, like it was fated. When they write about company doings in the ISEE Newsletter, Marcel Revenaugh's sister Yvette is the spokesperson. Good looking, even at her age. They met at a reception once. He hoped it was enough. 'Remember me?'

'Oh. Right.' That look, like she saw him, but she didn't notice.

'Tony? Tony Devlin?'

'Hello, Tony.'

'So, this is a big night for you.'

Good looking. Tough, too. 'Do you want something from me?'

'I came to see you do your stuff.' Grin, Tony. Like if you see enough of these jobs *just by staring* you will figure out how to do them as good as Pop.

'What, you blew in for the big bang just like everybody else?'

'No. I'm taking over operations at Devlin Dismantling and I . . .'

'Professional courtesy? As if.' She grimaced. 'You don't start these jobs at the last minute. You had to be on-site months ago. Or last week, while our crew positioned the charges and laid the wires. You wanted to see that, you hadda be here, and even then I'm not so sure.'

Tony tried to buy her off with a grin – works for most women. 'Tomorrow morning. I thought maybe you'd let me walk the site with you.'

'So you can rip us off? No way.'

55

His fists clenched but he ratcheted up the grin. 'Your brother's jobs are masterpieces. I just.'

'Yeah, your dad isn't too bad himself. Anything you need to know, Tone, your dad already knows it. And you're here because . . .'

Cover fast, Tony. Nobody knows about the trouble with dad. 'Special interest.'

For an old broad, older than him, Yvette Revenaugh looked slick. She always does. In the bar last night it was the black dress, cool makeup, plus diamond earrings for the party. Dark eyes, never on him. She was checking out the room. 'You and what army?'

'Oh, just me and my associate, Tom.'

Her eyes flicked down at him. 'You mean Bro. Your brother Tom's with Reponen now.'

'I mean Tom.'

'Tom is here?'

'And Tom's girlfriend.' Why not, how's she gonna know the girl is nowhere and Tommy shoved him out the door? 'I mean fiancée. Doubtless you're at the wedding.'

'Wedding?'

'Labor Day weekend. We could get a table together.'

Her eyes flickered over him; he was thinking, good looking woman, thousand dollar suit, should I hit on her? 'Excuse me, I'm expecting some people.'

'Imagine. Alexandra McQuarrie and our Tom.'

'McQuarrie. Like the bomber guy used to be a Weatherman?'

'Not Kieran McQuarrie. Pat,' he said like Pat McQuarrie was his new best friend. In business, rule one is, optimize the association. Connections are the whole thing.

'Yeah, right.' Yvette made it clear she was done with him. 'Nice seeing you.'

'So we've got some extra muscle now. New blood in the company.' Blood. It made him queasy.

'I bet you do.'

Tommy doesn't usually lie but Yvette Revenaugh pushed him, sleek, tough woman, she could buy and sell him and knew it. And just like *that* he rewrote the agenda. Wham. 'Really. McQuarrie Enterprises is paying us to bring down a resort hotel.'

'If you mean that big old thing in Florida, forget it. Revenaugh is already contracted. If.'

'If?'

'If the terms are right. What is this. Are you for sale?'

Could she see the idea made him drool. *Pop would kill me. Bro would kill me.* Tony wished! If they could only sell out Devlin Dismantling, or merge. He could get out from under. Take the profits and enjoy. He swallowed to stop his mouth watering. Choked on it. Finally said what Bro would expect him to say. 'We pre-empted your bid. Since we and Pat are practically family.'

'Yeah, right. Sure you did.'

'With that in mind, Pat sent me to parley.'

'No he didn't. What do you want?'

'Marcel around?' You bet he was making it up as he went along. He wants. Then and now he doesn't know what he wants. Up against it in the bar last night he grabbed something out of nowhere. 'I think Pat sees us working together. He wanted me here to observe. Since we're family.'

Turned out he didn't get anything from anywhere. Yvette didn't bother to answer. She flicked a bronzed fingernail at the bartender and turned away to settle her bill. 'This is for me and the little guy here. Nice seeing you, Tone.'

Tony slapped a fifty on the check before she could sign for it. Smooth, Tony, smooth. 'And with Tommy back on board we've got a lot to offer. Think about this for a minute. Devlin Dismantling and. No. Revenaugh and Devlin.'

'I didn't hear that. If I did I'd have to sock you.' She turned to go.

He reached out to keep her and this is when his hand slipped down on her breast: nice, he thought he could feel her leaning into his touch. She wheeled, elbowing him hard. 'Ow!' He called after her, 'Will I see you at the party?'

'You're not on the list.'

She didn't have to say it that loud, to the whole bar and half the casino.

One bad move and that part of the trip is a writeoff. Tough, if he and Yvette had hit it off he could have skipped over the secret part of the agenda, which he completed in the night after he gambled away the K that Bro gave him for contingencies and before he got back into the suit and went down to cut a figure at the big brunch at Caesar's.

But that's done and now he is out here on the asphalt, where as the morning wears on sweating locals and tourists start setting up lawn chairs and jockeying for an unobstructed view. Vertical implosions are about one per cent of your demolitions in America but unless that's your favorite landmark going under the wrecking ball, they're, like, the only thing the public notices. People come flocking like cockroaches when they think there's a building coming down. A controlled demolition like this one is a work of art, but, rock bottom? That isn't what brings them out.

It's a stock car race or a mass skydive or an air show where fighter pilots do their stuff, they are just waiting for somebody to wipe out. They don't care how well it's done. They poke and crane at the sky hoping for the worst. So this trip is a writeoff and Tony is adrift out here in the sun with all the other yoo hoos and weenie buns who bussed in from places like Paramus and the Belmar Wall for the big Memorial Day weekend gambling bash plus fireworks plus vertical implosion, and everybody here, maybe even Tony, is crazed with excitement and hungry for disaster. They are high on the possibility, waiting for the rush that comes when you're in at the kill.

15

In the rocky hours of the night Devlin hears Pop's voice. With Lexie gone he got through the rest of Sunday however. Fell into bed and crashed into sleep. Now he hears Pop's voice.

Tommyboy, we gotta get out of here. I think this hotel's on fire.

He shouts for his father but Pop is nowhere. He runs down echoing dream hallways trying to find his father but the voice recedes. Alone, he makes one more sweep of the building Devlin Dismantling is taking down right now. The charges are set and the wires laid, everything ready for the blast. Minutes to detonation and there is somebody in the building! Crash into a room where you though you heard a sound and hear scratching behind the next wall. The next. You already know you can't run fast enough. This building was supposed to be secured!

Either he's in a dream that's playing out in a hotel or he is at a coroner's inquest. Or both. Devlin is caught in an argument so rational that this could be daylight, harsh and real. The first thing I do on a job, he tells *someone*, is secure the site – local contractors put up a security fence before DD makes the first site visit or takes its core samples. You post security on all four corners during working hours. Once the explosives are on-site, you post security around the clock. You don't want anybody or anything getting in. Secure the building and tear out all but one set of stairs so nothing can get back inside. Post a twenty-four hour guard at the bottom of the one remaining stairwell. You sweep the building the night before the blast. Again. The day of the blast police close the streets surrounding. You make your last sweep of the building an hour before the blast – every room, every closet. You have to be sure. You do sweep because in these things your premier concern is safety. Do what you must to bring a building down, but the first law of controlled demolitions is: do it without harming anything that walks. Tom Devlin is careful. So rational.

Then the walls shimmer and fold in on him and he is trapped in the old, bad past.

It is terrible and strange.

In life Tom Devlin's planning is precise, the crew he trained to do the work is meticulous. There is no detail too small. But hotels like the old Armbruster in Boston are bigger than they look from the outside, the parameters deceptive, especially in dreams. Devlin is crazy with anxiety. Protective fences can be broached or tunneled under; should they have guarded the manholes in the street outside? There are a dozen ways to get into a deserted building after the company has cleared the site and sealed it. The old hotel is a warren of hiding places. It doesn't matter how many security people Devlin Dismantling sent in to patrol the building, no security is absolute. If a wino squatter forgets and blunders back or a crackhead wants a secret place to smoke or a desperate high school kid is looking for a place to get high or commit suicide – which, Freddy, which was it? – there is always a way in.

He shudders.

Somewhere in the abandoned hotel there's movement – a faint rustle magnified by empty corridors – probably an animal, but what if it's something bigger – could be the wind, but what if? If anybody gets hurt, he is responsible. He has to follow the voice and pull that person out! The source is impossible to pinpoint – coming from upstairs, the basement, he doesn't know. The timer is ticking, so hurry. Maybe this time he can save Freddy Slade.

Obsessing, Tom Devlin is circling the drain. Grinding his teeth in the rocky dawn on Memorial Day, he relives the Armbruster blast as if he can change what happened. Shuttling between sleep and wakefulness, he numbers the details as if by replaying the story, he can rewrite history and make everything come out all right.

The morning after these things, he can never be sure whether he was remembering or dreaming.

But tonight the boundaries blue and change. He finds Freddy Slade tonight, in the last room on the top floor of the old Armbruster. This time, he's going to save the kid! Sobbing, the boy puts his arms around Devlin's neck and is carried along. He's skinny, but the effort is tremendous. Devlin comes out into the sun staggering under the weight. Then his arms lift. He is holding nothing that matters. Startled, he looks down at what he's saved. It's a picture frame. The victim's high school graduation photo. Just the way it looked in the Boston *Globe* the day after the salvage crew found a hand sticking out of the rubble.

And inside the hotel, somebody is still calling. *Help*!

He has to go back in even though the search always ends in the same place. No matter how fast Devlin runs or how many doors he throws open, when the building comes down Freddy Slade will be in it. He's in it every time. But there is a difference tonight. Behind the next wall, somebody is screaming and he can run for the rest of his life and not reach the source. It is a woman's voice.

Flailing, he hurtles into consciousness shouting, 'Lex!'

16

There is a trigger in Devlin's personal operating system that can detect a glitch in his life before there are any outward signs that something is about to go wrong. Struggling out of the dream in the depths of four a.m., he heard the *click*. Things look OK to the naked eye but at the *click*, he snaps to.

Decisions come fast.

He's in the car. By the time light shows in the eastern sky he has cleared the city. It's Monday but it's a national holiday, so he's speeding along empty roads. For all he knows, Lexie's heading for New York by now, they could pass each other and never know. Reason tells him a sensible man would sit tight in Manhattan and wait for her, but this isn't about reason. Reason is too slow.

You are done waiting. Find out what's going on.

By midmorning he is threading his way through the pretentiously rural lanes of suburban Lincoln, Mass. Behind closed gates big, showy houses crouch on a couple of acres done up to look like more. Just the kind of neighborhood Pat McQuarrie would choose – every owner a country gentleman. For a price. The stone gateposts at the McQuarrie place have been freshly pointed, with cement urns planted on top. Somebody had faked a McQuarrie coat of arms. Copies are bolted to the stone and the wrought iron gates. Northern magnolia trees with their root balls still in burlap line the driveway, waiting for heavy equipment to roll in. Terracing, topiaries and yards of fresh sod all shout that the owner is a very big deal.

The excess is disgusting. He noses his car into a flowerbed in front of the house. Who does McQuarrie think he is? Who is he, really? All this money just to prove to the world that Pat McQuarrie is a winner. One man's vanity goes out of control and two people who only want to be together are clamped in the jaws of a million dollar wedding. It's like an axe blade in the bed between them. No wonder Lexie is lying low.

'OK,' he says to be closed front door. 'Where are you?'

He has to start somewhere. Three days of aborted phone calls is three too many. It's time to look into real faces and hear truths. He rings. Then he knocks. If Lexie doesn't come, at least let it be her kid sister. He and Maggie are cool. Maggie will level with him.

Worst luck. Plump Eleanor aka Lally McQuarrie/Lodge/Rami rez/ Whatever cracks the distressed Cypress front door and peers out. She so wrecked that she doesn't recognize him. 'Whoever you came to see, they aren't here. They're all at the picnic.'

'Lally, it's me. Tom Devlin.'

'Tom?' She yawns. 'Oh, right. Lexie's Tom.'

'I need to come in.'

Lexie's old sister opens the door for him with a dirty grin. 'Sure, Tom. See anything you like?'

'Hello, Lally.'

'Man, you're looking good.'

Blotched face. Bleary eyes, ringed with last night's mascara. That smile. What can he say? 'You too.'

'You know that's crap, but thank you.' Lally rides over him like a war wagon. 'It's about that girl, right?'

What girl? He ought to stop for a question period but he's fixed on Lexie. 'Where's Lexie?'

'Oh, Lexie.' Stretching, she scratches her midriff. 'I told you, nobody's home but me.'

'You're sure?'

Pat McQuarrie builds his life on appearances. Lexie says she grew up under orders: 'You girls meet my friends looking like ladies, or you don't meet them at all.' Pretty dresses when they were little. Matching hair ribbons. Later, expensive suits and perfect hair, to make him look good. Manners to match. Not Lally. Not today. The woman can't keep a day job; she slouches back here every time a marriage self-destructs, and in spite of Pat's orders, she is a parade of defiance in dirty K-Mart jeans and a strained sweatshirt with cuffs covering her grimy knuckles. She hates her father; she hates Lexie for being happy, but that's only part of it. Behind Lally's eyes something else is smoldering, and it is buried deep. She yawns again. 'She isn't with you?'

'Would I be here?'

Her mouth is working the way drunks' mouths do. 'Why isn't she with you?'

'That's what I'm here to find out.'

'You drove all the way from New York to find out if she's here? Didn't you ever hear of phones?'

'You think I'm that stupid?' Three days of waiting roar in on him. 'People lie on the telephone.'

'Well, don't get pissed at me, babe. I'm always good for the truth.' She bares her teeth. 'You never phone me. You damn well should have phoned me. You know as well as I do, she's long gone.'

'How long?'

'Yesterday.' She covers a belch. 'Wuow. Lexie. You really don't know where she is?'

'She said she was taking Maggie to some school.'

'Putney. Dad's idea. Pretend farm for rich kids, costs a bundle. Guess he's gonna buy her some couth.' Rage flickers. 'It's time somebody taught him that you can't buy everything.'

'Are you OK? What were you drinking last night?'

'So they're up there. Kid wouldn't let Mom drive her, and she sure as hell wouldn't go with me, so Lexie stepped in. Putney!' She snorts. 'It's a boarding school.'

'I know.'

'And good riddance, I say.' Lally is gnawing on her cuff. 'I could have taken her, but nooo. It had to be Lexie, and why?'

'If they left yesterday,' he says patiently, 'why aren't they back?'

'. . . because I'm the fuckup,' Lally snarls, 'she's the dependable one.'

He flashes on Lexie, poised on that windowsill. 'Yeah.'

'Me, they'd just as soon put a bag over my head, sweep me under the rug, but my saintly fucking sainted sister . . .' This is no hangover, the woman is still drunk.

'But they haven't come back.'

'Some kind of pre-frosh sleepover,' she says.

'They're staying at the school?'

'Whatever. Kids,' Lally says for no apparent reason. 'Kids.'

'At a motel?'

'You think I keep track? How am I supposed to keep track of her? I can't even keep track of myself.' It's midmorning, but the fumes coming off Pat McQuarrie's oldest daughter fill the foyer. Pink granite floor. Directoire chairs. Brass sconces. Everything here is brand new, except Lally. Devlin smells the morning after on her, plus hair of the dog plus whatever else is going on with her unwashed body underneath the sweatshirt. She was never pretty, but she used to look better than this. Tears grease her face.

'Hey, don't.'

'Don't what? I'm not doing anything.'

'You're crying.'

'No I'm not.' Whatever it is with Lally, it's probably Pat McQuarrie's doing. The big operator, the handsome, silvery-haired glad-hand would do anything to keep his daughters in line.

Devlin asks, 'Lally, what's going on with you?'

'Like I'm going to tell you about the hospital? Well, fuck rehab and fuck you too.' Lally's mind is only half on this conversation. 'If you can't find Lexie, that's your problem. You're marrying her, you keep track of her.'

'They could be back soon, right?'

'Not 'til tonight.'

'Tonight!'

'Big picnic. School sports day. Hah! Like Maggie cares about anything you play with a ball.'

He looks at his watch. Ten minutes here sawing back and forth with Lally. It seems like hours. 'If I leave now I can make it in time for lunch.'

'Cool. Let me pee and get my shoes.'

'Not this time, OK? Got to catch them before they start back.'

'Do you think I like sitting around here all by myself? It's not my fault they boosted my license.' There is a chill in her tone. 'Besides, I'm warning you.'

He gives her a sharp look. 'What?'

'Nothing. Oh, you know. Holiday weekend, traffic's a nightmare, why not just hang in here with me?' Shifting gears rapidly, Lally leans in as if she's forgotten what she looks like. The hair falls over one eye in strings but she is acting gorgeous. It's weird. Her tone is weird. 'We could have some fun.'

'Much as I'd love to,' he says kindly.

'They'll be back tonight. Hell, it practically *is* tonight. One drink and you won't even notice. Come on, I'll make you some breakfast. Mimosas and Poppin' Fresh croissants. Raspberry jam, you'll love it.' She trails her hand, waiting for him to take it.

'Nice of you, but I've got stuff to do.'

'If you're messed up about her, you could phone.'

What he says next comes to him from an odd place. 'This may work better if I surprise her.'

'Come on, there are better ways to spend a holiday. Dad's turned on the heater in the pool. Skinny dipping, what a hoot.'

He pries her fingers off his arm. 'Another time, OK?'

'Lexie's property, yeah, right. Well, not altogether,' she says spitefully. 'I know a little something about that.'

Devlin is too busy sifting through the information to pick up on that. What little information he has. Nothing wrong with it, exactly, but nothing rings true. By this time even the deaf, dumb and blind boy would know there is trouble. 'Sorry. Gotta.' He gives her a hasty hug. 'Look, if Lexie calls.'

'Why would she call? She'll be back in a few.' The next thing Lally says stops him cold in the doorway. 'So. What do you want me to tell that girl? If she calls back, I mean.' He jumps. 'What girl?'

'Give me a break. You know who I mean, I mean, your girlfriend from San Francisco.'

Zee? 'I don't have a girlfriend in San Francisco.'

'Sure you don't.' Lally runs her tongue around her lips and winks. 'So. What shall I tell her if she calls again?'

'Who?'

'Sexy voice says you and she are tight, real tight.'

Zee. 'She called?'

'Bingo.'

'When ?'

'Saturday, yesterday.'

'Which?'

'Both. What should I tell her?'

Both. Better not ask if Zee talked to Lexie. What was said. He needs to meet her not knowing. 'What did she want?'

'She didn't say. So, when she calls back?'

'Maybe she won't call.'

'That one? You got to be kidding.' Lally is crosseyed with respect. 'That kind doesn't quit. She won't quit until she gets what she wants.'

'Fine. You want to know what to tell her? Tell her forget it. Whatever she thinks she's got to tell Lexie. Tell her Lexie already knows.'

If he can drive fast enough, this will be true.

17

It is humiliating. Minutes to detonation and the special rep from Devlin Dismantling is on the streets, to the naked eye he looks like any other rubbernecker. Tony is in amongst the bikers and whores and pasty gamblers and fat moms with squalling kids duking it out with teen bikers and cranky old men for a good spot, like Pop's reputation and Devlin Dismantling stand for nothing. He is a half-notch up the food chain from the kids skinning up poles and onto Dumpsters and the tops of cars or scrambling for space on the roof of the Seven Eleven. Ironic, right.

Somebody gives him a shove. 'I found this spot, now move!'

'Whatever, lady.' Any spot is as good as any other. A blind man could see the hotel Revenaugh International is bringing down, it sits up ahead like an elephant on a dinner plate. A major implosion rocks the world. You can see it from anywhere. But there is a greater irony, and it is this that sours Tony's stomach and makes his teeth ache.

Every spot is wrong because when a building comes down you can never get close enough. It is like sex. The tension is tremendous.

'Oh shit!'

The woman who got Orange Crush on his suit snarls, 'Watch out where you're going.'

So it's tension that keeps Tony Devlin in place even though he is done here and it would be smart to get out of Atlantic City. He's blown his chance for the front row seat, the party favors and the opportunity to gladhand the Revenaugh family connections but he won't go home empty. There is this. The implosion.

It marches in on you like sex, but it's bigger. You know what's coming, you could strangle waiting and you will scream for joy when it comes but there's nothing you can do to bring it on any faster. Tony has been at a hundred of these things but his belly's tight and his dick is throbbing like this is his first time. Controlled. Demolition. You get in love with it. That moment after the detonations start but before the supports give and the walls shudder and start to crumble. You go crazy with anticipation: to experience the sequence, rock with every small explosion and roll into the big collapse. You want to crawl up inside and feel it clenching around you. When it begins you will shout and roll with the wave and the whole time you are panting, *more, bigger, faster.*

'Fox Five, do you want to answer some questions for our viewers?'

Photo op. Do a little company PR. 'As a matter of fact . . .' Tony's breath rushes out. Not now. It is too private. 'Sorry.'

OK. If cops carbon-date arsonists by the frequency of the fires they set, is this why Tony gets off on even bigger things? Not like your twitch and your shudder, wham and it's over. Nothing to ruin the Wanamaker's suit. What happens to Tony when he is present at one of these jobs is orgasmic but it is different. Deeper. It is profound.

He squints at the big old Sixties modern hotel with its broad, bland face flanked by two oblong towers. A quarter-ton of dynamite and plastic, he guesses. How much wire, how many charges? If he could figure that out that would be him up in the booth instead of Marcel Revenaugh. It's going to be a good one. The casino was built for the ages. Naturally it's coming down for a newer, bigger one. Look at her. He has to grin. The Revenaugh family has put bands of protective covering over the windows on three floors, where they set the bulk of their charges. The black strips bind the building like funeral ribbons.

Standing at either end of the twelve, thirteen-story building, the towers look like bookends or tombstones – reinforced concrete, a pretty problem for Marcel. Tony doesn't know how to plan these jobs down to the minute but he knows how they are done. It takes a little extra whammo to bring down towers like those and to bring them down synchronized, so you don't have to move in your large equipment later to finish the job. It takes more expertise than Tony has to topple the ends of a building precisely, so they fall in toward the middle of the thing instead of out and away from the center, where they could do some real damage. The art is in the kind and amount of explosive you use in each charge and how you space them and how you time the small explosions. The problem is exactitude. You have to make the charges big enough to do the job but small enough to break the supporting members instead of blowing out walls and sending chunks of concrete everywhere like unguided missiles. You want to do this right and you want to leave nothing standing. You want to crumple your building into pieces small enough for the salvage company to break up and cart away.

And this is the magic. The Revenaugh family magic, Pop's magic, Tom's magic, planning these implosions so large buildings come down swift and beautiful and safe without so much as cracking a window across the street. Beautiful. Fucking impossible. It isn't Tony's fault that the computer confuses him worse than all Pop's paperwork – original building plans and his careful blueprints for destruction, the sketches and endless hand-jiggered calculations.

'Timing,' Pop says, 'it's all in the timing. Place your charges just right and at just the right intervals and you still have to know exactly how big is each charge and how much wire and exactly what is the interval,' and it is this that drives Tony crazy, the beauty is in the exactitude which eludes him. It eludes him every goddam fucking time.

I may be out here with the scum of the earth but at least I am thinking like a professional.

But he isn't thinking like a professional, his mouth is dry and his chest is tight.

Hot, he thinks, and crowded here, ruined the suit and fuck he hates this, the band playing somewhere near the barricades and then the music ends which means that as soon as the speeches are over Marcel Revenaugh himself wherever he is will make his remarks and then he will give the signal and Marcel Junior will trigger the blast.

God it's hot.

God it's still.

A toddler cries. Its father growls, 'Shut *up*.'

Most of the people waiting will think that what they hear next is the band.

It is that regular. Crack. Crack. Crack. Crack. Small explosions drum in four-four time as multiple charges go off in the midsection of the building like synchronized drumbeats, close together and so exactly spaced that the sequence is sharp and regular. Crack. Crack. Crack. Crack.

Hardon. It gets Tony every time.

There are perhaps ten seconds in which nothing happens. Nothing changes. There is only the sound of ranks of small charges going off in relentless synch.

Crack. Crack. Crack. Crack.

People shift uneasily but before they have time to say what they think – *it didn't work!* – puffs of smoke and flame blossom and the black ribbons disappear in the blast. The solid old hotel starts to go. Tony's chest is so tight that he can't find the breath to shout. The middle part of the building goes first, separating from the tower on the left and starting to topple. As it does, explosions crumple the supports of the left-hand tower and it folds in brilliantly as the entire structure collapses in a smoothly coordinated left-to-right wave that advances like a tsunami until it hits the far tower and, God damn Revenaugh and his secrets, instead of falling out toward the hotel parking lot the tower on the right folds in on the ruined building so that the whole structure falls in on itself as it flattens and becomes rubble. The thing is leveled in eighteen seconds. Where there was a twelve-story resort hotel, there is nothing at all. The site is consumed in smoke and dust so thick that it will take minutes for the air to clear and all around Tony, watchers open their throats in a wild scream and the sound that comes out of his throat fuses with theirs.

'Now!'

Better than sex, he thinks, shuddering. Sobbing. He always does. Trembling and laughing. Bigger.

Different, Tony thinks, rocked by the destruction. This one better because it is different.

Big hotel like that reduces to a pile of rubble thirty feet high the very least, when the dust clears in a half-hour or so it will be easier to gauge. It'll be weeks before they find the item he left, Bro's surprise for the Revenaughs. He grappled the thing over the cyclone fence last night after the local contractor's guards gave up on patrolling and ducked into the van to stack a few Zs. He counted to a hundred and, like a black shadow, followed, staggering into the hotel with the thing. For once he knew exactly what he was doing. The nod from Tom, one kind word from Yvette and he wouldn't of had to do this. *Now*, he thinks. Listen, he's doing it for Tom. It doesn't matter how well you sweep, Tommy, or how carefully you walk the building. There are a thousand places to hide a body in a hotel that's coming down and who's to say whether the party was or was not well and truly dead before the implosion. Yeah, they can tar Revenaugh with the same brush, but there's more.

Now we're even.

18

A student with a striped flag maneuvers Devlin into the last temporary parking lot in the farthest field at the Putney School. It's half past mud season here in rural Vermont; the ground oozes under his feet as he walks the last few yards up the hill.

He could pick Lexie out in any crowd. Tall, blazing with energy, she's the kind of redhead who makes people stare. She can come into a new place with her head thrown back and that reckless grin and within minutes she's surrounded. All he has to do is look for the largest group. What he loves best is that no matter how many people she collects, she makes him feel like the only person in the world. He cross-hatches the field, starved for her. All he wants is to find her and lock hands. He needs her smile.

It doesn't take long to scope the place. Lexie isn't here. In town, maybe, at whichever motel. Maggie will know. Finding Maggie will be harder. One small, sullen thirteen-year-old on a hillside swarming with loud, healthy kids.

The school is about what he expected. Beautiful. Isolated. So exclusive that it can afford to be rustic – farmhouse, barn, stables. Pretty, simple, it's also a working farm. Perfect for the weird subgroup of the American rich that knocks itself out pretending to be just folks. Putney looks like their kind of place – a farm with an academic flip, where kids used to the A list life can forget that they're a minority and get down. Adolescents from rich families pay good money to bale hay, milk cows and muck out stalls as if, magically, this makes them just like everybody else. Pat McQuarrie is so hung up on status that he probably thinks he can buy Maggie's way into their ranks.

Everybody's outside today. The picnic is over but nobody wants to leave. The weather is too nice. There are games going on – baseball. Field hockey. Soccer. A cross-country run. The hilltop where the school buildings sit is crawling with students and faculty and subfreshmen and parents. In this part of New England winters are so cold that men on farms like these used to get sewn into their longies in October and it was May before they got cut out of them. The only differences now are central heating and Gore-Tex, washing machines and thermal underwear. Spring comes late to Vermont but when it comes it hits hard. It's unusually warm for this time of year. Devlin sees upperclassmen running around with their faces turned up and their arms spread as if this is the first time they've seen the sun since fall. Teenaged boys and sexy women the same age grapple in the new grass, laughing like lifers let out of jail.

All but Maggie McQuarrie.

There's no point in asking anybody where Lexie's little sister is. He knows her too well. Maggie is smart, funny, misanthropic, his kind of kid. She has Lally's blunt Irish mug, but on Maggie it looks good because she doesn't fight it with bad makeup and silly hair. She sweetens it with a warm, sardonic grin. The kid hates group activities. In fact, she hates groups, and unlike her sister, she's small and plain enough to sneak out of any crowd without being noticed. He starts looking in the library, the most logical place. In the dining room. In a deserted lounge. Anyplace where she can hang tight and wait to be rescued from all this wholesome fun. There are loud, happy adolescents everywhere – in uniform, mixing it up on one of the playing fields or coming in off one of the mountain trails or happily grooming large animals that stand like heavy equipment in the barns. Other adolescents happen to like trees and sky. They like running around. Not Mag.

It takes the better part of an hour to find her. She is sitting on the back steps of an eighteenth-century house reading a book. Zipped into her jacket in spite of the warm weather, flanked by her sleeping bag and her backpack, Maggie looks like a tightly wrapped package waiting to be picked up and moved out. When she hears Devlin's footsteps she draws up her knees, scowling. Then she looks up and sees that it's him.

'McQuarrie.'

'Devlin!'

'Maggie, for Pete's sake.'

'I though you'd never come.'

He responds automatically. 'Then why didn't you wait out in the open, where I could find you?'

'What, and get scarfed up in some stupid game? Did you know that everybody in this place has to play a sport?' When Maggie gets mad like this her chin sticks out and she starts running her fingers through her orange frizz. She can't wait to go.

'So, did you have a good time?'

'You've gotta be kidding. Look at this place, Devlin. Cows!'

'You have a problem with cows?'

'It's so healthy I could puke.' Maggie picks up her sleeping bag. 'Where the hell were you, I've been ready since ten.'

'How was I supposed to know?'

'Somebody had to come for me.' Maggie McQuarrie looks nothing like Lexie but her eyes are like her big sister's. Beautiful and clear. Sudden as quicksilver in that sallow, triangular face. She's fidgeting like an escaping prisoner. 'So. Are we leaving or what?'

When Devlin and Maggie talk no explanations are needed but he needs one now. 'Wait a minute, you were expecting me?'

'Somebody's gotta take me home. Mom's too tired and Lally's too drunk and Dad doesn't have time for this, so I figured it would be you.'

'Lally. She was kind of bent that she didn't get to come with me. Where's Lexie, at the motel?'

'Lally's always bent. Could we please just please go?' The kid is herding him along like a puppy lobbying for a walk. 'So, where's your car?'

'Maggie, stop a minute. What about Lexie?'

69

'What do you mean, what about Lexie?'

'She brought you. Isn't she supposed to take you home?'

'Like she's going to turn around and drive all the way back up here to get me?'

He says tightly, 'Back from where?'

'New York, I suppose.' Maggie is only half-here in the field with him; she fixed on escape. She says over her shoulder, 'Wherever she went.'

He grabs her arm. 'She didn't stay?'

'Like she would spend a night in this dinky town. Would you?' Maggie shrugs him off. 'I thought you knew. She left yesterday.'

Lexie, on the machine: *Don't look for me until Monday*. It doesn't mean what he thought it did. 'Where did she go?'

'How am I supposed to know?' Maggie says over her shoulder, 'I haven't talked to her since yesterday noon.'

'Noon!'

'At least she stayed through the brunch.'

'Maggie!'

'Come on.' Maggie leans on him, nudging. 'We'd better go. This place is a swamp and your feet are sinking in.'

19

Tony has to drive like hell to get to where he is going, which he's supposed to do before five so he and Bro can leave for the meeting together, present a solid front. The chief officers of Devlin Dismantling stepping out of the company car. It's a bitch, given the Memorial Day weekend traffic, his sour stomach and the fact that even though his day sucked, he scored after the Revenaughs' implosion. He actually had a bimbette lined up for tonight. Sweet girl in the acid green tank top and matching bike pants, Tony looking like a million bucks in the suit and he doesn't have time to take either her or the suit out on the town. Hours down here in the Jersey heat doing Bro's bidding and he isn't even going to get laid.

When he took this girl Roxy back to his hotel room the message light on the house phone was blinking. He said, 'You wait outside.'

'Five minutes,' Roxy said. 'Five minutes only.'

Like he wanted to return the call.

They didn't talk long. Bro asked if things had gone OK in Atlantic City.

Tony told him no on counts one and two, yes on count three. It's gotta be months before the salvage and removal crew gets down to the bottom layer of the rubble left by the Revenaughs' implosion. Twelve-story hotel reduced to a neat heap of rubble the size of a city block. And when the salvage company finds the body underneath the thirty-foot high plateau of disassembled parts of the demolished building, it's going to make the Revenaughs look bad.

'So. Good, right?'

'Could have been better.' Bro doesn't praise. 'How soon can you get here?'

'What do you mean, get there?'

'I need your butt.'

Then Bro told him what was coming down. He was crusty and close-mouthed about their new client but Tony knows. He knows.

By the time he came back out in the hall Roxy was locked on to a buff-looking guy half Tony's age, it pissed him off. 'Five minutes, you promised. That was only three.'

'Closer to five than four.' She ran a thumb under her shoulder strap.

Hands in his pockets, rummaging for something to give her. 'Wait a minute.'

'Bye.'

Never mind. He would have had to blow her off because of this job. He's supposed to get to New Haven and hook up with Bro so they can ride north together. Bro wants the officers of Devlin Dismantling to arrive in a body for the big meeting. Like that makes any difference.

On the other hand, he can't afford to drag his feet. This thousand dollar suit might pay for itself after all, if him and Bro walking into this meeting together all suave gets them the job.

He tries his voice. 'Hel-loooo Chief Silvertongue.'

Given that business is so bad that he and Bro had to start laying people off, they can definitely use the job. Especially given who they're doing it for, as in, connections lead to new connections. More work.

'Charm.' His voice sounds good to him. Good smile. All his own hair. This suit. He is pissed at Bro for yanking him home but it's flattering. 'He *needs* the good old Tony Devlin charm.'

Never mind how you're going to do the job once you get it, concentrate on landing the contract. Significant front money, which they need around now. Plus, the movie tie-in that their new client is brokering can only make the company look good. This could be as big as the hotel going down at the end *of Lethal Weapon 3*. If this thing comes down and it comes down right, Devlin Dismantling is going to be famous. Tony and Bro will be right up there in the public consciousness along with Revenaugh International. And, man, given the exigencies, Tommy will freak when he finds out. But he'll have to come back in with them so they can bring this off OK, no way he won't. This could be a very big thing for them.

20

It is late afternoon when they get back to Lincoln. Maggie scowls as if Pat McQuarrie had bought the oversized stone manor just to make her look small. 'I hate this place.'

'I can see that,' Devlin says.

Now that she's unlocked the front door, Maggie stalls.

'You're not going in?'

'In a minute.' She cracks the door and peers inside like a stranger. 'Mom?'

'Come on, Mag. It's your house too.'

'It's dark in there.'

'I'll get the light.' He reaches inside and flicks the switch. Maggie hangs back so he has to lead the way inside. The sprawling McQuarrie house is dead empty. Devlin feels it as soon as they step into the foyer. He can hear it in their footsteps on the inlaid marble – a skill he picked up in architecture school or something he just knows. In this overblown decorator's wet dream they are the only things moving.

'Mom?' Dwarfed in the twilight, Maggie stops in front of the beveled mirror. It takes Devlin a minute to figure out what she is doing. She's fixing up a thin, new-moon smile for the family. He doesn't have the heart to tell her they aren't here. 'Dad?'

He touches her arm. 'Um. Mag.'

'Maria? Oh shit, it's her day off.' Maggie drops her pack and bedroll on the inlaid marble compass in the foyer floor and yells. 'Lal!'

No wonder she hates it. The echo alone. The leaded windows. It's like a nineteenth-century tomb. 'Maggie, I think your folks are out.'

'Mom and Dad maybe, but Lally's like a vampire. She never goes out before it gets dark.'

'You mean she never goes out until she gets drunk.'

'Whatever.'

'Maybe she's found a new guy.'

'In your dreams.' Maggie is getting smaller. 'She never goes out this early. She can't even get her face working before dinner.'

'Cheer up, maybe she got drunk and decided to go wreck a car.' It would help if he could make her laugh.

'Lexie said she might sleep over with us.' She raises her voice. 'Lexie? Lexie!'

'Maggie, she isn't here.'

'How do you know?'

'Trust me. Nobody is. They haven't been here for a while.' He feels both good and bad about this. So what if he hasn't caught up with Lexie. They probably zipped past each other on I-95 at dawn today, which would put her back at the apartment. If he leaves now he can be in the city by ten, eleven at the latest. The trouble is, Maggie is standing here willing him to do something. When he leaves she'll be alone in this big house. He says reassuringly. 'But they'll be back.'

'When, do you think?'

'Soon, no problem.' He isn't sure why they're stalled in the foyer. 'Do you want me to help you get your stuff inside?'

Even her voice is getting smaller. 'Not really.'

'OK if I use the phone?' He is trying to ease her inside and it isn't working. 'Maggie, the phone.'

'The phone?'

'I need to call Lex. She's probably home by now.'

'Yeah right.' Maggie's tone is a surprise. It's right out of *Clueless. As if. Don't ask.*

'Don't worry, I'll put it on my phone card.'

'We're good for it.' She hooks his sleeve like a spelunker afraid of getting lost and nudges him into the octagonal study off the living room. 'I think there's a phone in here.'

'You don't know where the phones are?'

'Dad's office.' She makes a face. 'You know.'

'Not really.'

'It's kind of don't touch.'

'Like, you might break something?'

She shakes her head.

'Business secrets?'

'Something he's doing, or something I did? I don't know.'

Pat McQuarrie's home office is wood paneled, decorator perfect with leather chairs and uniform books with identical morocco spines. Whatever he has to hide is well hidden. There are a phone and a solitary silver inkwell on the antique desk. When he pulls the phone toward him he uncovers a fresh gouge in the glossy surface. Hanging over his shoulder, Maggie makes a little *whoosh* of surprise. He wishes she'd give him space to make this call. In fact he'd like to be alone to make this call, he and Lexie have some stuff to sort out. He clears his throat and Maggie backs off.

Come on, Lexie, pick up. Pick up.

Maggie is at his elbow by the fourth ring.

In New York, Lexie's machine picks up. If she's been home, she's gone out again without changing the message.

'Nobody's anywhere,' Maggie says mournfully. Behind her, shadows gather in the outsized living room. 'I wonder where Lally went.'

Devlin has an odd, bad feeling. 'I should go.'

'Yeah.'

'You're cool here by yourself until your folks come home, right?'

'Yeah. Sure. I guess so.'

The kid is almost smiling, so smile at her and split. Get out of Massachusetts, get back to the city, find out what's going on. He says carefully, 'They'll be back soon. It won't be long.'

'I hope not.'

'So, if you're OK?'

'Why wouldn't I be OK?'

Find Lexie and if you can't find her, call the police. No. Not the police. Somebody. But he can't leave Maggie like this. 'What about dinner?'

'Dinner?'

'Did you eat at the school?'

'Not really. It's OK, Maria probably left something, I won't starve. You know. Out in the kitchen.' She makes it sound like a long way.

'So you're all right?' All he wants is to get in the car and go.

'I'm always all right.'

'Fine, then.'

'You take care.'

'I will. You too.'

'I will. I'm cool.'

'No, you're not.'

The girl snaps, 'I said I was fine!' It's a question of scale. Five-foot-one Maggie in a forty-foot living room.

'Look, do you have friends in the neighborhood – somebody I could leave you with until your folks get home?'

'Friends? Me?' She pulls out a tattered copy of *Dune*. 'Don't worry, I'll just read.'

He sighs. 'Come on, Mag, let's go eat.'

'You don't need to babysit me.'

'I'm not leaving you in an empty house. How are you with sushi?'

'Yeugh.'

'OK, hamburgers. Something gross for dessert. Awful-awful, Fribble, a blizzard, whatever they call it up here. The sky's the limit. By the time we get back your folks'll be home.'

In the Brigham's ice cream parlor they find, Devlin orders cheeseburgers with fries for both of them, but he's too wired to eat. He waits until Maggie's dessert comes. When he finally has her smiling, he asks the questions he should have been asking on the drive down from Putney. The problem is making them sound casual. The poor kid is freaked enough by her model room in that decorator's showcase, by her absent mother and that hostile big sister, by the bait-and-switch that has funneled her into boarding school. What else, he wonders. What else is freaking her.

'So,' he says carefully, 'It was nice of Lex to take you up to Putney yesterday.'

Maggie repeats, 'She even stayed through the brunch.'

'But she had to leave?'

'Had to meet somebody. I thought it was you.'

'Um. She left in a hurry?' Better not ask if she was happy or upset. He's afraid Zee caught up with her.

Maggie nods. 'She said she had to get back.'

'Back where?'

Maggie sucks milkshake into her straw and creates a vacuum with her finger. Then she tilts her head back and shoots it into her mouth. 'Beats me.'

75

'I wish she'd said.'

'It's OK, she promised to get in touch as soon as she got there.' She answers a question Devlin isn't asking. 'Could have been some crisis with her play.'

'Her play?' He used to ask. Lexie didn't want to talk about it. At least not to him. *I want it to be a surprise*, she said. *When you see it, you'll know why.* He should have pressed. He should have made her let him into rehearsals, but he hated it. It was like having a rival in the bed. 'She never told me what it was about.'

'That's Lexie.' Maggie shrugs. 'Everything's gotta be a surprise. It's no biggie, probably you'll see her before I hear from her. So. Could we go?'

'You haven't finished your shake.'

'Please? They're probably wondering where I am.'

There are cars parked under the porte cochere. Devlin leans across the front seat and opens the door to hurry Maggie out so he can go. 'You take care, OK?'

'You aren't coming in?'

'I'm in kind of a hurry.'

'That's what Lexie said.' She says in that thin voice he's getting to know by heart, 'Ooops. Company. Could we go somewhere else for a while?'

'Not really. What's the problem?'

'Business. Dad hates it when I walk in on him doing business. It's like he thinks I'm going to ruin some big deal. But if you come in . . .'

'I really have to go.'

'Walk me to the door?'

'Mag!' Devlin has been spinning his wheels for too long. Five more minutes here won't make any difference. 'To the door only. As soon as you get inside, you're on your own.'

'Deal.'

Nothing is that simple. The door opens on three men clustered in the foyer. Three men who . . . It isn't Devlin's worst nightmare, but it's close. Even with their backs turned, he recognizes his old brothers, standing like tombstones in McQuarrie's front hall. *What are you doing here?*

Pat McQuarrie looks as if he just strode in from the pool but the other two are sober in business suits, leaning forward with their heads bent and their hands clasped behind their backs as if this is an ordinary day's trading instead of a national holiday.

Maggie says, 'Dad?'

The three men swivel. Caught in the act. Pat McQuarrie is in his foyer with the chief officers of Devlin Dismantling. Set next to smooth, manicured Pat McQuarrie in the middle of all this opulence, Bro and Tony look testy and out of place in their new ties and their tightly buttoned suits.

'Yeesh.' They are expecting more. Devlin sort of smiles. 'Hi guys.'

Bro rakes him with a calculating glare. Feisty little bastard, simmering like an unwatched pot.

Tony turns on a big smile. Like a lounge singer bringing on a class act he says, 'Wuow, talk about timing, heeere's Tommy! Devlin Dismantling on the job. You got all the chief officers now.'

'Not really,' Devlin says. 'I have to . . .' He wants to ask McQuarrie about Lexie – when he last saw her, how she was, but he can't do it with his brothers standing there. 'I have to go.'

Grinning Tony overrides him. 'All the officers except Pop. This is so great.'

'I'm not an officer, Tone.'

'So. Tom. This job. You're in with us on it. Right?' Bro scowls and waits for him to agree.

Maggie's voice fills the silence that follows. 'Daddy, I'm home. Do you want to hear how it was?'

Standing behind her, Devlin shakes his head.

'Well well, how about this. This is terrific. Great to see you,' Pat McQuarrie says. Ignoring the girl, who is desperate to be recognized, he pitches directly to Tom Devlin. For the first time since Devlin refused to bring down that white elephant in Florida, Pat McQuarrie is happy to see him. 'You couldn't have come at a better time.'

Tony says, 'You're just in time for the meeting.'

'I don't think so.' Devlin bends to give the girl a quick hug. 'Bye Mag.'

'You're not staying, right?'

'Sorry, Mag. You take care.'

Maggie says in his ear, 'You take care too.'

Moving in on him, McQuarrie puts the child aside like a household ornament that one of the movers left in his way. 'So, Tom. Son. What would you like to drink?'

'I'm in kind of a rush.' Devlin has lost track of Lexie for too long.

'Wuow, Tommy, you're not staying?'

Bro is quick and harsh. 'Shut up, Tone. He'll stay, all right. He can't afford to leave.'

'Sorry, Bro. I can't afford to stay. Big meeting in the city. Miss it and it'll cost me bigtime,' he says because money's the only thing Bro understands.

Pat McQuarrie's warning follows Devlin to the car. 'It's going to cost you if you don't stay.'

He's in the car when Tony comes running out. 'Tommy, wait up!'

'Sorry, Tone.'

Tony runs after the car, flailing. In their long lives as brothers, fifty-year-old Tony Devlin has somehow ended up being the kid. He flicks the switch that rolls down the car window. 'What!'

Tony's face is working. If he was going to beg, he knows it's too late. If he has some fresh argument to try on his kid brother, he hasn't thought it through. What he does say is so far off the wall that Tom Devlin won't take it apart until much later. 'That girlfriend of yours is something else! Give her a big kiss for me.'

21

Questions torture Devlin as he wedges his rental car into the stream. The last of the holiday weekend traffic is dripping into Manhattan like sludge in winter. Now that he's oozed across the bridge and onto the West Side Drive – twenty minutes from Lexie's – it congeals. Clamped to the wheel of a steaming car, he sits with his skin twitching. Trapped while his mind runs on ahead.

He doesn't know where Lexie is. Or why.

The nightmare is trying to pinpoint the transition. When did he go from expecting her back to this? When does 'away' turn into 'missing?' Is it an absolute state or a decision you have to make?

'Wait!' Shouting, he bangs the wheel. He'll get back and find her smiling, *Tommy, where've you been*? Or he won't.

Missing is a hard line to cut. Unless you're the missing person you can guess at causes, but you can't know. The Roanoake colony, vanished without a trace. The crew of the Marie Celeste. Nobody knows what happened. When a settler vanished from the stockade the possibilities were limited, but there were always possibilities. She could still wander in years later with feathers in her hair and an inscrutable smile. Sometimes the searchers found a mauled body or a neatly dressed skeleton, leached by wind and sun, lying there in its sunbonnet and tattered gown. At least you knew.

The gray area round 'missing' is broader now, when people travel at lightspeeds. It's as big as the world. People drop from sight. There are a thousand possibilities. What took them? Accident or murder? Amnesia? Cosmic kidnapping? Some people walk out of their lives for good reasons. Which is it, Lexie?

He could handle this if he knew. He'd be OK if he could be sure she's all right.

'Out of the way, asshole!' A driver cuts into line in front of him, scraping metal.

'Same to you,' Devlin yells, preoccupied. How do you know, he wonders. How can you tell if she's in trouble or if she segued from *just stepped out* to *gone for good*? If she's in trouble or if she has turned her back on you and walked away. Which is it? Four days and he still doesn't know. He should go to the police but they'll blow him off unless he comes in with details. Physical evidence. When a small child goes missing, cops hit the streets in a hurry, but without evidence of violence they aren't likely to get serious about a consenting adult, especially when the first rule is that most missing persons don't want to be found.

Manhattan police don't consider a missing persons report until twenty-four hours pass. No point in starting the machinery when she may still show up. If Devlin files a report, they'll ask him a few things for the record and send him home to wait.

He is considering: Should he go in tonight and file, just to start the clock, when the car behind him smashes into him so hard that his neck snaps. 'What!'

The driver leans on his horn.

He shouts, 'Shut up!' And in the next second, calls the shot.

Missing.

While he is stuck between exits, surrounded by overheating cars. What if he ditched this klunker and ran the rest of the way? Do it. Check the apartment. Go to the cops. He cuts off the motor and smashes open the door. It feels great to be moving.

'What the fuck are you doing!'

'Back in the car, asshole!'

Right. He won't make it past the cars embedded in the highway like insects in glue. Even if he could outrun the drivers, it's a half-hour hike from here to the subway. Longer to Lexie's place.

Use the extra time to think this through.

First, the apartment. Find a recent picture. Call the hospitals? Script the missing persons report. The first question the cops will ask is when he last saw her. *Officer, it's been two weeks. I came in and found her on the window ledge.* No. He can't take that into the police station. They'll ask if Lexie has a guy on the side, they'll ask if he does. They'll ask if he and Lexie parted on a bad note, like, did they have a fight. All three questions make him uncomfortable. When it comes to stepping out on your partner, he's the perp. *No officer, we didn't have a fight.*

Are the Manhattan police the right people to notify? Which precinct? Should he file with state police instead? Which state? Since she got in the car Friday, Lexie's driven in – bare minimum – five states. She went through Connecticut to Massachusetts on Friday, fighting holiday weekend traffic for the sake of a wedding dress. Then for the sake of her little sister, she drove through a scrap of New Hampshire on her way to Vermont. Beautiful landscape, hills. If something's happened to her, it could have happened anywhere along the way. The issue is, where. She could be broken down or piled up in a ditch, but he can't make the highway patrol in any of these states get serious until he has proof.

Missing. Nothing you know is ever enough.

There are no signs that he can point to. There isn't anything wrong, really. It's just that nothing is right. All he has to go on is this dirty, bad feeling. Lexie threw their lives up in the air last Friday and they came apart. The pieces haven't landed yet.

This is another problem with *missing*: the desperate little songs you sing when you don't know. He is spurred by the fear that when he finally makes it into town, he'll let himself into an empty apartment. Some time over the long weekend, Alexandra McQuarrie, who promised to marry him in September, dropped out of his life.

Unless she was stolen.

But this doesn't keep him from thinking, *relax, this could be a false alarm. Don't hit the switch until you're sure. She's fine.*

Unless she isn't.

He retreats into routine. Drop the car off and wait for the sleepy weekend substitute to run your plastic and check out the trunk. Grab a gyro sandwich the way you always do. Eat it on the subway. You'll finish by the time you reach her stop. Come up at her exit the way you always do and be reassured. Her corner looks just the same. The tousled super smells just as bad as he ever did and he lets you into the lobby with that same weary glare. Go up to the apartment and use your key but don't call out, you might wake her up; if the place is empty you'll just look dumb. See if she left you a message. Play the machine. Check out the phone pad and her desk calendar. Maybe she left you a note. Check again. Go spooking through every room looking for signs.

Unlike buildings, lives aren't built according to blueprints, which means you can't go back to the plans to figure out a fix. You can't take core samples of a person to find out how they are put together or what they are made of, even though knowing might help you keep them up instead of bringing them down. Lives aren't constructed or brought down according to schedule, either. In the territory of unknowns you can't be certain of anything. The only thing you can do is wait. Try to plan.

It's almost after midnight. Devlin has left off waiting and started making lists. Like a private detective in a B movie, he's pulled out a yellow pad and put down the names of everybody he's seen in the last few days and everybody he knows Lexie saw. Lists of places he knows Lexie went. Places she might have gone. People to call as soon as it gets light. He does all this with his body slanted forward, every reflex geared to the sound of Lexie in the hallway, Lexie's key in the lock. He is like a kid whistling his way past a funeral home on Halloween. Prepare for the worst, he thinks. Life is full of accidents and surprises. What keeps him here in the circle of light that bounces off the legal pad is this secret. It's a long way from the comfort of 'away' to comprehending 'missing.' He thought he'd made the transition but he is by no means there.

Until the phone rings. He shouts, 'Lex!'

'I'm so sorry, it's Maggie.'

'Maggie?'

'Devlin, this is awful. I think something's happened to Lexie. No, I know it!'

'How?'

Maggie can't stop crying. 'She was supposed to call me tonight at eight o'clock, she promised.'

He freezes. 'She promised?' *You didn't tell me.*

'You got it.' Maggie's voice quavers. 'Promised. She said not to worry about where she was going, at eight tonight she'd *call.*'

'This is bad.' It is. Sometimes Lexie gets a little crazy, but when she makes a promise, she keeps it. Devlin pulls out his Filofax. 'Hang on. I'll be there as soon as I can.'

22

So they're about to get the job but fuck, Bro hates the rich. He hates that rich, fat fuck and that loose daughter with the smeared mouth coming on to Tony like a party doll with attitude. The fuck with the lord of the manor, with his port wine in the Waterford glasses special ordered to fit in that fake stone house. Who does McQuarrie think he's fooling with the granite veneer and fifty dollar cigars? You can see what he is; it's written all over the man. Never mind what he claims, you can't fool another Irishman. Polished Pat McQuarrie is a hop, skip and a jump up from the bogs; that's potato field mud rimming the fingernails like the borders on a funeral note. So much for the Fordham education. So much for the showy house and the grounds and all the stuff he bought to make it look like the McQuarries are better than the Devlins, who do honest work. Stupid he is, and weak. Those watery eyes. Probably drinks a little on the side.

Bro Devlin, boiling on the McQuarries' front walk.

So fuck the man for making the Devlins wait and fuck him for treating them like they were dog shit that got on his shoe and he was deciding whether to hire DD or just scrape them off. Bro busts ass to hell to get him and Tony up to Massachusetts in time for this appointment, and uphill against holiday traffic, too. Drops everything and on a holiday, for fuck's sake, because this bigtime developer tells him it's a matter of piss while you've got the chance, you won't get another pot. Like if he and Tony don't hop he'll give the job to one of the big companies. The Revenaughs. *I'm giving you a chance at this because of the family connection.* Yeah sure, well fuck you too. Bro's seen the place. He got the on-site video in the FedEx and he got the photos too and he could tell the bastard a thing or two, him and his job. There's something hinky about it. He came to DD because McQuarrie's deal with the Revenaughs was never in place no matter what anybody said.

But DD needs it, so he and Tony ride out. With Pop down, business blows and they need everything they can get. Arrive on the dot. With Tony, and that took a little doing. After what he did for Bro down in Atlantic City he was a little pissed, but never mind. Park so the seal on the company car shines gold in the burglar light. Go up the stone steps and ring the bell. Fucking Windsor Castle, who does he think he is? Wait and listen. Ring again. Listen. Wait. Where is the motherfucker? It's seven-thirty on the dot. He and Tony are out front in business suits – *look your best, assholes, we need this job*. Standing in front of the company seal like a photo off a brochure and they are waiting. Stranded until this Pat McQuarrie or one of his people answers the door and shakes hands and takes them into the meeting.

Bro hocks and spits into a flowerpot. 'You'd think he would have a guy standing by to let us in.'

'Look at this place,' Tony says, 'man, Tommy's marrying all this?'

Bro says coldly, 'I wouldn't know.'

'The fuck you wouldn't.'

'Tom and me ain't speaking.'

'Well take it from me. You and me are invited to the wedding, Bro.'

'So they tell me.' He rings again.

Fucking big house, who is he trying to impress? *Suck in your gut, Tone. Stand tall, Barry my boy. We are coming on like major players here.* Fix the pocket handkerchief, Barry Devlin. Act like you wear a suit for a living. Get Tony to stop smiling that fuck-me smile. Look your best, assholes, we need this job. Standing there in the yellow bug light waiting for whoever. They are dressed for business, Tony and his brother, and who comes to the door?

A woman. Not bad looking in the shiny red thing, younger than me, but definitely over the hill. She doesn't look drunk, exactly, but Bro gets a whiff. *Our Tommy is marrying a drunk*? He mutters to Tony. *'This* is the lucky girl?'

'Naw, I saw her picture, that isn't her.'

She cracks the door and gives them this tight, wise look. 'What do you want?'

Bro gives back the cold, business eye. 'We're here for the meeting.'

'Meeting?'

'Mr . . .' *Correct that. Don't make it like you want something.* 'Pat McQuarrie. He sent for us.'

And this babe comes back all cold. 'And you are . . .' Like she learned it on TV.

Fakes them out, she does. Bro answers in the company voice. 'Devlin Dismantling. Doesn't that ring a bell?'

'Not really.'

He follows up with the Devlin scowl. 'Well it should. Now where the fuck is McQuarrie?'

Tony smiles like it was him and not Bro swearing, 'Pardon our French.'

From inside a woman calls, 'Lally, who's out there?'

'Nobody, Ma.'

'Nobody!' This is bitter, bitter. 'The hell we are.'

She grins and explains. 'Nobody for her.' Nice in the red dress, what little he can see through the crack.

And his brother Tone? For a minute Bro has no idea what the fool is doing, leaning into the door like a cat fixing to lick butter. Then he does. He is coming on to her.

'Ma, it's somebody for Dad. He *claims*,' she calls, all snide.

The other woman calls from inside, 'Well, tell them to wait.'

This babe pushes Tony back so she can close the door. 'Not in here. Out there.'

And he and Tone stand outside for a fuck of a long time before they hear the man. Close, like he's standing right behind her in the hallway. *About fucking time.* 'Lally, Lally, it's the Devlin brothers. Why didn't you let them in?'

'They look like Jehovah's Witnesses to me.'

'Dammit!'

'I'm not kidding. The suits.'

Her father has the grace to be pissed at her. 'Get a grip, Lally.'

'Plus I don't know what they're selling.'

'Something I need. You don't know who they are?'

Bro pushes the door open. 'You don't know who we are?'

Tony barges past him like a star, with the slick hair and the porcelain smile at three hundred dollars a tooth. 'Well, hello, Lally. We're your new brothers.'

She is too buzzed to figure this out. 'You got to be kidding.'

'Well, brothers-in-law. Almost, anyway.'

'Shut up, Tone.' If they weren't watching Bro would punch the shit out of him. But two McQuarries are witnessing and besides, Tony did a thing for him in Atlantic City and Bro owes him. 'Mr McQuarrie. I'm Barry Devlin and this is my brother Anthony.' Bro sticks out his hand.

'Sorry not to shake but as you can see, I just got out of the pool.' This Pat McQuarrie that summoned them? This Pat McQuarrie that they bust ass and burned rubber to get to this meeting with is standing there half naked and dripping on the floor. Tiger stripe bikini bathing suit! 'I wouldn't want to get you wet.'

Now, this is serious business. Bro and Tony rode in here wearing dark suits. Looking fit for business. For this? Walk into a meeting where the real world for God's sake keeps its clothes on, and this Pat McQuarrie comes out in a fishnet shirt and a fucking bikini bathing suit! The arrogant bastard is standing in his front hall in his bare feet, still wet from his fucking heated swimming pool and son of a bitch the question is, do they need him more than he needs DD?

Bro Devlin doesn't think so. He can hear the weakness, buried deep. Those watery eyes.

Fucking son of a bitch.

But McQuarrie is holding the money.

And he gives Bro that look just like their fuckwad of a kid brother, ten cents worth of education and that makes them better than Tony and Bro, when at least they got their hands dirty doing honest work. But fuck that shit, they got the job. Good thing, too, because right before he got in the car to come up here, Bro got on the phone with this guy he knows at the Globe because he had a beauty idea. Beauty idea!

Now, here is the insult. The insult is, fifteen minutes on the place and they are still standing in the man's front hall. The big country gent doesn't think enough of the Devlins to ask them in. And son of a bitch! A car stops out front. People get out. Somebody busts in the front door like they own the place. A little girl, must be McQuarrie's although she doesn't look like him. And behind her, looking like he just saw death riding down on a horse? The brother Bro lost the best part of his life helping through school, through college. Did all that and what thanks do they get? Any other day he would drag Tommy down and beat the crap out of him.

Tony lights up. *Just in time.* 'Tommy. Hey Bro, it's Tommy!'

McQuarrie lights up. 'You're just in time for the meeting.'

Tommy does not exactly smile.

Bro says to the kid, like, *this is an order*. 'So. You're coming with us.'

'Sorry, I have to go.' Like that.

In and out, never mind that Tony wheezed like an asshole and followed him out to the car. *Adios arrivederci mañana*. With hardly a word for his big brother, that he owes. *Well, I will darling Tommy him.*

In a way, it put them at an advantage for the meeting, which Bro did not much like holding in that marble front hall. After McQuarrie lost Tommy – how does Bro know he lost Tommy? That watery look. After he lost Tommy, he invited them in. His office. Like the inside of a music box. Port wine even though he and Tony were in such a hurry to get here that they never got dinner. Cigars.

Hotel he wants brought down, McQuarrie says. Spanish stucco, five stories, a couple of hundred rooms. 'You got the video, you know the deal. Can you handle it?'

'With a little help we can.' Not huge, so fine.

Not so fine, the man has a timetable. Here it is the end of May and from a standing start he wants the building to come down on July Fourth. The fourth, as in the glorious Fourth. So, wow.

Tony shakes his head, 'Six weeks, we can't do a . . .'

'We'll do it,' Bro says.

McQuarrie says, 'I understand that with your father down, your brother Tom plans the jobs.'

Tommy that just left. 'He does and he doesn't,' Bro says.

'But you'll have his cooperation?'

'Count on it.' Tony starts to say otherwise and Bro axes him with a look. 'He's in.' Although no words passed between them after Tommy left Bro says, 'He just told Tone.'

Tony's voice hits that Tony whine, 'But July Fourth.'

Bro hisses, 'We've got it nailed.'

'The timing is key,' the man says. 'The movie company wants it to tie in with the city's Fourth of July celebration.'

'Movies.'

'Global Productions.'

'Global!' Tony is slavering but he knows as well as Bro how long it takes to prepare a building. To do it right you can't be rushed. 'But that's soon.' He is looking at Bro. *What would Pop do?*

Bro doesn't have to tell him Pop is out of it.

McQuarrie is going on like they aren't there. 'It has to come down right after the fireworks. Something about the script.'

'What's the matter with Labor Day?' Bro is sparring for time.

'Production schedule,' he says. 'Shooting schedule. Setups.' He has too many reasons. 'Plus the wedding. You're both coming to the wedding, right?'

So Bro has the invitation from his own lips. 'I suppose so.'

'We wouldn't miss the wedding.' Tony grins like a girl at a prom. He is thinking about that sister in the red dress, loose-looking, like he likes. Who is Bro to do anything but wish him well of it? 'But the Fourth July is soon.'

'Action picture with a Fourth of July hook. Posters. Product tie-ins,' McQuarrie says. 'Licensing.'

Tony grins. 'We can sell our footage to TV.'

But Tony is also right. It's very fucking soon. Still, Bro is watching the man's money. His money is on *now*. 'It's not too soon for the likes of us,' he says, even though Tony is right. 'Thing is, if we had a little more lead time. We'll do the job all right, but we could lay on some flourishes that would get us an Oscar if we could strike for Labor Day instead.'

'The producers have their schedule.' Pat McQuarrie snips the end off his cigar with a pair of gold shears. 'And I have mine. After all, the wedding.'

'The wedding.'

'Rigid timetable. A big wedding is hard to set up. But look what's in it for you. Important contacts. People for you to meet. Of course if you aren't in, I can always call in another company.'

Bro makes a shrewd guess. 'You've spoken to other companies.'

He clears his throat. 'I decided to go with you.'

They are sober now. Him. Tony. Bro.

'But if your brother doesn't want to be. A . . .'

'Site planner. No problem. Pop plans the jobs.'

'I heard he was sick.' McQuarrie clears his throat. 'I research these things.'

'Never mind what you heard. These days it's all computers. My brother Tony here is on top of it. Right Tone?'

Tony's look says the hell I am. 'Sure.'

'Besides, we're counting on your brother, right?' That smile. 'Now that he's practically in the family.'

Tony is with the program now. 'You bet.'

'I wasn't sure.' God damn blam surprise. Fifty dollar cigar in the man's hand and Bro can see it leaking out. The weakness. Those watery eyes. Uncertain tone. 'The way he took off just now.'

Bro growls, 'I'll see to it.' So what if it's a lie?'

Then Tony surprises the shit out of him. 'We'll have Tommy in on this, Pat. Don't worry, we talked.' Tony, backing him up.

And McQuarrie falls into their hands.

Their mark. Their money. They take him over the jumps once more. He puts up the front money. Startup costs. There is a little hesitation. Then the three of them agree that Global Productions will pick up the rest of the tab. That is, Global is picking up the tab if. If it comes down right and the Devlins bring it in on time. Kill fee, in case. The whole nine yards. Bro negotiates while Tony wanders out in the hall what is he doing out there, swimming in the shadows with the daughter, is she single, is she up for grabs? Better not ask. Bro says, 'We'll need to get down there to start planning. We'll need front money in the amount of.' He names it. Sets the figure high.

He agrees.

Gotcha. 'Fine. We'll get in there and start preparing. It means you front for subcontractors around the clock. And we'll bring it down bingo bong. Right after the fireworks.' Bro says everything except what's really on his mind. With Pop too sick to make a site visit let alone a site plan, he knows DD will do it but he doesn't know in God's name how.

So they got the job. Bite and scratch your way up the brick wall of life, come up the hard way and by God you'll see who's tough enough to come out the other side.

'God,' Tony says when they get back in the car. 'You are one mean bastard.'

'Fuck you,' Bro says, 'and watch out.' They don't have to have the rest of the conversation. Tony knows what Bro is like when he gets mad; he lunges and pounds on a person until he forgets what he's pounding on. One of the things Tony had to do in Atlantic City was dump the other one, sharp-nosed bastard from the old days, hit on Bro for money he said the Devlins owed, it didn't get bad until . . . Vile things he said about Bro's mother that Bro had to smash the man before any more words came out of that toilet of a mouth, never mind that he couldn't stop – smashed the mouth into a bloody smear and didn't stop until his face went away, one more thing Tony had to do in Atlantic City. So what if he fucked up with the Revenaughs, at least he got that part of the business right.

23

It's his second trip to Lincoln in twenty-four hours. Worry keeps him shuttling up and down the coast. The idea that if he just keeps moving he can find Lexie and settle this. This time he flies. It's marginally quicker. He can pretend to sleep on the plane. At Logan Airport he climbs into a rented Chrysler with the radiator still warm from the last user. The car smells of dead starfish and there's a wet bathing suit bunched on the floor in the back.

What did he expect to find going on here at the McQuarrie house at five in the morning, light blazing out of every leaded window? Plainclothesmen taking notes in the flickering dome lights from massed cop cars or Pat McQuarrie taping a plea for the Channel 8 mobile unit? Black car signifying the FBI is on the case? Is there a case? Even that is uncertain. The urgency here is all his.

He is alone with it.

The sprawling house is dark. The sensors turned out the security lights at the first sign of dawn. His rented Chrysler is the only car in the driveway. As he shuts off the motor, something stirs in the shadows under the porte cochere. He knows without getting out of the car what it is. Lexie's little sister is hunched on the stone steps in a sleeping bag. She pulls it around her and gets up. Like the winner in a sack race, she shambles into his arms. 'You took forever.'

'Maggie, you're freezing. What are you doing out here?'

'Waiting for you.'

'Have you been sitting out here all night?'

'It's OK, I had a book.'

'It's a long trip.'

'I'm sorry. I didn't know who else to call.' Wild expressions skate across her face. 'I think something's wrong.'

'Look, can we go inside?'

'No!'

'Come on, you're shivering.'

'Don't make me go back in there.'

'Why not?'

She is trying hard to squeeze her face into one place and make it stay there. 'Because I just hate it.'

'What do you hate, Mag?'

'I hate everything about it.' She isn't ready to say why. She may not know.

'Look, we can't talk about this standing out in the driveway.' Devlin does what it takes to iron the urgency out of his voice. One sharp word at this point and the kid'll start crying. 'We need to sit down somewhere. I have to ask you some questions.'

'But that's the whole trouble, I don't know anything!'

'I bet you do,' he says gently. 'You just don't know what it is until you say it.' *God*, he thinks, *God I hate this*. He tries to turn her toward the front door. 'The way this works is, people know a lot of stuff without knowing what they know?'

'Yeah, right. You got that out of some mystery novel.'

'I don't read mysteries.'

'TV, then.' She pulls away. 'This isn't TV.'

'Hold still! Could we just sit down and do this?'

'Just not here.'

'What's the problem with here?' Stopping, he turns and looks up. All those dark windows. The rest of Lexie's family inside. Polished, relentless Pat McQuarrie. His fading wife. That strange, angry sister. McQuarrie's entourage people, masquerading as butler and driver. What are they protecting anyway? Is one of them awake and watching from a darkened window? Trying to hear? He has no idea what people like the McQuarries are really like. Or what they are thinking.

Maggie says, 'It's hard to explain.'

'Get in the car.'

So Tom Devlin and Lexie's little sister Margaret sit down together over breakfast in the same booth where they sat last night. The place is overheated, snug and bright. Except for the counter kid, they're alone in here. When Maggie's finished her coffee and her face is pink instead of off-white he says, 'I should have done this last night.'

'Done what?'

'Asked the questions. When I picked you up at school I wanted to grill you, you know, where's Lexie, when did you see her last, how did she look, upset or what, but I didn't want to scare you.'

Relieved, she nods: *there*. 'So you don't think I'm crazy.'

'I'm here.'

'Lally says I'm crazy. Sometimes I think I am.'

'Well, you're not. So. Should we work backward? Like, what was the last thing Lexie said to you?'

'She said, "When I get there, I'll call you . . ." '

'But she didn't say where.'

Maggie's face crumples. 'She promised.'

'For God's sake don't cry again.'

'I'm not crying.'

He waits for the kid to quit scrubbing her face with the paper napkin. 'OK, let's start there. Let's start in Vermont. You got to Putney and Lexie checked you into this inn?'

'No, she was going to. But we came in and the desk clerk had this phone message for her, you know, pink slip, X person called at X time? No I don't know who. Or what.'

'Was she upset?'

'She was fine. She just got in a hurry is all, I thought it was a problem with her play.'

He snaps forward. 'She told you about the play?'

'On the way up there, yeah. Is that a problem for you?'

Hurt, he says, 'She wasn't telling anybody until it was done.'

'Except me,' Maggie says with a loved, smug look. 'She said last month that she was doing it for me.'

'And not me.'

'Turns out she wrote it for me. Family stuff.' Maggie makes that face he knows. Shadowed. Too sad for a kid of her age. 'She said there were things about it that she was still figuring out, but there was stuff I needed to know.'

He wants to stop her for question period, but she rushes on.

'Then we go to check in and she gets this call. I should have paid more attention, but if you want to know the truth, I was so bummed about boarding school *at all* that it went right by. I mean, bummer. She said she had to go and I could sleep over in the dorm! And all because of this phone call. So OK, we had a fight. You don't think she split because we had a fight? Is it my fault for not telling you?'

'Don't beat yourself up. Now, remember. What did she tell you about the play?'

Maggie looks embarrassed. 'Not much. This. Not everybody wants the play.'

'It's only a play.'

'She's right. I heard them talking about it last night.'

'Who?'

'So she left, just when we were having fun. Gags about the lord of the manor, you know. My God my father bought a hunting coat. About how Lally's never a bridesmaid, she always has to be the bride. So Vermont was the great escape for us. You know, from all of them. Daddy's like a great big rubber shoe that we have to scoot from or he'll mash us flat.' She looks up. 'And then all of a sudden she has to go off and,' she breaks off. 'I don't know.'

He proceeds with care. 'Did anybody come looking for her on the weekend? I mean, anybody you don't know? Somebody named Zee?'

'Who?'

'Lally told me some woman kept phoning, she asked for Lex.'

'Oh, Lally. Don't pay attention to anything Lally says, Lally's got her own shit. Besides. Lexie wasn't around that much.'

'Where do you think Lexie was going?'

Maggie shrugs. 'With Lexie you never know.'

He is pushing hard and Maggie is trying hard but what she has to tell him is minimal, slippery. Talking, asking, changing ground gently, Devlin tries to surprise a fresh answer out of her. 'OK, OK, Maggie, what is it exactly? I probably need to talk to the cops, but I can't until I know what to say.'

'She never called.'

'So wherever she was supposed to be going, she's either still on her way . . .' Chilled, he begins. 'Or.'

'See?' Maggie is done trying to stop the tears.

He slaps down two twenties and reaches for her hand. 'OK. Time for the police.'

'It won't do any good.' She pulls away. 'If you call the cops, Daddy will just call them off.'

'This isn't his thing,' Devlin says angrily. 'It's my thing.'

'That's what you think. You're only in love with her. The cops, they know who our father is, he's their new best friend. Like, he's hiring half of them to work the wedding.'

'That's months away!'

'Daddy plans ahead. The first thing the cops will do is check with him.' She's used to defeat. 'And Daddy, he'll tell them the same thing he told me last night, so you might as well sit down.'

He slides back into the booth. 'He spoke to you last night?'

'Sort of.' It is getting harder for her to talk. 'Last night, when she didn't call and I got so scared. I told Daddy.'

Devlin's head comes up. 'Before you told me?'

'I was so worried! He said it was nothing. He said he knew where she was so forget it, we should all go to bed. Do you think he knows where she is?'

'What about your mother?'

'He wouldn't let me wake her up. You probably don't believe it but they still sleep together. Like, in the same bed?'

'I don't care what they do.'

'I mean, he went in their bedroom and shut the door.' She is working through something. 'Oh! Like he didn't want Mom to know.'

'When we tell the cops everybody's going to know. They'll send officers out to the house.'

'And Dad'll tell them the same story he told me. That Lexie's out at Aunt Costanza's place.'

'Your Aunt Costanza lives in a convent.'

'Yeah, I know. So I'm all, Dad, I'm worried about Lexie. And Dad, he's, like, Don't you worry about Lexie, Lexie's out there on a retreat.'

'Retreat?'

'Retreat. You know. OK maybe you don't so I'll tell you. It's a Catholic thing. You go somewhere quiet to shut out the world so you can think.'

Eight years of Parochial school. Sundays with Tony and Bro shoving him up the aisle. 'You don't have to tell me.'

'And pray. And stuff.'

'That doesn't sound much like Lexie.'

'It's a lot like her. When things get too heavy she takes off,' Maggie says. 'She's done it before.'

But he is fixed on the next thing. 'You really think she's out there in that convent?'

'That's what my father says.'

'Then let's go.'

Maggie shakes her head.

'What, Maggie?' He is pushing her hard. 'What?'

So Maggie arrives at the place she's been avoiding ever since they sat down at this tiny Formica table. Unless she's been avoiding it all her life. Pink and miserable, she is gnawing her fingers with embarrassment. What she has to say is costing her plenty. She mumbles over bunched, raw knuckles, 'My father tells lies.'

90

24

The place doesn't look anything like Devlin expected. The Sheraton Tara, a phony Tudor pile looming over the Mass Pike looks more like a convent than this Sixties blockhouse tucked into the side of a hill. Surrounded by woods, the L-shaped building could be anything – motel, doctors' offices. The only sign that this is different is the brushed steel cross bolted to the yellow brick above the door. It's barely seven a.m. but there are a half dozen cars nosed into the border of the little gravel parking lot. 'I don't see Lexie's car.'

Maggie shrugs. 'I told you it was a lie. Can we go now?'

'Not yet. Do they have switchboard or a receptionist or what?'

'It doesn't matter, it's too early to bother them.'

'Why are you whispering?'

'It's too early to bother anybody.' She looks little and anxious in the morning light.

'Come on. I'm going in.'

'It's partly a cloister. You can't just walk in.'

'You were here Friday.'

'That was a family visit.'

'You think Lexie isn't family?'

'I think she isn't here.'

'I can't let this go until I'm sure.'

'Like she was ever really here. Like my dad would ever give me a straight story.' Now that she'd arrived at the truth about her father, Maggie can't stop repeating it. She's like a toddler gleefully repeating its first four-letter word. 'Sure, you bet he would. Yeah right.'

'Whether or not.' Devlin squints through the small glass square in the door. From here it's a straight shot down a long empty hallway – several yards of bleakly gleaming floors. He presses the button. Nothing. Not even the sound of a bell ringing somewhere deep inside. He turns to Maggie. 'Where is everybody?'

'Don't you know anything?' They're all in church. This is stupid, we should go.'

'Shut up or wait in the car.' He rings again.

Through the glass square he sees a door open at the far end of the hall. He half-expects to see a cliché nun pop out in an old-fashioned habit with white starched linen around the face. She'll have a big, clanking rosary hanging from her belt along with a pen holster, just like the mother superior at his old grammar school. The woman coming down the hall is dressed in a long-sleeved blouse and dark skirt – standard for contemporary nuns. She puts her face close to the glass.

91

Devlin fixes a disarming smile and puts Maggie in front of him. 'Wave at her.'

'You gotta be kidding,' Maggie mutters. Then she waves. 'Lo 'Stir.'

Surprised, the nun unlocks the door. 'Margaret. At this hour?'

'I'm sorry it's so early.'

Devlin says, 'I know this is weird, Sister, but could we come in?'

But she is studying the girl. 'Are you all right?'

'I'm fine, 'Stir. I just.' Maggie is fresh out of words.

'I'm afraid this is my fault,' Devlin says, surprised by how young the sister is. Authority: it's interesting. The woman is his age but that sharp look and the stance, with her arms folded, put him back in third grade.

She says to Maggie, 'And who's this?'

'This is my friend, Tom Devlin? Um.'

'Something's come up,' Devlin says.

'I kind of need to talk to Aunt Costanza.'

'Margaret, everybody's at Mass.'

Devlin says, 'It's about Lexie.'

She turns, surprised. 'Lexie! I was really glad to see her the other day, I'm just sorry we couldn't talk.'

'You don't know me, but I'm going to marry her.'

'Really. As I said, we didn't talk. Maybe if she hadn't had to rush off.' She steps back, assessing him. 'Tell her I'm sorry she left before we could talk.'

Maggie gives him the elbow. *See*?

'You haven't seen her since Friday.'

'No. Friday is visiting . . .' She is looking at him straight on. No hidden agenda here. 'If I had seen her, I'd tell you.'

'And she hasn't been back?'

'I'd know.'

'Like, for a retreat?'

'Lexie? Hardly. Even *if* we had a retreat going this week.'

Next to him, Maggie stirs.

'Is there a problem?'

Devlin leans on the doorknob to signal that he isn't through. 'Sister, I need to come in.'

'Everybody's at Mass.'

'Fine. He moves them into the little foyer. 'That's why we came, Sister. For Mass.'

'You should have said so,' she says with that sharp look. 'This way.'

'Maggie. You coming?'

The kid shrugs and follows. Once the door closes behind them, the air gets close. He can hear the low mumble of people praying in unison. Maggie is very much at home here – visits with Aunt Costanza over the years. For Devlin, however, it is something else. A part of his past that he hasn't been back to since grammar school. A community of women, with strong women in charge. He pulls in his elbows and tries to look small enough to fit in this narrow hallway where the nun moves with such confidence. He hasn't been inside a church in years. But if everybody in the convent is in chapel now, logic tells him Lexie will be in chapel, retreat or no. If she's here. He can scope the place and cross himself and go.

The nun opens a door. 'In here.' She sees them in and then goes in by another door.

In the public part of the tiny chapel he sees four old people, one yuppie and a young woman lined up at kneelers in front of folding chairs. There are enough chairs for fifty people but these six are the only civilians here. They glance his way with the affronted look of insiders. An ornamental grill separates the congregation from the sanctuary, where the members of the community kneel in pews flanking the altar – a gesture to the fact that the order is cloistered. To underscore the separation, someone has put up a gauzy scrim drawn open just far enough to expose the altar. Devlin sees the kneeling women behind it, but he can't see them clearly. If Lexie isn't in here with the civilians, would she be up there? He and Maggie have come in late. In another minute the sisters will be filing up for communion. If Lexie is with them, he'll see.

He is struck by the disparity in the sisters' habits. The younger women going up to communion are dressed like the one who answered the door – in what Devlin thinks of as civilian clothes. The older ones are divided, some looking strikingly dowdy in street clothes and the others resolutely clinging to long brown habits with wimples and cinctures, intent on preserving the difference between what they are doing and what goes on in the rest of the world. It is as if even in this retreat house, where outsiders come looking for peace, expectations are in collision. His relationship to all this is ambiguous at best. And Lexie? He'd know her even in a nineteenth-century habit – coif and wimple, dark brown homespun habit and rope cincture. Lexie isn't here.

Next to him, Maggie is fidgeting; should she go up to communion? Does branding her father a liar mark a fall from grace? *Listen, kid, compared to the things I've done* . . . He gives her a little shove: *Go.* When she comes back with her hands folded and her head bowed he gives her a minute or two to kneel and pray for whatever Maggie McQuarrie prays for. He waits for the last blessing. Then he shifts, rasping, 'OK. You were right.'

Now it's Maggie who doesn't want to let go of the chance that they can find Lexie here and escape all the other, grimmer possibilities. She whispers, 'You don't think Aunt Costanza?'

'No. No I don't.' He stands. 'Let's go.'

25

Tuesday morning and Gerald Slade gets good news along with his coffee and the morning paper, which he reads from top to bottom in the Student Union. He comes here for breakfast every day. When he first moved out of his old life and into his office at the junior college where he was teaching accounting before Freddy was born, he never ate here, he ate at home. Freddy is dead now, and this is all he has.

He is finishing the paper at an hour when most professors are still in bed. Gerald sleeps well enough, but he can't be in the office past six a.m., when the college cleaning people come in – swift Vietnamese. Relentlessly thorough, with their stern, judgmental looks. If they find him sleeping on the floor, they'll sweep him out. He has to dress and roll up his bedding and clear out ahead of them. He shaves and showers at the gym. Then he walks around the campus until six-thirty, when the cafeteria opens. It's as good a place as any to get a cheap breakfast and enough free coffee to keep him here until the Vietnamese clear out and he can walk in to work just like everybody else.

Without a newspaper to protect him, he and the student counterman would have to make eye contact. Worse, they might have to talk. An informed mind is an armed mind, so Gerald gets *The Globe* out of the coin box and raises it like a shield. He makes the paper last until eight, when the first students come trickling into the cafeteria and he has to leave. The trick is an organizational skill essential to any accountant. Thoroughness.

Reading page for page, column for column, line for line straight down to the want ads occupies the time ordinary people waste on living their lives. It is the by-product of simplifying. Read while you are waiting for the others to finish breakfast with their lovers, families or brothers and sisters or housemates, the time they waste talking, maybe even hugging goodbye, all the useless acts they have to perform before they can get down to business. This is a pared down, no-fault way to fill the time. No accidents and no losses, no surprises but no worries, either.

The secret? Keep the particles at a minimum. Finish what you started and you can throw the newspaper into the recycle bin on your way out of the cafeteria. Check your box in the college post office and stuff the contents into the trash barrel as you leave; it's all official garbage or junk mail, you never get anything personal. Exercise vigilance. Keep paper from piling up on you.

It is this kind of conscientious thinking that keeps Gerald on top of things. God, if he hadn't been blind and heedless to the tyranny of small objects, could he have kept Freddy alive? If he had left off filing his papers and rearranging small objects and paid more attention to what Freddy said, could he have kept him off drugs? He doesn't know. What he does know is that he is extremely careful now, he keeps the number of particles to a bare minimum so he will never, ever again be caught short. They had to shovel out the house! He keeps a careful inventory of his few pairs of socks. Shirts. Underwear. The number of jars of instant coffee and almond crisp graham crackers he has stored in his desk. Never open a fresh one until the last one is finished. In the same way, he limits the things he does on a given day. Breakfast. Newspaper. Office and classroom. Carefully scheduled meals. Evenings when he distributed his time among public events at the college and movies and hours spent in college lounges and nearby bars where he can watch TV, making sure that nobody notices that he's been there too long.

When Gerald gets up these mornings he doesn't expect much. His days march in a thin, unvarying pattern and he likes it that way. He is comforted by monotony. But now!

To the naked eye, the item doesn't look like much – a long paragraph at the top of the Hot Deals column of the real estate section, the last section in the stack. But to Gerald Slade, father of Freddy Slade, lately deceased because of criminal carelessness on the part of Devlin Dismantling, this is astounding. He is blindsided by good fortune.

Local Developer Contracts to Demolish Florida Property.

'Oh. Oh!'

Perhaps because he spends his working life with figures or perhaps because his brain has been rubbed raw and the contents refined by greed, Gerald's find faculty is as finely developed as any computer's search function, and almost as fast. *Demolish. Demolition. Demolitions.* The words are powerful magnets. He can find them in any page.

In a business marriage of two distinguished family firms soon to be united by the marriage of Alexandra McQuarrie of McQuarrie Enterprises and Thomas Devlin of Devlin Dismantling, the two companies inked a deal yesterday, according to a DD officer. A Florida hotel owned by J. Patrick McQuarrie of Lincoln,, MA will be taken down by Devlin Dismantling of New Haven, CT, according to a surprise announcement made yesterday afternoon by Devlin CEO Barry Frayne Devlin, head of the demolitions company. The collapse of the Twenties landmark will be brought about by vertical implosion, a DD specialty, the CEO says. The implosion, which involves weeks of planning and careful preparation, will climax Fourth of July festivities in Cleotha, Florida this summer. It is also slated to climax Damned to Blow, *a forthcoming action picture now in production, Devlin said in an exclusive phone interview with this columnist.*

There's more, but he's too excited to read. Gerald is choking on it, blind and deaf to everything but the blood rushing behind his eyes. His heart clenches.

His shout cracks the silence. 'Look!'

'What?' Behind the counter in the Student Union, the work-study waiter glances up. Younger than Freddy, if Freddy had lived.

'Nothing.'

The kid's eyes skim Gerald's face. *Nobody.* He turns back to his laptop, stifling a yawn.

95

Humiliated, Gerald stands. It's too early to go but he can't stay here. Ritual. Freddy's death cut him loose in the world and left him exposed, regretful and guilty and wide open to grief, but by God he is protected by ritual. When you go out, don't take anything and don't leave anything behind. Be sure you haven't accidentally pocketed a packet of sugar or kept your paper napkin. Fold up the newspaper and slip it into the recycling bin as you leave.

Not today.

For the first time since he began to simplify, Gerald goes counter to ritual. Riffling through the paper, he rips off the top half of the page. He uses the nail scissors on his Swiss Army Knife to cut out the item. Then, more radical, he folds it to put in his wallet. To keep! After years of nothing Gerald Slade finally has *something*. Is it too good to be true? He takes it out and reads it again. Risky while he's being watched, but he has to commit it to memory. Too good to be true, yes. But true. An implosion, the Devlins, a wedding, perfect. Deep in bitterness, he has been working on a plan, but nothing as good as this. This woman his enemy Tom Devlin cares so much about, and on the Fourth of July, an implosion. An implosion! Gerald's hands are wet and his belly is shaking. He is sweating and aroused.

Something. Yes. Something will come of this.

After years of emptiness Gerald has a definite date to put on his calendar. An event that he can target. As if fate has taken a hand in his revenge. He can forget about waiting, the world has given him a new, exciting course of action. Something big, that he can look forward to. Better than his original plan. Symmetrical. No, perfect. And it dropped into his hands like a gift.

Trained in precision, Gerald will be meticulous, making a schedule he knows he can keep. The Fourth is a long way off, and that's a good thing. It will take considerable time and thought but what he does next will be exquisite. After years of nothing, he has something to live for. And he will make Freddy proud.

26

'You have got one weird family.'

Maggie shoots Devlin a look. 'Daddy worked hard for what we've got.' She hates her father but she loves him too. His lifetime of big meetings and bigger deals. All this. They are parked in front of the house. If somebody followed them from town, if he's watching from the bushes, if he sees them together and understands that Devlin and Maggie are close, they are too preoccupied to know.

Devlin sighs, 'And he lies.'

She blushes. 'Yeah.'

'OK.' He pulls the hand brake. 'We both know he's lying about Lexie. I lean on him until we get the truth.'

'Maybe I'd better do this.'

'Confront him with the lie?'

Maggie McQuarrie is a strong, tough person but after everything they've been through she comes out sounding like her mother. Cautious. Tentative, sweetly uncertain. 'I'll just say we dropped in at the convent because he told me that Lexie . . . I'll tell him Aunt Costanza asked me where Lexie is, and we said Aunt Costanza, Daddy said she was out here at the convent with you, and she said . . .'

He cuts her off. 'More like: Lexie hasn't been near that convent and you know it. What's the story here?'

'You can't be that direct with Daddy.'

'You're scared of him.'

'Go to hell.'

'Don't cry! Look, I'm sorry I said that. I keep forgetting who you are.' She's only a kid, gawky and fragile, and he's been hacking away at her as if she's another grownup. 'I know you can't just shove him up against the wall.'

'Could we just go in there and do this?'

At the door, Maggie hands him a key he didn't know she had. When he opens it she ducks under his arm and goes inside. The hall is filled with sound. Somewhere inside, Pat McQuarrie is yelling. He follows Maggie through the hall to the archway leading into the room where her father paces as he shouts.

Pat McQuarrie is dressed for business and loaded for bear. He is ranting in that bowling alley of a living room, working the space like a stage. It's the only room in the house big enough for this scene. Two of his entourage people stand with their heads bent, taking the flak. Defeated, they have put away their Palm Pilots and flip phones. The boss is beyond apologies and explanations. He is not interested in documentation. He is beyond noticing that Tom Devlin and his little girl are standing in the archway. Raging, Pat McQuarrie is swinging a rolled up newspaper like a man punishing a dog.

'Did you see this? Did you see this? Did you?'

Momentarily distracted, one of his men glances at the pair in the doorway. Quickly, he looks back at the boss; he can't afford to miss a beat. 'Yeah, Pat. We did.'

'You saw the item?'

'It isn't much of an item.'

'Shut up! You saw it and you didn't call me?'

'Look at it, three inches. It was too small to bother you.'

'My point!'

The other man tries, 'Too small to be noticed, right, Pat?'

McQuarrie wheels on him. 'You wish.'

Pat McQuarrie is standing with his back to the door. Standing with Devlin in the archway, Maggie clears her throat. 'Um?' If she thought she could get her father's attention, she was wrong. She couldn't move him if she hit him with a truck.

'I was going to give Channel Eight an exclusive! Do you fools see the difference between that and this?'

'They could still . . .'

'You think it's exclusive now that it's been in *The Globe*? The word here is exclusive. And one of you idiots . . .'

'Not us.'

'No way.'

'Somebody did.' McQuarrie is raging. 'Now, let's get down to it. If I didn't call *The Globe*, who did? Where the hell did this item come from? Who leaked to the papers, and how did the son of a bitch columnist get it so early in the day? Mal Fletcher happens to be a friend of mine, and I know his deadline schedule. He wrote this story before the Devlins and I even met on the damn thing. So which of you creeps jumped the gun and called *The Globe*?'

'Pat, we didn't . . .'

'Somebody had to call them, Graver.'

Graver says, 'The story quotes this Barry Devlin.'

'Don't tell me the Devlins thought of this all on their own, they don't have the brains! So which one of you retards tipped those Neanderthals that they were my first choice here? Was it you, Graver? Mulligan, did you tell them that they had the job?'

'Why would we do that?'

'Not why.' Graver scowls at Mulligan. 'Who.'

McQuarrie snaps, 'Whoever was on the take. Bro Devlin knew they had the job before we even met on it, you can see it smeared all over *The Globe*. "Two distinguished families," that's crap! And where am I in the story? Like the Devlins get all the credit here, them with their cheap suits and dirty necks.'

At Maggie's touch, Tom starts. She mouths, *Don't*. Bristling. Nods and tries to unclench.

'This shanty Irishman announces before we even have the meeting and

I'm supposed to think it's an accident? What did he have if he didn't hear it from you guys, ESP?' he is too angry to notice Devlin and Maggie fidgeting in the archway. 'Major announcement, like Bro Devlin and that idiot brother are some kind of players, when they're nothing but a couple of . . . how do you think that makes me look?'

With a swift look at Tom, Maggie says, 'Daddy . . .' She would do anything to cut him off.

'And they blow our chance for some real publicity!'

Both of McQuarrie's people speak at the same time but he taps the newspaper angrily.

'Shut up! Exclusive means exclusive, you think TV is gonna touch us now? *The Globe*. Last page. And I ask you, where am I in the piece? Look at this. Look! My biggest project ever, big tie-in with Global Productions, Fourth of July blast date so shoot the works, major money hanging on it, and the whole thing gets reduced to this. Crap clipping so little that you couldn't even roll a joint and why? Because some glorified junk man out of New Haven makes an end run and calls Mal Fletcher, what was he trying to do, preempt? That's your bog Irish thinking, they're born poor, and they think small . . .'

Devlin growls a warning, 'McQuarrie.'

'Pinhead thinking and what do we get? Two inches on a back page, wham, bam and that's that! And where am I in the piece? I ask you, where am I in the piece?' 'Dad!' Maggie is tugging on Devlin's arm, trying to hold him in place.

'So. What, Graver? Did the bowlegged weasel have to blow you to get the information, or did he slip you a little something on the side?'

Over his employer's shoulder, McQuarrie's man Graver sees Tom Devlin bunched, collecting himself to lunge. 'Pat.'

'Don't you Pat me, you sniveling swamp Yankee.'

'Mr McQuarrie . . .' Mulligan makes a wide gesture to signify that they aren't alone here.

'Who did this, Mulligan, did your father sleep with their mother, or did your mother do the nasty with one of them?'

'McQuarrie!' Devlin grabs McQuarrie's arm so sharply that he can hear the joint pop. 'That's enough.'

'McQuarrie snarls, 'What!'

Devlin spins him around. 'I *said*, that's enough!'

And his tone changes. 'Tom?'

Mulligan and Graver exchange looks. It's part of their job to prevent this kind of confrontation, but they don't.

'Don't hurt him, Tom.'

In another context Tom Devlin and his father-in-law would tangle in a fight. Devlin's not a fighter, but he's angry enough. But this is Pat McQuarrie. The smooth developer isn't yielding, exactly, but he lets Devlin complete the turn so that they are facing like partners in a waltz. McQuarrie is flushed with anger. Rigid, Devlin is pale and furious.

Maggie says to both of them, 'Just don't hurt him, OK?'

As if Pat McQuarrie has willed it, his red rage recedes. 'Just rhetoric, Tom. And always present company excepted, of course.'

He'd like to kill him, but he needs him. He says tightly, 'I have some questions.'

'Questions?' McQuarrie turns, gesturing expansively. 'For you, my friend, anything.' He rolls over Graver and Mulligan like a Bentley heading for somewhere better. 'But. A little coffee first.'

27

Pat McQuarrie has reassembled since they walked in on his tantrum. At ease in his starched shirt and expensive suit, Lexie's father looks comfortable in his body. Sleek, like a bird that smoothes its feathers with a single shake. Devlin has laid it out for him and all he says is, 'Tommy, don't hit the switch.'

'Don't call me Tommy. Nobody's seen her since Sunday. It's time to call the police.'

'Wait a minute, Tom. What makes you think it's been since Sunday?' They are in Pat McQuarrie's office – shelter-magazine perfect and as empty of signs of occupancy as the owner's face. Whatever he is thinking doesn't show. The face is handsome now that the angry flush has receded, strikingly young. Like a lot of the American Irish, the man probably started going gray when he was still in college. The hair is dead white now and the eyes are a predictable blue. Graver and Mulligan split while McQuarrie's attention was diverted. If Maggie had left the room as ordered instead of clinging grimly to her friend, they would be alone.

Devlin turns to her. 'She said goodbye and left right after the brunch, right, Mag?'

Now that they are in her father's office, Maggie has shrunk. 'I saw her get in the car.'

'Sit down, Tommy, there's no point in doing this standing up. Maggie, go tell Maria to hurry with the coffee.'

'Your daughter is missing and you're offering me coffee?'

'Who says she's missing?'

'I told you, we went out to the convent and checked.'

'Maggie, I thought I sent you for the coffee.' When Maggie doesn't leave her father says, 'Wait a minute. Did I tell you Lexie was at the convent?'

'No. Maggie did.'

'Why, Maggie, where did you get that idea?'

Devlin stiffens. 'She says you told her. And she doesn't lie.'

Maggie elbows him, baring her teeth. Easy. Go easy!

Pat McQuarrie blinks. 'That's ridiculous.'

'The nuns say she hasn't been back since Friday. McQuarrie, it's Tuesday.'

'I know what day it is.'

He wants to grapple Lexie's father to the rug and pound on him until he hocks up the truth but Maggie is squinting wildly. He can't touch the man until she leaves the room. 'I don't know where she is.'

'That's not unusual,' McQuarrie says in that practiced, reassuring tone developers use. *The contractors will have this done in no time. No, the property is nowhere near a fault line. Bedrock, all the way down. In the next quarter, this project will go through the roof. It's going to double its worth.*

'It is to me.' *Sure, the check is in the mail.*

'She doesn't tell you everything. That doesn't mean there's anything wrong.'

'What, then? What does it mean?'

Smiling, he shrugs as if it's obvious. 'Why, that she went off by herself?'

'Why should she do that, McQuarrie?'

'Tommy, Tommy, you'd better get used to calling me Pat. We're practically family now.'

Devlin snaps, 'Not yet we aren't.'

McQuarrie chooses not to escalate. 'Please, just Pat. After all, the wedding.'

'There isn't going to be a wedding.' He is startled by the finality.

'Trust me. There will be a wedding,' McQuarrie says. This isn't reassurance, it's a flat statement. 'I know my daughter and I know my plans. There will be a wedding no matter what. Now, about Lexie. You're so certain something has happened to Lexie. What makes you so sure?'

'Everything! I don't. It's.' Never walk in on a bigtime operator with your speeches unwritten. He shakes his head 'I just know. Something's going on.'

It may come with the territory – this ease with the rhetorical question. The developer's tone is neutral, his manner pleasantly curious. He is slippery, impossible to pin down. 'What, son? What's going on?'

'You know better than I do, I haven't see her since . . .' Since Chicago. 'We haven't talked since Saturday, and Sunday I was out when she called, and that was the last . . .'

'Oh, that. Women. They get busy with woman things.'

'She took Maggie to Putney and when I go up there I find out that she dumped the kid Sunday and took off. She isn't in the city and she isn't here. Work with me here, McQuarrie.'

'Pat.'

Gauging his enemy, Devlin amends. 'Pat.' If he's ever going to do this, they have to stay friends. 'Pat, Lexie's gone.'

'Gone doesn't mean gone forever.' McQuarrie goes on in a genial, us-guys tone. 'Let me tell you about my daughter.'

'There's nothing you can tell me about . . .'

'Maggie, I told you to go check on the coffee.' He shoots Devlin a loaded look. 'Little pitchers.'

'Daddy, I can't believe you said that! If you want coffee, get it yourself. Or get Mom.'

McQuarrie slips into his chair behind the big, empty desk and lets one hand rest on the TotalPhone. With a complete office setup in front of him – bells, buzzers and six phone buzzers, he shouts, 'Maria. Maria!'

As if she's been lurking, Maria comes and goes.

'Let me tell you about Lexie. This is going to take a while, stop

102

scowling and sit down.' Then he turns to his daughter. 'Margaret, I've
asked you to leave and now I'm telling you to leave. Tom and I are man to
man now, unless we're *mano a mano*. Understand?'

The girl looks at Devlin. He doesn't have to tell her that when they're
done here he'll find her and report. She gives him a shy little smile and
ducks out.

'That's better,' McQuarrie says.

There is a long silence while they wait for the coffee. Devlin came on
strong with his questions and got nothing. It is time to wait the bastard out.

Pat McQuarrie clears his throat. The buttons on his phone are lighting up
like blinkers on a pilot's control panel but he ignores them. A signal to
Devlin that this meeting is his top priority. He angles his head, sizing
Devlin up. Since Lexie decided to marry him, the two men have tried to
play family or about-to-be family, but that never worked. They are
adversaries, facing off.

Devlin's first weapon is silence.

So McQuarrie has no choice but to begin. 'Lexie is a very independent
girl.'

'She's not a girl.'

'Trust me, she's been this way since she was five years old. She's always
drawn a circle around herself, step too far into it and she takes off. My best
bet is that this whole wedding thing is crowding her and she needs a little
space right now.'

Tell him nothing, not even that you tried to get her to elope.

'But the wedding is important and there *will* be a wedding. Count on it.'
McQuarrie waits.

Let him wait.

'You know, Alexandra's always been my favorite, but she's done this
before. She took off the summer before she went to college – she wanted
Hampshire, I saw to it that she accepted Yale. She ran off to visit one of the
relatives. Do you get the picture now?'

Devlin's mouth dries out. *Relative*? 'That uncle?'

No response. 'And then there was that time after college, she turned
out to be in Tijuana with a couple of girlfriends – came back with a pair
of maracas and a California tan. When she broke up with her last
boyfriend she went off to Maryhurst, you can never tell with that girl. I
know, you think she isn't a girl but they're all girls, aren't they? When
you turn them upside down? Sorry! Nothing personal. So my best
suggestion to you is to lay back. Go home to New York, give it a week or
two, hang loose, let it play.'

Devlin looks at his fingernails until the silence gets to McQuarrie and he
starts talking again.

'So now I've demystified her for you, right? Don't call out the cavalry,
don't go chasing after her or she'll despise you for it, take it from me.
She'll despise you for invading her privacy and she'll dump you because
you're weak. *Capiche*?'

'No.'

'I have a very complicated operation set up here, Devlin, and if you
knew anything about women you'd know a wedding is a very complicated

103

dance. And believe me, I want this wedding to come off on time just as much as you do, and I'll do everything I can. So take my advice. Stay loose, Tommy, give her a chance to work this out. Let her work it out and come back to you on her own.'

McQuarrie is good. Very good.

What he says next has the ring of perfect truth. 'As for the convent, I'll tell you what the story is with the convent, Tom. I told Maggie that Lexie went on a retreat because I didn't want her to worry. You know how kids are, especially at Maggie's age. They worry over every little thing.'

Devlin grimaces.

'I just wanted you to know where I'm coming from. Do you see where I'm coming from?'

He nods. McQuarrie has left him with nothing to do. Unless he's left him with instructions to do nothing. This is going to take some thought. He stands. He hasn't figured out where he's going next but he needs to find someplace quiet, where he can rethink.

At the door, a woman speaks. 'Pat, what are you . . . Oh thank God, it's Tom.'

'Moira!'

'I thought you'd never . . .'

'Don't!'

'Never what?'

'We've been so worried!'

'Shut up, Moira.'

Pallid, jittering and tremulous, like a factory reject of the model they designed Lexie on, Moira McQuarrie plunges into the room. With her fading red hair down and anxiety scoring her face, she traps Devlin in a hug. 'I'm so worried about Lexie, we haven't heard from her since Sunday and we don't know where she is!'

She doesn't get to finish. Her husband moves with the finesse of a stage director, taking her by the shoulders with an affectionate squeeze and turning her as he mutters into her neck. Devlin can't hear what he is telling her but the woman throws him a sad, failed look as McQuarrie says brusquely, 'You girls can have him to yourselves later, dear. Tom and I are talking business.' He pushes her through the living room and into the hall. Coming back into the office he barks, 'Devlin, what are you doing?'

'Calling the police.'

'Don't bother. They know all about it.'

'They what?'

'I've already called the police. You might as well put down the phone. Trust me, they don't want to hear from you.'

'Why the hell not?' Tom Devlin is ready to do murder and her father, who claims he knows Lexie better than anybody else, responds with that bland, professionally crafted smile. The man who may or may not know what is going on with Lexie is stonewalling him. He's been stonewalling ever since they began.

'They already know. I had an idea you were coming, Devlin, and I took some precautions. I called the Lincoln police station and asked for Missing

104

Persons. I told them they'd be hearing from you. And I told then we were worried about you.'

'You. What?'

'I warned them about you. Oh, don't worry, they'll be civil, they just won't . . .' He is trying to look grave but he is smiling. He can't hide it. 'I said you were just out of the hospital and your medications hadn't kicked in.'

28

Bro went out early to buy a copy of the Boston *Globe* without saying why it was such a big deal. He is showing Pop the newspaper clipping even though he knows as well as Tony that Pop doesn't notice much. Pop hasn't said anything.

'Look!'

All Tony can find to say is, 'We're in the papers?'

'You bet. We're news. Big news.'

'You sure that's good?' Tony is thinking about the thing he did for Bro in Atlantic City. He's not certain they should be getting their names into the newspapers right now. He'd just as soon keep a low profile, in case.

'Damn straight. Pop, get a load of this!' Bro's timing is questionable in every respect as Pop is not having a very good day. While Bro was busy folding the paper back to shove in front of him, the old man went into spasm and slid, so he is leaning all crank-sided in the chair. Tony rearranges his father, prodding until he's upright, but no matter how carefully he props the pillows or how many he uses, Pop slides. One of his eyelids is drooping too. Still, he appears to be listening as Bro reads the news story aloud for the second time. 'Two distinguished families, Pop. Do you hear that?' Bro turns to the nurse. 'Does he hear that?'

She nods.

Some time while his sons were enroute to or from Boston, where this deal was struck, Pop appears to have lost the ability to speak. His eyelids squeeze shut and then open. Tears stand in the corners but they may be from the medication. Unless it's the effort to communicate. Accident? Intention? It's hard to know.

Tony mutters to the nurse, 'This is terrible.'

She tightens her mouth into an angry line. 'Shh or he'll hear you. It comes and goes.'

Bro has his own concerns. 'Distinguished families. How about that, Pop? Pop? How about that, Tone?'

'How did you get it into the paper so fast?'

'Oh, that.' Bro flashes that swift, jaunty Devlin grin and quotes *The White Album* from when he and Tony were still young. 'Mother Superior jumped the gun.'

'What did you think you were doing?'

'What do you think I was doing? I faked the bastard out.'

'You did *what*?' Tony should not be questioning, him being Pop's second son, especially with Pop down and Bro sitting in what lawyers call First Chair. He shouldn't open his mouth, but he is.

'You heard me. What they used to say in the TV war news about Nam. Preemptive strike.'

'McQuarrie wasn't definite.'

'He was by the time we left.'

'He wasn't definite when you called *The Globe*. Piss him off and he'll ditch us.'

'No way.'

'He could sue.'

'He can't afford to.'

'He can afford to do anything he wants.'

'That's open to question,' Bro says.

'The whole deal could blow up on us.'

Bro shushes him with an angry look. 'Not in front of Pop.'

'Pop doesn't know.'

'Don't say that.'

'Well, he doesn't.'

'Of course you know, don't you Pop?' The old man in the chair coughs wetly and Bro grins. 'See?'

The last two days have left Tony borderline. He still doesn't know borderline what. He snaps, 'Go to hell.'

'You don't get what's going on here, Tone. You let yourself get fooled by the big house and the string bikini but I kept my head set on the main chance.' Pacing in the morning light, Bro looks narrow and mean. 'I took a long, hard squint at the man. It's in the eyes. He can't afford to lose us. I didn't only see what he wants, Tony, I smelled it on him. We're the best he can get to do this, and I can tell you, he needs to do this. Who else would he get?'

'The Revenaughs.'

'You think he can afford the Revenaughs?'

'You saw the house.'

'You don't know spec when you see it? The house is shouting, *quick turnaround*. You think the sacred, holy Revenaughs would agree to go in there and do the job on that guy's smile and a shoestring and do it in six weeks, give or take?'

'They'd have to be crazy.' *We'd have to be crazy.*

'There. Ergo. QED.'

Tony pokes at the paper. 'You don't think he'll be pissed?'

'Who cares if he's pissed?' Bro's laugh is a little crazy. 'It's in the papers now. This makes it official. Him and us. Tommy and that girl. You don't get it?'

'Not really.'

'Everybody knows about it. Everybody. He can't go back on it now.' Bro bends over Pop and leans close, so he can speak into their father's good ear. 'Did you hear that, Pop? He can't go back on it now.'

Pop gurgles.

'See, Tone? He's proud of us. You're proud of us now, right, Pop? Name in the papers, and the big city papers at that. I'm telling you, Pop, DD is back in the swing of things.'

The old man blinks.

'I don't know if he hears you, Bro.'

Bro shows sharp teeth. 'And look at this here, our blast is going to be in a Hollywood motion picture. Famous forever. DD. You. Me. Think of the publicity, they could put our names on the end of the movie, I'll make them write that into our contract. Our names at the end, signed and delivered. Pop, are you proud of me?'

Tony says, 'I'm not so sure he's here right now.'

'The hell he isn't. He just a little under the weather is all.' Leaning closer, Bro yells. 'A couple of days and you'll be just as good as ever, right, Pop?'

'Don't shake him, Mr Devlin.'

Bro wheels. 'Barbara. Beverly.'

The nurse sniffs. 'Bethany.'

'Whoever. The fuck with you. Get the fuck out!'

The woman hates Bro but he pays her well enough, so she leaves. Bro Devlin straightens then, looking at Tony over their father's head. 'This is bad.'

'Very bad.'

'We've got one hell of a great big job ahead, and Pop . . .'

Tony shakes his head.

Bro's teeth looked jagged, like a little ring of broken plates. 'We've got to plan the thing without him. Me. You.'

'I'll do what I can, but I can only take it so far.'

'All the way. We've got to take it all the way.'

'I can't,' Tony says.

29

'There's not a lot we can do for you without something substantive,' the police lieutenant says. This is a small, rural town; this office knows everybody else's business. The lieutenant looks up from his empty notepad. 'What did you bring?'

'I didn't bring anything. I told you, I came to report a missing person. Alexandra McQuarrie, here's her picture. Hasn't been seen since Sunday. Two days! She's five eight, red hair, gray eyes . . .'

'The McQuarrie family? At Stoneforte? I just got off the phone with the father. He says there's nothing wrong.'

Stoneforte. God. 'You called him?'

'He called us.'

'When?'

'Right before you walked in.'

'He called you to tell you nothing was wrong?'

'He called to say you'd probably be in.'

Something in the lieutenant's tone makes Devlin ask, 'What did he say about me?'

'That you were coming. Why?'

Resting on his knuckles, Devlin leans over the desk. 'You don't think that's strange?'

'Not really.' The lieutenant rolls his chair back to keep the distance between them. 'We've had business with Mr McQuarrie before. About the other daughter. Trouble outside a bar. She's used up her last DWI, that kind of thing. We're old friends.'

Devlin is so loopy with fatigue that nothing tracks. 'How long ago did you say he called?'

'I told you. Just now.'

'And this is the first time he phoned you on this?'

'I don't see anything else noted here, so, yeah.'

Then Pat McQuarrie was lying to keep him from coming here. *Don't bother with the police. I warned them about you.* What was that about? 'You're sure that's all he told you? That I was coming?'

'Yeah. Oh right.' The lieutenant grins apologetically. 'And. He also said we should tell you his daughter's fine, she just phoned in.'

Devlin's heart jumps but he knows better. 'That's a lie.'

The lieutenant shrugs. 'We don't know that.'

'I just told you.'

'Mr McQuarrie is local. We don't know you.'

'And you're not ready to believe he might be lying?'

'He's always been very good to us.'

'I brought this picture.' Devlin slaps it down on the desk.

'Nice.'

'It's been forty-eight hours.'

'That's not what the father says.'

'I know what the father says!'

'He ought to know, he's her father.' The lieutenant hands the picture back. 'Now if that's all.'

'Look, the woman's been off the map for two days now. For all I know, she's off the planet. I'm worried, her little sister is scared shit.'

'Kids. You know how kids are. And those McQuarrie girls. If your girlfriend is anything like the big sister, what's her name, Eleanor . . .'

'She is nothing like Lally.'

'You hope.'

'All I need from you guys is a little cooperation. If you could put out a bulletin.'

'I'm sorry. We don't have enough to go on.'

'I gave you a picture!'

'Not what I mean.' The local cop looks as bland as Pat McQuarrie. Is he as big an operator? On the payroll? No way of telling. His voice thins out to a suspicious twang. 'Where did you say you were from?'

'New York City. Why?'

'And Ms McQuarrie lives in . . .?'

'New York.'

'Then if you're worried about her, you should probably start with the authorities there.'

'She was last seen here.'

'In Lincoln?'

He groans. 'Vermont!'

'Then maybe you should . . .'

Pass the buck, officer, pass the buck. Exasperated, he parrots, 'Start with the authorities there. That's all you're going to do for me, lieutenant? Is that all you're going to do for me?'

'Mr Devlin, we're doing everything we can.'

'This may not mean anything but I should tell you. The last time Maggie saw her . . .'

'Who's Maggie?'

'The kid sister! The last time Ms McQuarrie's little sister saw her, she was getting in the car.'

'The car. Did she say where she was going?'

'No.'

'If I run the plates for you, will you back off?'

'It's a start.'

'Fine. Give me the make and model. We can run the plates, notify the state police. In case the car turns up.'

Devlin gives him the particulars.

The lieutenant scribbles on his pad. 'OK, I'll put this into the computer.' He is waiting for Devlin to go. 'Now if that's all.'

'That's all you're going to do?'

'I should warn you, based on what we've got . . .'

'I know!'

'Here's where we are, Mr Devlin. We can send a cruiser out to the house but the father's not likely to tell us anything we don't already know. Especially since she's been in touch . . .' The police officer shrugs.

'If I tell you she hasn't?'

'The father claims she has.'

'So you're not going to investigate.'

'Not until there's something to investigate. Look, Mr Devlin. We have all we need on the girl.'

'Ms McQuarrie.'

'We have all we need on Ms McQuarrie. You've done all you can do, so why don't you leave your particulars with us? Phone numbers. Where you think you're going to be. If we hear anything, I'll be in touch. And if you hear anything . . .'

'Right,' Devlin says bitterly. 'I'll get in touch.'

'Oh yeah,' the cop says as he walks out the door. 'He said to tell you she forgives you.'

'He *what*?'

'He didn't want you to get all bent over a little fight.'

30

'I went to the station, Mag. Your dad told them Lexie called the house and everything's OK. I'm making a . . . Reality check?' Devlin is phoning from a stall outside a Seven-Eleven. It's an empty exercise, naturally McQuarrie lied. Lexie never called, try and tell that to the lieutenant with his flinty stare.

'If she'd called here, don't you think I'd know? Don't you think I'd tell you if she'd called? Do you think . . .' The kid's scared and getting shrill.

'Don't, Mag. She's probably fine. If I had your family I'd need a little space.'

'Space?'

'You know, someplace your father can't follow. Where he isn't in tight seeing that things go his way.' He tries out an idea. 'Do you think she split just to get him off her back?'

'Probably. Don't get mad at me, I didn't know until the fight.'

'There was a fight?'

'Yeah. Mom and Dad. After you left.' She says, 'You think it's so weird that parents fight?'

'It's not like I'd know. I only had Pop.'

'I forgot. Listen, they don't fight that much. Mom is too much of a wuss, but when they do . . . If it makes you feel any better, Mom is freaking over Lexie, just like us.'

'I don't know if that's good or not.'

'Mom is all, "Patrick, we have to call the cops." And he knocks her hand off the phone. "The last thing we want is cops swarming all over us, not with our history . . ." '

'History?'

'Yeah, something happened.'

'When?'

'I don't know. Back then, I guess.' Maggie's teeth are rattling against the receiver. 'All I know is, Dad is all, "Moira, shut up." And she's, like, "My daughter's missing, and you want to hush it up?" He goes, "No cops, Moira do you hear me? No police. Ever." She's, "What do you mean, ever!" and he's all, "Don't worry, this is nothing." So she totally nails him. "Like the other things were nothing?" '

'What other things?'

'Don't know.' She's wound too tight to interrupt the instant replay. 'Anyway, Daddy goes, "Moira, don't dig that up." '

'What did he mean?'

'Did you know Mom was gone once, and nobody knew? Before I was born. And Lally . . .'

He leads her carefully. 'What about Lally, Mag?'

'I don't know. Something happened with her, maybe that's why she's so weird, and Lexie . . .'

'What about Lexie?'

Her voice shrinks to nothing. 'I'm not sure.'

'Maggie, I can't hear you.'

'Please don't yell at me.'

'I'm sorry. I didn't mean to yell.'

'I'm not exactly over this, OK? I mean, it's not like my folks fight like dragons and I can't find my sister every day. My mom is like, "Patrick, we've got to call the police," And he goes, "No. It would go on the blotter and the press would pick it up. Moira, we can *not* afford bad press right now." '

'Bad press!'

'That's what he said. Then he goes, "Not when there's so much hanging fire." '

'Lexie's gone and he's worried about his image?'

'That's when Mom freaks. She says he cares more about McQuarrie Development than he does about his own flesh and blood and then he says no way, he loves her. Then he whispers something I can't hear and . . .' She swallows her breath in a wet gulp. 'They make up. I know you don't like Daddy, but they always make up.'

He is considering. 'If I wanted to find that guy your uncle Kieran, where would I go looking for him?'

'Nobody knows,' Maggie says. 'He's probably dead.'

Priorities. No room in his life for false leads. 'Look. I have to go back to the city now. Stay in touch?'

'Give us a break,' Maggie growls. 'Get a damn flip phone and I will.'

'I promise.'

He beeps the machine at Lexie's apartment. Empty, what were you expecting? He checks his office voicemail. Call from Zee, trilling sweetly. Forget it. Skip to the next. It's Abe Reponen, demanding a callback. Sure, Abe, as soon as I do this. At state police headquarters in New York, Connecticut, Massachusetts and Vermont, he gets the knee-jerk response. 'Did you and your girlfriend have a fight?' Go ahead, deny it. How does that make you look? Dispatchers in four states take the particulars without much interest: age, height, weight, coloring. Make and model, plate numbers for Lexie's car. When last seen. 'Can't find your girlfriend, eh? This kind of thing happens all the time.' Skeptical. Sarcastic. 'You know how woman are.' They tell him to start with the area hospitals. Even with accidents, they say, the police aren't necessarily the first to know. Thank you for calling, we'll keep you on file. Translation: file closed until you come up with something better. Pass the buck, guys. Go ahead and pass the buck. Without a ransom note, wreckage— God, a corpse, all his encounters with the law are going to play like the one in Lincoln. It crosses his mind that he'd be better off hiring a private detective. He needs somebody to scope the atlas and the phone book and call every hospital within ambulance range of the major roads, but that has to wait until he gets back to the city.

113

He returns Abe Reponen's call.

'Tom! Where've you been?'

'Sorry. Family crisis.'

Abe says, 'With our client expecting sketches this week? Where the hell are you?'

'Boston.'

'Boston! We meet tomorrow at ten.'

'Don't worry, I'm on it. I'll run the sketches past you first thing in the morning.'

'Be here at eight.'

It means pulling an all-nighter when he gets back but Devlin can't sleep anyway. The work will help him make it through the night. He is good at what he does. In addition to the sketches he made at Lexie's, he'll draft a couple of elevations for a second approach. Old tactic. Give the client two alternatives. Give him a dummy sketch to turn down so you can stampede him into taking the plans you want to build. Easy work. Fun, in a perverse kind of way, planning for oblivion. He'll complete the thinking on the road. After four days of knowing nothing he's grateful for a job he knows how to do. First, he has business with his brothers. He's driving back to New York because he has a stop to make. Cut to the chase, Devlin. Check the bastards out.

The surprise is, when he pulls into the industrial park outside New Haven his brothers are glad to see him. Bro comes as near to smiling as Bro ever does. 'You must of heard. Pretty big deal, right?'

Tony bobs at his older brother's side with hands rising like the Pillsbury Doughboy's. He is nudging Bro: *See*? 'I told you he'd come.'

'Shut up and let me do this. So, Tommy, you saw the papers?'

'I heard.'

But Tony can't stop. 'I knew you'd come.'

'Don't hug me, Tone.'

'Tommy. Babe.' Tony's eyes are glistening. 'I knew we could count on you in a pinch.'

'I'm not staying.' He is skimming the office like a high resolution scanner. Looking here, there. What does he expect to find? Not clear.

Tony blinks. 'You didn't come about the job?'

'I'm fulltime at Reponen Associates.'

'That, that's nothing,' Tony says. 'This is really big. Movies, kid. We're going to be in the movies. We can do it, but we can't do it without you.'

'You've been doing fine without me,' he says.

Bro says bitterly, 'If you didn't come back to pitch in, what did you come for anyway?'

Devlin's eyes are like gun slits in a fortress. He can see out but nobody can see in. 'Nothing much. I just came to see Pop.'

'Pop. Well, Pop.' Tony gets misty. 'Pop's not doing so good right now.'

'He's having a bad day.'

Devlin is surprised by relief. The old man is a hard ticket even when he's well. 'OK then. I wouldn't want to bother him.' He could leave, but he can't. He is listening for something. He can't say what. When he hears it, he'll know. Crazy to think his brothers have anything to do with Lexie's disappearance but the suspicion has brought him here. 'How did your meeting with McQuarrie go?'

Bro says coldly, 'It was in the papers. You should know.'

'Implosion,' Tony says with that Death of a Salesman smile. 'Miramar hotel in Cleotha, Florida.'

'When?'

'Fourth of July.'

'Too soon.'

Tony says, 'I know.'

'You can't buy more time?'

Bro says, 'He has his parameters.'

'The movie. The bigtime, Tom.'

'Not enough time. Bad idea.' He should leave but there is the off chance that. What? They are holding Lexie hostage until he agrees to come in with them?

Tony says, 'It's all in the family. We thought you'd be pleased. We thought you would . . .'

'Well, I won't.' He looks for clues, but if his brothers are hiding anything, they are hiding it deep.

Bro snaps, 'So, fine. Now that you've gone uptown for good.'

'You know that isn't it. I love you guys, but I'm done with this.'

His brother gives him an ugly grin, 'You mean you're chickenshit because of what happened to that kid.'

'Fine, you want me to say it? I'm chickenshit because of what happened to that kid.'

'So fine, fuck you. Tony can handle it.'

'Pop isn't?'

'Not for about a month, no. Probably never again. But fuck you,' Bro says. 'Tony can handle it.'

'Tell you what.' These are his brothers, after all. 'Draw something up,' he says to Tony. 'Run it past me and we'll see.'

'You mean you'll help us?'

'Not exactly. But I can keep you from blowing yourselves up.'

'Don't do us any favors.'

'This isn't for you. This is for me.'

Bro surprises him. He barks, 'That's not enough!'

'You want more?' *Why do I think we are bargaining?*

'Onsite visit, just one.'

'When?'

'Saturday. We've got to work fast.' The last of the big spender adds, 'DD will pick up the fare.'

Devlin nods. He can almost hear the *click*. He is studying his brothers' faces but their faces don't change. He clears his throat. 'About the McQuarries. When you had the meeting. Was there anybody. Um, did you meet her?'

'You mean the sister?' Tony grins. 'I think she likes me. How are you with a double wedding, kid?'

'Not that one.' Draw your line through thin air, see if anything bites.

'Don't be stupid, Tone, he's talking about his girl.'

Devlin turns to Bro, but Bro is busy looking at something else. Nothing to pin suspicions on but nothing that makes him any easier. Everybody is under suspicion now. One more thing he has to do. 'I probably ought to try and tell Pop hello. But he's where. Home?'

'No way. He comes to work.'

'Just like always.'

'Come on.' Tony is standing too close. 'I'll show you.'

'Just like always but he's not exactly.'

'Thanks. I know where he is.' *One more thing I need to do.*

'Don't say I didn't warn you,' Bro says.

He goes into Pop's office and shuts the door. He has to do this alone. Pop is here all right, but he's nothing like he was. The wheelchair has been rolled up to a window and parked facing out. Devlin can see the tufted white crown of his father's head sticking up above the back of the chair. He speaks but Pop doesn't move. He turns the chair so he can look his father in the eyes.

'Pop?'

Pop's still in there. He's sunk a lot since March, when Devlin came to tell him he was going to San Francisco. He is struggling toward his son, but from such a great distance that he won't make it today.

'Pop, it's me. Tom.'

Pop's expression doesn't change.

'Hey, you're looking good. I know you don't think so, but you're doing a lot better than you think, you could be heading for a remission. Just in time for the wedding, right?' No matter what ugliness came down the last time you saw him, this kind of encounter is hard. When a man like Pop dwindles to this you have to keep talking; you think about taking him by the shoulders and shaking; you think about jabbing him with a pin to see if there's anybody inside; it's always easier to hate than pity. Always easier. 'You know, Pop. The wedding?'

Pop's foot twitches.

'If there is a wedding. She's gone. Lexie is gone.' He bends too close. They are alone in Pop's world now. 'OK, Pop. I've got you where I want you so don't shit me. Did they take her, Pop?'

31

A woman Lexie never met and wouldn't want to know is probably the last outsider to see her before she dropped off Tom Devlin's map. Best not to ask her what she thinks she's doing in New York. Zee is not your basic stalker. No sir, not successful Zee Wellaver, with her suits from Emporio Armani and her top of the line Prada bag. She is the farthest thing from a stalker but she flew across the map to have it out with Tom Devlin and she isn't going home until she's left her mark.

Take him away from me, will you? Nobody does that to Zee.

Thursday Zee got a good, close look at her. How it happened was: in love and war it's always smart to scope the opposition, which is why she left San Francisco before Devlin did. Happy hunting! Alexandra McQuarrie was right there in the phone book. A couple of calls and Zee knew where she lived and where she shopped. Deli, right near the apartment. Best to run into her on the street, where strangers are the rule. She was outside the deli when Lexie came out. It's not hard to bump into another person, especially on a long weekend when New York closes for the holiday by Thursday noon and everybody's in a rush. It isn't hard to drop a Prada bag creatively, as in, spill the contents so the other person stops to help you pick them up. So just last Thursday, Zee looked her rival straight in the eye. It could have been like an oldtime Western standoff, 'You better get out of here, this town ain't big enough for the both of us.'

Or the man isn't big enough.

But Zee laid back. Listen, she has the goods on Tom Devlin and he knows it. Things he said, what they did, but she thought as soon as she talked to him, he would do the job.

Lexie smiled and everything in Zee was screaming, *Tell her* but she laid back. He'll tell her after we hook up. Oh rage, oh despair, oh sure.

It doesn't help that the bitch is good looking – tall, damn her guts and slender, with that perfect Irish skin and pale gray eyes, down on her knees looking straight at Zee without a clue. Beautiful hands, wearing that ring Tom showed her before they fucked – Tiffany standard, so big deal – pretty face. Well, Zee could have wiped that perfect face off her face with three words. Would have, if she had known Tom was going to blow her off. If she'd told Lexie she was fucking Tom Devlin would it have made her cry?

But she laid back.

How was she supposed to know he was going to blow her off? So she just took her scattered change from Lexie and thanked her and left. Zee, who thought he'd tell the woman it was over and take back his goddamn ostentatious engagement ring that he was so proud of and give it to her.

By the time she found out otherwise, Lexie had left New York. Well, fuck Tom.

If you want anything done well, you'd better do it yourself.

So Zee phoned the house in Boston. Listen, somebody had to break the news. Yes she is resilient. It's her stock in trade. She forgets, sometimes, but she never forgives. Yesterday she did a little shopping. There is a store in the Trump Tower that sells expensive knockoffs of diamond jewelry. Zee found exactly what she needs. A solitaire in a Tiffany setting is so common that she has a duplicate in hand. Now she's found her way back to the deli where the woman shops. She pulls it out of her Prada bag. Says to the counter guy, 'Lexie McQuarrie asked me to leave something?'

The clerk looks into the Tiffany bag and sees the jewelry box. 'It looks like a.'

'None of your business. It's for a guy.'

'Ring.'

'It's for this guy that she goes with, Tom Devlin?'

'Oh shit, she's not . . .'

'Don't ask questions. Just give it to him.'

32

Devlin expects the worst without knowing what that is. Lexie's actor friend is on the machine – the only sign of life in the empty apartment. Good, he thinks, *Maybe I can ask him about this play.* But the message is about something else and when he follows up, it drives everything out of his head. 'Yo this is Clay, Clay Presnell from *Death Duties*? I've got a message for, Tom Devlin? So, Tom, if you're there? I've got something for you, I'm holding it down at the deli? I'm working the late shift and this thing. Um. You might want it tonight. Hate to do this, man.'

He goes down to the deli.

Yeah, Clay Presnell is holding a thing for him. A tiny shopping bag. The end of life as he knows it. 'Where'd you get this?'

'Moke says a woman left it before I came in. Lexie, I guess, she didn't leave word so I guess she's bailed on us, sorta sucks since the play is just starting to shape up.' He cranes as Devlin opens the little blue Tiffany bag. 'It looks like a . . .'

It's a little velvet box. He flips it open. He snaps it shut. Stunned, but he says, 'Yeah.'

'Wuowww. Man. You all right?'

'Never been better.' He is squeezing the box. If he could crumple it to dust, he would.

'I bet. What are you, throwing it away?'

Devlin rethinks. 'No. Hold it for me till she gets back?'

'Who knows when that's gonna be? Sorry, man.'

He sticks it in his pocket. 'Phone me if she checks in?'

'What makes you think she's going to check in? It's weird,' the actor says. 'I think she's gone as far as she could with the play. And. The ring? Personally? I'd go for the refund. That thing wasn't cheap.'

'I'll put it in the bank.'

'That's cool. Don't be a stranger.'

'Right.' Stunned, he follows up insofar as he's able to. Hard work when you've been smashed in the heart with a brick. The part of him that is still functional says, 'The play. Open rehearsals?'

'Sorry. But you're on the list for the first preview,' Presnell adds thoughtlessly, 'Unless you can convince Lexie to let you in.'

He can't convince anybody of anything. He's not sure he'll make it out the door. Coughing to cover the shock and misery, he blurts, 'I gotta go.'

Kidnapping he could have dealt with, some unknown secret lover that she left him for, car wreck, phone calls to hospitals in four states. Not this. The ring. Lexie has returned the ring. She did it via a third party without

119

bothering to attach a message. She didn't need to. The message is clear.

When he was eleven, he broke his wrist. He remembers looking at the zigzag bone ends sticking out and thinking, *This is going to hurt like hell.* But it didn't, because of the shock. Then it did. That's where he is right now. In shock.

It's like being trapped under a mountain. All he can do is put one foot in front of the other in this dark tunnel; all he'll be able to concentrate on is finding the way out. Like the soldier who gets hit and keeps walking, he can only manage next steps. He needs to move his stuff out of her place. Only a psychotic would stay. Only a psychotic would be crazy with questions – why, Lexie? Why? It seems important to touch base with Maggie. Maybe she knows.

'So, I, ah. Heard from Lexie. I got a kind of message from her. I guess it's over,' he says miserably.

Maggie says, 'Yeah, and it sucks.'

'How do you know?'

'We heard from her. I tried to call you but the machine's busted. Get yourself a damn cell phone!' She's having a hard time breaking it to him. 'She talked to Mom.'

His heart zigzags. 'She did?'

Her funny little sigh fills the receiver. 'So I guess she's all right.'

'Where do you think she went?'

'Too soon to tell,' Maggie says unevenly. 'Agh. One other thing. She gave Mom a message for you.'

'What? What!'

'She says not to look for her.'

'Mag!' His voice breaks in two. 'Something I did? Something somebody told her that I did?'

'I love you, but you're yelling.'

'What if something's happened to her?'

'Dad says not to worry,' Maggie says, but she's shaky too. She says uncertainly, 'He says wherever she is, she's fine.'

'How the hell does he know?' His breath comes out in a *tschuh*! Don't. You're scaring her. 'OK Mag, I'm cool. Love you. Bye.'

Numbly, he prepares for Wednesday's meeting. After everything, he needs a concentrated all-nighter just to make it through. Focus, man. Survive tonight and maybe you can handle tomorrow. He is weighing it: whether to take off for Lincoln now, pillage and burn and shake the truth out of the McQuarrie family or whether to wait until he can talk to them without losing it and starting to yell. First, OK, he has to survive tonight. Try not to think about the two of you together – all the sweet moments – Lexie killing herself to make Szechuan chicken for him when they both know she can't cook; her helping him hunt down and bring home his first power suit. Get busy, man. Get so busy that you can pretend to forget. Put all the good things behind you or you'll die of it and then you'll never get her back.

Never mind that you are running on fast food and no sleep, open your laptop and work. Do the meeting. Make all the calls it takes to line up a sublet. Be grateful when your big brother phones, telling him you owe him one last favor. Get down with Bro, get into it, agree to go where he says and do what he wants. For the weekend. One way to get through.

'Cleotha,' Bro says, 'Cleotha, Florida.'

It is sad and terrible, sitting here in a place that Lexie's left behind, surrounded by her things. Anything is better than this. Even flying to Florida with people he loves but doesn't like to make a site visit on a job he wants no part of. Bro and Tony aren't hiding Lexie, never were. Wherever she went, she took off on her own. He can do everything his brothers want and it won't help him get Lexie back. Pleasing Bro and Tony is an empty exercise, but. Lovers can walk out on you but brothers are brothers until the last one of you dies. He can't be at Lexie's place, he can't even be in the neighborhood where everything used to make them laugh, even a trip to the laundromat. Not now. More: he can't be in a half-furnished sublet when the weekend rolls in like an empty hearse. He can't be in New York. He can be in the world, maybe, but just. Anyplace but here.

33

'I'm only here for the day.'

'I know that,' Bro says sourly. Fine white sand is clinging to his black socks and dribbling into his black shoes.

'We could have driven.'

'We need to talk.'

'Without Tony?'

Bro gives him a look.

Devlin and his wiry old brother are slogging through a Florida landscape as strange as the surface of the moon – blinding sunlight striking reflections off white sand and open water, low dunes tufted with sandspurs and grasses he's never seen before. In the inlets, mangrove trees with weird, glossy leaves drop roots that grip the bottom in a stranglehold. Down by the water, the sand is packed hard by the tide. 'Why don't we walk down there?'

'What, and get our feet wet?'

'You always did hate the outdoors.' Herons start up. A cigarette boat tows a parasailer offshore; kids on JetSkis go screeching back and forth across the wake. Unlike Bro, he shed his jacket. Even out here on Mars, he can feel the pain. 'Cleotha. Yeesh.'

'This is noplace, kid.'

'But Pat McQuarrie thinks it's someplace?'

'I don't know what he thinks. I think he thought restoration. High ticket item. The works, but nobody would touch it.' Black socks. Bro is wearing black socks. Even in this heat he doesn't sweat. 'Now he wants us to blow the place.'

'Tax writeoff?'

'Bigger. He says.'

'Condos? Theme park? What?'

'Whatever. Plus big money for the shoot.'

Right, *Soon to be a major motion picture.* 'How much are they paying?'

'Who knows? Your father-in-law keeps his cards close to the chest.' Bro is like a tropical monkey with an agenda. Spidery. Quick. *Same gene pool as me. I think. But a different genetic set.*

'He's not my father-in-law.'

'After the wedding.'

'The wedding's off.' If he can find Lexie and straighten this out, they're going to elope.

'Hell no, he invited Tony and me.'

Something inside Devlin makes a swift three-sixty. It's Pavlovian. Miles

122

between and Pat McQuarrie can still get him going. *She's back, she loves me, it's still on.* In your dreams. With a snap he reverses, landing back in the same bad place. 'Packaging! It didn't cross your mind that he lies?'

'I could show you the invitation.'

'And you tell him I'm back in the business just to get the job.'

'We need the work, Tom.'

'You know I'm out of demolitions.'

'You're here.'

'You should have put on some sunscreen, Bro. That skin.'

Bro points. 'There's our mark. Some heap!'

The shoreline curves from this point and the hotel shimmers at the far end of the arc like a big pink wedding cake. At this distance it is still gorgeous, a monument to some Twenties developer's dream gone bust. Right, McQuarrie. Let this be a lesson to you. In the woods behind them, eighty-year-old streets trail off into nothing because the last dream got too big. Cement lions on crumbling pedestals mark the intersections of nothing and nowhere. When he bought the place Par McQuarrie was dreaming twenty-first-century dreams. 'And you're here to bring it down.'

'Think of the movie. Blam! So.' Bro waves grandly. 'This is where the city puts the bleachers for the fireworks, X thousand people coming in from all over the state. T-shirts, maybe, posters of the blast. National TV just like the Revenaughs.'

'The difference is, the Revenaughs know what they're doing.'

'That's where you come in.'

Reflected sunlight dazzles. It's hard to see. 'Surrounding buildings?'

'Hospital. Retirement city. Last developer sold off part of the hotel grounds for tract houses. Hey, the surroundings are not all that many or that close.'

'If.'

Bro snarls, 'If what?'

'If you can bring the thing down instead of blowing it up.'

'That's your department,' Bro says.

'I'm only here for the day.' Something about being with Bro makes him talk like Bro. It always has. 'He's gonna build out here, how's he gonna get people to come out here?'

Bro makes a dry sound that passes for a laugh. 'You know that and I know that. You think I'm gonna tell him that?'

'Where's Tony?'

Bro steps out onto the causeway. 'At the hotel.'

'Why are we walking?'

'Vantage points. It's a movie thing. Plus I need to do this, Tommy. Brothers are brothers but some things you've gotta do alone.' His voice drops to a gritty whisper. 'I need to sweeten the deal without Tony finds out, you see where I'm coming from? He thinks we're fifty fifty, but we aren't.'

'You've been holding something back?'

'You got it. Something for you. By this time you've figured out that Pop is out of the equation.'

A sign they should sell Devlin Dismantling, he thinks. Retire. God knows they're old enough. 'It might be time for you guys to get into something different, Bro.'

'Like what, brain surgery? So. What I am thinking is this.'

Easy, it is so easy not to hear Bro's Amazing Free Offer, whatever it is. Tom Devlin has learned over the course of a lifetime of lectures to shut out his brother's monologs. Where he used to hand out advice, Bro is trying to hand out money. Flat fee in six figures? Fifty per cent? Piece of the business? What? Whatever. To him Bro is like one of those sound machines from Hammacher Schlemmer, white noise. Do you want the standard wind sounds, or would you rather hear the surf? Bro drones on and he zones out until he hears his cue. It is always the same line, the end point to thirty-something years of speeches. *After everything we gave up for you.*

'I'm walking the site with you, Bro, that's all. Now let's do the rest of this in the car.'

Unused for decades, fenced and boarded up as it is, the Miramar hotel is an architect's vision: a Mizener landmark like the others that sprang up all over Florida in the Twenties when the money was new and nobody thought it would ever go away. Up close, it looks like a wedding cake after the party; chunks are falling off. Devlin is struck by the contrast: the raging undergrowth and creeping decay, and the purity of the design. The destruction is worse inside: leaded frames sag; the stained glass is long gone. He sees broken rods where tapestries once hung and pale squares on the stucco walls like ghost paintings, stay here long enough and he'll hear Twenties cocktail music wafting out of the bar. It's like the shell of an old movie star, empty, except for traces of what it used to be. It used to be beautiful. Not any more. It's like walking into his life.

They find his other brother in the cavernous foyer. Tony is grinning too hard. He fans a clip board in front of him like Adam with the fig leaf. 'So, Tommy.'

What are you hiding? 'Tone.'

Oh that grin. 'Wuddiyou think?'

'I'll need dupes of the plans.'

Bro jogs his elbow. 'Just walk the place for us, kid. That's why you're here. What to bring and where to put it. You know the deal.'

'I think you should pass on this one.'

'No way, kid. Get with the program.' Tony taps his pencil on the clip board.

Bro prods. 'Top of the head.'

'Top of the head? You'd better front for a new fence out there. With razor wire.'

'Expenses.' Bro scowls. 'We're going to shore up existing.'

'I mean, this is going to make one bitchin movie, right?'

'Tony, show me the plans.' The floor is thick with sedge from years of flooding. Broken pint bottles and plastic food cartons crackle underfoot. 'What are you doing for a crew?'

'Our guys are coming down.'

'It's going to take more than our guys to sweep the place. You're looking at a longtime squat here, Bro. You don't know who or what's living upstairs.'

'That's not your problem. You want to start here or start upstairs and work down?'

'The plans.'

'You heard him, Tony, go get the plans.' Bro snatches the clip board and wheels, scowling. *Get with the program, this is costing us.* 'Your problem is checking out the site and telling us how much of what and when and where. Core samples?'

'That's supposed to be Tony's department.'

'We don't have much time.'

'Damn straight you don't. Six weeks is shit for time.'

'I mean you, kid. You're not down here for your health, so start with the notes. Here.' Bro thrusts the clip board at him. He could be telling him to hand over his school lunch money or do his Saturday chores.

'No thanks.' Devlin takes out his Palm Pilot. 'You can't sweep this place by yourselves. Where's the crew?'

'Local contractors A-OK. Local salvage company, local plumbers, lo . . .'

'We're talking about security.' Last night he had the dream. Numb, he is going through the motions here. Without Lexie to steer by, he's lost in space.

Bro snarls, 'You do your thing. I'll take care of the rest.'

'While we're at it, that fence is sitting in quicksand. Pay the two dollars, Bro. Get new posts. Sunk in cement.'

'Fuck that. The costs. How do you think we got the deal?'

'Do it or I'm out of here.'

Bro spits, 'Done.'

They are at the bottom of the grand staircase. 'The stairs. I'd leave this stairway, it's the easiest to guard. You want to get somebody in here first thing Monday to rip out all the rest.'

'Who's gonna know about the other stairs?'

'My point.' He's supposed to be going down Bro's check list but instead he is standing quietly the way he does in empty buildings. Listening. He is getting the lay of the place, a sense of the complications. The geography of rooms in the warren above. As if, if he listens hard enough, he'll hear Lexie's voice. He shakes himself. *Get a grip.* 'Post a guard starting tonight.'

'Who'd bother? There's nothing left to steal.'

'Those are the ones you have to worry about.' The dream. The dead kid again. *Offed himself on my watch in spite of the care I took. The last blood I want on my hands.* With Lexie gone, he is doubly at fault.

'Tommy, get real. Just because you got stung once . . .'

'Post a guard or I'm gone.' Do this. Get done. Get out while you still can.

'All right. *All right!*'

It takes the rest of the day to scope the building and even then he can't check every room. The second floor is all mezzanine, a decaying balcony that overlooks the lobby and the grand ballroom where the parquet rotted to nothing years ago, exposing the cement flooring underneath. The other main floor hallways and anterooms are tiled – the tiles are cracked, worn,

125

loose in some places but still magnificent. It would take an artisan with a toothbrush to bring back the detailing in the ornamental tile that runs, waist high, around all the rooms on this floor.

Tony comes back with the plans and Bro sends him off to Kinko's to get dupes. He is oddly jealous of his youngest brother's time. 'You belong here, Tommy. It's in the blood.'

'I'm here for Pop.' Surprise. It's true. 'What I need from you is your pledge. You do what I tell you here.'

Bro says, too fast, 'Fuckin A.'

'Chapter and verse?' It is time to listen carefully.

'We're brothers, kid.'

This time his old brother is on key. He thinks Bro has always been straight with him. He nods and moves on.

They finish in the decaying clock tower at the top of the hotel. Below them, the surrounding land is laced with little waterways. To the far west the sky turns rosy as the sun prepares to slide into the glittering Gulf. It was a beautiful site in the Twenties; it's beautiful now. But things happened while the building was asleep. Tacky development houses crept up on one side and on the other, there is the hospital. Pat McQuarrie was probably thinking Venice when he went into overcall to buy the place all those years ago. Venice Italy on the coast of Florida, big backers with big money building a new world for the jetsetting Eurotrash. He wanted the rich and famous arriving in launches – with its cement balustrade and inlaid floor, the dock below looks like a veranda on the Grand Canal. What else did he imagine? A helicopter pad. Top of the line fittings in every room, and more, little villas springing up in the abandoned property beyond and beyond that condos, all in the Spanish style. Look out Palm Beach, here comes Pat McQuarrie. Tuck in your elbows, Vero Beach and Hobe Sound.

The view from the tower also makes clear exactly what went wrong. As seen from here, Cleotha is a nothing town. Jello mold ranch houses set on a grid, fast food restaurants and K-marts stretching into infinity. And here in the shadow of the hotel, dozens of old people in big hats and beach shoes spill out of their retirement houses and shamble back and forth on the beach like refugees from the city of death. Some are sweeping the sand with metal detectors and others drop to their knees, looking for something they'll never have. This is nothing like Palm Beach. Restored in any other location, the gorgeous ruin would be a standout. A magnet for the big spenders with their flip phones and arm candy, sleek, pretty girls with nothing to lose. Or smart, successful women with boy toys clamped to their arms. But, here. How can you project glamour and eternal happiness in the city of the walking dead?

Bro nudges him. 'Are we done?'

'Good thing this place is coming down.'

'Tell me about it.'

He won't. It used to be so beautiful. It is so fucking sad. 'I'll send you some specs, but then I'm done.'

'You can do it that fast?'

'This part. Look, Bro, there are some things you should be aware of.' Do this right. Talk the talk. He still thinks you're a baby. 'Number one, the proximity of the surrounding buildings.'

'No problem.'

'Believe me, it's a problem. You accidentally blow this place up and you're going to kill people. If you've gotta do this you have really got to do it. Take care. Every step. I'm giving you sketches and estimates only. You need an expert to bring it down.'

Bro shoots him a sly look. 'You think I don't know the business, Tom? Bet your sweet ass I know the business, I was in the business before you were fucking born.'

'I think you should get on the phone with the Guido Speziales. They quit Revenaugh – fight over methods, whatever. They might have an interest in helping you.'

'The Speziales!'

'Hire a Speziale to consult.' Do this fast and maybe Bro will forget his boneheaded pride.

Bro manufactures a cough so he can cover his mouth. 'The Speziales? If you say so. Sure.'

Get assurances. 'And give him my specs to work from. Promise?'

'Promise? You betcha. Sure.'

'Number two, which is also number one.' Keep talking. Drum it in. Do this so you can walk away. 'Security.'

'That's covered.'

He needs to get out of here. He needs to catch his plane and go back to New York. He has to find a sure way to jump-start his new life without Lexie but before he does any of that, he has to do this. 'No.'

Bro is waiting.

Devlin says in Pop's tones, 'Even when you think you're covered, you're not covered. Whatever you put up here, anybody that wants to can tunnel under it. No matter how many guards you post, there's always a way in.'

34

Strange, ending up here. Unless it's logical – Alexandra McQuarrie, at the only possible end point. Miles from home, wherever home is. Even that is open to question. The overpriced stone pile that her father bought for the wedding? The apartment in Manhattan that he used to keep her in place? Here?

In this tight place, even her voice sounds strange. 'Did I want this?'

Maybe. At first. The silence alone! All month there have been people tugging at her, yammering. Who wouldn't want to be alone with only the sound of her own breath? Lexie has managed to spare Tom the knowledge that when things get bad she goes back inside her head to hide. Tom doesn't know it, but she has kept part of him there too, so they can be safe.

Now there isn't room.

The wedding machinery is chewing her to bits. She tried to stop it. 'Four hundred people! This is disgusting.'

Her father rode right over her. 'Nothing but the best for you.'

It isn't. It's for him.

Cabot relatives, Lowell and Lodge descendants, Athenaeum library board members invited, along with representatives of the best Boston clubs, with the hum of anxiety running along underneath – will they come? There's the society Pat McQuarrie has always aspired to and there are people he owes and people he needs to seduce into believing in him. Debtors and investors. Media people. Nothing stops a Pat McQuarrie production once it's launched. With Lexie's father, there's always been a bottom line – the family finances stand or fall. He borrowed on the Newton mall to put this gaudy show on the road, so the family's hanging by a thread again. A Diana Spencer/Princess Grace/any-Kennedy wedding, unless it's a Malibu Barbie wedding, staged in Lexie's name. Even her mother bought in. Pins in her mouth and her lips trembling: 'Turn the hem this way, sweetie, you're going to make this family proud.'

She can't stand the pressure of their expectations. Then there is the play. Lexie is crazy with a secret that she doesn't know herself. Why can't she break through to what really happened?

She's trying!

This play about her life is eating up her life. Voices from her past are whizzing around inside her head nonstop and she can't make out what they say. She's *this close* to discovery, no closer to what happened that night, behind closed doors. In New York she and the cast wrestled with it. Rehearsals crowded out everything else: concentration, so there's trouble at the office. Love, so there's trouble with Tom.

You bet the stranger *she thought she knew* looked good to her. He walked into her life and offered an escape. It all came down in a sweet, logical progression. He got in touch. She was so glad. He came to Chicago. She was afraid to see him, she was glad to see him. He came up to the hotel room. 'You!' she said, and hugged him tight. He said, 'I was worried. I've been hearing about you.' She should have asked, *from who*? But she heard Tom's key in the lock and she had to hide him on the fire escape. *Come with me*, he said, and she trusted him but not enough to leave with him.

Then he turned up in New York.

He found her on the corner outside the Second Stage. She'd stalked out of the storefront rehearsal, crazy with frustration because the words wouldn't hold still. She had her forehead pressed against the plexi wall of a NYNEX phone box. If anybody asked, she was just making a call.

Then he touched her arm. You're crying.

Nobody sees Lexie cry. 'Don't tell anybody. Go away.'

I won't tell anybody, but I won't go away either. Don't you know me?

Rubbing her eyes, she turned. 'You were sitting in the back.'

Look closer.

She did. 'Oh, it's you!'

Of course.

'You cut your hair. You lost the beard.'

It was time.

'You look terrific.' She smiled.

He smiled back. *So*. Death Duties. He even knew her working title for the play. *Why are you doing this to yourself?*

'You ought to know.'

If you're doing it for me, it's too late for me, he said with that nice smile.

'I'm trying to figure it out!'

He took her arm. *Don't. There are things you don't want to know about.*

'Let go.'

You are better off not knowing. His tone chilled her. *It would be better if you left this alone. All this old, sad stuff.*

Sometimes you know a thing without knowing what you know. It's killing her. The dream, or partial memory. Lexie in the dark in a strange place. Then? Now? She doesn't even know how old she was the first time. Lally called her into the room, their ruffled bedrooms were connected by a door. *Want to see what I have in this box?* Daddy came in and caught them. Daddy was furious; he roared and chased her out but she could still hear him shouting. His voice was terrible. That was the first time she went back inside her head to hide.

Now she's been warned by the stranger she thought she knew. *Secrets, families march over the dead bodies of secrets*, he said. *Sometimes it's better to let dead secrets lie.*

She got older; she forgot. Then in the night, one night, she heard something. In the sliver of light that came in through her bedroom door (when?) she saw something. A struggle. What? It was like connecting with a live wire. Somebody slammed the door on her, shouting. 'Go back to bed.' Shaking, Lexie went deep into herself, looking for that safe place to hide. It was too late. Her skull was buzzing. Electrified. The next morning her life went on, but at the most unlikely times she feels that jolt. As if she's on Death Row, strapped into the chair with the metal cap clamped on her head.

What were they doing, there in Lally's room? She doesn't know. She has run at the question from every direction and she still doesn't know for sure. She is writing a play with no last scene and no curtain line.

And, standing there outside the Second Stage, he tried to warn her *You are skating too close to the chasm. It isn't safe.*

'I don't care!'

Please. Why can't you just drop it and walk away?

'I have to do this. I have to know how it comes out!' She scanned his face for signs of approval.

The play?

'The story. My story.'

Back off, it isn't your story. Alexandra McQuarrie, you're in danger.

It was the last thing he said that night. It left her drained and shaken. Sometimes you know a thing without knowing what you know. She was wild with it. She doubled rehearsal time, ordered a closed set until she figured it out. No copies of the script outside the Second Stage, only one outsider allowed in, and he never came. While Clay and her cast worked through the first act and some of the second, she hung on every speech. She was listening for her unwritten curtain line.

Toward the end of the week Clay took her aside. 'Lexie. We've been talking. Everybody's whipped. You're cool, the play is extremely cool and I hate to say this, but this thing is making you extremely weird.'

'Weird?'

'Starting with the eyes. You look like a raccoon on speed. You need a break.'

'It's the end.' She looked around at the others but none of them would look back. 'I can't figure out the end!'

'Maybe it's a case of the Zen archer,' Clay said kindly. 'Sometimes it's better not to aim. You did your job, now it's time to back off and let us do our job.' He was very nice about it. His tone told her how crazy she was. 'How about you leave it to us for a couple of days?'

She fled to Boston. Holiday weekend, the extra fitting Moira wanted for the wedding dress, perfect, Lally's a fuckup so Lexie's wedding has to be perfect. She really went to see Maggie, poor kid feels orphaned without her. If only she felt better about the new house. She never felt anything but bad, going in. Lally greeted her with that edgy, spiteful grin. Maggie was off somewhere. Her mother gave her an absent-minded hug and rushed her into the car. 'Your nails,' Moira said, as if appearances were the only thing that signified.

Which is how the stranger Lexie *thought she knew* found her two steps from the breaking point. She was too pressed to ask how he knew where to look. He found her in a weakened condition. Admit it, crying. Again. She was crouched on the front steps of the bridal boutique, an early Memorial Day weekend wreck. Car crashes, you can deal with. This was her heart. OK, he caught her in tears. Alexandra McQuarrie, who does not cry.

Crying again?

She looked up. 'You!'

It's the play. You're under a terrible strain.

'I have to do it.'

Why?

'I think it's for Maggie.' She thought, now why did I say that? Since childhood memory has been battering at her like a bird on a window. It can't break through the glass.

Some secrets are better left buried, he said oddly, considering. *Look at you. Are you all right?*

'Yes. Not really. No.'

At the time she thought it was wedding fever.

The fitting had gone badly, the dressmaker fussed endlessly while Lexie fidgeted. Fixed in place and weighed down by several pounds of wedding dress, she had found four lines of dialog. She was desperate to write them down before she forgot. The dressmaker trilled but Lexie lurched off the little pedestal and stepped on the pearl-encrusted train.

'Stop!' Moira yanked her arm. 'Hold still.'

Lexie jerked away. 'Leave me alone. I'm making a note.'

'Lexie, this is your *wedding*.'

'It isn't a wedding it's a show. Welcome to Pat McQuarrie's flying circus. Take Three.'

The dressmaker gawked.

Pretending they were both happy and everything was fine, Moira started warbling the first few bars of the eternal mother's song. 'Don't talk like that. You know you've been looking forward to . . .' The middle varied but it always ended with, 'the happiest day of your life.'

'Don't. It's Daddy's show, Mom, I just happen to have a walkon. It's always been his show and the rest of us are only bit players. It's all we've ever been.'

Moira's teeth locked like prison gates. Words escaped in a bitter hiss. 'You think I don't know that?' It was a terrible admission.

'Mom!'

Moira McQuarrie has a thing about making scenes in public. That Fifties upbringing – her job is to hold the ladder while he climbs. Her thunderous look said, *Not now.* 'Now get back up on the platform so we can finish this.'

In the dressing room, Moira helped her out of the gown and draped it over the clerk's arm. It looked like a fainting princess being carried away. Lexie skinned back into her jeans and the black T-shirt. Over time she had studied her parents' marriage, looking for signs. What kept them together, she still didn't know. She dropped her voice so it wouldn't carry outside the booth. 'If it's that bad between you and Dad, then why are you still married?'

She could see Moira thinking. 'You support your man. Whatever happens, you support your man. You support him even when he . . .'

Deep in her mother's eyes, she saw her father's secret flickering. 'What, Mom. What?'

'Shh.' Moira shook her head. 'Shhh! They'll hear you.'

'Aren't you going to answer me?' She gave her mother a shove.

'I said, shhh!'

'Why do you put up with it?'

Moira's face crumpled like the tissue the clerk had pulled out of the front of the dress. It was just as pink. After too long, a word popped out. 'Embarrassment.'

They were close to something. The heel of her hand thudded into Moira's shoulder. 'Embarrassment? Embarrassment!'

'Stop!'

'What, Mom? What are you telling me?'

'Don't. Forget it. That's all I'm going to say.'

'Forget it? Give me a break, Mom. I'm getting married here. If something came down that I don't know about, you'd better tell me.' She shoved again. 'You have to say.'

'What makes you think you have the right to know?'

The bride, freshly peeled out of a six thousand dollar wedding dress. Shouting. She didn't care who heard. 'You spend your life dressing up for him, making parties for him, shilling for him and doing God knows what else for him because you're *embarrassed*?'

This time her mother shoved back. 'Shut up, Alexandra. Just shut up and go to hell.' For a moment there, Moira had forgotten that they were mother and daughter. When she saw Lexie's shocked face, poor, faded, used-up Moira McQuarrie stuffed her hand into her mouth and ran away like a child who's just made a terrible mistake.

Which is how Lexie ended up sitting on the front steps. Crying, admit it. Never mind that she's spent her life trying to be strong. He sat down on the step beside her. And right there on Commonwealth Avenue, he made an offer that overturned her. *You can walk out on this whole mess any time you want.*

It was starting to sound good to her. 'They left without me. They took the car.'

I'll give you a ride to the house. You'll understand why I can't come in. I'll let you out at the gate.

She did. They didn't talk about any of it on the way. He was that kind of gentle. She told him goodbye, she thought for the last time.

Maybe they both knew he'd find her again, pacing outside the convent chapel late that night. Crying. *Alexandra, this makes three.* Interesting, how he always knew where to find her. Where she was most vulnerable. It was midnight: the chapel was locked. All she wanted was a quiet place to think. Troubled and needy, she pounded on the door. 'And call yourself a church!' She didn't hear him come up. He touched her arm and she jumped. 'What are you doing here?'

Looking after you.

That's supposed to be Tom's job. But right now their situation is ambiguous. Her breath zigzagged. 'You don't need to. I'm OK.'

Just for a while. You need some quiet so you can sort this out.

Oh, yes.

Let me take you someplace quiet. Where it's safe.

Crazy, what you do when you're in overload. She thought about it. She thought carefully. In the territory of distress everybody reaches a point

132

where the impossible looks good to you. Anything but this. Anyplace but here. 'I have to do something first.'

Of course. Take your time.

She said, 'I have to take Maggie. But after that . . .'

My time is yours.

'Only for a while.'

Of course.

What do they say in the want ads? Best available offer. Everybody wants to walk out of their lives at some point in their lives. Look. Only for a while. A day? Two? Be back in New York Tuesday morning, first thing. They made a plan. Why not? She loves Tom but there's no way she could explain what's going on with her to Tom. No need to explain to Tom. She'd be back before he found out she'd been gone.

She met him on Sunday at the place they agreed on when he called the motel. He was waiting at a rest stop on the turnpike not far from Putney; she left her car. They went the rest of the way in his truck. After everything it was a relief to lean back and let somebody else drive. They didn't talk much. Crazy? Probably, but as they rode along she took apart the silence. Companionable. Essential. Safe. Just as he promised. Quiet. The kind of quiet she needs so her mind can go out and come back with the ending to her play. For the first time since she opened her chest of secrets and tried to put some of them into dialog, Lexie felt safe.

I know this is hard for you, he said when they got there. *It's hard for me too*. He stopped the car.

Strange looking place, but she was OK with it. 'This is it?'

For now. Come in.

Everybody wants to walk out of their lives at some point in their lives, but this is impossible.

It's been days! Lexie is here and Tom is alone in New York. The world is going on without her. Her wedding is probably going on without her, if she knows Dad. Rehearsals of *Death Duties* are going on without her, and if she doesn't get back they'll do it wrong. For all she knows Tom is going on without her, and all because she trusted this stranger *she thought she knew*.

It was strange, but for the first two days it was wonderful. He was so kind. The silence. Good food. Long, quiet car rides to places where they could walk miles in the woods. In high school, Lexie and her mother used to go out to Aunt Costanza's place on retreats. Three days of silence. Meditation. Prayer in the chapel and rest in single rooms empty of ornament except for the crucifix above the door. Sensory deprivation of a kind, like those immersion tanks where customers escape their anxieties by floating in salt water in the dark. This is a lot like that. With the world shut out, there's no telling what new awareness will come in. Relieved of responsibility, she felt a hundred pounds lighter. Free. *This isn't a rescue*, she told herself, *it's a retreat*.

Until she found she couldn't leave.

35

As soon as he got the Devlins and the McQuarrie family in his sights, Gerald Slade quit his job. He has made notes on the time he spent in Lincoln, Mass. Solidifying his special friendship there. It angers him that Tom Devlin, *who let his Freddy die* spends so much time with that little McQuarrie girl. *If he had spent any time at all on Freddy* . . . Take note. It's time to focus. Get ready.

It takes everything he's got. The plan demands complete concentration. He can't waste time in stupid faculty meetings or talking to stupid kids, no wonder he had to quit! Gerald is deep in his plans. He has a lot to do between now and the Fourth of July. There isn't room in his head for anything else.

Quitting has worked out well for him.

When you quit your job, naturally you move out of your office. It presented him with a dilemma: where to live. He has solved the problem with Holiday Inns. It's expensive, but what does he have to spend his money on? The best part is that Holiday Inns are interchangeable. Walk out of your room in one and into another and it's as if you never left. The decor is the same. The placement is the same. The uniform surroundings are gorgeously impersonal. A perfect way to simplify so you can concentrate on the plan. Concentrate and you can make it all up to Freddy in the ecstasy of revenge.

These places are made for concentration. He can make his own time. He can hang a Do Not Disturb sign on the door. No more rolling out at dawn to avoid the prying custodians. No more breakfasts in the Student Union. He can make instant coffee in his room instead of having to go out. He skims *USA Today*, the daily complimentary copy. Then he can watch TV in his pajamas or get right down to work. There's a shower right here in the room; no more dressing at the gym. If he wants exercise he can run in place or go out and walk laps around the parking lot. He can do anything he wants.

For the first time since Freddy died, Gerald's life is full. On days when he isn't traveling, he has his list. He is researching in public libraries on his way down the east coast. He started with newspapers on microfiche but now he's advanced to using library computers to search the web. He needs more than InfoSeek and Dogpile.com can give him, but it's a place to start. There isn't much on Devlin Dismantling, but there's plenty on the Revenaughs. News stories. Photos. Video plugs of majestic collapses as buildings prepared by the Revenaughs come down. Always meticulous, Gerald is researching controlled demolitions. Things he needs to know and what to buy so he can move in at the last minute and do Freddy proud.

When he's done for the day he eats in the Holiday Inn dining room. Back in his room, he takes grim pleasure in filing printouts and ticking off items on his list. Phase one. *Locate her*. Done. *Gain her confidence*. Also done. *Research*. Almost complete. Now he is entering phase four.

He never stays long enough to draw attention. When the clerks start using his name, he moves on. It keeps him pure. Things had begun piling up in the office in spite of him. Student papers. College junk mail. Gifts from secretaries who felt sorry for him. Flowers. Hummel figurines. Junk you can't throw away because the donor will hold it against you. Now he travels light. There is no room for clutter in his life. There's only the plan.

He is working his way south. He took his time until he crossed the Georgia line. Now he is moving faster. When the Devlins bring down that hotel in Cleotha, Florida, Gerald will be on the scene. He'll be there with a bang. For the first time since Freddy died, Gerald Slade is what passes for happy. These days when he gets up in the mornings he has something to look forward to.

36

Since Lexie sent back the ring Devlin has been to Lincoln twice, trying to get information. He's spent as much time looking as he can and still keep his job. He has to find out if she's OK. If she's done with him, he wants her to tell him to his face.

The first time he drove up to Lincoln, he asked questions until the chief ordered him out of the police station. 'I told you, Mr Devlin, this isn't a police matter, this is a family matter.'

'I'll try again.' For all the good it did. He'd tied up the lines for days, trying to get some kind of reading from the family, but they closed ranks. Maggie was away at canoe camp in northern Canada and the others stonewalled him. Pat McQuarrie was charming enough, 'I should have warned you, my daughters dance to their own tunes.'

'You aren't worried that she's missing?'

'Trust me, she isn't missing,' McQuarrie said on the phone. 'When she's ready, she'll come back.'

It was time to go to the house.

He found Moira McQuarrie in the cut flower garden. 'Don't worry. She's been in touch and she's fine.' She was blinking like an albino rabbit in the shade of her big straw hat.

'Please, Mrs McQuarrie, I really have to see her.' Touch her. Hear her tell him what's going on. 'Where is she, Mrs McQuarrie? Where's Lexie?'

'I can't tell you.'

'Why not?'

'If everything's fine, everything's fine.'

It took all his self control to keep from shaking it out of her. 'Mrs McQuarrie, everything isn't fine! So why the hell aren't you looking for her?'

OK, he pressed too hard; for a second there, he saw anger flare. Her voice shook. 'Now, why would I want to do that?'

He couldn't speak without yelling so he stood in the sunlight, waiting her out.

'She loves retreats,' Moira said finally. She could have been weaving a story for herself, not him. 'Those cottages on the Provincetown dunes, you know, anyplace where she can hear herself think.'

He wished he had some of whatever the woman was taking that made her so mellow and detached. 'Provincetown? Is that where she is?'

'What makes you think I know?' Then Moira McQuarrie said with amazing honesty, 'I thank God that she's young enough to get away.'

When he cornered her by the swimming pool, Lally slid down the scale from flirtatious to steely and hostile. 'Why should I tell you anything? Men are rats. You of all people ought to know.'

'I still love her.'

'Yeah, you would.'

'Can I get a message to her?'

'You can fucking get off the property or Our Father will call the cops.'

On his second trip to Lincoln he talked to the garden guys, who knew nothing, and he talked to Maria, the housekeeper. When he gave her a fifty her voice dropped. 'Don't let them know I said so, but I think it was the wedding. Terrible fights over it. He-saids, she-saids. Terrible fights.'

'Is Maggie here?'

'They sent her to Canada.' The maid's eyes softened. 'Poor thing.'

He tilted his head, listening, but that was all she'd say. 'Help me,' he said. 'I just want to talk to her.'

But she'd given all he was going to get. 'Miss Maggie? As soon as she's home from camp. Quick,' Maria gave him a push. 'That's his car. You'd better go.'

He wanted to kill Pat McQuarrie, not hide from him. Maria got him out by saying, 'If you leave now, I'll have her call you as soon as she gets back.'

He was back on the shuttle before he faced facts. She was talking about the little girl.

In the weeks since, Devlin has badgered troopers in three states and made junkets to three resort towns where Lexie just might have gone. He's been to the Second Stage and talked to every member of the cast and come up empty.

'She was freaking over the play,' Clay said. 'Too much pressure and she split.'

'Without telling me.'

Then he said an interesting thing. 'Plus, when the family sees it, she'll be in deep shit anyway.'

He is too upset to ask why. It looks as if Lexie has left him cold. Look what she did. She just bailed. Whatever happened to goodbye? She blew him off with a Tiffany's shopping bag. Just the ring. No note, so he can't tell what is driving her. He's trying to stop worrying and get mad. If he can get mad enough at her, maybe he can turn his back on this and walk away.

Now it's the end of June and Maggie is on the phone. 'You're there!'

'You're back!'

'I hated camp. I miss you so much!'

'I miss you too.' Devlin has been trying to hang tough. No walking past her building, looking for a light, No dropping in at the deli or at the Second Stage. Time to start over. But he can't. 'Have you heard from her?'

'You wish. And nobody will tell me anything. I hate not knowing where she is.'

'So do I.' The hardest part is waking up without Lexie. The second hardest is walking into places where Lexie used to be. It's hard enough talking to her little sister. 'But she's all right.'

'They say she is.' If the kid isn't crying, she's close. 'You'd better come up.'

'I can't right now, it hurts too much. The wedding's off.'

The next thing she says flattens him. 'No it isn't. That's why I called. I. Ah. Thought you ought to know.'

'Know what?'

'Like, you wouldn't want to just read it in the paper,' she says unhappily. 'OK, the invitations are out, so you'll find out soon enough anyway. Get this. They're going ahead with the wedding.'

He stiffens. 'They can't.'

'They are. Dad paid for the new house and the dresses, plus the caterer, up front. Do you really think he'd let it go by?'

'That's crazy.'

'Like, they have to go through with it.'

'Without Lexie?' There's that knife again, twisting under his heart. 'Without me?'

'Sure. All they did was change the names on the invitations.'

Anger shakes him. 'She's marrying someone else?'

'No. Somebody else is marrying somebody else.'

'Who, Maggie? Who's getting married?'

'Lally. They scraped up some bozo for her,' Maggie says, and Devlin goes rigid. A wedding he never wanted. No. A wedding that put his relationship on the skids, and Pat McQuarrie's treating it like one of those PlaySkool toys with glossy, interchangeable parts. Lose a couple of pegs? Hey, any old pair will do. Maggie is saying, 'Some guy, works in a gas station. She met him at a bar, *not* good and all Dad cares about is her getting skinny enough to fit the dress so his money isn't wasted and she'll look good in the pictures. Don't you think that's weird?'

His voice is tight with rage. 'I can think of a couple of other words for it. Hang on. I'm there.'

37

Life's a bitch and then you die, Lally thinks.

Yeah wrong. Here's the bitch. Lally is the bitch. *Hear me roar. Look at me crooked and I'll rip your ears off. Make something of it? Go on. Try. I'm the bitch, OK, but it doesn't matter a stake in your bunghole who's the fairest in the land, I'm the one that's getting married so fuck you.*

This is what's on top with her. She is in trouble about the dress.

Here are the McQuarrie women minus Lexie, trotting around the Bridal Boutique in dresses and high-heeled shoes. Moira dragged them down here for the fitting, another command performance. That would be her in the organza. Mother of the Bride pink. Twitchy little Maggie is so skinny that they're stuffing padding down the front of her blue organza dress. Here's Lally in white, what a joke. Eleanor McQuarrie at her age just about to close on happy-ever-after, and the dressmaker is crapping it up.

'I'm sorry, Ms McQuarrie, this dress was made for somebody much smaller.'

Fucking Lexie. 'Make it fit. Hell, if you have to, you can always cut off my boobs.'

Lexie got everything Lally ever wanted and now by God she's going to get it back. Lally never fit anything the sainted Alexandra wore but she will fucking do it anyway. She will do it because things happened and Lexie split so Lally is all they've got. When you're mounting a show and the star flakes, you roll out the understudy. Fuck no Lally doesn't know where Lexie went and she doesn't give a fuck. Now she's the one getting married. So, tough if she doesn't fit the dress now, she will fit it sooner or later. She will fit it one way or another. Even if . . . Take *that* Cinderella. Even if they have to saw her boobs off with a butcher knife. Listen, she would be a size six too if it wasn't for certain things.

It's not her fault, what happens later. It's not her fault that before the day is over she's going to try to hit Maggie with the car. Blame the dress. Blame Moira, she won't quit fussing. When Lally sucks in the roll between her bra and girdle line and tries to wrench the zipper closed, pearls pop off and roll.

'Don't!' Moira cries. 'Let me help.'

Lally smacks the mother's hand away. 'Fuck off, you're in the way!' Lally's fat face is streaming. She is pink and shaking with rage. Nothing to drink since last night, you bet she is pissed. She hasn't lost it yet but she will, she will.

The dressmakers are polite enough – have to be, for what they're getting paid. *Whereas Moira services my father for free which means everything is an issue with her*. So for Pat McQuarrie's sake, the loyal wife is pleading, 'Please be careful dear. Eleanor, stop,' *story of my life*. It follows her around like Muzak, her own personal white noise. The clerks and the other customers, she could handle. *Never see those twats again*. But this!

Blame the time of day, five p.m. and Lally's dry as the desert outside Palm Springs. She's usually boiled by this time but instead she is trapped on the dressmaker's platform like a fish washed up on a dock. But she's getting married, so she's cool with it. Or she would be, if it wasn't for skinny little Mag.

Looks like me, big jaw, but skinny, the bitch, but skinny, like a Kate Moss wannabe. Go ahead, flaunt it, whereas I . . .

This is what tips her over. Lally and Moira are grappling over the zipper and Mag? Maggie has the nerve to laugh. 'Watch out, jerkoff.'

But the kid is snorting through her fingers like this is funny! Listen, she's been warned. Maggie knows the look: *Wait till I get you home*. Nobody pisses Lally off. Maggie of all people should know. So she sticks her fist in her mouth but Lally can see she is still laughing. 'I'm warning you . . .'

She should let Maggie have it right there, but she has to wait. See, the McQuarrie women don't make public spectacles, in the McQuarrie Armed Forces, that's Rule One. From the minute Lally was old enough, the mother would say, 'Wear this dress for the cocktail party, Lally. Not those shoes, the ones that match the dress. Do something about your hair.' She had to suck up to the company. 'Business friends of Daddy's. If they like you, it may do Daddy a lot of good.' In the next life, Pat McQuarrie will issue uniforms. Stripes, because life in this family is like jail.

Payback time is coming, but not yet.

So what if the cops boosted Lally's license on the last DWI and Pat took away her keys? Fuck them all. When they get to the house Lally lingers in the car. She waits for Moira and that dumb kid to get out. Then she slips behind the wheel. Maggie knows to watch out for her, but she has her arms full of packages. Lally releases the brake and starts the car.

Let this be a lesson to you.

'Shit!'

Like quicksilver, Maggie slips out of the way and the car rolls into the bushes and crunches to a stop. Brushing herself off, the kid gets up and without looking back, stalks into the house. Moira is another story. Moira is hysterical.

Moira pulls her out of the car. Her voice is trembling with rage, 'Eleanor, how could you?'

'Back off. Back off and go to hell.' *Take that, you cow*.

And Maggie? Maggie got hers over supper. The last of the big spenders and his lovely wife have Consolidated Malls at the table in the dining room and Pat is scared shit Lally will embarrass him and queer the deal so she and Maggie are sent to the kitchen to eat. The children's table, in spades, neither of them talking, Lally going sour under the yellow light.

She's a little tense anyway. After the thing with the car she needed a drink but some time today Maria uncovered her next-to-last stash and her father, the grand Patrick McQuarrie himself stood over Lally while she

140

poured it down the bathroom sink. Mumble-something years old and her father has to stand guard and make her pour perfectly good vodka down the sink.

She dusts off every word that makes him flinch.

He pushes her away with the flat of his hand. 'We need you dry for the wedding.' You'd think he was standing over one of his mall sites with an army of bulldozers. *We need this hillside cleared.*

So if she's hard on Maggie tonight, blame it on that. Blame it on the crap dinner in the kitchen with no wine.

Maggie is saying, 'I know you were only trying to scare me with the car.' No point in talking after that. Maria says a few polite things to Maggie and Maggie perks up.

They eat. Lally gets up. She's about to walk away when everything piles up on her and she wheels. She draws back her arm and *smacks* stupid Maggie with a roundhouse right that knocks her off the chair.

'That,' she barks. 'That's for the last thirteen years.' And turns and stalks out.

When Lally was the only daughter she was the favorite. And then she wasn't. Damn perfect Lexie came along. And then. Damn that baby and above all, damn the secret they all keep.

What did she know, she was only a kid. A couple of things happened. Big things. Lally kept it in the closet but they found it the very first night and God all they care about is appearances. Whatever it takes to make the family go. Looked at it. 'This? How inconvenient.' All smiles. 'Don't give it another thought, sweetie pie, Daddy will take care of this.' Wrenching out a piece of her heart and *giving it away.* And later is was, 'Be nice to the Cabot boy, Eleanor. Forget the little wop you brought home, he doesn't love you. If you're going to pull down your pants for somebody, do it for one of the Lowells.'

Daddy, so practical, so condescending. 'If you're not good enough to get into college, Eleanor, there's still a place for you, there's always a place for women, if you do your job.' He made clear what her job was. Her job was to marry up. 'You only think you're in love with that spick you picked up at the disco. No daughter of mine gets yoked to some greaser for life. You're going to marry the Lodge boy.' In spite of the other thing that happened. It should have cracked her out of this jail of a family, but they found out and covered that up too. Shut her in her room. 'You stay in here until you're back in your right mind.'

So she is a lifer, locked up in this family. In jail, they teach you morals. Daddy brought Lally up right. She doesn't just fuck her men, she marries them. When she can. And if she can't. Well, that's something else. She did everything she could to please him. She even snagged Bernard Lodge. It wasn't her fault that the Lodge family didn't want a big wedding, *what, were they ashamed of me?* Just families, registry office, like they were trying to sweep her under the rug. That one ended fast. Pat blamed her. 'Did you tell the boy something about yourself, Eleanor, something that scared him off?' He grabbed her neck and shook. 'What did you say to them?' *Nothing. I didn't tell them anything.*

Lally has spent her life not telling. No wonder she needs a drink. *If I start talking the world will scream and cover its ears.*

With no college, the jobs she could get were jobs he wouldn't let her take. 'Think how it would look! I didn't bring my daughters up to wait on tables. Stand behind counters in department stores. McQuarries don't sell liquor for a living.'

She thought she could get married for a living but it didn't work. Things happened. All four of the marriages blew up, her temper, don't ask. The ones he didn't approve of were the worst, Pat McQuarrie has his ways. If a watch doesn't work right, he gets rid of it. Time for a new one. Same with men. And she's out of work again – divorced – so she ends up back on the goddam hearth.

Stuck. In stir until she can find a man to ride out on. Well she just did, with a little help from Dad. He didn't come cheap but what the fuck, they never do. And this one, after the Blessed Event they helicopter to the Vineyard for the honeymoon and damn all, she is going to keep this one. When the honeymoon's over and they get back on the ferry to Woods Hole, she's going to save her life. She can tell him everything. Then they'll get in his truck and head out west to some small town where nobody knows the things Lally has done and where her father's money doesn't reach. She'll get her new man to some new place where they can be safe from Father Dearest *and then by God we're going to turn my man upside down and see. I love looking at their works.*

There's a knock on the door. Moira comes in. 'You shouldn't have hit Maggie. If your father and I were speaking we'd have an intervention.'

'Been there. Done that.'

'You can't go on the way you are.'

Lally is waiting for her to leave so she can look under the mattress for her pint of peach brandy. 'I can go on any way I want.'

'You can't get married in this condition. We need to take steps.'

She whirls on her mother. 'You mean Twelve Steps.'

'When you get like this, you know how you get.' Wonderful, the way Moira looks at her. Like the bomb squad when they see the timer click down to zero. Afraid. She puts on a happy voice. 'It wouldn't hurt you to go to Silver Hill until the wedding.'

'Been there. Done that.'

'Four hundred people, you want to be at your best.'

'No. You want me to be at my best.' Snarling, she adds, 'If I have a best.'

'Look at it this way, you can get your nice figure back. They have a wonderful gym. I can have the dress brought down for fittings. You met that Ahlquist nephew at Silver Hall,' Moira says, the woman would do anything to lure her back into rehab.

'And you remember what happened with that.' Lally can get men OK, but when she tries to keep one, they fight back. She gets the way she gets sometimes and it's ugly. *Pathetic, huh, long hard life and every time you look around you've lost another goddamn man.*

Moira says, 'If you could just stop drinking, maybe you wouldn't have this problem.'

Listen, I can quit drinking any time I want. 'Put on a new tape Moira, and fuck you.'

142

'You can't go on this way.' Great. Tears again. Her eyes are red most of the time now and the Kleenex has left her nose raw.

'I can go on any way I want.'

'Not after . . .'

'After what, Moira? After what? After everything you've done for me? Or is it everything I did?'

Moira is thinking about something the family never found words for. *It's her secret as much as mine.* 'Eleanor, don't.'

'Is there a problem, Moira? Do you owe me one?' Lally is like a Rottweiler bearing down on her. 'Everybody in the room that thinks they owe me one . . .' She is on top of her mother now, gnashing at her ear. 'Roll call. Everybody that owes me one had better get out. Now.'

'.' Moira is fresh out of words. She goes.

Lally needs that brandy. A day without a little hair of something sucks. Thanks a lot, Dad. *What do you care if I get the shakes?*

But in the context of the heat death of the universe, Lally is feeling better now. A little violence now and then does a person good. See, in spite of the dress not fitting and grease popping out on her forehead even after she scrubs she feels pretty, just like in the song. She feels pretty in spite of the fact that she will never look like the great and holy Alexandra and life's a jail unless life is a bitch.

She feels pretty because if there's a bitch in the woodwork it's going to be her. *Fuck the fairest in the land. She's gone. There's only me.*

38

Given where his head is, this is an obscenity. Torcheres line the McQuarrie driveway, two full months before the wedding. An ersatz Calder sits in the garden next to what looks like a real St Gaudens bronze. Somebody has garlanded the front door. There's a bouquet wired to the front of Moira McQuarrie's Beamer like a trophy. As if the driver bagged a May queen during hunting season and mounted the antlers on her car. Lally McQuarrie is an obscenity, bobbing in the doorway in baby pink with her hair tortured into some hairdresser's idea of a 'do.

Unless the whole thing is a joke. Devlin was in Cuernavaca once on the Day of the Dead: Mexican graveyard humor spelled out in gaudy flowers and candy skulls. It's just what this is like. Except what's dead here is whatever he and Lexie had. He may never get it back and the McQuarrie wedding rolls on.

Lally is buzzed on Haldol, Xanax, something; there are bubbles in her grin. 'Couldn't stay away, could you?'

'Is your father here?'

'Kiss the bride?'

'I can't stay.'

'If you came crawling after Lexie, you can forget it. She isn't here.'

'I didn't.' It is safer to lie. He needs to crack this family open and break Lexie out.

'Then you came for the party.' She is sort of smiling. She is wearing a three strand pearl choker. 'Imagine. An engagement party, for moi.'

'I have to see your father.' He's trying to get past Lally and Lally is like a little engine parked in his way.

'Oh, I get it. You're here about the job.'

'I already have a job.'

'Come on in anyway. Party down.'

'I'm not in a celebrating mood.' He wants to get past her, she wants to keep having this conversation.

'You'll take the job. My father always gets what he wants.' She says bitterly, 'Sooner or later, he always gets what he wants.'

'Are you drunk again?'

Then Lally surprises him. 'Don't fuck around. I know what you think of me.'

'You're cool, Lally. Now let me in.'

'But I wasn't always this way. Things happen to people . . .' There's a rumble somewhere inside Lally like a truck starting. Her teeth flash; a hair closer and she'd gnash away part of his face. 'And they change.'

'Whatever it was, I'm sorry, OK?' He puts his hands on her shoulders and turns so that she's in the doorway and he is standing inside. He gives her a pat. 'Later.'

In the paneled study, McQuarrie raises a smooth, unreadable face. 'What are you doing here?'

'God. Damn. You.'

'Well, Devlin. Nice to see you too.'

'God damn this wedding.'

That polished smile. Decades raising money out of thin air have taught Lexie's father how to keep his adversaries from knowing what he's thinking. 'I assume you've decided to take the job.'

Devlin wants to lunge across the desk and murder him. He's not surprised when Graver and Mulligan materialize, standing quietly on either side of the door. He is shaking with anger. 'I'm here about your daughter.'

'Sorry about that, Devlin. Luck of the draw.'

'She drops out. Disappears! And you aren't even looking for her.'

'Should have warned you. She does that,' McQuarrie says with that same smile. Condescending, the smile of a man who always knows more than you. 'People in our family do.'

Angry as he is, Devlin is watching him carefully, as if he expects to see Lexie's status registered in her father's face. 'And you aren't even worried about her.'

'No, I know my daughter.' Now Pat McQuarrie looks at him dead on. 'If I was worried, would I be sitting here?'

Devlin registers this: remember and try to feel better. Then he pushes on. 'So instead, you're running this bogus wedding.'

Smug bastard. Cool tone. 'I have my own concerns, Devlin. Projects. Investment to protect.'

'And you don't give a rat's ass who gets married as long as the wedding comes off.' It is an obscenity.

'First things first.'

'You bastard.' As they talk Devlin is studying him, trying to get some clue. What to do here? Play along, he thinks. Get the tune and try to play along.

'Sorry about your little engagement, but you know women. Women!' Pat McQuarrie snorts. 'They're always gumming up the works.'

'But nothing stops you.'

'Don't worry, we'll have our wedding.' Does he practice that smile?

'It's obscene.'

'It's a business necessity.' The beginning frown is for Lexie, who forced Pat McQuarrie to initiate wedding plan B. But it passes and he says, 'You know, we've got a deal with Global Productions for this implosion down in Florida. Movies! Local coverage and CNN. You know, it could be a very big thing for you.'

Is he bartering? Lexie for my cooperation? Lexie would never sit still for that but he'd better ask. He is weighing it when Maggie hurtles past Graver and Mulligan and plows into him. 'Devlin!'

'Maggie!' He hugs her hard. He looks over her head at her father. 'Florida? Count me out. With or without Lexie, there's nothing in it for me.'

'Money isn't enough?'

'You know what I want.'

McQuarrie sags. 'I've never been able to make her do anything she doesn't want to do.'

So Devlin knows what he needs to know.

Lally thunders in, screeching. 'Come here, you stupid little jerkoff, you have to get dressed for this fucking party.'

'No way!' Maggie hides behind Devlin. 'Could we please just please go?'

'You might as well go, Devlin,' McQuarrie says coldly. 'I'm done with you.'

Lally follows them out to the car. She stands in the driveway screaming as they scratch off.

'That poor guy.'

'Who, the husband?' Maggie shrugs. 'He's just part of the package.'

'Package?'

'Whatever Dad is putting together. Mall, multiplex, whatever he wants this time. He's all about packaging. But you know.'

Pulling away from the house Devlin nicks the corner of a flower bed that's been planted to look like an American flag. 'And this Fourth of July blast is just part of the package?'

'Whatever it is. Yeah. God, it's soon.'

'Too soon.' Devlin heads out of Lincoln. Glad to leave.

Maggie says wistfully, 'I've never seen a building come down.'

'There's always TV.'

'No way,' Maggie says. 'Daddy's taking us all down to Florida for the show. That's what he calls it. A show.'

'He thinks it's a show?'

'I never know what he thinks. It's all about money is all I know.'

'Everything is.' Hope jabs him. 'Shit, for all I know, he paid somebody to take Lexie away.'

'I don't think so.'

He flinches. *Something I did*? Now that he has Maggie here, he's crazy for any detail he can follow up on. 'Why not?'

'He was too big on this wedding. He was all, "There's a lot riding on it" so he was pissed when she left, he kept yelling, "First Kieran, and now this." '

This turns his head. 'Kieran?'

'You know, our uncle that went underground, Daddy never got over it. Lexie either, I don't think.'

Lexie: *Some family stuff I have to work out.* 'Kieran.' He is thinking hard. *God help me break through.* 'Maybe that's what she was trying to do with the play.'

Maggie jabs his arm with two fingers. 'The play?'

'She didn't tell you? She's been digging up some stuff for this play of hers. Ugly stuff.' *When it's ready, they'll know. Until then I don't want them to know.*

'She didn't tell me that part,' Maggie says sadly. 'I thought she told me everything.'

'Maybe she wasn't ready for you to know.' They are on the Mass Pike now; if he has a destination, it hasn't come clear to him. He is thinking hard. 'Maybe the play is about this Kieran.'

Maggie considers. 'Naw. I don't think so. No, she wouldn't write about Uncle Kieran. She wouldn't do anything to get him caught.'

'Caught?'

'You know how the feds are. They never give up.'

'Kid, all that stuff's been over for years!'

'Unless it's a bomber. The feds won't leave that alone. They keep coming back. They watch the family at weddings, funerals, anything that might bring them back.'

'A bomber!'

'Sure, you didn't know?'

'I thought he was just a peacenick. Old hippie, underground.' There are footsteps in Devlin's head but he can't tell what's coming. Trouble in Chicago, someone hiding on the fire escape. And the package he thought Lexie left for him, that worn tweed coat. He asks. 'Your Uncle Kieran didn't just turn on and drop out?'

'There was other stuff.' She grimaces. 'The explosion. You know.'

Footsteps in his head. The weirdness in Chicago.

She says, 'It's supposed to be a secret, but Aunt Costanza told me. They were close.'

He turns the car. 'Do you think your Aunt Costanza would talk to me?'

'Not really. But she might talk to me. Like, you think Aunt Costanza knows where Uncle Kieran is?'

'I don't know.' He pulls off onto the exit and takes the long road uphill to the convent. 'Just ask, OK? I don't know what's going on, but I've got to see him.'

'You'll have to find him first.'

39

He waits for a long time in front of the convent. Except for the hum of traffic on the Mass Pike far below him, the convent grounds are still. They could be in another century. Flowers bloom. Birds dart. The ground is alive with the shadows of leaves. It's too fucking sylvan to be real.

'She doesn't know,' Maggie says when she finally comes out. 'But she has at least one idea. This place where he went the first time?'

'The first time he blew something up?'

'He didn't do that, he was just there. She means the first time he went underground. She says he never blew up anything in his life and then she started to cry.'

'So he's in touch with her.'

Maggie nods. 'He was her favorite. After the Weatherman trouble they hid him at the convent for a while. Then he went to this place in Connecticut, she wrote it down.'

He takes it from her. Aunt Costanza has drawn a map of northwestern Connecticut, the directions are pretty vague. About what you'd expect from an ancient nun who wants her favorite back but is afraid of what will happen if he's found. 'You think she knows what she's talking about? She's pretty old.'

'She's also pretty sharp. She's the one that got him back for my christening.'

'How do you know?'

'She said. Anyway, this place? She says he isn't there any more, but maybe they know where he is.' The girl worries a spot on her sweet, blunt face. 'Why do you want to see him anyway?'

Just to rule something out, he thinks, but he can't tell her. They are sliding between concern and fear. *Questions*, he thinks, *I need to ask him some questions*. He says, 'Maybe just to find out if it's his coat.'

'Like he's going to blow his cover to tell you if it's his coat?' Her voice sinks. 'It's late. I guess I'd better get back.'

'Look, Mag. You don't have to go home if you don't want to.'

'Yes I do. I have to be in this lousy wedding.'

'You could come with me.'

'No way.' Unwittingly, she echoes her drunk sister. 'My father gets what he wants. He'd call the cops or file charges. You know. Kidnapping or child abuse.'

Something about the girl makes him protective. He could adopt her if that's what it takes. Tough, but he can handle it. 'Look. I'm serious. What if you never went back?'

She turns away quickly but he sees the tears. 'They're my family.'

The last time he went to see Pop, Pop didn't exactly know him. Just being there, he could feel the tug of all the years. 'I know what that's like.'

'So you might as well drop me off on your way.'

'I'm sorry.'

'It's OK. But, hey. It can't go on forever, and besides.' She brightens. This is a kid who's survived on pulling herself together. Like Lexie, Maggie is expert at keeping going. She keeps going no matter what. She tries a smile. 'Besides, Friday we go to Florida. Cleotha Motel or something, Daddy says they have a pool.'

'Florida, wow.' He grins.

'Yeah, and guess what, I'm meeting a friend there, how about that?'

He is too preoccupied to hear what the child has just told him. 'Have fun.' Something makes him say, 'I gave my brothers all the specs so it should be fine. But. OK. Your dad has bleachers or something, outside the perimeter. But. Um. Could you stay back from the blast site, just in case?'

'But I'll miss it!'

'No you won't. Those things are huge. Promise?'

'I promise.'

'I love you, Mag.'

'Me too.'

40

Devlin is driving into the woods of Connecticut, north of the pastel PostModern casino that looms over rural Ledyard. Bro and Tony took him to Foxwoods once when they were trying to lure him back into the business. They led him through the Mashantucket Pequots' gambling paradise like a kid. PeeWee goes PostModern in spades. Bro fixed him with that grim, anxious grin: *Are you having fun yet?* On the coast in Mystic Seaport, malls spread their glitzy skirts and cigarette boats and catamarans bob like toys in the water next to an authentic nineteenth-century whaler. Here outside rural Putnam, it's as if ugly America never happened. Roads are narrow, studded with mailboxes and rustic general stores and two-pump gas stations. As he goes farther inland the woods get thicker. The road kills get bigger and bigger: possums. Raccoons. Deer dart in front of the car.

He's heard that Ku Klux Klan members still meet in these woods – their blue collar lives glamorized by white hoods and hatred by torchlight. Conservative swamp Yankees are suspicious of outsiders of every color and stripe. They're defending the same rocky plots of land their ancestors worked. This outlandishly rural landscape within shooting distance of both New York and Boston is an odd place for a pacifist colony to locate, but their community is marked with an X on Aunt Costanza's spidery map. Devlin is heading in.

He needs to confront Kieran McQuarrie. Stick it to him. *Was that you in Chicago? What is it with Lexie? God, is she all right?*

He turns at the mailbox and drives in. He sees a couple of shacks in the woods as he takes the dirt road in to the middle of a sad looking circle of shacks. Once when he was a kid on summer vacation with a great aunt, Devlin got dragged to visit a Shaker colony because he was too little to be left alone at the hotel. Maine, he thinks it was. What was it about the Shakers that made her want to visit? Unclear. She lured six-year-old Tommy with promises of cornhusk dolls and candy, the kind of things Shakers sold at their roadside stand. When there were enough of them to man a roadside stand. The place was spooky and sad. Except for a few very old people, it was deserted. A sect that forbids sex doesn't have a big chance of making it. Driving in to the collection of A frames and log cabins that ring the central clearing, he thinks this looks a lot like that. He has come into the shell of a dying community.

The aging men and women staking out tomato plants or slouching on front porches look up briefly and then go back to what they were doing. Devlin noses the car into a row of logs felled in a decade when there were more cars to park. Pacifists, he thinks. They won't hurt me. But will they talk to him?

Behind him somebody says, 'If you came to do a Where Are They Now, *Hard Copy* already has it.'

'What!'

'Sorry. Didn't mean to scare you. Yeah, every few years somebody remembers us, this time it's *Hard Copy*. Anniversary of the Kent State Bombings. The March on Washington, Cambodia, I forget now. There were so many terrible things.'

'I'm Tom Devlin.'

'Dave Rasmussen.' He looks like a bleached-out Willie Nelson. 'Just Ras, if you want to use my name in whatever story you're doing. Hey, we could use the publicity.'

'I'm not doing a story. I—.'

'Listen, we need any press we can get these days. It gets harder, keeping the message in front of the public. If you're trying this for *The Day* or *The Norwich Bulletin*, though, you might as well forget it. We're old news to them.'

'I'm not a reporter.'

'You dress like one.'

'But I do need to talk to whoever is in charge.'

'I should have known. Nobody's interested in a bunch of old hippies. Not any more.' Even veiled by the thick hair and untrimmed beard, the smile is nice. 'Not since they came in and shot us up thirty years ago.'

'They shot you up?'

'You know, that should have been a big break for us. If the world was put together right.' He shrugs. 'Stupid hicks thought we were Communists. It was a search-and-destroy mission, shoot 'em up and save your country. Do we look dangerous to you?'

Proceed carefully. Don't spook the guy. He shakes his head.

'They came in the night, killed two and blew the buttcheek off a woman I was in love with. Now, if you want to write *that* story.'

'When I get back to the city I'll call a friend at NBC.'

'I'd like to say it was the Klan, but it wasn't. It was farmers. They sent their kids to die in Vietnam and it didn't matter that it was wrong, they were damn proud of it.' The clear gray eyes are focused on the past. 'See, when their sons got killed in that abomination of a war, we were the nearest thing they could shoot. Crazy, isn't it? But you're too young to study that.'

'I guess.'

'Pacifists. You can't even fight back,' Ras says. 'Plus protecting certain people we were hiding.'

Devlin's jaw crunches. 'You hide people?'

'That plus going out of our way to get arrested. You don't know very much, do you?'

'Look, Mr Rasmussen, I'm looking for someone.' Devlin is thinking, *Why are we out here talking about this*? Ancient Mariner time, maybe. Everybody has to sob out their story.

'You get hurt or get busted and you get your message to the people.

Nickel and dime stuff, lie down and hope to hell some cop will bash you and hope it happens on TV. These days we have to knock ourselves out to make a statement. Nobody cares any more.'

'I admire what you're doing, but that's not why I came.'

Ras shakes his head. 'I should have known. It's never about us. Not any more. At the beginning, we had *such fire.*'

'I'm looking for somebody, got in trouble in the Eighties, dropped out of sight?'

'Everybody would like to get involved and stay involved, but people are only people. They don't have the concentration.' Ras sighs. 'You give your life to principles but over time, the pain in the ass factor is too high. Christ in the Garden of Olives. Everybody went to sleep. You can't solve all the problems in the world. Sometimes I think you can't solve any of them.'

'I think he used to live here.'

'You try to keep going but sometimes . . .' Rasmussen's pigeon breast inflates and the clean, frayed blue work shirt rises. A sigh comes out. 'You just get tired.'

'Kieran McQuarrie,' he says.

Ras stiffens. 'You don't look like FBI.'

'So if you've seen him, if you can put me in touch.'

The answer comes out too fast. 'He was framed.'

'What?'

'You heard me. When he lived with us, they didn't have a thing on him, which is why we're still living here instead of serving time. Then in the Eighties . . . Listen, he was framed.'

'I don't suppose you'll tell me what for.'

'I shouldn't even be talking to you.'

'Or where he went.'

The old hippie's eyes change for a split second. It's like a stroboscopic flash. 'Not even if I knew.'

'If you guys had a fund or something, I could . . .'

'No. We have parameters. You take a gift and you're obligated. So we can't be bought.' Ras looks around. 'The plumbing's shot to hell. We could use some new wiring.'

'I could contract . . .'

'No. Just no.' Ras says. 'But I'd be careful if I were you. Our Kieran is an extremist.'

The scenarios flashing behind Devlin's eyes are too wild to sort out. He says in controlled tones, 'Translate. Please.'

'When you believe in a thing the way we do, you follow it out to the end. Look, I don't know what you want with Kieran McQuarrie or why you think I can help you but you should know, when you live by your principles you're ready to die by your principles and sometimes we . . .' His voice drops. 'Take things to extremes. Now, if you don't want to sit down and have some wine with me and whoever I can convince to come and sit down with you, I'm going to have to put you back in your car. OK?'

'OK, just, is he living near here?'

'You'd better go.'

'It's. Look. It could be urgent. I have to find out what he knows about my fiancée.'

Then this Ras guy, tired old hippie nothing like anybody in this generation pulls a, slow smile. 'Oh, love stuff,' he says. 'When you get as old as I am, it won't hurt so bad.' Seeing Devlin into his car, he bends down and peers in the window. 'Tell you what. Why don't you give me your card?'

'My card?'

'Particulars. Phone number. Some place where you can be reached.'

'You don't know where he is.'

'If I did, I couldn't tell you. If he gets in touch I'll tell him you were here.'

41

What Bro hates most isn't that his bastard brother Tom is tall where Bro and Tony are short, or that women get the hots for him. He doesn't even hate him for backing off this job, why do anything hard when you've had it easy all your life? The top ten reasons Bro hates his baby brother are that he doesn't have a care.

When Tom looks in the mirror he sees *pretty*, whereas Bro looks in the mirror and he sees *old*. It's the worry. One day your whole life passes before your eyes and it is over. There's a prize at the end of the road and you haven't made it out of the gate. That can't be Bro's face looking back at him, all wrinkles and chimpanzee eyes. It's Pop's. Shriveled, from too many tough winters. Pinched nose, that squint.

Fifty-four years and nothing to show. Well, that's about to change. You grown up thinking this can't go on forever. Fifty-four years later you turn around and in spite of the good things you expected, everything's the same. Except for your socks and underwear the things you have are the same things you had twenty years ago, same leather jacket, same suit. House the same, furniture the same. The only new thing is the company car, gotta show clients that you buy top of the line. The things you do outside of work you can number on your thumb. The women you've had you can number on your goddamn toes and all but one of them were one-fuck babes don't ask me what went wrong.

At Bro's age, his worries get worries like head lice. Any diversion would be welcome. Any diversion, he thinks, but it's just his life, day after day after goddamn fucking day. Same job. Same face in the mirror. Same house. Minus one Daisy Menafee Devlin, who took off in the Sixties. Taking important parts of their father. When she went Devlin hearts got sucked down the tubes. *And the bastard doesn't even know*. Tom doesn't know it, but he isn't blood. Save that information until you can use it, Bro thinks. Their mother's yeah, but not Devlin blood, which is why he's so fucking tall. He isn't family. He never was. Some guy their mother met while Pop and Tony and he were off at an ISEE convention, the bitch. She dumped the baby on them and ran off God knows where with her new man. Well, Bro hopes they're happy. He hopes they rot in hell. *And wherever they're rotting, they can damn well see us on TV*.

See, even flat lines can be changed.

You go all your life putting one day after another like two left feet on the long march to death. Then you look into the mirror and you think *This has got to stop*. Bro saw there was a worldwide block party going on out there without him so he took the McQuarrie job. Without Tom to backstop, it's

154

risky. Well, fuck that. DD has prepared the site without him. They did what he said, where he said. Tomorrow they roll in the drums of explosives and set the charges and lay the wires. Timing, now timing's tricky, but hey, he thinks, surprised by an erection. *It's going fine and it will go fine.*

'How's it going?' The first words out of Pat McQuarrie's mouth when he walks onto the site. Where, incidentally, no civilians belong. Except for the guard. The last of the big spenders here moves his whole fucking party into a motel outside Cleotha and comes bombing out to the site like this is a country club and Bro is supposed to bow down like the *maitre d'*. Look at the overweight bastard walking in where he doesn't belong, slick in his pointy toed shoes. Pat McQuarrie doesn't know what he's looking for but Bro can see he is surveilling. As in, he hired the Devlins, are they doing it right? Damn straight. Yes he's paying through the nose and yes he wants his money's worth.

Bro growls, 'I can't talk. We're doing a job here.'

'And I'm paying for it.' Pat McQuarrie, trying to act casual. 'So how's it going?'

And by God Bro is easy with him. 'Fine,' he says. He manages the glad hand for this big Irish fuck. 'Everything is going fine.'

'Excellent. Brom and I are coming in later to coordinate the shoot.'

'Brom?'

'I told you about the movie.'

'You did.' Now, the movie people are staying in the nearest big town because Cleotha isn't good enough for them. Listen. DD is going to put Cleotha on the map.

'We're talking about Bromwell Tyne.' The big man is waiting for Bro's jaw to drop.

'I don't have time to go to movies.'

'He makes action pictures. Golden Globe nomination for *Battering Ram Three*. And Global Productions is distributing.' He puts his index fingers together. 'We're like *this*.'

'I can't be having outsiders tramping through here.'

McQuarrie is not happy. 'It's a must.'

'Safety.' Bro sets his jaw.

'We'll be careful.'

'Nobody comes in here but company.'

'I'm here.'

'Not for long. Security.' Security. The best they can afford. Shit. One old man and a teenaged kid.

'He's a director, Devlin. He needs to see what he has to work with.'

'Sorry. Trade secrets. I can't have him here.' Truth? Bro doesn't want anybody around when they move the explosives in. Placement is the issue and there are some questions Tony is still figuring out the answers to.

'He's paying a lot.'

Bro shoots him a look. 'And so are you. While we're at it, your check hasn't cleared.'

Watch the man fumble. 'I have that covered!'

So he has him where he wants him. Bro says indifferently, 'DD can still walk away.'

'You understand my position. For what Brom Tyne is paying, we have to give him a first class ride.'

'He'll get the ride he's getting.' Bro waits for McQuarrie to give up and go away.

'He doesn't want just one of your usual implosions.'

'No implosion is usual. Didn't you read our fucking brochure?'

'He needs the hotel to blow in a particular way. It's in the script.'

'Fuck,' Bro snaps, 'you want bespoke implosions you go to the Revenaughs.' They both know they're so close to detonation that McQuarrie has no choice. More: that the Revenaughs refused to touch it for a lot of the reasons that Bro was scared to touch it and Tommy refused to touch it. Not everytime. Not enough money. Too many buildings, too close. But the Devlins need the money, they need the press. A part of Bro is running on ahead: *safety is safety but this is going to be big*. He feints. As if to walk out.

McQuarrie grabs his arm. 'We have a deal. We have two days.'

'That's right.' Bro shakes him off. 'My way or not at all.'

'Whatever you say.'

'And you keep him off the place,' Bro says with a flinty glare. 'And you stay off the place.'

'Have it your way.' Like a quick-change artist, Pat McQuarrie shifts positions. Slick in the white linen suit. He says carefully, 'You're OK with me telling Tyne it'll come down just the way he wants it, right?'

'It'll come down how it comes down,' Bro says. The truth? *I wish to God I knew*.

Ugly, flashing on the conversation with Tony. Are we OK?

Fine, Tony says. *I jiggered a little here and there but it's prepared like Tommy told us.*

Chapter and verse? Bro had to ask.

Tony smiled at him like a choirboy. *Chapter and verse*.

'So, fine. I tell Brom it's going to come down this way,' McQuarrie says. It is not a question.

The bloody man is waiting for Bro to finish his instant replay and agree. 'Tell him what you want.'

'Exactly.' McQuarrie turns on the high horsepower smile with the chrome-plated hubcaps and the foxtail plume. The man's steering wheel probably has a necking knob. He is the master of smooth. 'After all. What's he going to do after the building is down, cut off our left hand because he doesn't like what he got?'

Bro narrows his eyes. 'You want to make sure he uses the footage.' The company has been in trouble ever since the accident at the Armbruster. Worse since Pop fell out. They need the publicity.

'What choice does he have? They're pouring thousands into this shoot. Steadicam crew. Cameras on helicopters . . .'

Warily, Bro says, 'I'd be careful with the helicopters.'

But McQuarrie rushes on. 'Cameras on the far side of the inlet and cameras on a barge offshore.'

What was it Tommy pointed out? That this job is spongy because anybody who wants to sneak in could come in by the water. But what kind of fool would do that the night before a blast? Face it, Tom's accident has left everybody twitchy. Since this is DD's first implosion without either him or Pop, Bro is not too comfortable himself. But he can talk a good game. 'To say nothing of TV cameras.'

'Sky Eight,' McQuarrie says. They are both smiling.

Funny, how he is feeling. 'Sky Ten, Eleven and Twelve.'

'I have a lot of important people coming.'

'Fine,' Bro says. 'The more the merrier.'

Aroused. He is fucking aroused. Look, they are doing it. God, are they doing it. Security in place, sort of. Hire a night man, do it fast. He has this secret fear: that the locals are not quite up to snuff. As in the contractors, did they really pull out all the stairs and if not, how soon and what about the fire ladders and other egress, Bro is only one person here, Tony is a putz and he has to depend. If he can find enough types on short notice he wants to make a four-alarm sweep after the explosives come in and if the fence in the left rear quadrant is a little shaky, nobody has to know. Tonight he and Tony and the DD core people sweep the building as well as you can sweep with just a few men. Tomorrow, the explosives roll in.

Fireworks on the beach tomorrow night, party, band, who cares. He and Tony will be going over things in the booth. By God this job is going to go off snap-snap-snap. Let McQuarrie have his day.

The next one belongs to me.

And when it's done Devlin Dismantling will be famous, so fuck the director, Mr Bromwell Tyne and fuck the movie, what is it, Asshole Four? What you see is what you get. *You'll use our footage and be damn glad of it, nobody in Hollywood knows how to bring down a building like us.* Plus, the job is plastered all over the TV. At the end of the day's trading the Devlins will be right up there with the Revenaughs. No more begging for notice, or tin-cupping for jobs. And when it's done Bro can forget about the sameold, sameold, he thinks bitterly. Sameold all these years because of Tom.

So fuck you, Tommy, think you're too good for us. Some day Bro is going to sit him down and stick it to him, *You think you're so special, well, we fucking did it without you. You think you're so special, well, you aren't. All you are, kid, is our tramp mother's illegitimate son.*

42

There is no logic to it. She thought they understood each other but they don't. Lexie would be easier with this if her rescuer hadn't stopped speaking to her. You came to a place of your own free will and you wake up one morning and tell him you are feeling better, it's time for you to get back to your life and he just smiles. It's still early so you blink and smile over your coffee but there is the fact that he hasn't spoken.

After weeks of life on the razor blade, she was relieved to let him take charge. When you finally let down, you're reassured by routine. From the beginning he kept the place locked, and at the beginning she was OK with it. During the daytime he gave her the run of the apartment and apologized for keeping the front door locked. When he first brought her inside and shot the dead bolt she asked:

'What's that about?'

For your own safety, he said, *there are a lot of weird types doing business downstairs and I'm afraid some of them are people you don't.* He broke off and corrected. *It's just better if they don't know you're here.*

Fine, she thought. I am sick of people. 'If you say so.'

It's for your own good. Trust me.

That lovely smile. 'I do.' She was so grateful to be here that she would have agreed to anything.

That was before. He made a nice dinner. She was puzzled when he told her he was going to lock the bedroom door. *For your own safety.*

'But you locked the apartment.'

Such a nice smile. *In case they get past the first lock.*

There's no telling what the place used to be, factory, workers' housing. Maybe the latter, there are a toilet and wash basin in the room where she sleeps. So she couldn't use that as an excuse. She gave him a long, careful look. Sweet man. Lovely face. 'I can take care of myself.'

You have enough to worry about. His tone was grave.

'God knows that's true.'

Odd, being locked in, but she lives behind locked doors in Manhattan so she didn't press. If the rest of the building where he has his tight, neat little apartment was as weird as the jumble she saw on her way in from the truck, security made sense. Coming upstairs, she thought she could hear rats running under the boards. By contrast, his apartment was clean and tight. The room was nice. He was only trying to be nice. She rather liked feeling protected. It'll be all right for a few days, she told herself. When I'm ready, I'll just thank him and go.

She thought. Until the third morning. She smelled coffee. Still sleepy, she dressed and tapped on the bedroom door: her signal that she was ready to come out. She came out wearing her jacket and shoes.

What's this?

'You've been wonderful, but it's time for me to go.'

He just smiled and gestured at the table. He had breakfast ready. Orange juice and coffee. Bacon and toast.

She shrugged and sat down. She liked sitting down like that at the little kitchen table. Two good friends with the light from the glass shade shining on her hair. Friends eating together in silence, nothing to say, nothing that needed saying. Later, she told herself. When he takes me out. Interesting how listless she was. Relief, probably, at finally being able to let down.

'Later,' she said. 'Later will be fine.'

He smiled and made more toast.

Somebody you trust, so you tell yourself it's a companionable silence. Let him take you out in the truck the way he does every day, he is trying to be nice. Go walking with him in the woods and think only later in the day that you are still here and the silence is a little weird. Still you and he are comfortable together so you let it go, no problem, tomorrow you'll get him to take you back to your car or to town, if driving to Putney is out of the question. Anyplace where you can get a cab or a bus to some town where you can rent a car. Or hitch a ride. Wake up the next morning planning to put it to him and wonder why you have zero energy. Mention it and when he doesn't respond, yawn and put it off until a better time. Ask to go out for a ride; his apartment is in the middle of this big building and there are no windows, so you're starved for some natural light. As it turns out, by the time you get back from your ride down to the store and the picnic and the long walk in the woods you are too drowsy to bring it up. Days flow into more days until you wonder why you are always so sleepy and where the time has gone. After years of struggle you have lost all sense of urgency. Eventually you start wondering what day it is and the whole time you are under an illusion that you are fine and everything is fine.

After all, this is a person you trust.

Smile at him when he lets you out of your room the next morning and mention it again. 'I should go soon.' Then smile when he pours you more coffee and puts more honey on your toast. Smile at him when he takes you out in the truck and smile when you see an opening and start to run and he comes crashing after you in the woods. Smile when you open the passenger door as the truck turns onto the highway and he snatches your arm before you can leap out; the next time he takes you out for some air you will get in his side of the truck because the door handle on your side is wired and when he catches you screaming and hammering in the night it won't matter that you aren't smiling because he loves you and no matter what you try to do he is quicker and stronger, and no matter what you try to do to him he takes it with that same lovely, well-meaning smile.

159

43

Devlin doesn't know what made him think he could find Kieran McQuarrie when the feds can't find him and the state police can't find him. Chutzpah or desperation? He thinks it was compression. Too much worry over Lexie over too much time. He went a little crazy. Two days badgering town police, talking to farmers, cross-hatching this part of Connecticut. Two days driving past defunct factories and nonfunctional mills, crumbling brick buildings that look as if they've been deserted for a long time. Two days following leads and he's come up empty. It's no surprise. What makes him think Kieran McQuarrie would be circling the same drain thirteen years after the blast? God knows where he is, or whether it matters. For all he knows Lexie is in Cuernavaca or Vancouver. But this is all he has.

He's sitting in a battered chrome diner outside Putnam, checking off roads on a strip map of the area. Over the last two days, he's been up and down most of them. His coffee is cold and his stomach is sour. He's been sitting here for so long that the high school kid in the tight peach nylon apron is trying to decide whether to flirt with him or turn him in. If he starts driving now he can be back in the city in just under three hours, but he hasn't finished with the map. Is there some hamlet he's overlooked?

The more he doesn't find the guy, the more he wants to find him. In a month of unmanageable loss this is something he can manage. Or thought he could.

'Your coffee's dead.' The high school girl has decided to flirt first, then call the shot.

'I'm looking for a guy. Do you . . .'

She cuts him off fast that it sounds like a gag line. 'You're not from around here, are you?'

But she isn't waiting for a laugh, she's pulling the slithering peach apron strings tighter over her round little body as if he cares. He goes on. 'Let me put it another way. If you wanted to get lost around here, where would you go?'

'You want a refill or not?'

'If there was money in it?'

'What does he look like?'

'Tall, I think.'

'What kind of tall?'

'I don't know. I think he looks like. Oh hell, check please.' Too bad they don't have milk cartons for missing grownups. Should he come back to this neck of the woods with a photo from the McQuarrie house that he can flash? HAVE YOU SEEN THIS MAN? Should he Xerox the thing and staple it to telephone poles and get storekeepers to tape it in their windows?

'I knew you weren't from around here.'

'How could you tell?'

Her boobs brush his bicep as she leans over him. She overfills his cup and leaves coffee sloshing in his saucer. 'If you were from around here, you wouldn't be eating here and you sure as hell wouldn't be asking dumb questions.'

He grins. 'OK, I'm not. Is that a problem for you?'

'It's a problem for some people.'

Two days. He even doubled back on the colony. If Rasmussen knows where Kieran is, he isn't telling. If anybody else has seen him, they aren't telling. Mention the pacifists in these tight little Yankee towns and they shake their heads. *They shouldn't be running around loose. Those people are all crazy.* Mention Kieran McQuarrie, for all the good it will do. Never heard of him. The bombing he's wanted for? What bombing? If it didn't happen in this town, it never happened. Describe the man from the scraps you have and understand that you don't really know who you're describing. You've never seen the guy. Big, you think. Deduction based on the coat. If it's his coat – what is it, were he and Lexie in touch? The off chance keeps him going.

While his mark could be anywhere – rattling around the map like a loose pinball or holed up in the northwest, sleeping in a shack with his hair frizzed and his beard wild – the Unabomber look, but with Pat McQuarrie's face. He could be dead by now. Or hitting all the stops on the underground railroad. Utah. Canada. Beyond. For all Devlin knows, the underground man spilled out into a brand new life. Shaves with a triple-blade razor at six and goes to work in a coat and tie at eight, sits down at a desk and does something boring. Gets up at five and comes home to a wife and a nice new family. Oh hell, he could be living in a carton under the next bridge.

You can spend only so much time asking questions in towns like this. The kid in the apron is in the back. He calls. 'You were coming with my check?'

Go home and cut to the chase. Do a web search on Kieran McQuarrie and then hire a private detective, if you really believe the trail leads to the lover you've lost. Start with the feds. State police.

She sticks her head out of the kitchen. 'You want what?'

FBI will bring up his own file on the computer before he's even cleared the outer office. *And why, exactly, are you asking?*

'My check!'

She brings fresh coffee instead. She's also put on fresh lipstick. 'You want pie with this?'

'No thanks. Just tell me what I owe.'

'Wait a minute. I'll have to.'

'Don't bother. Keep the change.'

'But that's a twenty.' Nice smile. 'More pie?'

Smile back. 'Love to, but I have to go.'

'Holiday weekend,' she warns. 'Drive safe.'

'Thanks, I'll try.'

'Later.'

Plan A has blown up in his face. Time to go back to the city and figure out what's next.

44

It's a brilliant day, shot with sunlight. Reflections glisten in the palm fronds and the glittering water off Cleotha, Florida. For Gerald Slade, it is like opening Door Three on a TV quiz show, or walking into a post card. After years of the marginal life, Cup O' Soup on the hot plate and showers in the college gym – after weeks in the sameness of a dozen Holiday Inns, it's almost too much. Dazzled, he squints into the light.

When you can't get what you want, Gerald Slade thinks, *you take what you can get*. And he has her in place. It's time to move.

Control, he tells himself, clamping both hands on the steering wheel. He can't afford to get caught in a Florida speed trap. He wants to be early for this interview but he needs the extra few minutes to think. *Take haste out of the equation*. This is the accountant's first rule of life: *Always double check your figures. When you can't get what you want, work with what you've got.*

Turning off the highway and onto the service road that will take him to the company trailer, he takes inventory.

Costume: silvered blue jeans a size too large, straight from a consignment shop. Work shirt to match. Not the usual for a college teacher but he has to look the part if he wants to get the job. He likes the feeling and besides, when this is done he doesn't expect to go back to teaching junior college. He doesn't know if he wants to be around after this is done. What happens to him doesn't matter. All that matters is letting Freddy know how much he loves him. When this is done, Freddy will be proud.

Car: his same car, but without the Massachusetts plates. He is using a set of Florida plates he picked up in a junkyard. Can't look like he's from anyplace they've heard of, that they can check.

Newspaper: The St Petersburg *Times*, county edition. Open to the want ads, with a couple of Help Wanted ads dutifully circled. Can't look like this job is the only job he wants.

Expression: bland. At this, Gerald Slade is a master.

Wristwatch: take it off. It's the gold Rolex his late wife gave him on their last anniversary together. He doesn't want anything to make them look twice, or start asking questions. If he needed a hat to crunch in his hands to make this performance more convincing, Gerald would have one.

What else? Invent your last two jobs. Make up names of two previous employers. Done.

So he has all his ducks in a row now, one, two, three. The things he needs and the people he needs are lined up neatly. Even her. When he lost Freddy, he vowed it was the last time he'd let his life get out of control.

Now he's reduced the particles to these essentials. First he has to get this job. Do a few things on the inside and he's ready. Then he'll go back for her. The central element in his plan. Like a machine when the last piece clicks into place, Gerald's construct will start ticking.

For the first time since Freddy died, Gerald Slade is what passes for happy.

Control. Don't count your chickens yet.

There are risks attached. Even without the beard, he may be recognized. Maybe they've filled the job. He was up so early that he thinks he'll be the first. But what if he gets there and he's one of a dozen? What if there are fifty better men in line in front of him? A hundred? He sets his jaw and drives a little faster.

When he gets to the temporary headquarters, there's only one car parked outside the company trailer. Nobody in line ahead of him. Good, because he is the first and only. Bad because they'll look at him more closely.

He knocks on the screen door. The wiry little man inside jumps like a fisherman at a twitch on his line. 'Come in!'

'It's locked.' Gerald holds his breath as the guy comes to unlatch it. It's a tight opening. He'll have to squeeze past to get inside. Holds his breath. Will he recognize? They are *this close*.

'Not any more.' The eyes flick over Gerald's face as indifferent as a scanner. It doesn't matter what the bar code says, only that there is a bar code.

In seconds Gerald is answering questions. The name? At this stage one name is as good as another. 'George Sepelvin.'

'Experience?'

'I was the night man at Pierce Preston in Bladensburg, Maryland.' He has made up an answer for the logical next question but the man doing the hiring is in too much of a hurry to ask it.

'Firearms?'

''Nam.' The lie makes him feel only slightly ridiculous.

'OK, I'm going to need your Social.'

As if he's going to let this narrow-assed bastard see anything with his name on it. He could claim he'd lost his card and make up a Social Security number, but. 'Could we keep this off the books?'

'Trouble with the law?'

Gerald shakes his head. 'I don't want to lose my disability.'

'Sure. Cheaper for me, cheaper for you.' But the interviewer gives Gerald a look. 'Now, this kind of work. You understand we don't pay disability. If that's a problem for you.

'When do I start?'

'You can go on over to the site now and get familiar. My brother will see you get a uniform, introduce you to the day guy. Today the real work kicks in.'

Damn straight. Gerald's heart leaps but he manages to control his expression. 'Sir?'

'Today we move in the explosives. We'll need security round the clock.'

Reality check. He's gotten this far but he has to be sure he can go the rest of the distance. This isn't the only brother he has to get past. It's time

164

for the real test. He plants his fists on the desk and gives whichever Devlin brother a long, hard look. *Do you know me? Do you know who I am?*

For the first time, the Devlin looks directly at him. Interesting. Gerald doesn't know which Devlin it is. They're like the enemy in any war. They all look alike to him. The Devlin says, 'So, what are you waiting for?'

One more minute, Gerald thinks, if he still doesn't get it, I can do this. *You don't recognize me, do you? Do you?*

The only change in the man's face is a look of increasing impatience. 'You want me to spell it out? So fine.' He stands. Like a club bouncer, he starts moving Gerald to the door. 'Congratulations. You're our new night man.'

You don't recognize me, do you? You killed my boy and you don't even know who I am. Well you'll know soon enough.

Leaving, Gerald keeps his shoulders high and his elbows tight to his sides. It takes all his self control to keep from shouting, *Not just you. The world.*

165

45

Look at them. Pat McQuarrie has his women where he wants them. Clustered in the lobby, Moira like the suffering Virgin in white linen, Lally shrink-wrapped in a flowered dress that exposes her fat belly; Maggie, so plain and withdrawn that you never noticed what she had on. *My family, my jewels, that's a laugh.* Even at a disadvantage the way he's kept her ever since he got her pregnant and forced the marriage, Moira is all elegance. Lexie would be all elegance, but she had the bad grace to cut and run just when he needs her most.

He could haul her back but with so much at stake it's better to leave her where she is. On ice. She's safe there. Lexie running around shooting her mouth off – that isn't safe. Bury a thing and keep it buried at great cost over a dozen years. Think she's forgotten and find her digging it up, his favorite daughter, how could she? If he hadn't found the page she left in his office copier, he wouldn't know. He wouldn't know! So good riddance, for now. Off where she can't throw a monkey wrench into the works. Graver and Mulligan are a lot better than that fool Devlin at finding people, so McQuarrie knows perfectly well where she is. What he doesn't know is what frame of mind his daughter is in or what she'll do next so let the dead stay dead and let Lexie stay where she is until this wedding is over and the immediate problem is solved. Send Lally off to Maccu Pichu on her honeymoon and figure out how to keep her there. Lexie? Retrieve her and talk sense.

But meanwhile, what does that leave him to work with? This. His sainted, suffering wife who can't stand to have him touch her, and this. Oh God, the only thing he has to work with is the rock bottom layer of his family, the dregs. Lally, that tramp. Maggie, keeps rolling out from the bed no matter how hard you sweep. He knuckles her between the shoulders. 'Straighten up!'

Maggie goes red. Margaret, who came along in the worst possible way at the worst possible time.

Lally stands there with that red slash for a mouth, looks like a slash of something else, well, *that* has caused plenty of trouble. The woman is smoldering like an unspent match.

He hisses, 'Smile, they're watching.'

Nobody smiles.

A matter of great urgency and they're standing around like a bunch of useless women. 'The governor's car will be here in ten.'

Prosperous man, with family. It's all he's trying to do here, make that picture, and what kind of picture do they make? At least Moira droops in the shadows like a deposed queen. And Lally passes. Just. *But, you*! Maggie, like a dead weight attached to his arm.

Soft little voice. 'Dad.'

Just as well Ms Lally's fiancée isn't along on this one, the last thing the governor needs to see is that sleazy dude with his shirt open to the sternum and the python boots. Should have figured out how to keep Lexie on board, but it could have been dangerous – things she knows, that she isn't supposed to know. Should have done better in the bridegroom department too, but it's a crunch situation and face it, his substitute bride here is no prize. It doesn't take two-bit arm candy to make Lally look cheap. In spite of everything he's spent on her, in spite of all the grief! In spite of the lifetime he's spent covering up for her, Pat McQuarrie's eldest daughter always looks cheap. By Labor Day Weekend when the hired band plays the wedding march on the marble terrace in Lincoln, it won't make a dime's worth of difference. There'll be so many important people wedged into the party that nobody will notice that the groom is coked to the eyeballs and the bride is a lopsided drunk. Pat McQuarrie is an entrepreneur with long experience. He's learned how to optimize any situation. Even lead looks like platinum when the music's loud enough and your audience is going by at a dead run. Or enough like it to do the job.

'Dad.'

'Margaret, be quiet. You're distracting me.'

But before the wedding and certain deals he hopes to close, they have to get through this dinner, when certain allegiances will be firmed up for the Miramar event. All the power people in one place. And he has hopes beyond the event, truth to tell. He shrugs her off.

But Maggie whispers, 'Dad, do I have to go on this?'

'Everybody's here.' Family he's spent his *life* keeping in line. 'Everybody goes.'

Five p.m. and Lally's voice has already begun to slur. 'Fuck that shit. You mean anything goes.'

'Language!' He studies his eldest. It isn't the smeared lipstick that's the problem, and it isn't the red patent sling heels, even though he fears for her life. It's the dress.

She glares. 'What's your problem?'

'Pull that top down, your belly's showing.'

'That's the point.'

'Not at your weight. Are you sober?'

Surly. All this money, all this effort, everything he has *done* for her and the woman is snarling, 'Do I have a choice?'

'It's the governor's party we're having dinner with tonight, so smile. Them and Global Productions. And a vice president from the studio.' Packaging. Pat McQuarrie will play one against the other to cut whatever deals he can. Truth is, he needs a little extra to make it through to Labor Day. Adnan Kashoggi may be coming to the wedding. Whether or not he is, other major players are.

'Well you can take the governor and shove . . .'

'Lally, don't start.' The state film commission is a bonus. Official circles have started to look good to him. Pat McQuarrie is sick of dealing for dealing's sake. Too much input and outgo, too high a risk. He's sick of living on margin. It's time to float to the top, which he would take to be politics. Compared to the way he's had to live, a real cliffhanger since the money ran out, swinging from deal to deal . . . Compared to that, politics is safe. It's what he needs to make his life perfect. That last touch of class. He nudges her. 'You bet the governor will be there. And certain private interests I've invited down for the blast.'

Lally growls, 'What if I kick your private interests in the private parts?'

'Don't be coarse.' To think he had the woman married to a Cabot, for a minute and a half. At a cost too terrible to assess. If that marriage had taken, Pat McQuarrie would already be welcome in the best places. In the front door at any club you could name. He wouldn't be hanging by his fingernails, which is what he is.

'Be careful,' Lally says. 'Watch what you say to me.'

'You try to make a nice life for your family and what do you get?'

She is getting louder. 'Is that what this is, a nice life?'

'Quiet, Eleanor. After everything I've done for you, the least you can do . . .'

'Done for me?' Lally's voice is loud enough to turn heads. 'You mean after everything you've done *to* me, don't you?'

Poor Moira takes in her breath in a little sob.

'Moira, are you going to let her talk like that?'

'Doesn't he, Mother? Isn't that what he really means?'

He turns to his wife. 'Moira!'

It's Maggie who tugs. 'Dad . . .'

'Dammit, Moira.'

Moira stares past him like the first mate on a becalmed cruise ship, looking for land.

'Dad . . .'

He turns on her, barking. 'What do you want!'

She's only thirteen but Maggie shakes her head like a much older person. 'Dad, Mom is kind of upset.'

'Upset? Why would she be upset? She looks OK to me.'

'I think she's sick.'

'No she isn't. You're not sick, Moira. You can't be sick now.'

And then his wife of forty-three years looks at him out of eyes he doesn't recognize and says, 'Sick of holding the ladder.'

Unless he recognizes the look from a long time ago. He says in a low voice charged with menace. 'The governor's car will be here any minute, Moira. Pull yourself together.' He has never been a wife beater, but.

'Leave her alone!'

'She's fine, Margaret. Fine,' he says, turning on the source of all the family miseries. 'As for you, I don't want to see you.'

Maggie's trying not to cry. 'You mean I don't have to go tonight?'

'You don't want to go?' Fine, he thinks grimly, I'll try a little *don't have to go* on you. 'No, you don't have to go and I'll tell you something else. You don't have to go to any of the rest of it. Not the fireworks tomorrow night and certainly not the blast.'

'Dad, I never said . . .'

'Fireworks.' Dear God Lally's hands are twitching.

He says, too late, 'Not for you, Eleanor.'

'About time we got some fucking action around here.'

It is the last straw. Pat McQuarrie turns to steel. 'Did you ever hear of the Man Without a Country, Margaret? He told them he hated his country so they put him on a boat offshore and he stayed there for the rest of his life. Exiled.' He glowers. 'Do you know what exiled means?'

'Daddy, I'm sorry!'

'What they told this Philip Nolen was, if you hate it so much, you don't have to see it at all!'

The kid's trying to apologize. 'I didn't mean it.'

That's more like it, he thinks. 'Too late.'

'I'll go to your damn dinner.'

'You're staying here.'

'I'll even smile.'

'I said, you're staying here. Call room service for a hamburger. You can charge it to the room.'

Lally elbows the girl. 'Lucky you.'

'But I wanted to . . .'

'And you can stay there until the weekend is over and we all go home.'

Moira touches his arm, 'Pat, the child hasn't . . .'

He shakes her off. The girl has his complete attention now. *All these years*, he thinks angrily. *All these years.* His voice is low and terrible. 'Do you think I care what you want?'

'You said I could see the fireworks.'

'Upstairs. Now. Go!'

She's about to cry. 'You said I could see the blast.'

'Well, you can forget it. Go!'

'But, Dad!' Maggie is having a hard time finding an expression she can live with. She looks from him to Lally to Moira, who is off on her own little cloud. Her voice breaks. 'Mom?'

Helpless, Moira shrugs.

'Dad . . .'

'We'll talk about it tomorrow.' *Enough*, he thinks. *I've had enough of you.*

Maggie gives him a little push. What does the girl think, she probably thinks he's unfair. Let her. Let her think this is only unfairness. 'But I want to talk about it now!'

Thinks her father's being mean to her when Pat McQuarrie is so tired of keeping the lid on that he can hardly stand the sight of her. Everything boils up in him. The pressure of his expectations. Certain things he's had to do to get this far. Secrets he's had to keep. Thirteen years of resentment boil into his throat and he shouts, 'Well, I don't want to talk to you!'

'Dad.'

'I don't even want to see you! Go to your room.'

46

'So. Devlin. I thought you'd never come in here again.' Clay Presnell, the actor/counterman grins his I'm-not-really-a-counterguy grin.

'Nice to see you too.' After his failure in Connecticut it's a relief to see somebody he knows.

'Since this is where she left the ring and all.'

'It's kind of sad, isn't it? Turning up in all the old places just to see if Lexie's here.' It's a problem. Is he an ex-lover who'd better get over it, or can he make things all right with her – if he can find her – or is he a man bent on rescue? Knowing is always better than not knowing. Worry drove him to Lincoln, again and again. Rural Connecticut just now. It has brought him back here. Devlin is in the delicatessen where Lexie used to shop, might run into her, knows he won't but has to come anyway. Landing in the city in the depths of the holiday weekend, he could have bought food in a dozen places. He came here. Secret mission, maybe. He's explored everything else. Now it's time to crack Presnell open and shake out the play.

Clay Presnell says, 'Hey, the service is good.'

'It's not like there aren't other places to buy food. I don't suppose you've seen her.'

'Not here, not at the Second Stage. Sorry. But, hey. Our Nova's the best in the city,' he says. 'Primo smoked salmon.'

'Not too hungry.'

'Better stock up,' the actor says. 'Holiday weekend. Tomorrow we're closed.'

'New York is closed.'

'Meanwhile, boy, do I have a meanwhile.' Clay Presnell slips a quarter of pastrami into oiled paper and tapes it shut. Then he tilts his head and turns, three-quarter profile. The actor's body is here on Third Avenue doing its job but his head is off at some celebrity photo shoot. 'William Morris and ICM are penciled in for the first preview.'

His hands jerk like a puppet's. 'You're opening the play?'

'Finally. She didn't let you in on it because. You'll see. So, hey. This is your big chance.'

Pain rolls in. *It's a workshop situation. I can't miss a beat or it will never open. I'm sorry*, Lexie said, *some family stuff that I have to figure out. When you see it, you'll understand.* Go to all the old places and you find out that the important part of your life stopped dead but while you were out, life went on. Business as usual. The news creeps up on him and taps him on the shoulder. 'You finished it without her?'

'Truth? It went a hell of a lot better after she split. There was stuff . . .'

He leans over the counter, boring in. 'Stuff.'

'Stuff she was trying to get at that she was scared to face. When she split, the lid came off.'

'Maybe that's what she was afraid of.' The play. *Maybe it isn't anything I did. Maybe she left because of the play.* 'Maybe she wanted to walk away.'

'I don't think so. She FedExed us some new pages.'

'When!'

'From Boston. She's very brave to let it all hang out.'

'I need to see it. Now.'

'A lot braver than me. I mean, some of it is pretty private. As in, Secrets of the Rich. You'll see it, don't worry. Here are two comps for the first preview, bring a friend.'

He looks at the date on the tickets. 'No. It has to be tonight.'

'Sorry. Can't be done. Cast weekend on Fire Island, everybody's out there but me and I'm out of here as soon as I close.' Presnell pulls off his apron. 'Which is about now.'

'The script, then. Give me the script.'

'Locked in the theater. Owner's gone. Sorry, man. If you run into Lexie, tell her I sent those invitations to her folks?'

'Wait a minute, Presnell.' Should he lean on him? Shake it out of him?

'Man, you'll see it next week.'

'This can't wait until next week.'

'Gotta rush or I'll miss the ferry,' Presnell says, pulling down the shutter over the front window.

'Life or death, Presnell.'

'Sorry, guy.' He pushes a button and the metal grillwork starts rolling down over the storefront. 'Better duck out fast, it's coming down. And watch your head.'

47

One of the inventions that makes this a good time to be alive is also a big minus. The biggest and smallest things in life present as sound bytes on answering machines.

Devlin plays his messages as he puts away the food. One message from one member of the cast and he'll hunt them down and start asking questions he should have asked a week ago.

The first call is a long-winded message from his boss; he's out in the Hamptons until after the holiday.

Some people know how to lay down a short track that does the job – like Maggie, calling from some motel in Florida. 'Hey Devlin, it's me. I'm bored out of my gourd. If you're bored too, you can call me at 813 . . .'

There are three calls from Zee, which he skips as soon as he hears her voice. *Buzz off, lady. You are done bothering me.*

He plays two more messages from Reponen. 'Our client called. Likes the specs you sent him, but he wants one more tiny change.' And, 'Incidentally, I like the sketches and the specs. On the changes, let's stonewall him, have a good weekend and I'll see you Wednesday about phase two.'

Next: 'It's Maggie again, call me at . . .'

One great thing about machines, he thinks. They're here when you can't be. And when you don't want to be. Good to know Reponen likes his work without having to wait until he gets back from Southampton to hear. Better, he can live a lifetime without having to deal with Zee Wellaver. He can screen calls until she gives up.

Maggie, he'll phone as soon as he clears the rest of the tape.

The terrible thing about machines is that you can be sitting in your new living room and have a bomb drop on your life.

The man's voice is light, neutral. New to him. 'Thomas Devlin. Are you screening your calls? If you are, you'd better pick up.' The caller waits, assuming Devlin is home and hiding behind the machine. 'Do you know my voice?'

He doesn't.

The mild, dry voice marches into the room like a small man pretending to be bigger. 'Come on, Thomas Devlin, pick up.'

'Who are you,' he says to the machine. *'Who are you?'*

The caller continues. 'Do you know who I am now? If you know what's good for you, you'd better pick up.' There's a silence on the tape: the caller concluding that Devlin isn't home. Then he clears his throat and regroups. He scripted this call for Tom Devlin, live and responding. 'OK, so you're

172

not there.' He says ominously, *'But when you pick this up* . . .' Another long silence while the stranger writes the rest of his sound byte.

Devlin shouts at the machine, 'What do you *want?*'

'. . . you'd better get down here. And if you don't? So, fine. You can just read about it in the papers, lovely person, ugly death. Too bad you won't be around for this, I'd give a million to see your face . . .' Then the caller drops the other shoe. 'I wasn't there when you murdered my boy and there's no reason why you should be here when she dies because fair's fair, you know?'

'Slade?' God. Gerald Slade.

The caller is hyperventilating. 'You do know where *here* is, don't you?' Damn his brothers, damn Pat McQuarrie, he does.

'And you know what's happening down here on the Fourth.'

'My God.' Devlin's belly freezes solid, *lovely person, ugly death.*

'But it's not your job, it's your brothers' job, so you can't stop it. Don't even think you can stop it. All you can do is watch it come down.'

'Slade!' Cleotha, Cleotha Florida. APB, whatever, what kind of police do they have, how much security did his brother hire? Get down there, but first get on the phone and replay this message for the local cops.

'And if you try to call off your brothers . . .' Rage roars out of the machine. 'I'll kill her. And if you contact the police, I'll kill her.'

Devlin grabs his jacket, wild to go. *Lexie, my God!*

But the machine talks on; with the threats laid out, the caller gets his voice under control. 'Want to know what it's like to love somebody and see them die? Well, now you do. So you can come down here or don't come, it won't make any difference, she's dying either way.'

'And don't try to stop it.

'Don't even think about stopping it.

'One sign of police or federal agents, one sign of *anybody coming from anywhere* and I don't wait for the implosion.' The tone is cold now. Even. Terrifying. 'I shoot her in the head.'

48

Fireworks, Lally thinks, you bet I need fireworks, lying spreadeagled in the sand just beyond the parking lot of the Pelican Bar and Grille, she came out here to get it like she likes it from some guy. So what else is new, she gave holy mother Moira the slip and probably she's a little drunk. Couldn't escape the governor's do last night, stuck up there at the head table like a boiled owl. Hard to sneak away from them tonight too, she thought, who knew the dirty Devlins would put up a reviewing stand so they could have the party right here at the beach? Hot dog, front row seats for the fireworks and tomorrow morning for the blast, and plenty of cheap bars lining the road. And the Chamber of Commerce party? Slipping out is a gas. Plenty of guys on deck, bankers, dentists in white suits, but much as you need the sex and what sometimes follows, you don't do it with people you know. Drift out to the nearest bar where the trailer trash collects, target your bikers and fly-casters getting drunk, troll a little, Ms McQuarrie, of all people you know how. Size them up. You can feel it building oh right, this isn't one of your nightly usuals, tonight we get the real fireworks. And when everybody stumbles down to the beach for the big bang Lally has glommed onto her mark, he likes her and the two of them hold back. Her and some guy.

Hey look, she gets off on the sneaking and she gets off on the hunting down and snagging and then there's this. The sex. It's only sex. Sand grinding in all the crevices and sand in her hair and shells and sandspurs cutting into the back of her designer dress well fine and take that and let's do some more of it, whoever you are because I love fireworks but we're not there yet.

While on a barge offshore outside Cleotha, Florida, the Grucci brothers deliver the optimum bang for the buck. Fireworks! Roman candles and twizzlers and starbursts folding out and overlapping in the deep night sky and it is going fine, wham, bam, crack out there in the universe and if there is a problem this is the problem. All creation exploding over your head and nothing going on with you.

Plus whoever this is, his greasy hair got loose from the ponytail and it is hanging in her eyes. Fireworks. Out of my way, asshole, I have to see!

'Get off,' she growls, with him making that noise that they all make and her coming up empty so she rolls him over when he's done and brings her knee up the way she knows and digs her sharp fingers into a soft place that she knows and this is easy because he is smaller than she is – she is always very, very careful how she picks them because you never know. There is this, that Daddy knows about.

And there is this, *that daddy doesn't know about*. Most of them she just boffs and they wander off but sometimes, there's this. She was frantic that first time, if she hadn't been desperate it never would have happened – too young! – terrible accident, that once. But after that, oh, after that. Something changes in you and every time after, you are fucking the possibility. You hardly ever, but this one, the way he grunts and rolls . . . When you are a horny drunk looking for any old fuck you don't expect her to come armed, you don't expect the sharp point in your eye or the explosion in your head while she— Still isn't there, working so hard and she isn't there! It's killing her. *Why am I so mad*? The third one of these and even with this she is still dead cold. Last time it was easy, woods outside the bar, had what she came looking for and, panting, finished him off with a rock but this is flat, sandy Florida, Lally too drunk to tell if she's ever going to come off, fireworks down on the beach, everybody going oooooh and nothing happened here except her getting cold and black blood filling his eye. She finishes with a cement block.

175

49

Explosives. This part, Tony Devlin is comfortable with, moving in the explosives. It's what he does best because it's what he's always done for Devlin Dismantling. He used to bring the stuff in and put it where Pop told him to put it. For a while, he brought the stuff in and put it where Tommy said. Never mind that the kid is practically young enough to be his kid if he'd ever had the damn time or liberty to have a kid, Tommy knows his stuff.

So yesterday started good. Tony went in with his DD crew – four hardbitten Irish boys from New Haven, been working for Pop for almost as long as Tony has. And when he went in, he was pretty confident. Now he's not so sure. Building's prepared OK, parts ripped out in just the right places, Tony can do that standing on his head, as long as you tell him where.

They spent the first half of the day rolling in the drums – five hundred pounds for this job, dynamite plus plastic. Everything's in place. He thinks. For this job, Tony and his boys drilled eight hundred holes in supporting walls to take the explosives, and then he had them string his wire and set fuses. Tony would be the first to admit that this part is somewhat problematic. Is eight hundred blast points enough? And are they all in the right place? And what about the timing? Pop was always a hands on guy. One detonator linked to the next, the next, the next. There was logic to it, like a string of fire crackers. On the other hand, Tommy's detonations were computerized. Triggered completely by remote. Now, as this is his first solo job, Tony has decided to wear a belt plus back it up with suspenders. You can't be too careful, right? So he has laid in his own blend of the old and the new. Fuses. Wires. Computerized dinguses. Hey, it could make him famous, if things go off like he hopes.

Positioning is something else. Bro was smart, making Tommy walk through the old hotel before he got away from them. Pick his brains, get his expertise and then the hell with him. Tony was not so smart because he picked Tom's brains well enough, but he forgets where he left the pieces. He should have taken his damn Perlcorder and had Kathleen transcribe it.

Never mind. Everything's in place now, it's looking pretty good. God, he hopes it is. TV, film company, the world out there is watching. Slick your hair back and never mind how hot it is, give them the black silk shirt. Never let the people see you in cotton.

It is the morning of the day.

Tony Devlin is up early. Too early – party flutters. A little hung over, so what? He and his guys swept the dying hotel last night, standard operating

176

procedure since the dawn of Devlin Dismantling. Sweep. Then celebrate. You don't hang with the suits after a job like this, you hang with your crew. Three hours at the deserted Flamingo Bar in downtown Cleotha while everybody else was watching fireworks out at the beach. Too many Margaritas, time slid. Bro hadda storm in and drag him. *Where were you when the mayor made his speech?* Well, tough. Today he and the guys get stoked on coffee and roll back out there for the final sweep. So what if he doesn't have enough guys to hit every nook and crevice in the old wreck before quarter to ten, when Bro wants them off the site?

Timing! This producer guy has DD on a tight schedule, doesn't hurt the movie to have CNN live plus prime time news coverage, Revenaugh family, take cover. So it's speeches at ten, photo ops, everybody with everybody. Tony is good with his new smile, he's spent enough on it. Chamber of Commerce band and then *blam*, with cameras on helicopters and LSTs, he thinks, whatever those people use – after a long haul on short rations, DD implosions finally bump noses with stardom. Look, we swept the place last night, OK? Safe is safe, Tommyboy, but there's such a thing as getting too picky. Tony and his boys will make a good show of it and get back in time to press the flesh at the reviewing stand. Send the boys back to town with the truck, he and Bro can come home from this baby in the governor's limo. At quarter of, the Devlin brothers take to the booth, OK, outside the perimeter but closer than anyone, let the mayor and the governor stay behind the velvet ropes with Pat McQuarrie. They'll see him and Bro going up to the booth, fixed for The Big Moment, *God. I wonder which one of us is going to push the button.*

He is maybe a little nervous, but he's feeling pretty good. Babes going oooooh instead of yeugh, great women of all ages following him, like, 'Oh, big man. He can bring down tall buildings at a single bound.' After a whole life flying solo, Tony will get loved in large numbers.

Then he runs into Bro in the hall and Bro snaps at him like a fox. 'What!'

'Just going out for the final sweep.' Tony spreads his palms like a kid: *I wasn't doing nothing.* 'What's with you?'

'McQuarrie,' Bro says. 'We're the whole show around here and the bastard says he can't manage a seat for me in the governor's box.'

'You mean you're not going to be in the booth?'

'I'm counting on you for that. I say no seat, no implosion.'

'We should both be on the job, Bro,' Tony says uneasily.

'We've done our part. Now all you have to do is throw the switch.'

He has a couple of questions for Bro but Bro is too pissed off to be bothered. Still, he tries. 'I need you in the booth.'

'Fuck the booth,' Bro says and pushes past him.

'Wait a minute. Hey, wait a minute!'

Bro doesn't bother to look back. 'Don't worry, you'll be fine.'

50

Never mind what Tom Devlin is thinking as he thuds onto the broken cement causeway to the doomed hotel. Every step he takes eats time. His car is behind him, nosed into the police barrier. No cars allowed on the causeway. *Don't come near*, Gerald Slade said, *if I see anybody coming, I'll shoot her.* Then what has he been doing out here, waiting for the blast? Where did he hide her during the final sweep? DD rules are: no intruders. Not this close to detonation. An hour and fifteen minutes, to be exact.

The cops almost stopped him at the barrier and he's one of the Devlins, like it or not. 'Sir, you can't go out.'

'Emergency.' The fear driving him surfaced and took shape. *That could be Lexie out there.*

'Sorry.'

'Somebody's out there.'

'Authorized personnel only. No unauthorized personnel allowed.'

'There's somebody hiding in the . . .'

'You from TV?'

'No.'

'Reporter?'

'No.'

'It wouldn't matter. You want to stay back here, dude. Where it's safe.'

'Don't be so sure it's safe.'

'Safe distance. They're blowing it up.'

Bringing it down, I hope. 'That's what I'm afraid of.' Tony, with his halfassed plans. He flashed his old DD card. 'Tom Devlin, of Devlin Dismantling.'

'Oh, you're with the company.' They finally let him through.

'My car!'

'No vehicles this close to detonation. You can ride back in the company truck.'

He starts to run. From here he can see people jumping into the DD pickup outside the security fence. The crew, the last security guard. Everybody off the site before the blast. Thank God for the truck. He can intercept it, make them take him back out . . . He waves. The truck keeps coming. He shouts and runs into the road, trying to flag it down. The driver honks and keeps going. He stands fast. The truck rolls on until it's either or. Then it stops so sharply that the DD crew riding in the back are almost jolted out. Tony jumps down, and Tony is pissed.

'Tony, thank God. There's somebody in the . . .'

'Couldn't stay away, could you?' Black silk shirt in spite of the heat,

178

RayBan wraparounds, DD hard hat under his arm because he doesn't want to wreck his hair, Tony looks like a hustler on the way to score a rich widow at a ballroom dancing class.

'Why the fuck aren't you answering phones?'

'Busy,' Tony says with that hung-over grin.

'Why didn't you put Kathleen on the . . .'

'Couldn't afford to bring her.'

'Why the hell didn't Bro pick up?' Devlin phoned his brothers before he left the city; he phoned from the airport, he phoned from the plane. You don't call the feds in a case like this because they won't listen to you. What phone call, what threat, this sounds like a crank call to us. You don't call the police because they'll bust you, on suspicion, police are touchy about anybody that even smells like a bomber. You call your brothers, because they're the only people who can stop the blast.

'Bro? He was consulting with the director.'

'Director!'

'Remember, we're in the movies.' Tony's face is oiled behind the sunglasses and his hair is black again for the first time since Devlin was ten years old. 'Bigtime, Tommy, get in. We have to get out and get this thing rolling. Their helicopters are on the way.'

'Call them off.'

'Get out my face here. We're clearing the site.'

'It's an emergency. Call off the blast.'

'You've got to be kidding! After all the work we put in?'

'Just do it.'

'No way. We're already counting down. Everything just like you told us, your charges will go off in perfect synch.'

Tony turns to get back in the truck. Devlin shoulders him away. 'There's somebody in the building.'

'The hell there is, we made the sweep.'

'I have to see.' Lexie! Lexie? He has to see.

'You think you're going to find something we don't know about?'

'It's happened before.'

'That was on your watch! This is mine.' Tony muscles past. 'We just came from there. All clear and ready to roll.'

Devlin grabs his brother's shirt collar, digging hard knuckles into his throat. 'I said, stop the blast. There's somebody in the building.'

'If you let go, I'll run it past Bro.' Tony spends a long minute muttering into his flip phone. Then he looks up. 'He says it blows at eleven, we got no margin here.'

'Tony, Goddamit! I got a call.'

Tony covers the mouthpiece. 'When?'

'Some time yesterday.'

'Oh, yesterday. We swept after that. That makes twice.' Lexie may be trapped in there and Tony is giving him an argument? Tony shouts into the phone. 'It's cool, Bro, I just told him. Two sweeps, no way the place isn't clean.'

'Tell him I'm going out to check.'

Tony mutters into the phone and listens for a minute. He looks up. 'He

179

says you do it on your own responsibility.'

'Fine!'

'Fine? You're running the risk of, and that's fine?'

'It's fine! Now are you going to give me a ride out or do I have to walk?'

Tony snaps the phone shut. 'No way are we going out again. So you might as well come in. Nice ride in the truck, front row seats for the . . .'

'No.'

'What, you don't trust me?' Oh no, you do not trust Tony when he gets that look in his eye and tells you, 'Trust me, if I say we swept, we swept.'

The past repeats itself. The dream repeats itself. 'Every room, every corridor?'

There is an edge of arrogance to the grin. 'Get real.'

'Get out of my way.'

It isn't much of a fight. Tony isn't much of a fighter. Sitting in the back of the pickup, Pop's guys cheer him on. He pushes Tony down and starts to run. Everything hits him at once. It's all mixed up in him – fear and desire. He would kill Tony if he had to, if it meant he could see Lexie again.

'Have it your way,' Tony calls after him. 'But don't go in there thinking that Bro's stopped the clock.'

Devlin turns in the road and gives his old brother a long, cold look. 'What is this, a bluff?'

'You're warned.'

'You'd blow the place and you'd blow it regardless?'

'Fuckin A.'

'You think you could blow it with me in there and the cops wouldn't stop you?'

'Man, this is show biz. They know we're blowing this thing for a movie.' Some time since Devlin saw him last, Tony has had his teeth capped. The grin he flashes is straight off the pages of *Dude*, or *Gent*. 'For all they know, you're one of the stunt guys.'

'You would, wouldn't you?'

'So come on. Get real and get in the truck.'

Devlin wheels.

Tony shouts after him. 'Now you know what it's like when you look at the stars and somebody steps on your head.'

It's too late for words.

'You have fifteen minutes,' Tony says. 'Thirty, tops.'

51

Calculation, everything is calculation. Precision is Tom Devlin's home town. Look, he grew up on these jobs. Bro runs DD operations by the clock. It's taken him ten minutes to make it out here to the point, and that was at a dead run. Allow fifteen for us to make it back, Devlin thinks. *Us?* Yes, she's here, yes she needs him. Fifteen minutes. Unless he has to carry her. Count the five minutes it took him to cut through the cyclone fence – yes he came equipped. And the time he spent scoping the building from the outside. Two wings and eight stories plus the tower, there's no way one man can cover all that so he'll have to target his search. He numbers the black bands belting the windows where Tony's charges are set. The middle three. For a job this size he should have set charges on four floors, must have been short handed. His own situation is worse. One guy, with thirty minutes to sweep and get her out and safely away. At eleven a.m. sharp, they trigger the blast. Unless. Bro is like a ferret. Small, but with a savage edge. When push comes to shove, don't count on faking him out.

Devlin goes up the stairs to the entrance. He crosses the broad porch and steps into the grand, gutted lobby. Sand silts the tiled floor and vines grow in niches where statues have been ripped out. The place is a jumble of broken stucco and wrecked furniture.

Precision drives the architect. It serves him now.

Start by listening. Get a sense of the building. Whether there's anything moving overhead or running along the corridors. Figure out whether the building is still breathing. Stand in the lobby until you think you know.

No. You are not alone in here.

Shout.

'Lexie?'

'Slade, you bastard.'

Uncertainty rattles through him. 'Whoever you are, if you can hear me, shout!'

Nobody answers.

Twenty-five minutes left, and that's conservative.

Scope the place.

Frayed wires hang from breaks in the ceiling and the walls where sconces have been ripped out. Forget the elevators, forget the lights. The power's off. Standard operating procedure in these jobs. Daylight filters in on the lower floors, but on the floors Tony has covered, he'll be operating in the dark. There isn't a light strong enough. Tom Devlin is alone in a dying building looking for the last living person in the jumble of abandoned rooms. And she is here. He can feel it. He can still hear Gerald Slade's threat. *Now you'll know how it feels.*

Love-death, he thinks. Is Freddy Slade's bereaved father in here with his victim, waiting for the blast? Does he want to die like Freddy or only have Devlin feel what he felt?

He shouts. 'Listen, Slade, I feel it! I always have.'

He is cross-hatching the first floor at a dead run, shouting as he runs. 'Lexie. Lex! Are you here?' He checks the dining room, looks into the grand ballroom and moves on. Even on the main floor with its open spaces there are a dozen places to hide a woman. And to hide. Gerald may still be here – it he's crazy enough. 'You might as well come out, Gerald. I know you're here.'

He waits, listening. On a column next to him, a green lizard flicks its tail.

'If you hear me, you know you've got me where you want me, OK? So if you can hear me, let her go. You and I can finish this.'

He has no idea what he'll find. The crew swept the building less than an hour ago, they should have found the bastard. Or seen him running away. They should have found her. Is Lexie struggling to free herself or did Gerald kill her or drug her or tie her and tape her mouth shut and leave? He doesn't know.

'Slade?'

There are no footsteps shaking the floors overhead, no voices. There's only the whisper of stucco dust sifting down and the creak of a weakened building settling in on itself. He isn't bargaining with God, but he is bargaining.

Devlin shouts, 'Me instead, Gerald. Gerald! Do you hear me? Me instead!'

Maybe he brought her in last night. Put her in a place no crew would think of. She's here. He can feel it in the back of his throat and in his bowels and in his belly. She's somewhere in this crumbling building and the building is going to blow. Time. He has no time. Should he go down to the ground floor and search the dank rathskeller and the drained swimming pool or should he go up?

Devlin's heart and guts are in collision.

Step back. Calculate.

Focus on the hotel floor plan, which you memorized the way you do all projects. Ones you create. Ones you have destroyed. Zero in on its obvious byways and its secret places. The doomed building is like a dying woman. You can find her treasures in time, if you know how. OK. He counted three black bands. Tony belted the middle three floors. DD always covers the floors where the charges are set to contain the blast and keep the windows from blowing out. Fine. Start there.

Devlin bolts up the shaky central staircase. Supports weakened, yeah, at least Tony did this part right. He is running on hope. As in: she's right here and he finds her. Or she hears him and calls out. On Two, he shouts.

'Lexie. Alexandra?'

He thinks he hears banging. He thinks it's coming from above.

'If you can hear me, bang again!'

182

But the sound is too regular. It sorts out into drumbeats. There are drums thumping at a distance, a sweet sad sound straight out of autumn nights and high school football games. The difference is that this time it's coming in on the hot, dry air of July in Cleotha, Florida: the Chamber of Commerce band is playing a march tune.

'If you can't bang, scrape!'

Maybe she can't hear him. Unless he can't hear her.

Be cool.

Think. There's the outside chance that you can cut to the chase and disarm the operation. Then you'll have all the time in the world to search.

If Tony has done the job right, he really can end this. On Three he'll locate the key charges. He can yank wires, pull fuses and disable the detonators, simple work. He can disarm the operation and take his sweet time looking, find her and amble away. Let his brothers pick up the pieces with McQuarrie and the press. They created the problem, so fair's fair.

Hope hurries him along until he comes out on Three and see what Tony's done. Running, he shines his flash into the lounge, into several rooms. The complexity of Tony's arrangements makes him groan. This is not an operation he can abort. There is no making any sense of what Tony has done. The hallways and lounge tell him Tony has laid in a mishmash of remotes and random drums and snarled wires. It would take hours to figure out exactly what he did. Whatever he did, he did a lot of it. Classic Tony: overkill. Disable some part of Tony's jackass arrangement and it won't stop the detonation, it will just botch it. You run the risk of blowing up the building and sending chunks out to frag the old folks' home and bystanders and everything else for miles around.

So, search and hope you can find her and pray that you both get out in time. This is the ugly old dream all right, but the dream in spades. In the dream, he saves Freddy over and over and every time, the kid is just as dead. Devlin's back in hell, running down the hallways in a crumbling building, opening doors, searching on that familiar, never-ending loop. The difference is that this isn't Freddie Slade he's looking for. It's someone he loves – Gerald: *somebody you care about*.

And he only has one chance.

Devlin covers the floor as well as he can, calling. Flashing his light into corners, stopping to listen, thinking, *ok shit*. Fifteen minutes left and as he runs up the next flight of stairs he is aware of a distant *whap whap whap*.

Ignores it and runs on.

'Lexie!'

'Slade!'

But the sound gets bigger, coming in on him like a flashback straight out of *Apocalypse Now*. It's the movie company's helicopters, coming in. Another few minutes and the things will drown out any sound Lexie could possibly make. God, he thinks, skirting one of Tony's oversized drums. Desperate, he comes thudding back to the single flight of stairs.

Counting down to the blast.

He doesn't have long.

He's no closer to finding her than he was when he walked in.

He needs time to find her and he needs time to get her out and get away.

183

He's running out of both.

'If I can't find her, what the fuck,' he shouts to his brothers, to God. 'If I can't find her, go ahead!' If he can't find her he might as well die. He is ripped apart and screaming with passion, 'Go ahead and blow me away!'

But at the same time he is searching methodically, calling, shouting louder because he has to make her hear over the approaching machines. On the sixth floor his flashlight fades to nothing; the long windows stand open and uncovered and he makes a quick circuit before he comes skidding down the end of the last hallway into the hotel's bridal suite. The remains of the bed still rest on its heart-shaped pedestal and the bathroom door stands wide. He sees stained marble counters and the old fixtures.

The fixtures. Plumbing.

The pipes. Idiot. You forgot to listen to the pipes.

Where is your head?

'Stupid. Stupid!' Calculation, organization, yeah, right. All this method and Devlin has lost it so completely that he forgot to listen to the pipes. He throws himself on his belly and puts his ear to the lead waste pipe that links this toilet to the hotel's toilets above and below.

And he hears it. Scratching. Remote scratching. Somebody somewhere is scraping on the main conduit. She must have heard him calling. She's here.

'Lex!' He pulls out the bolt cutters and bangs on the pipe.

Time. I've wasted so much time.

Then he holds his breath. He is about to die of it when he hears somebody scratching in response. In seconds the sound is drowned out by the movie company's helicopters coming on their first arc to shoot some preliminary footage. He starts to run.

You bet I heard scratching.

It is coming from somewhere deep.

Devlin hurls himself onto the grand staircase and goes down, deaf to everything but the approaching helicopters. The machines veer off as he plunges into the lobby. It's silent except for the sound of his own breath and stucco dust sifting down and then my God. It almost overturns him – the sound of civilization.

It is his pocket phone.

Desperate, he pulls it out. Five more minutes, he thinks, maybe less; he flips it on. 'What. What!'

'Next time you'll be more careful,' Gerald says.

The words roll into Tom Devlin and strike where he lives. He throws himself down the last flight into the hotel basement in a flood of confusion. Everything is mixed up in him now: Gerald and the tragedy with Freddy, his guilt; Lexie and their missed connections and his fuckup with Zee, all of it shaken loose by Gerald Slade just when he's at his most vulnerable.

He'd fucking forgotten he was carrying a phone.

He tears down the last flight of stairs and thuds to a stop in the tiled hallway. In the dimness, he sees her standing with her arms raised. Naked and beautiful.

'Lexie, my God!'

The thing does not move.

184

Statues don't. This isn't his lover, it's one of the three graces, extending her stone arms to him. Groaning, he skirts the ruined fountain with his heart running out of his ears and resumes the search.

Stop, asshole. Stop and listen. Walking on light feet he goes into the room with the drained swimming pool. Nothing. The locker room. Again, nothing. Wait. Stop here in the women's locker room and listen to the old plumbing. Put your ear close to the pipes. He hears scratching.

Close.

Very close.

On the other side of this wall. Devlin is so close that he can hear her voice. She is wailing through the gag.

'Lexie, I'm here!'

Shouting, he runs around the divider. Then he sees her.

It breaks him in two.

'God, thank God.' Supercharged, wrecked by surprise, he pulls the girl out of the shower. She's been tied for so long that she's rigid with it. It's like handling a log. He cuts the wires with the bolt cutters and yanks the tape off her mouth.

'Hurry,' he says. 'Get up, we have to hurry.'

'It hurts,' Maggie McQuarrie says. Wincing, she rolls onto her hands and knees and tries to stand. 'It's awful, but I'll try.'

Five minutes. They have five minutes to get out of here and no time to get away before the blast; noplace to run where they will be safe from flying chunks of stucco and metal and concrete. At close range the air will be filled even if the building comes down the way it's supposed to instead of blowing up. There is no counting on anyone to see a man and a girl running out of the building at the last minute and stop the blast, no counting on Bro to back down, not Bro with his vindictive streak – *don't know why he always hated me*. Devlin and Maggie may make it to the water but they'll get trashed just as badly in the water. There is danger in the water and danger on the beach but there is more danger here.

They have to get out. He has to think fast.

52

The St Petersburg *Times* wants photos before, during and after the implosion. Fine, Pat McQuarrie thinks. Anything for the enterprise. Executive and family, with the Miramar hotel still visible on the point. It's taken some doing to get this far. Pat has suffered some losses in his time; he's juggled funds and danced the dance. Right now he's a hop, skip and a jump ahead of the knacker. But he's about to improve all that. Solidify his investments. Pull his family together for the march into the next century.

'OK, everybody.'

There are only three McQuarries here. Lexie? She's on ice for the moment, and given the circumstances, it's a good place for her. It's taken some manipulation but Pat McQuarrie has kept it together this long and by God he isn't going to let Lexie get in the way with her passion for old scandals. Not his fault she doesn't get it. When things threaten the enterprise, you do what you have to, anything to get past them.

So let her sit, until we get through this. Work with what you have. Let the people see you standing together. Executive and family, in full color. Make certain they see you smiling. They are lining up the first shot.

He pokes the sleepy, slovenly cross he has to bear; she's scratching her belly and yawning like a waking grizzly. 'Eleanor. Where's Maggie?'

Lally blinks. 'Who cares?'

'I do. This is supposed to be a family picture.'

'Family picture. That's a laugh.' She snorts. 'Some family.'

'Who roughed you up last night?'

Fumes rise off his oldest daughter. Everything about her is rank with the morning after. Everything about her says, *don't bother me.* 'Say what?'

'Whoever he was, he left you in a bad mood.'

'Don't they always.' The tone.

Give them everything you've got, Pat thinks, do everything you can to keep them happy and keep them in place in society and they glare as if you're the only thing standing between them and everything that makes them happy. Whatever that is. With Lally, it's probably the next drink. McQuarrie pushes her into place. 'Let's just do this.' He looks around. 'Where's Maggie?'

'What, you can't keep track?'

'That's your job. Now find her. We're already minus one daughter, we need her in the shot.'

But Lally won't be budged. 'Who gives a fuck if she's in the rotten picture?'

'And do it fast, detonation's in five.'

Moira's mind comes back from wherever it's been wandering. 'Eleanor, your language.'

'She doesn't belong in the picture, she doesn't belong in this family.'

And with that airy way she has of ignoring things she doesn't like, Moira says, 'Pat, where's Maggie?'

'I though she was with you.' Surprised, McQuarrie turns to look at her. 'Moira, are you sure you haven't seen her?'

Moira McQuarrie is cool in white linen, not a wrinkle unless you count her face; she turns sad, violet eyes on him. 'Why no, Pat. I thought she was with you.'

53

'God. Tom, you're so smart!'

Even though Maggie is scrunched on his lap, Devlin has to strain to hear. The child is shouting over the heavy heartbeat of helicopter blades as the machine lifts off the point where the hotel stands. Sand clings to her hair and her sweaty, trembling body.

'Not smart,' he says to her even though she won't hear him over the racket. 'Just an asshole who should have used his cellphone sooner.' His call to 911 started the chain of command decisions that got them off the sand pit and away from ground zero. On his lap, Maggie buries her head in his shoulder. She smells like Lexie. God he misses her.

Next to him, the director's second AD shouts into his mike and waves at the pilot. The rented chopper banks in a wide arc so Bromwell Tyne's cameraman can pan the desolate spit where the finished hotel sprawls, waiting.

He must have gotten some excellent shots of me and Maggie running out of the hotel, Devlin thinks grimly. *Now let's get the hell out of here.*

He knows how Bro is on these jobs. Any delay kills him. He'll be jumping around in the booth like the Gnome King because the blast is delayed.

It's five minutes past eleven.

If Devlin and Maggie are safe now it's because Pat McQuarrie will do anything to wring publicity out of the Cleotha job. Anything. The man wants maximum coverage on TV and an end credit on this movie, and if a last-minute rescue means some spectacular footage, fine. *With thanks to McQuarrie Development Inc.* Never mind that Bro Devlin is probably jumping up and down on the beach like an angry gnome, McQuarrie makes DD delay the blast so the director can get this excellent rescue on film.

Tom knows how these things come down. Thank God he knows or he and Maggie would be stuck in the building. Thank Maggie for bullying him into carrying a phone.

The second AD jabbered nonstop as he and Maggie dodged in under the thwapping blades and came up the ladder. Devlin caught just enough to get the picture.

This is how it came down.

With minutes to go to detonation, you don't try to run because you'll never make it. Instead, you phone 911 for helicopter assistance and you're damn glad you aren't put on hold. Tell the cops you're talking from the belly of the dying hotel, tell them you need a lift off the sand spit and you only have a few minutes to make it. Tell them to order DD to stop the blast,

188

but don't count on it. It would be just like Bro to shut down the company phones, he's that bent on bring off the blast on time. *If you can't reach me, you can't stop me.*

Smart cops. The dispatcher radios all four helicopter pilots, who radio the director. After all, Bromwell Tyne and Global are paying for the choppers. Anything for the shoot, the great director says when they reach him. You want action in your action picture, well, here's some extra. He'll probably write the rescue in, to hell with the writers, they're only writers. He'll just add a character, pick up some shots during post-production. All because Pat McQuarrie will do anything to get into the movies.

'Thanks, Pat. Thanks for the rescue. Good thing you didn't know it was me.' He grips Maggie a little harder. Didn't the man miss her? Does he miss any of his daughters really, or are they only pieces in his game?

At the pressure, Maggie turns and puts her arms around his neck. He can feel her sobbing.

'I miss her so much,' Devlin says precisely because Maggie can't hear him. But his throat is tight and his knees are jittering. They are still at risk here.

It's clear Bro delayed detonation, but for how long? How many minutes to the blast? Do they have enough time to pull out and away before he presses the button?

The second AD is howling at the pilot to go back in on a lower arc so the camera can pick up another angle but he is only an assistant director and the pilot is concerned for their safety. So is Devlin. If Tony did this wrong, the decaying stucco heap will blow up instead of caving in. The sky and the bay will be filled with flying chunks. One wild scrap of metal or piece of cement or flying stucco in the blades and they are smashed to oblivion.

Even if the building comes down right, as if by the numbers, the shock waves will be tremendous.

Most of Tom Devlin's calculations are made from the ground, but even at this height he knows their position is risky. 'Back,' he shouts, 'higher!' but nobody can hear him. He leans forward and screams, 'Get the fuck out!'

The pilot is no dummy. In spite of the director's orders coming into his earphones and the second AD shouting halfassed instructions, he pulls up and away to what may or may not be a safe distance. And from here, even over the sound of the motor and the thump of the revolving blades Tom Devlin and the others hear the *crack* of the first detonation. Then in rapid progression they hear the regular drumbeat of small blasts as the other charges go off like a chain of firecrackers in what turns out, in spite of Tony's jumbled, jackass rig of wires and remotes, to be a neatly controlled implosion.

It's going to work, Devlin thinks as the hotel lifts slightly like an athlete getting ready to start running in place. For a few seconds, nothing happens. It's going to work! But there's the tower. Different height, different density, did he warn Tony to figure that in? The Moorish tower tops the right-hand wing. If Tony did this job right, it will be the last thing to fall. The wall supporting the tower will shudder like the walls of the other wing, and after that pause that stops hearts, it will collapse inward, falling into the wreckage. There's still a chance that it won't. If it falls the wrong way, it means disaster. Waves will swamp anything that floats offshore and if that doesn't kill the boaters and their passengers, flying debris will finish them.

Devlin's fists turn to stone. Maggie squeaks as his arms tighten.

Go, Tony.

The hotel stands still. Then as smoke billows and flames shoot up the right-hand wing of the stucco heap begins to fall inward as the building ripples, collapsing. Perfect, Tony, gorgeous; Devlin's belly is quivering and even with his long history in the business he is aroused and screaming, 'Go, go, go!' and Maggie is screaming and the second AD is screaming and the pilot is screaming. The right wing falls into the middle which begins its collapse with house-of-cards perfection, everything disappearing into the smoke until only the tower that tops the left-hand wing remains standing so that there is still the risk until:

'Yes!'

The tower lifts and instead of falling outward – the last thing Devlin has to fear here – it hesitates like a living thing and then with an orgasmic shudder, collapses inward.

And here is Tom Devlin, a strong man – tough in most cases – reduced to screaming and cheering along with the others. 'Lexie, my God!' Sobbing. She's still alive, she isn't here! 'Oh my God, Lexie.'

190

54

From where he is hiding, Gerald hears the helicopter drop and hover. He hears the heavy beat as the big machine stops hovering and whirs away but he has no idea what has just happened.

Time passes, but he is beyond knowing how much time.

Alone in the dark, snapped into fetal position, Gerald Slade tightens his arms around his knees and waits.

Then the first detonation sounds. The next. The next. At the first crack of the tiny, controlled blast he bit through his lip, but he won't know it. Stucco dust and rotted wood and the detritus of years sift down on him and turn into an avalanche as the regular *crack crack crack* of controlled detonations continues. The small explosions come in perfect sequence. Gerald Slade is at the threshold of death. Complete, or close to it. He is stopped here with Freddy waiting and the man who did this to them – Tom Devlin – and somebody Devlin loves *and can't save* both trapped elsewhere in the building. *Yes* Gerald thinks. Everything where it belongs. At last. And the building will come down on them; buried deep as he is, he feels the first seismic rumble.

Yes.

He has avenged Freddy. Found a way to make it all up to him. And Freddy is proud.

Fused in the transition between heaven and hell, they will meet!

Yes.

Gerald Slade shudders in the rapture of destruction.

55

Devlin has a lot to process. The expression on Pat McQuarrie's face when the helicopter sets down on the beach and his youngest daughter tumbles out. He should be excited and glad. After all, this is his youngest child, after all, she's just been picked out of the ruins of an ugly death. Why isn't he shouting with joy? At best he looks relieved, as if at the return of a small, unimportant article. He gives her a perfunctory hug for the camera and hands her off to Lally. The other thing Devlin has to take apart: McQuarrie's sour look when his youngest child jumps down and Lexie's lover comes down the ladder after her.

Does he blame me for Lexie leaving?

God knows what Pat McQuarrie is thinking, but it becomes important to find out. He sees trouble in Lally's congested face as she yanks poor Maggie back into the McQuarrie family circle. The play: *some family stuff.* There is pathology here. Maggie waves goodbye with a sad, triangular grin. Then there are his brothers' faces. Tony's is glazed with success but Bro's glare tells another story. *Fuck up my blast, will you?* One look makes Devlin want to scoop up Maggie and flee for their lives.

Nothing tracks.

He needs space to figure it out but he is caught up in the sideshow here in the white sand in Cleotha, Florida. The dust from the blast is at its thickest. It will take an hour for the last particle to settle. A noisy hell boils up around him – cops, TV cameras, Bromwell Tyne's flacks shouting while the drums and the brass in the Chamber of Commerce band play their tin ears off like ringers auditioning for the bigtime. Shit, maybe they are. Pat McQuarrie and Global's publicists turned out plenty of print media and television people to cover the blast. This Devlin Dismantling implosion is as big as anything touched off by the Revenaughs. Sleepy Cleotha has never lived so high. Locals are lurching and laughing drunkenly, screaming with excitement. The beach is a mass of rebounding bodies.

Foam-covered TV mikes bob like bright nerf balls, everybody wants a statement. Fortunately, the sharks are feeding on Pat McQuarrie now. It's clear the bastard loves it. There's so much confusion that lucky Devlin can slip away and walk free.

If he hurries he may even make it out in one piece. The world knows there's a hero out here on the spit somewhere but the cameras didn't get close enough for them to see his face.

You bet the cops will want to talk to him, you bet he doesn't have time for that right now. He's buzzing with urgency and crazy to get away. He has nothing to hide, he has Maggie and Gerald's phone threat on his machine to back him up. It's the delay that's killing him. He wants to cooperate but not as much as he wants to get someplace quiet. Boarding lounge. Tourist class bathroom on some outgoing flight, anyplace where he can process his material. He has questions he needs to sort out. Questions about Lexie and her place in the McQuarrie family. In his life! It's past time. He hunches his shoulders and tries to bulldoze his way through the mob. 'Sorry, excuse me, sorry, ex . . .' Nobody tries to stop him.

He's almost in the clear when Lally McQuarrie straight-arms a cop out of the way. She is heading straight for him. 'Not so fast, asshole!'

Like half of a touch-tag team, Bro is closing in on his other side, gnashing. 'What the fuck were you . . .'

He mutters so nobody will hear, 'Wrong, Bro, you wanted to kill me. What the fuck were you?'

Somebody shouts, 'That's him!'

Devlin freezes: quarry caught in the cross-hairs.

'There he is!' But shouting, the blind crowd surges past him, heading for the one guy they recognize from the TV. The locals flow around him and Lally disappears in the crush.

Bro, he can still see. Tom Devlin sees his flinty old brother rising above the crowd; excited Cleothans have picked him up and now they're moving him along like a dancer in a mosh pit. His hard hat flies off and for the first time in his life Devlin sees his brother's old face unclench in a helpless grin.

OK, Bro, you got your success. You don't owe me and I certainly don't owe you.

He can turn his back on DD, with all accounts squared. If he can ever get out of Florida. Out on the spit the dust has almost settled. Through the clearing haze he can see a thirty-foot plateau of rubble, almost hotel-shaped. *Better to be out there*, he thinks. *Gerald wasn't so dumb.*

Running, he looks for Maggie. The girl is scrambling up the reviewing stand with a paramedic following. Poor kid! While her husband sells himself, Moira McQuarrie stands halfway up the bleachers, wailing as if she thinks Maggie got herself trapped in the hotel on purpose. Cop cars are circling, there's a guy heading Devlin's way with Detective stamped all over him. Hours of questioning ahead when as far as he can tell the case is closed. Gerald snatched the girl but the cops won't believe him until he shows them the stuff on Freddy's death and plays the machine for them. No. They won't really believe him for months, not until the salvage crews get to the bottom layer of rubble where Gerald Slade's body waits.

He can't be here right now.

A woman tugs his arm. 'Barb LeFleur. News Channel Eight. Did you see any . . .'

He sees a way out. 'Keep it quiet and I'll give you an exclusive.' He leans closer. 'I'm him.'

'Lance. Lance!' But News Channel Eight's camera guy has gotten separated from her by the crowd. 'Hang on a minute until I find Lance.'

'I can't wait,' Devlin says.

They strike a deal. Ten minutes for News Channel Eight. Conditional. She gets an hour of his time, exclusive, in exchange for a ride in the News

Eight van from here to Tampa International. At the airport he'll jump on the next departing flight, spare no expense, first class if that's what it takes to get a seat.

Funny how far you can travel while pretending to talk to the reporter. 'It's OK, you'll have all the time you need with me when we get into the van.'

Lead her, with one eye on the news chick and the other on Maggie, who is being hurried into an ambulance. At the last minute he veers and hops in the ambulance instead. Grinning at the sight of him, Maggie lies to the woman cop climbing in after them. She lies to the paramedic, who's trying to get her to lie down on the gurney. 'It's OK. He's my brother.'

'I don't care if he's . . .'

Maggie's face crinkles. 'I need him!'

'OK.'

And the girl is so clearly glad to see him that the police officer and the orderly buy it. While the woman from News Channel Eight fumes, Devlin rides into Cleotha in the ambulance with poor Maggie, who is enroute to the local hospital.

He talks politely to the cop, who has no way of knowing that he and Maggie are both coming from the same place. 'Is she OK?'

The woman shrugs. 'That's what we're going to find out.'

Alarmed, he asks, 'Mag, are you OK?'

'Well, last night was a little scary.'

Devlin knows not to say any of the things he is thinking. If he could bring back Gerald he would murder Gerald for what he did to her, Freddy Slade's father tied the child up and kept her all night in that huge, crumbling hotel, who would do that to a thirteen-year-old kid? She had to be scared shit and he knows it, but she is trying to be brave. 'Really, Mag. Are you OK?'

Her grin is shaky, but she nods. 'I'm cool.'

He turns to the paramedic. 'Is she OK?'

'Nothing serious. The family just figured out that she was gone all night, so they.' He finishes with a significant nod.

'Gone is an understatement.'

'So they want her checked over. You know.'

Like, you think Gerald raped her? Get serious. But he looks to Maggie. 'He didn't . . .'

She shakes her head. 'Of course not.'

'And,' the orderly says, 'she was with a man when they found her.' They are at the hospital.

'I heard he rescued her.'

'You never know,' the orderly says.

Do they really think I would touch her? The back doors open. 'I love you Mag, but I've gotta go.'

She nods. 'Take care.'

'I will.'

He jumps out of the ambulance at the hospital and snags a cab as the driver gets paid off by a frantic mom with a wailing toddler. The driver is happy to make the fare – fifty bucks from here to Tampa International. Plus tip. Leaving, Devlin doesn't know whether the cops are after him or if it's only the piranhas with the nerf balls, 'How does it feel, saving a girl's life?' 'How does it feel, being trapped in a building that your own brothers are imploding?' He has one-word answers prepared, in case. 'Good,' for the first. And for the second? 'Bad. Very bad.'

The cops? When he gets home he'll check in. Let the Cleotha police send somebody up to New York to take his statement. He'll offer to pick up the fare. If they want, he'll get a lawyer, file a deposition, whatever it takes.

It's just as well he managed to dodge the cameras. It will be several hours before somebody digs up a mug shot and Tom Devlin is temporarily famous. The last thing he needs right now is instant fame. Talk to the Cleotha police, OK, but on your turf, not here, not with Pat McQuarrie bopping around like a pinball on the loose and his brothers playing backup and Lally McQuarrie frothing.

Get home, man. Keep your head down until you figure it out. What to do next. When the plane lifts his head clears and he knows. First things first. Since they first fell in love, Lexie's been trying to tell him something. It's in the play. It must be in the play.

56

Fourth of July air traffic keeps Devlin tied up at Tampa International until late that night. He's on the last plane out, which gets him in early the next morning. To his surprise, the Cleotha police are at the door when he finally makes it home. Looking tickled to be in Manhattan, the detective comes in and after some hard back and forth about leaving the scene, takes his statement. By the time they are done talking, the detective will be satisfied.

The detective has brought Maggie's statement. Everything she says corroborates Devlin. The rest breaks his heart.

Not counting Tom Devlin, Gerald Slade was the sweet kid's only friend in the world. The details of their meeting in Lincoln, the promises he made and the moonlit trip they took to the old hotel make Devlin shudder. In Lincoln, where he first made friends with the kid, Gerald was gentle and sympathetic. On the scene when Devlin couldn't be. He seemed so lonely and kind, she was lonesome and trusting and nothing bad happened to her until the end. Alone in the motel in downtown Cleotha, Maggie was tickled to hear from him. Grounded while the rest of the world was out watching fireworks, who wouldn't want to sneak out and visit the scene of the blast? She felt so safe. Gerald was, after all, a security guard. How could you be in danger from somebody who wore a uniform because he was working on the project?

The mint chocolate chip Blizzard Gerald bought her at the Dairy Queen was laced with Valium, it was still in her blood when they checked her out at the hospital the next day. By the time Gerald unlocked the security gate and led her onto the hotel grounds, she was pleasantly sleepy. Relaxed. Nothing scary, they were just seeing what the place looked like from the outside, she knew she shouldn't be there, it was exciting. 'My father would die,' she told investigators, giggling. *You must be tired*, Gerald said nicely when she staggered against him. Talking softly, he helped her to the lip of the Spanish fountain in the courtyard. He was so quiet there in the moonlight, so not like her father. *I'm a father too*, he said. She felt so safe. He was so nice. *You can sit down and rest a while right here*. She didn't wake up until midmorning. She was tied in the ground floor bathroom and her mouth was taped. And somewhere overhead, Tom Devlin was shouting.

'He rescued me,' she told police. 'He could have been killed but he rescued me.'

Gerald's phone message clinches it.

After Devlin plays it for the detective he disconnects the answering machine and hands it over. Let the Cleotha police tag and file it, along with his statement. As it turns out, they have bigger problems. There was a man

196

killed in their town the night before the blast. They were so hung up with the McQuarries that they didn't find the body until the day after. Local guy, very popular, they're under a lot of pressure to find the killer. They think it's Gerald, but they can't prove it until they dig him out. They took skin samples from under the victim's fingernails, all they need is a DNA match. Devlin offers to undress – see, no scabs, no scratches, but since he was in transit the night before the blast, he's out of the running. By the time he checks his statement to be sure he hasn't left anything out and signs it, it is late morning.

The he calls Maggie. On the tenth ring, somebody picks up in the big house. 'Maggie, it's me.'

'We just got back.'

'Are you OK?' He wants to hear everything, he wants to tell her a few things; more than anything he wants to stay connected because even though Maggie isn't her sister, his love, this is as close as he can get unless he finds her.

But in the background, Lally McQuarrie/Cabot whatever is ranting. Maggie whispers, 'Can't talk long, OK? It's trouble with Lally.'

'I hear. Drunk?'

'That isn't all,' Maggie says.

'What do you mean?'

'She's been worse ever since we got back.'

'Worse?'

'Something's come up and they won't tell me. And she's being just awful.' He can almost feel her wet breath in his ear. 'Get this. She thinks she knows where Lexie is and she won't tell me.'

'She knows?'

'I wish I knew!' The girl's voice tightens because she doesn't want to cry. 'I don't know what's the matter with her!'

'Has she hurt you? If she hurts you I'll kill her.'

'Not yet.'

'Maggie, my God!'

'Shh. Here she comes!'

Devlin hears Lally shouting, 'Who are you talking to?'

'Nobody.'

'Is that Lexie?'

'Ow. Let go!'

'OK, Lexie, get your butt back here, we have to get ready.' Lally screams into the mouthpiece. 'All right, slut, what have you written about us?'

His vision blurs and his ears hum. He can't speak to the bitch. There's too much to say. He clicks her out of existence.

And in a strong sense memory, feels Lexie's fingers trailing down his arms. They lock in his: *don't go.* She didn't say anything that last night in the Chicago boarding lounge but he could feel her fingers begging. *Don't go.* She fills his life and he hasn't seen her since.

He gets through the day on work. Work complicated by reflection. Tom Devlin, taking his life apart and examining the parts like the insides of a machine that has mysteriously stopped working.

197

He goes to the Second Stage an hour early.

Director-actor, and, as it turns out, stage hand, Clay Presnell puts down the table he is carrying. 'Hey, you're an hour early.'

'Tom!' A woman he ought to know gives him a Xeroxed program. 'I was hoping she'd come with you.'

'What?'

'We've worked so hard and she hasn't seen it yet.' She hands him over to an usher.

'Up front,' the usher says. Around Devlin, scruffy yuppies in Saturday clothes are already in their seats.

'Who are all these people?'

'Invited dress rehearsal.' Clay Presnell points to a folded sheet of paper propped on the seat of the folding chair. Block letters: TOM DEVLIN. 'Glad you could make it. You'll miss them.'

'Miss who?'

'You ought to know.' Clay grins. 'The family. She let it all hang out in this one, and with her gone, we pushed it the rest of the way. The uncle helped. Amazing detail!'

Every muscle and nerve in Devlin tightens. 'The. *Uncle*?'

'Yeah. Like he wanted everybody to know but he didn't want Lex to have to face the music.'

'Because . . .'

'When it came down he took the rap. Weird, I'd say.'

Jangling, Devlin gets up. 'Where is he?'

'Better sit down, it's starting.' Presnell adds, 'Tomorrow night it really hits the fan. The family's supposed to come.'

198

57

It would kill Lexie to see what's going on here, Devlin thinks. Or she'd want to kill somebody. It'll be hard cutting through the crap to find out what she was trying to do when she wrote it. Whatever it was, Clay Presnell grabbed her script in his teeth and ran with it. There are so many layers of gauze draping the stage that it's impossible to make out what's going on.

'Good evening.' Presnell has come downstage to make a shiteating speech about art and the intentions of the writer. And, he adds, he has a surprise for them. 'We owe special thanks to our mystery collaborator, who supplied the last details.'

Riveted, Devlin gnaws his knuckles.

It's the worst kind of play. Murky. Arty, with people in white canvas shifts playing Greek chorus and out of control actors waving wildly and spraying the front row with every speech. Clay's cast has padded the script Lexie gave them: if you get a laugh, string it out; if you accidentally get a gasp, write it in. Devlin doesn't know whether to grieve because Lexie lost their lives together over this or mad for her sake, because she was trying to do so much and they've made a mess of it.

It will take him forever to find the truth and pull it out.

Death Duties starts like most of the worst Irish plays. The McQuarrie family story begins so many generations back that he has to take notes to keep up. Drowned fishermen lurch back from the dead; widows keen; the first McQuarrie to pull himself out of the muck deserts his family to go to America. There is a pageant of McQuarries lying and stealing to get where they are. So much for Pat McQuarrie's pretensions.

Go, Lex!

Then the lanky blonde girl Presnell cast in the lead comes downstage and everything changes. Her hair is wild and she speaks in a child's voice. Who is she supposed to be then, Maggie?

'And my big sister called me into her room and when she called I always came because I was only six and she scared me. Sometimes she hurt me but I had to go because I was little and she was my big sister so much bigger than me that I had to obey her. She dragged me out of sleep.' Childlike, she rubs her eyes. 'My sister said, "Alex, come here!" It was the middle of the night.'

Ice knifes down Devlin's spine and the chill spreads. Alex. Lexie. *Lexie?* He can't be sure.

And the play goes on. ' "It's in my room," my sister said and I went with her. She had something new and I was already scared to go in there.

"Want to see what I have in the box?" she said. I didn't, but I went with her.' The actress stops breathing so the audience will stop breathing.

Devlin's jaw opens. *Clank*. Something terrible is waiting to come in and he can't rush it. He can only wait.

The actress playing 'Alex' goes on in that light child's voice. ' "OK," I said, because she was so much bigger than me. Understand, nobody says no to my big sister.

' "Come on," she said. "I'm so proud and I want to show you." '

Her eyes go wide. 'She had it in a box. The box was on her bed. She pulled me along by the hand. "Come on. Look in. It won't hurt you." '

As 'Alex' speaks, three performers move into place upstage. One is supposed to be the child. Another represents the big sister. As 'Alex' goes on with her monolog, the big sister character looms over the child. The threat is so evident that Devlin flinches.

'So I looked. She had it lying on a towel.'

A man walks into the tableau. Clay Presnell, playing the father. But the two sisters don't see him.

'The eyes were closed,' this 'Alex' says. 'It was so little and so quiet that I thought it was a doll. Then it began moving.'

The monolog segues into a riff that Devlin guesses Clay wrote – it's much too flowery for Lexie. 'Alex' rhapsodizes about the perfect round head, the pretty arms and legs and toes and fingers. Meanwhile, the trio upstage acts out the scene without dialogue. The father pushes the woman and the child away. He takes the baby in the box away from them.

'Alex' goes on. ' "It's all right," our father said, "I'll take care of this." But my sister was crying "nonono" until he said, "Stop that. I promise, I'll find a good home for him." Then he shoved me out of the room. "Go back to bed," he said, "and if you say one word to anybody, I'll kill you." I went back to bed and the next morning I prayed that I had dreamed it.'

Maybe she did, he thinks. Six years old. Poor Lexie!

But doubt skitters in. The ages don't track. For all Devlin knows, the little girl is supposed to be Maggie. Is Lexie trying to tell him that she had a baby and her father gave it away? *God*, he thinks, writhing. *Is that what she's been trying to tell me*? Doesn't she know he could love her baby too?

Unless the baby is Maggie. It doesn't track. It doesn't track!

While 'Alex' goes on in that light voice actresses use to keep your attention. 'I found out later that he had given the baby to this girl Bridget, who cleaned for us. Mother told us Bridget had quit her job and moved back to Ireland. They said she'd stolen some silver, I think.'

During the blackout that follows, Devlin hears footsteps in the back, chairs sliding. A group has come in late. The ushers finding seats for them.

Waiting, he broods. *Whose baby, Lex? Who had the baby*?

Then the lights come up again. Clay Presnell strides in wearing a suit that Lexie may have lifted from her father's closet. He's made up to look like Pat McQuarrie but the monolog is nothing like him. Too flowery and detailed. It takes the first McQuarrie off the boat at Ellis Island ('my nails were black with the mud, I was wearing cardboard shoes') and trudges on, tracing the chain the McQuarries climbed to get where they are. Now that he's started, Presnell can't stop. Maddened, Devlin can't know whether

200

this is Lexie talking or just an actor padding his part.

Lexie, what are you trying to tell me?

Troubled, he keeps skimming the text for clues. Presnell details the McQuarries' rise to the top of Boston society, which clubs they need, which families. Then he crunches through to a point that Devlin recognizes. The wedding that almost catapulted the McQuarries into polite society.

Pretending to be Pat, he says, 'My daughter was engaged. One of the Cabots, I was so proud! Our daughter, marrying a Cabot. We invited the Cabot parents for a weekend, I had the house painted for it, furniture upholstered, new dress for Moira and . . .'

Then. 'Shit!' Presnell says, and now he does sound like Pat McQuarrie bellowing. 'Not again! A baby. Another damn baby.'

And he crosses left to walk into a scene with the actresses playing Pat's wife and his daughter.

Lally?

When the rest comes down, Devlin can't credit it. Pregnant, yes, Lally is pregnant again. Some biker she met, and at the worst time. Pat has gotten her engaged to marry up. 'The Cabots. Listen, girl. If you have this baby, it's over with the Cabots.'

Father and daughter fight. 'I gave one baby away, Daddy, that was one too many.'

'You could have an . . .'

'Daddy, Daddy, what if the Cardinal found out? No,' she says, 'I'm keeping this one.'

Devlin can't know what really happened or what Lexie wrote when she started this scene, he only knows what Presnell and his runaway thespians have made of it. The efficiency, the level of expedience rings true but, God! He is aware of the rest of the audience sitting behind him in the dark; a little scuffle in the back row and then a charged silence as the drama moves downstage. Father and daughter fight while the younger daughter hangs back, the only witness.

They have started using real names.

'Trip to China, you and your mother, Eleanor,' the father shouts, pacing as he plans. Trip to India and Singapore for Lally and Moira, 'You can have the baby in Tokyo, don't rush back on my account; string it out and when you get back Moira can present me with a brand new baby. He pretends it's out of love, but he is furious. Some dirty stud's child, another lie they have to tell for the good of the family. And this father will do anything to keep the family's position. He lays out the plan. Easy to pass off Lally's baby as their youngest daughter, Moira's miracle child. 'We'll do magic here. And you will come back and marry Henry Cabot and then we'll see who thinks Pat McQuarrie isn't good enough. And one word to anybody, and I'll kill you.'

Then Lexie wanders into the light.

'Back to your room!' he shouts. Instead she comes downstage, spreading her hands to the audience.

Lexie, Devlin thinks, relieved. This is what Lexie knew. What did she say? *Some family stuff I have to sort out.* She did it for Maggie.

201

'I saw it all,' the Lexie character says. 'I saw them go and I saw what happened after they came back, Lally and Mother and the baby. I was thirteen years old and I knew. My sister, my niece and I loved her. I chose her name. I named the baby Margaret and if you're here, Maggie, you know I love you.'

No question about who's talking here. It is Lexie.

Fine, he thinks. *She wanted Maggie to know*. This is more like Lexie. Settle your scores before you start anything new. Show your little sister how much you love her. You love her enough to tell the truth.

He is wide open, waiting for the rest to come in. *Do you love me enough to explain why you are missing*.

But the lights come up for intermission.

You're not supposed to go backstage during a performance but Devlin doesn't have time to sit in that folding chair for another hour, snapping up whatever scraps Clay Presnell cares to hand him in Act Two.

'Tom!' The actor starts up as he barges in to the backstage toilet that serves as the star's private dressing room. 'What are you doing back here?'

'Gotta talk.'

'Not now, I'm preparing.'

'Sorry.' He pushes Presnell down. 'This is urgent.'

Out in the hall, the women in the cast are running their lines for the new ending. Somebody giggles. Somebody else shrieks.

The actor looks up. Devlin is big enough to keep him in place and he knows it. 'OK, what is it?'

'If this is about some fucking family secret, I need to know the family secret.'

'You can't wait another hour?'

'No.'

'The second act's short.'

'Not short enough. I think Lexie's in trouble.'

'Oh,' Presnell says. 'So that's why . . .'

Devlin leans closer, listening carefully. 'Why she dropped out?' Out of sight. *No, out of my life*, he thinks.

'No. Why her uncle was so worried.'

'Uncle!'

'Big shaggy guy, started coming around when she wasn't here?' Presnell looks up. 'I thought it was because he was in the play. I mean, because in the second act I play him. Then he started giving us stuff. Terrific stuff.'

'He's in the play?'

'Pretty much. He gave us some notes.'

'He wasn't, like . . . *molest*—' Devlin shudders.

'Naw, nothing like. If that's what's crawling up your ass you can chill. Neither was the father. The way it comes down, the uncle is entitled.' He trails a hint like bait. 'After all, he took the rap for what she did.'

Devlin takes him by the throat. 'What did she do, Presnell? What did Lally do?'

'Let go! See, the way Lexie had it, this stuff was all kind of submerged. Like she knew about the baby but there was some other stuff she didn't know.'

'For God's *sake!*'

Ego boils. 'You want to know how a director works, right?'

'Sure.'

'Cool, but my audience is shuffling out there. If we don't go on in the next five minutes, they're gonna start throwing chairs. Could we do this after?' Presnell tries to stand.

Devlin pushes him down. 'No.'

'OK, all right? Let go of my ears and I'll tell you. What I think is ... How it came out is ... To tell you the truth, we were going nuts with it until the uncle stepped in and handed us the rest.'

'What?' he digs his fingers into the actor's shoulders.

Presnell yips. 'The part Lexie didn't know. Ow!'

'Sorry.'

'See, the dude that got Lally pregnant the second time didn't go away, he died. He found out about the baby and came back when he heard what they were doing. He threatened to tell the Cabots and blow the whole deal unless they paid through the nose and kept paying.'

Devlin lets go and Presnell stands. 'There was a fight and this Lally— whatever. I don't know how she did it. Accident? Not. The father covered it up, like, they find the body after an explosion.'

'Kieran!' Devlin wheels, heading for the stage door.

'The rest ...' Presnell begins like a barker trying to keep the audience in the tent. When Devlin doesn't stop Clay calls after him, 'The rest, we kept for the second act. You'd better hang in if you want to see what we did with it.'

By the time Presnell finishes Devlin is on the street, running for a taxi.

58

In the back of the house, Lally McQuarrie's head turns so fast that for a minute her father is afraid it's going to rip loose from her neck and start spinning. Spit almost strangles the girl, but Pat McQuarrie can hear his savage daughter, dear God, he can hear her.

'How dare you walk out before it's over.'

'Shh,' Pat McQuarrie hisses, horrified by the risk of exposure now, just when everything is so close. 'ShhShh!'

But Lally is out of control. As Devlin leaves she growls, 'Motherfucker, this is the story of my life!'

Close this thing down, he thinks, *close it down and lock the place*, but he is grasping at air, *can't stop it now, get too much attention, get in all the papers then there would be no keeping it quiet or shutting this down.* Pat McQuarrie bent on his lifelong quest to get things the way he wants them and keep them in place. *Money, if that's what it takes*, he tells himself, he got where he is by thinking fast, *give them whatever it takes to stop this. Shut it down right after this performance.*

But when the lights come up he has worse problems – his wife Moira in tears and Maggie looking at him out of smeared eyes, and Lally? My God!

The girl is missing. Gone from her seat on the aisle.

The girl, whose hands were filthy from the beginning. The bitch who brought this scandal down on us. The girl who knows as well as her father does where he sends the monthly checks. Where Kieran is. The girl who, when he reaches the garage where he parked for this atrocity, has already taken off in the family car.

59

'OK, you lied to me.' Devlin is breathing hard. He has the blade of his forearm clamped to Dave Rasmussen's throat. They are both studded with sand and twigs. He can't be sure which of them knocked the other down before he grappled the old hippie to his feet and backed him into the closed front door of his house. 'Now, tell me where he is.'

Rasmussen pushes on the arm. He rasps, 'No.'

'It's an emergency.' Give the guy just enough air so he can talk. Devlin tried to ask nicely, but there is no nicely in this thing. They argued to a standoff. It went on for so long that Devlin lost it and hurtled into the old pacifist, pinning him to the door.

'I told you, I don't know.'

'Don't lie to me.'

'I'm supposed to tell you, just because you charge in here in the middle of the night?'

'You're supposed to tell me because I have to know.'

'I can't tell just anybody.'

Devlin is trembling in the early morning cold. When he spilled into the street it was after midnight. It took longer than it should have for him to find his way back here. His voice shakes. 'I'm not just anybody.'

'You think nobody ever asked? Feds? The cops?' For a pacifist, Rasmussen is pretty tough. In spite of the pressure on his throat his voice is strong. Passive resistance got a good look at Tom Devlin loaded for bear and left without a goodbye wave. When he pushed for information, the colonist pushed back. They tangled. It took too long to get him to this point, and the guy's look tells Devlin this isn't a surrender, it's a policy decision.

'This pacifist thing isn't a default setting, is it?'

Rasmussen doesn't smile. 'No. It's a choice.'

'Kieran. Did Kieran choose?'

'He was forced underground.'

Devlin trails the bait. 'It wasn't the Weather thing. It happened when that house blew up. Fucking amateurs.'

Rasmussen doesn't respond. The eyes are like freshly licked plates. All surface.

Devlin says quietly, 'I know he didn't do it.'

There is no change in his face.

'I can help him.'

'No you can't. Whatever you think you're going to get from me, forget it.'

Devlin loosens the vice slightly. 'I know who did it. Now where is he. Are you going to help or what?'

There is a long silence while Rasmussen gets his breath. He keeps his voice low. 'Do you think I'd tell you?'

'So you really are covering for him.'

'No.'

'Yes.'

'It doesn't matter what I'm doing,' the old hippie says wearily. 'The outcome is the same.'

'Not this time. This time it's urgent.'

'That's what they always say.'

'Life or death.' Glaring into his face, Devlin is distracted by a wedge in one brown iris. Scar in the eyebrow. Pigs, in the Sixties, when Devlin was a little kid? It's barely visible through Dave Rasmussen's thick hair.

He sighs. 'It always is.'

'Look, I don't want to turn him in or anything, I just want to.' It's too complex. The contents of the play boil up in him – so much to tell her, and he doesn't know if he can tell her anything because he's afraid she's found out about Zee. Words dribble away. 'Arg! Please.'

'What?'

'It's family stuff.'

'That's a new one. You might as well let go now, I'm not going to tell you anything.'

So close. Days wasted days tearing around Connecticut and flying to Florida when Kieran McQuarrie is so close that he might have answered if Devlin shouted his name. 'OK, so you won't tell me. Could you at least get a message to him?'

No change. Not a flicker.

'It's for somebody I love!'

'Whether or not.' Damn you, stop sighing. 'Whether or not.'

'A fucking message. If you won't let me help him, it's the least you can do.'

'Help him?'

Bingo. 'Listen, you think you're so holy, underground network world peace whatever, well listen. You think you're protecting him.' Devlin bears down hard. 'You're going to get him fucking killed.'

'That's a new one.'

'No, it's old.' He groans. 'This thing is thirteen years old. She is. They had to . . . They thought they had it buried and she dug it up again. Oh shit. I love her and everything's gone bad and now nobody's safe.' He doesn't know why, exactly, but he knows it's true.

The eyes are changing. Rasmussen says in a low voice, 'You know he was framed.'

'I know who did it.' He does but he doesn't. If they killed a guy so Pat McQuarrie could engineer the Cabot wedding, what will they do to keep this one on track?

Rasmussen slips out from under Devlin's locked arm and steps away. He says mildly, 'It's probably exactly who he thought it was. He'll be interested to know for sure.'

The scenario unfolding in Devlin's head is ugly and short. 'They'll do anything to keep it from getting out.'

206

Rasmussen points to the place on the map. He offers to go with him.

'Thanks, but no. I'll be OK.'

'He doesn't know you.'

'Lexie does.'

'Be careful.'

'We're OK.' Not his fault he rushed out of the Second Stage so fast that he didn't see the McQuarries massed in the back, or hear Lally's guttural yip. Lexie. Oh, Lex*! When I see her again we'll get past all this. We will.* For the first time since he lost her, his voice is bright with hope. 'They haven't seen it yet. They aren't supposed to see it until tonight.'

60

Lexie is sleepy all the time. When she wakes up these mornings she doesn't bother to turn on the light. She likes lying here in the dark until she smells coffee and her uncle Kieran knocks on the door. Decaffeinated, she thinks. Must be. She can't clear her head no matter how much she drinks. At the moment – *what is he giving me*? It doesn't much matter. Whatever he's giving her is so powerful that she could be dying and she wouldn't care. A woman who lives at the pace Lexie usually does welcomes this kind of stillness. Sleep. In an old movie, some long-dead star called it, 'those little slices of death.' Whatever it is, it feels good. She can sleep away the nights until the play has opened and they've all seen it – did Clay send the invitations she left for him? No way to know. Her sense of things is that the opening is soon, but she's lost all track of which month they're in, what day.

Never mind.

When the play's safely opened she can focus on getting out. Good, she thinks drowsily, *Maggie will know who she is, I'll go home and we can get past all the lies*. She knows Kieran has locked her in here because he loves her but it's too quiet. Her uncle has been living like a monk in here, where she's used to the world. Here, he says, *where you'll be safe*. Once the truth is out they can go head to head and she'll make him let her go.

In the meantime, she dozes. She has stopped worrying about who or what is running loose in the cluttered, sprawling building outside Kieran's rooms. Scavengers, junk dealers. The fat guy Kieran works for, but she thinks he goes home at night. Rats, she supposes. You don't have an unoccupied space this big without getting rats. But Kieran's rooms are tight. He wakes Lexie up in the morning and smiles at her over breakfast. Somebody must have told him about Seasonal Affectiveness Disorder: they breakfast under a double bank of lights. Kieran brings her sandwiches from the deli and fresh magazines at lunch. His library has been salvaged from a thousand houses over time and she is going through it. The big stuff brought in for auction is lodged in the warren downstairs – she has no idea how far the building goes; back when he still trusted her out on day trips, Kieran used to drive the truck into a bay in the back before he let her out. The china and glassware the dealer has accumulated occupy one of the rooms they pass through on their way upstairs. The books have found their way here. So when she isn't sleeping, Lexie reads.

Not a bad day for a woman who's lived her life in overdrive. Read, eat and sleep. In an inner room with no light coming in the windows or leaking around closed window shades to remind her how late it is, she can sleep for hours. Given the way she feels, she'd rather sleep than think.

When she was still herself and jamming on the theater piece, Lexie used to promise that some morning she'd give herself a present. Wake up and go back to bed for the day. This is some variety of that.

She and Kieran don't talk much. They don't have to. She stumbles out in the morning and he smiles. She smiles. It's like being a little girl again. Everything taken care of. Decisions made for her. He loves her and he would never hurt her, so there's that.

One of these mornings she'll prod him until he starts talking. So much unspoken, so much lost time. *What were you doing all these years, Uncle Kieran? Things happened and you left us, but I never really knew why.* That isn't the real issue and she knows it. There is all that stuff she tried so hard to bury as a child and then scratched up with her fingernails. Memories, suspicions. Dropped into the play like shit on a Xerox. *Copy this. Enlarge until I understand.* Missing pieces of the story.

Don't worry, Kieran says when she tries to ask. *Rest your soul. I'll carry it for you.*

The drug – what drug? – is working on her but even submerged in a perpetual dream, Lexie is goaded by details she needs to think through. Then dark thoughts overwhelm her and she slips back into sleep. When Kieran calls her for breakfast today, she mumbles and he closes the door, leaving her to retreat into the safety of the dark. She is roused by noises in the other room. Kieran shouting. The thump of an overturned chair. Other noises. Silence.

She hears the key turning in the bedroom door. The light from the other room is so strong that she can't see. 'Who's there?'

A new voice marches into the room. Strong. Urgent. 'It's me. I came to get you out.'

61

Loser, fool, you drove through this town a dozen times last week. Hours wasted. You saw the place from the road and you never thought to check it out. Crazy with worry and too stupid to ask the right questions. Stewing, Devlin is too distracted to notice that there was a car following him or that in the one spot where the road widens, it passes him.

The road winds downhill into a northeastern Connecticut mill town planted on a hairpin bend in the river. The town is a strange mixture of cheap housing and architectural treasures from the late eighteenth century. Car parts and washing machines rust in the front yards of some of these places and others have been refinished and painted to look like wedding cakes. Half the houses layered with asbestos siding and junked up with plastic are real Colonial treasures and other owners have dropped thousands on dinky, crap houses that are an offense to any architect. It's as if the owners can't tell the difference.

He hates himself for being so blind. Everything here looks familiar. Face it, after his last hunting trip this whole part of the state looks familiar. God knows he scoured every small town in a hundred mile radius in the two days he wasted looking for Kieran McQuarrie. He just passed the diner where he lost half his last day asking the wrong questions. Now Dave Rasmussen has sent him straight to the place. His destination is right where it's always been, at that bend in the road. He was just too stupid to see it.

Either that or it was too big for him to see.

The converted factory building is a long, three-story brick affair that occupies a city block, but its boundaries don't stop at the corner. The street dividing two blocks has been closed so the owners could add a two-story shed that is almost as long as the converted factory. It wasn't much of a conversion. Whoever bought the place just put up a sign.

ARBOGAST WORKS: ARCHITECTURAL ELEMENTS, FIXTURES AND DESIGNS.

Dave Rasmussen offered to call ahead. 'It's still early.'

Devlin scowled. 'He can't know I'm coming.'

'Al Arbogast doesn't work that way.'

'I'm talking about Kieran. Kieran can't know I'm coming.'

'Second generation in the business. If I don't call Arbogast, you won't get in the front door.'

But there are other ways in. A building this big has back doors, loading docks. Windows. Anybody could get in anywhere. Or out. He should ditch the note Rasmussen gave him for Al Arbogast and find a back way in. Sneak up on Kieran. Wherever he is. What does Dave think

210

this place is. Airtight? Alarmed? He parks across the street gets out. He can get in, no problem, but the place is so big that he doesn't know where to start looking. It could take hours to find Kieran or Lexie. If he can find them at all. There's a dayglo cardboard sign posted at the entrance. ROTTWEILERS LOOSE. BETTER ASK.

OK. Do what the man says. Find the office. Finding it turns out to be an issue. The warehouse is vast. Dust has been sifting down from these ceilings for more than a hundred years. The dim open space ahead is filled with massed large shapes. Could be anything. He should have brought a flash.

He calls. The building swallows his voice.

To his left, he sees artificial light. He circles stacked crates and finds a door open. The office.

He knocks on the door frame.

Al Arbogast stirs, but not much. Sitting in the oversized desk chair, the owner of all this is tremendous. Hard to tell how long it's been since he last moved. The fat man's voice starts somewhere deep inside him and takes a long time getting out. 'That way,' he tells Devlin before he asks. 'Past the columns and the pediments. If you get to the rubber tires, you've gone too far.'

'Dave called you.'

'He said give you a work light.' He points.

Devlin takes it. 'Thanks.'

'You'll need it. Lotta crap back there.'

Like a polite Boy Scout Devlin volunteers, 'Don't worry. I won't take any of your stuff.'

'You couldn't begin to take my stuff.' The fat man could care less.

'Is there anything I should watch out for?'

'My stuff has stuff,' he says.

'I mean are the dogs tied?'

'Dogs?'

Devlin gestures. 'Out front. Rottweilers, it says.'

'Oh, that.' A laugh struggles through Arbogasts's pipes and pops out. 'Dead.'

'I see.'

'Watch your step.'

'No problem.' He goes. Footing is a problem. Navigation is a problem. It helps that the two men carrying a sofa out of the second huge, junk-filled room he blunders through have opened double garage doors and daylight is coming in the back. *Lexie, in this terrible place.* He can hear things moving behind the cartons in the next room. Could be woodpickers, antique dealers, could be Kieran, armed and waiting, he has no way of knowing. He passes a deep bay filled with rubber tires and comes into a room where destroyed wooden columns lean like drunken ghosts. It's a bad place to be alone in.

My poor Lexie, in here.

Finding the stairs to Kieran McQuarrie's apartment should be harder. He doesn't have to look far in the room where some Arbogast stored pediments and banisters and fireplaces ripped out of old houses. There is light overflowing an open door upstairs and light spilling down the unfinished staircase. Kieran McQuarrie's place. Exactly where Al Arbogast said it was. *Oh God*, he thinks, running upstairs. *Don't let them be gone.* At the top he waits for a minute, listening. Nothing. He looks in. Empty. There's nobody in the neat little living room. Nice room with a bank of lights over the eating area. Table neatly set for breakfast. He can smell the coffee. He heads for the kitchen door. He knocks. He calls. 'Mr McQuarrie?' Clamping his lower lip between his teeth, he opens the door into the kitchen. He doesn't know what to say to Kieran McQuarrie or what he's going to do.

Not an issue. Somebody has smashed in his face. There is a dent in his temple. Devlin thinks he has stopped breathing.

Except for Kieran, the tidy little place is empty. If Lexie was here, she's gone now. If she was ever here.

Stop, Devlin. Stand still. The Arbogast warehouse is smaller than the hotel in Cleotha, the clock was ticking and you found Maggie. Get the lie of the building. How the rooms extend upstairs and on this floor and in the shed at the end of this floor. OK, savvy architect. Listen. If you know how, pray.

For a moment he is completely still. Close to breakthrough, if he can only think hard enough. He thinks. Then he hears Kieran groan.

His concentration snaps. 'You!'

Kieran stirs.

Devlin drops on one knee. Looks for the eyes and tries to look in. 'McQuarrie, are you in there?'

'I only wanted to protect her.'

'You're alive!'

Then he isn't.

The door to the warehouse still stands open. In the darkness out there, something drops. Devlin can hear it roll.

The sound gives him the shakes. He picks up the work light and the bloody baseball bat and walks out into the vast second floor.

It doesn't take him long to find them. The lantern Arbogast gave him lights up a trail in the dust. Lexie dragging her heels, he hopes. He hopes she's leaving the trail for him. Unless she is out cold and being dragged. He shouts.

A woman answers.

He follows the sound and shouts again.

From somewhere ahead, she answers.

'Lexie?' He is uncertain.

Raising the work light, Devlin goes through a corridor in the maze of chairs and tables, crates and cartons, bicycles and old sign boards to the far, outside wall of the warehouse. It should be a straight shot from Kieran McQuarrie's front door to the end but these two points are separated by so much heaped junk that there are no straight shots in this building. A woman is calling, but he can't make out who it is or what she is saying. All he can do is follow the sound. Close to the end, he passes a Rolls Royce sitting up on blocks and shines his light into the last place. Coming around the corner, he calls.

212

'Can you hear me?'

Then he sees them. They are sitting on the floor in the one area where the junk thins out to make an open space for metal chairs with heart-shaped backs and little marble-topped tables. They are sitting backed into an old-fashioned soda fountain. Lexie and her sister Lally, sitting at the base of the long dead soda fountain.

Lexie is sitting in front, almost on Lally's lap, as if she expects her big sister to take care of her. Lally has her arms around her younger sister. Devlin thinks he sees blood lacing the whites of the woman's eyes. His blood. She is waiting for him. All this and Lexie sits quietly, dreamy and not quite smiling. At the sound of his voice she makes a half turn and Lally tightens her grip. The two women cling like orphans.

His breath compresses into words. 'What? What are you *doing*?'

Lally's tone is ugly. 'Go away.'

'What have you done to her?'

At the sound of his voice Lexie looks his way, startled. The light makes her blink.

'Are you all right?'

'She's fine,' Lally snarls, 'Now, go away.'

'Are you all right?'

Lexie's eyes are glinting like a dog's in a bad snapshot. She isn't all right. Work light, baseball bat, what does he think he's doing here, yelling in the dark and bumping into things? For a man who has been taught to listen to buildings, he's making a hell of a lot of noise.

'Lexie, it's me.'

'Tom!' She blinks again but does not smile. 'What are you doing here?'

'I came to get you.'

'No need. Lally came for me.'

Lexie's tone tells him that she doesn't know what Lally just did. The woman got her out without letting her see what she did to Kieran. Carefully, Devlin sets the work light on a carton and puts down the bat. He holds out his hands like a hunter approaching a trapped hound that may try to bite him. 'Um. Lexie. Some stuff has happened.'

She sounds tremendously sad. 'I know.'

He is studying Lally. The woman's face is empty, her mouth a cruel smear. Drunk? Sober but drunk on hatred? He does not know. He has no idea what she's going to do. Padding forward in the near dark he says to Lexie, 'So maybe you should come with me?'

'No, Tom.'

Lally still has one hand around her sister but the other one has disappeared. She is groping in her pocket.

Watching her, he says, 'You can do it. For me?'

'No way.' She sounds groggy but her words cut deep. 'Lally told me what you did, and who you did it with.'

'Oh God, Oh Lexie, I'm sorry.' He knows not to move any closer. Not to try any heavy lifting. He asks carefully, 'Did she tell you what she did?'

There is a silence. If Lexie's drugged, the drugs must be powerful. He can see her trying to think.

Waiting, he makes quick calculations. Lally is hugging her sister protectively, but her right hand is busy with something he can't see. Can he pounce and pull Lexie out before Lally hurts her? Should he back off and reason with the bitch?

Then Lexie says, 'You mean that boyfriend, right before she married Henry Cabot? That was an accident.'

'No, I mean just now. I don't want to upset you, but your sister just . . .'

Lally stirs. 'Shut up, Devlin.'

'I'm afraid for you.'

Lally starts up. 'Damn straight.' Blood in her eyes. It could be Lexie's. Drunk, crazy, neither or both, she wheezes, 'I saw the play.'

Devlin is afraid to move. He tries to make his voice do the work for him. Projecting. 'Let her go.'

'You think I'm holding her?'

'Let her go!'

Lally laughs. 'I'm not holding her.'

She isn't.

'She came with me on her own,' Lally says. The woman still has one arm around her younger sister. Lexie's eyes pop as Lally tightens her hold: *see*? And loosens it, prompting her sister, 'Right, Lex?'

Lexie smiles to prove they are together here.

Devlin hangs in place.

Then with a sour, wet smile, Lally McQuarrie shows him what she has in the other hand. If Devlin tries to move in she will drive the ice pick into her sister's neck.

He says in a low voice, 'Lexie, I know you don't trust me right now and I don't blame you, but please. Don't ask questions, OK? Just get up and come away from her, OK?'

Both sisters look at him. They are fixed. Still.

Waiting, Devlin listens to the building. It has been trying to tell him something all along but until this moment he hasn't caught the vibe. He is listening to it for once and all. He has a sense of somebody moving close by. Some part of him is counting to a hundred, just to keep himself from moving too soon. The counting stops. Everything stops.

Somebody's breath comes rushing out.

Lexie says, 'I can't.'

The worst day. 'Oh my God, oh my God, Lexie.'

'I can't, Tom.'

All this worry, all this anxiety and effort and rushing around and this is what it comes down to. *The worst.* 'I'm sorry.'

Lally shows all her teeth. 'Now, fuck off.'

'OK,' he says quietly. Turns. 'OK. I'm going for the cops.'

'Don't!'

'Somebody has to.'

'Tommy, she's my *sister.*'

Lally again: 'We're sisters, asshole.'

Devlin stops, but that's not why he stops.

The sound that comes out of Lally may be laughter. There's no making sense of it. She has raised the ice pick. If he moves or if Lexie moves she will drive it in. 'Sisters for life,' she says. 'What do you make of that?'

Crack. The sound come from behind him.

Lexie cries, 'No!'

Nobody would have taken Pat McQuarrie for a good shot. He hits Lally in the shoulder before Devlin sees him or registers the sound of the shot. Screaming at the insult, Lally drops the ice pick and rolls away. She is bleeding, writhing and out of control.

Released, Lexie stares, paralyzed.

Devlin wheels. He is struck by how together Pat McQuarrie looks, standing there in the clean shirt, with the beautiful white hair shining in the light. The gun, which he is still holding. 'McQuarrie, my God.'

He reaches out, begging. 'Let it stop!'

'Just because I didn't get here in time. All my plans,' McQuarrie says and continues in a dying fall. 'The wedding. My investors, the newspapers . . . All this *mess.*' In that moment Devlin sees what McQuarrie sees. He can almost see the developer's empire toppling.

'The gun, McQuarrie. Can you put it down?'

'I don't think so. Look what we've done. Look what we've come to.' His voice wavers. In the glow of the work light, Pat McQuarrie has the blind, bludgeoned look of a man who knows he is ruined. 'The papers, there's too much to keep out of the papers.'

In the background, Lally is howling. Lexie hasn't moved.

Devlin says, 'I'd better get somebody.'

'No.' McQuarrie raises the gun. In a triumph of recovery, he regroups. 'We can't let this get out.'

'You can't stop it.'

'Our plans, Devlin, I can't let you wreck out plans.'

'I didn't do it.' Whirling, Devlin points to Lexie's sister the drunk, the tears and the blood, the ice pick she is still gripping. To Lexie, who is studying all of them. And brings his arm around, pointing to Pat McQuarrie. 'You did.'

The big man jumps as if he's been hit and then pulls himself together. 'Alexandra, get yourself up. Shh Lally, stop crying, we'll find a way to fix this.'

'Forget it.' Devlin lies. 'The police already know.'

It stops him.

McQuarrie falters. His gun hand sags. Devlin grabs the bat and bunches himself to lunge. Shouts. 'OK. OK!'

Then Lexie's voice startles him. Like velvet in the dimness. 'Tom, don't!'

'I have to!' Hit the man once, go for the cops when all he really wants is to stay here and pound the crap out of him.

Lexie, crying, 'Don't hurt him, he's my father!'

'Lexie, my God.'

'It's all right, Lals, we always kill our father,' Pat McQuarrie says in a new, sweet voice. And jams the gun into his left eye and blows out the back of his skull.

215

62

'I guess Dad got his party after all.'

'It isn't exactly what he wanted.'

Lexie sighs. 'It never was.'

They are sitting on a stone wall outside the family's old house in Auburndale, the one McQuarrie sold because it wasn't grand enough. After the cremation, Moira McQuarrie used her own money to buy it back. The showplace in Lincoln is tied up in probate along with everything Pat McQuarrie bought to make it look like his family had ancestors they could be proud of. Decent of him to leave everything to Moira; she can't file for bankruptcy until the whole mess has cleared Probate Court. At least he figured out how to get shut of his creditors. Pat McQuarrie is scattered somewhere off Boston Harbor. Devlin Dismantling doesn't get paid until his corporate finances are settled but that's not Tom Devlin's problem. It's not Moira McQuarrie's problem either. She is laughing in the autumn light as if she doesn't care. The weather is still good so they are having the funeral party outdoors.

Up on the terrace next to the old house, Moira has seen to it that a handful of Pat McQuarrie's friends are gathered in his memory. There aren't many left. The ones there are have come to have drinks and make speeches in his name.

Devlin and Lexie have come down to the far end of the yard because they don't want to hear what any of her father's mourners have to say. He hasn't let go of her hand. It's taken this long for them to make it this far and he isn't about to let this get away from him. Last week, for the first time since Lally's arraignment, they talked. She made the first phone call. It was to tell him about this event.

'It would mean a lot to me if you came.'

'I'm there.' Devlin's heart leapt.

It may take him the rest of his life to repair the damage. He doesn't expect them to talk. It's going to take them a while to get past all the lies and secrets and mutual grief that separated them. He's content to sit here with her, looking out at the late summer sunlight on the grass. Linked.

But Lexie tugs at his hand. 'I never thanked you for what you did for Maggie.'

'It was. Ah.' His big moment, for all the wrong reasons. 'I thought it was you.'

Devlin is trying to tell her something but she takes it in a different direction. 'Um. That day?'

'When the hotel came down?'

'No. When Lally came after me, and you . . . Agh.' Neither of them needs to hear her finish that sequence. 'Lally told me you slept with that woman because you were pissed at me for running away.'

Time spirals and loops in on itself. Running away. Is Lexie talking about San Francisco? Chicago? Memorial Day or all three? 'You weren't running away from me, you were taken.'

She takes too long to say what she says next. 'Both.' She looks up. 'The woman . . . I already knew.'

'I'm sorry.'

'That's over. You didn't send me out the door, Tom, it wasn't even the wedding. Maybe it really was the play. The pressure, what I was trying to do.' Lexie sees her little sister lurking at the fringe of the party and waves. Maggie lifts her head and comes running their way. 'Mostly it was for Maggie, and I blew it.' Her breath is heavy in the summer air. 'I was trying to say so much.'

'It doesn't matter what anybody tries to say,' he says. Dying. 'It always comes out wrong.'

The kid calls, 'Devlin!'

'Mag!' He drops Lexie's hand and jumps down to hug her. She still loves him, whether or not Lexie does. 'Maggie, hey.'

The kid hugs him so tight that he can almost feel what she is thinking.

Then Tom Devlin realizes that he's done the one thing he vowed never to do if he got Lexie back. He has let go of her. In a minute, he'll look over his shoulder to see if the woman he's always loved is still sitting there, but right now he's hugging this little kid in all her little kid grief and confusion; Maggie needs him and he loves her too, and he can't let her go right now.

If Lexie stays in place for him today – if she's still waiting on the wall when he finishes with Maggie and turns back to her – it can't be because of anything he says or does. It has to be her choice.